THE **12:57** KILLER

Andy Shaw

THE 12:57 KILLER

CONTENTS

THE 12:57 KILLER

Andy Shaw

1

If Eddie Edwards had learned anything from his military career it was neither be early nor late, and so, with precisely five minutes in hand, he drove through the open gates of Fenn Farmhouse. The gates broke up a thick hawthorn hedge so high that only when through them could he finally see the house. It was typical of its type: an old red-brick farmhouse, extended over the years; once, but no longer, part of a working farm. The hedge continued along the front of the property and around the right-hand boundary, enveloping the lawned front garden. Left of the drive, after a narrow grassy strip and a few plants, came a dense row of ivy-covered trees, nicely concealing the property from the hill rising on the other side.

At the end of the drive, Eddie Edwards swung right in front of the house and reversed to park around the corner; he might need to make a fast getaway. Before climbing the stone steps to the front door he checked his watch, straightened his tie, and brushed his hand through his hair a few times. He needed to look in control. He climbed the steps, rang the bell and waited. After a while, he heard footsteps approaching and the door being unlocked. It swung open. The house owner wasn't at the other side. This made things easier.

"Edwards," he said. "Eddie Edwards. Here about the candlesticks."

Hector Munro checked a list on his tablet. Eddie Edwards' name was there, at the top, and he showed him in.

"I'll let my employer know you're here," Hector said, sending his employer just such an email, leaving the visitor to look around.

The reception hall in which they both stood led into a narrow inner hall with doors off, all closed. The stairs were across the hall, opposite the main door. A grandfather clock stood in one corner. Chairs and small tables stood against walls festooned with cartoons of political figures, below Toby jugs hanging from wooden beams. Someone's done all right for themselves, Eddie Edwards thought. Hector Munro's employer took a while to reply, forcing the two men into a conversation about cricket.

When the reply eventually came, Edwards read it over Hector's shoulder: "Send him in." Eddie grinned. What a show the man puts on, he thought.

Hector ignored the sound of footsteps climbing the outside steps and led Eddie Edwards across the main hall. A short ring on the front doorbell, followed by a longer and angrier ring, persistent knocking and the bell again, made him stop and throw an anxious glance over his shoulder.

"First door on the left, sir," he said, pointing. Eddie nodded, and Hector abandoned him to scuttle back to the front door.

Eddie Edwards let himself in, closing the door behind him. To his right and taking up about two-thirds of the space, was a beamed sitting room with faded, slightly chintzy upholstery, a TV in the corner, deep shag-pile carpets, rugs, an unlit fire laid with logs and dark wooden furniture to match the beams. To his left, taking up the remaining third, was an area of raised decking made from pale wood and divided from the rest of the room by a tall shelf, the side facing the decking, lined with books. The area was accessed by wooden steps close to where he stood, and encased with more book shelves. Each part of the long room had its own window, looking out over the grounds to the side of the house. The furniture in the library consisted of deep, high-back leather recliners, bases an inch or so from the ground, and more occasional tables. Eddie wasn't interested in any of this, nor in the sound and aroma of coffee percolating in the background. Barely noticed it. He was only interested in the man at the top of the wooden steps, hands on waist, jacket pushed back, a leather chair just visible behind him.

"Hello Stafford, long time no see," Eddie said, striding up the little library's steps.

"What the hell are you doing here?" Stafford Mills said.

"That any way to greet a friend?" Eddie leapt up two steps at a time until he was able to thrust his face into that of his host. His eyes fell on two silver candlesticks in the middle of a round coffee table and from there to the partially open window. "You might want to close that, Stafford, old fruit."

The identity of those responsible for the thunderous knocking and ringing took Hector Munro by surprise. It was Aidan Stanton and his fiancée, Jenna Nesbitt. Hector knew the young couple well. They lived just down the road in the village. Hector sang in the choir with Aidan, and hairdresser Jenna cut his wife's and his sister-in-law's hair. Jenna hung back awkwardly. Her fiancé, normally so easy-going, looked angry. "He in?" he asked.

"I've just shown someone in," Hector said. "I don't know how long he's going to be. He's got various people coming to look at those candlesticks he's trying to flog on Craigslist."

Aidan took Jenna by the hand, and pushed past Hector into the hall. "We'll wait," he announced.

Rather than argue, Hector quietly closed the door behind them. "Is he expecting you, Aidan?"

"You know very well he isn't. How many messages have I left?" Jenna just gave an embarrassed shrug.

"You'd best take a seat," Hector said. From behind a door at the end of the inner hallway came the sound of scratching, a door swinging open, and tiny running feet. Jenna Nesbitt broke into a smile, squatted down, and stretched out her hands.

"Hello Dandelion," she said to the small dachshund scampering across the hallway towards her as quickly as she could, tail furiously wagging, paws slipping under her in her haste. Dandelion pushed past Hector and nestled against Jenna, who scooped the animal into her arms and carried her over to a chair. With the dog on her lap, Jenna searched through her bag for a treat, telling the dog how pretty she was. "Yes, you are," she said, "yes you are."

What was it with grown women and tiny yappy dogs the size of rats, Hector pondered. His wife and sister-in-law were just as bad. He turned to Aidan, who was still on his feet. "You might be waiting a while. Can I get you some refreshment? Bridget's made a fruit cordial. Brenda can easily warm it up for you, or there's tea or coffee."

Aidan Stanton's ears pricked up. "Bridget's made a fruit cordial? I don't normally imbibe at this time of day, but I could do with some Dutch courage."

"It's non-alcoholic, Aidan," Hector said.

"Bridget's not made an alcohol-free drink since Adam was a boy," Aidan said.

"Aidan!" Jenna said.

He broke into a smile and took a seat beside her. "Cordial would be nice, thanks, Hector." Jenna looked up from the dog, and nodded that she'd like one as well.

"I'll let Stafford know you're here," Hector said. "Can I give a reason for your visit?"

"He knows full well why we're here. I've rung enough times."

Without another word, Hector messaged: *Aidan Stanton and Jenna Nesbitt are in the hall waiting to speak to you. They say you know why.*

"I'd better get her back to Brenda," he said, holding his arms out for the dog. "You know what an awful fuss she makes of that animal." Jenna Nesbitt gave the dog one last cuddle and passed her over.

Hector, the dog under one arm, left the couple where they were, and made his way towards the rear of the house. At the end of the inner hallway, a door to his right opened

5

onto a utility room which led to the kitchen. He'd done no more than turn the handle when, behind him, he heard a door open violently. He spun round and saw Eddie Edwards. He was a lot less cool and collected than when he'd arrived. Seemingly oblivious to the bystanders, Eddie yelled over his shoulder, back at the room he'd just emerged from: "Don't think this is over."

An expletive came back in Mills' unmistakable voice and the door was slammed, or possibly kicked shut. Eddie Edwards stared at it for a few seconds, leaving Hector wondering if he was going to try and force his way back in. Hector put the shaking dog down just inside the utility room, and closed the door on her. This appeared to snap Eddie out of it, and he turned to stride across the hallway back to the front door. Only when level with Aidan Stanton and Jenna Nesbitt, now on their feet, although hanging back, did he seem to realise they were there.

He stopped and looked about him shamefacedly, throwing them a guilty look and another at Hector.

"Apologies for the scene, particularly you, young lady," he said. "Hadn't realised anyone else was about." He fiddled nervously with his jacket, gave a cough and continued to the front door with Hector in close pursuit, himself throwing a glance at the living room door, wondering if Stafford Mills was going to burst out, ranting.

At the front door with Hector still advancing on him, Eddie Edwards mumbled, "Don't put yourself out. Er, I'll show myself out, thank you." He stepped outside but went no further, waiting on the porch for Hector to reach him. Aidan and Jenna nervously edged forward, still keeping a safe distance. Dandelion yelped from inside the lobby.

"I don't envy you your job, mate," Eddie told Hector at the door. With this he turned and marched down the steps. Hector moved to the porch, joined there by Aidan. The two men watched him: click, click, click, went metal heels on stone. Click click click, went metal heels on the tarmac driveway. By now Eddie Edwards was striding towards the car whose bonnet jutted from around the corner. He didn't look back until he reached it. Here he stopped, paused, and after a few moments slowly turned. Hector and Aidan were still watching him.

"Show's over, gentlemen," he said.

An embarrassed Aidan slipped back inside, mumbling, "Well, since he's free…" and he headed for Stafford Mills' living room.

Hector stayed put. He glanced over his shoulder and saw where Aidan was heading but left him to it. Stafford Mills would soon tell Aidan Stanton to clear off if he wanted to. Hector was more concerned about this Eddie Edwards causing further ructions. He'd disappeared around the corner. Hector heard a car door open and close, and an engine start. Even when the car moved along the drive, Hector still didn't move. He stayed right where he was as the car turned through the gate. Only when he could no longer hear it did he return indoors.

Apart from Dandelion's barking, all appeared calm and peaceful. Jenna Nesbitt had resumed her seat but didn't look at all comfortable perched on the edge of it. She gave Hector a little shrug and slapped her hands on her knees a couple of times.

"I'll get you that drink, Jenna," Hector said, thinking it the least he could do.

As he opened the utility room door, Dandelion bolted, running between his feet and along the inner hallway, back over to Jenna, ignoring Hector's shout to come back. Jenna scooped the dog up and he went to collect her. They met halfway and he carried her back to the kitchen, aware of voices coming from behind the living room door, but deliberately not listening, not wishing to get involved. He'd crossed the utility room, its door left open behind him, and got as far as the kitchen when he heard the living room door open. Hector set the dog down again. This wasn't doing his knees any good. He thought he heard Jenna say, "Did you get it?"

He locked the dog in before returning to the hallway. By the time he got there, the young couple had reached the front door. Stafford Mills was nowhere to be seen. Hector didn't go over to them, but stayed at the end of the inner hallway. Aidan let his fiancée leave first, pausing to say, "Ocado are here, Hector."

Weren't Ocado here yesterday, Hector asked himself. Aidan followed Jenna out, leaving the front door slightly ajar. Aidan hadn't looked very happy, Hector noticed.

By the time he'd reached the front porch, the Ocado van had passed Aidan and Jenna walking in the opposite direction. Whatever Aidan was telling his girlfriend involved a great deal of gesticulation. Hector turned his attention to the van pulling up outside the house. Its driver lowered his window. Hector pointed and said, "Can you take the stuff around the side? I'll meet you there."

The driver nodded and continued around the corner. After ensuring the front door was on the latch, Hector quietly descended the steps and set off after the van. Once round the side of the house, he found three blue shopping boxes deposited by the side door, and the van reversing

8

towards him. He stepped out of its way, raising a hand in acknowledgement to the delivery driver as he passed, who reciprocated the gesture. Everyone's always in such a hurry nowadays, Hector thought, ambling towards the boxes. He carried the shopping inside, a box at a time, leaving each on the kitchen table, before returning for the next. From elsewhere in the house came the sound of a vacuum cleaner. That explained where his wife was, but where that sister-in-law of his was, he dreaded to think. Probably still asleep. It was just a little after eleven, and it wasn't unknown for her to sleep half the day.

Hector was again summoned by the door bell at just before quarter to twelve. He opened it expecting to find either a T. Smith or a Leslie Gallagher (the two remaining Craigslist buyers on his list) but instead found a woman, clutching a car key. He wondered if Leslie Gallagher was in fact Lesley Gallagher? Gallagher had called the farmhouse's landline to make the appointment. A call Hector had taken. He'd made the appointment in the name given, using the masculine spelling Leslie, as the caller was a man, but maybe the appointment had been made on behalf of a woman?

"How can I help you?" he asked.

"I'm Sylvie Laurent," the woman said, the hint of a French accent almost, but not completely, lost over the years, just discernible in the background. Her tone suggested he should know who she was. He didn't. "I'm slightly early," she continued. "Stafford said to come for midday. I dropped my son off at school and it didn't take as long as I thought." Hector checked his candlestick list – Sylvie Laurent wasn't on it. "Are you here to have a look at the candlesticks?" he asked.

"I know nothing about candlesticks," Sylvie said. "Stafford invited me for lunch." She paused, to consider her words before continuing: "We're friends."

Hector took in her outfit: skintight jeans, a long-sleeved top, also skintight, and low-heeled stilettos. They really were friends, he thought. He glanced over her shoulder. A post office van was in the process of pulling up next to her car. At the van's wheel was the area's postman, Vaz Banks. Vaz grinned at him and mouthed the word – parcel. Brenda or Bridget have been online shopping again, Hector thought, returning his attention to Sylvie.

"You'd best come in," he said, stepping to one side. He left the front door open. "Do take a seat. I'll just sign for the parcel," he nodded towards the post van, "then let Stafford know you're here."

"May I use your cloakroom?" Sylvie asked.

"Be my guest. First door on the right under the stairs," he said, indicating a door leading from the inner hallway.

Hector moved to the porch, the door ajar behind him. Vaz was already throwing open the back of his van. He climbed inside, emerging moments later with some post and a parcel. He jumped out of the van and strode towards the steps. Hector stayed put. Vaz was younger than he was; he could come to Hector. At the top of the steps, Hector took the post and parcel and laid them on a chair next to the door. He'd just reached out to take Vaz's chunky tablet and stylus from him, to sign for the parcel, when the living room door flew open again, with such force that both men jumped. Hector spun round expecting to see Stafford Mills emerge, but instead a man he hadn't seen before, wearing pink trousers and a purple jacket, stormed out. "Rot in hell,

Mills," the man yelled, promptly colliding with Sylvie Laurent, drawn from the cloakroom by the commotion.

"I'm terribly sorry my dear," the man said, taking her by each arm and not letting go. "Didn't see you there. Are you all right?"

"No harm done," she said.

He continued to grip her by both arms, as concerned as she was astonished.

"Who on earth are you?" Hector asked, taking a step forward.

Vaz stepped inside and after giving a double take at Angry Man's outfit, stood next to Hector to show support.

The flamboyant man let Sylvie Laurent go, and swept speedily across the hallway, stopping when he reached them. "My name is Tim Smith. And yours?"

"Not sure that's any of your business."

"Work for him, do you?" Tim Smith gave a backwards head jerk towards the room he'd just exited.

"If it's any of your business, I do."

Tim Smith straightened his cravat, and said, "Then you have my sympathy."

Vaz turned his attention to the woman Tim Smith had nearly knocked over. She hadn't moved. She cast a confused glance along the hall then back to the room Tim Smith had emerged from. "Is everything all right?" she asked.

"I think you'd better leave, sir," Hector told Tim Smith.

He raised his hands and said, "Don't trouble yourself squire – I'm going."

Vaz suppressed a giggle. Hector's own tablet, left by him on the chair next to the post, pinged. Hector glanced at it. It was a message from Stafford Mills: *Get rid of him. Call the police if nec.*

Tim Smith also read the message. He snorted in disgust, pushed past Hector and Vaz and hurried down the steps, Hector and Vaz following. He hadn't reached the bottom when Stafford Mills' voice rang out. "Sylvie! Come in my dear, do please."

Tim Smith froze. He turned slowly and tried to push his way past Hector and Vaz. When they wouldn't allow it, he yelled across their shoulders, "Still fancy yourself as a ladies' man, do you Mills?"

"Mr Smith, please," Hector said, arms extended, hands raised.

"I'm on my way, squire," Tim Smith said. "Wouldn't buy silver candlesticks from that man for all the tea in China." He continued to the last step, where he stopped and turned again. "Where can a man get a decent beer around these parts?" he asked.

"The Old Speckled Hen on the high street," Vaz replied. "Take a left through the gates, five mins on your left."

Tim Smith nodded and turned away, only to turn back yet again. His eyes fixed on Hector, he retraced his steps. Again barred from going any further by the two men standing shoulder to shoulder, he leaned uncomfortably close to Hector Munro. "I hope you're paid well for your troubles," he said.

He didn't wait for a reply. He spun round and pointed his key at the car Vaz had parked next to. The car doors unlocked and he marched down the steps. He got in and reversed up the drive and into the road, without another glance at the property or the two men.

They remained where they were, halfway down the steps, neither taking his eyes off Tim Smith's car as it passed the front hedge on its way to Osborne Tye high street.

"Whatever was all that about?" Vaz said. Hector's response was a confused shake of the head. Even though the car had vanished, they remained there in an uneasy, bemused silence, neither clear about what had just happened.

It was Hector who finally said, "Can't be standing here all day."

"Then you'd best sign for the parcel and I can be on my way," Vaz said, handing Hector the tablet he'd clutched throughout. Hector took it and scrawled his signature across the screen.

"You'll let me know if you find out what the hell that was about?" Vaz said, as from inside the house, came the sound of a woman crying out: "Stafford, please!" The men looked at each other.

"Now what?" Hector said, running back up the steps, Vaz on his heels.

They burst through the front door to see a dishevelled Sylvie Laurent outside the living room. "Stafford please, be reasonable," she said. She hadn't finished her words, when the door was closed in her face. Initially, she looked more astonished than when Tim Smith had nearly knocked her off her feet, but then the look on her face changed from astonishment to anger and defiance. She narrowed her eyes and marched back to the door and flung it open.

"Stafford Mills, don't you dare…" she said fiercely, stepping back inside, only to come straight back out again, pushed backwards with such force that she hit the wall opposite, her keys flying down the hall. She gave a cry and crumpled to the ground. Vaz and Hector ran over to her.

"I said no," Stafford Mill shouted at the top of his voice, and slammed the door shut, turning the key in the lock.

Vaz reached Sylvie first and helped her to her feet. Hector went to get a chair.

"I'm alright, thank you," she said. (Despite her assurances, both men would later tell the police that she looked far from it.) Vaz sat her down. "You catch your breath," he said. On the chair by the front door, Hector's tablet pinged to announce an email. He ignored it.

"What the hell is his problem?" Vaz said. "I've a good mind to go in there and punch him!"

"Please don't," Sylvie Laurent said. "It will make things worse."

"Mme Laurent, I can't apologise enough," Hector said, returning her keys to her. "I can't think what's got into Mr Mills. You stay there, and I'll get my wife to bring you a nice cup of tea."

"That's very kind of you, but I'd rather be on my way." She got to her feet, and shook her keys as though they were a religious icon. After pulling her top back into shape, and running her hands through her hair a few times, she said, "I must look a state."

"Are you sure you don't want that cup of tea?" Hector said.

She shook her head and made her way shakily to the front door, Hector and Vaz on either side of her. At the door, Vaz said, "Now, you're sure you're okay?"

"A little shaken," she said, "but nothing more serious." She turned to Hector. "Please tell Stafford this is *au revoir*, not goodbye."

"You want my opinion," Vaz said, "that man in there," he pointed along the hall to the living room door, "assaulted you and you should get the police on to him. Me and him, we witnessed it." He moved a finger back-and-forth between himself and Hector.

"I'd really rather not, but thank you," she said.

"Your choice, but you're not doing yourself any favours," he said.

"Stafford Mills is my son's father," she said brusquely.

The two men looked at each other, mouths open. Only when her car had pulled out through the gates, watched by Vaz and Hector from the porch, did Vaz say, "You know he had a kid?"

"No disrespect, Vaz, but I think you'd better be on your way, before something else happens,"

Hector Munro said. He didn't care to see his employer right now and pausing only to collect his tablet from the chair by the door, exited by the front door, closing it behind him. With Vaz disappearing down the drive to his right, he turned left and made his way towards the kitchen side of the house, reading the latest message from Stafford Mills en route: *get rid of that woman*.

2

"Dora," Eden Hudson said, trying to hide the exasperation in her voice, "eat your porridge." Her nine-year-old narrowed her eyes and pushed the bowl away, folding her arms across her chest.

"I don't like it your way. I like it Nanna's way."

"There wasn't time to make it in a saucepan, Dora. I have to go to work and you have to go to school. Now eat." On the kitchen top, Eden's phone started ringing. She glanced at it. It was the station. She snatched at it, "Eat something, Dora," she said, moving to the next room to take the call. "Eden, it's Judy McDermott," the voice on the other end of the line said. "I don't believe our paths have crossed before." Eden's pulse raced. Detective Chief Superintendent Judy McDermott was the head of the region's homicide team and the highest ranking officer in the country to work part-time following a year-long maternity leave. She was Eden's role model. There could only be one reason for her call. "The Fire Brigade attended a house fire and found a woman's body. We're still waiting on the post-mortem, but it looks suspicious. Her husband most likely started the fire as a cover up. He's in custody. I want you on the team. As of now, you're acting Detective Sergeant Hudson."

"Who's the DI?" Eden asked.

"Guido Black."

Eden had heard of him. A high flyer. Fast tracked, a DI at thirty. He was a bit Marmitey, the force being divided in its opinion of him. This would be their first meet.

"I'm on my way," she said.

She returned to the kitchen to find her step-grandmother, Dottie, in the kitchen and Dora devouring an eggy muffin. Dottie must have rustled it up in the microwave. It was okay when she made breakfast in the microwave. Oh well, it had all the major food groups, and she really didn't have time to argue. "When you're finished, get your bag. I've got to go."

"We're taking Amy don't forget," Dora said.

Eden had forgotten. Amy was a girl who always ran late. "Well, I hope she isn't much longer. I have to go to work." She looked over to the woman she'd named her daughter after: Dorothea – Dottie – Hudson. The woman who'd co-raised her, called Nanna by Dora even though technically she was the child's step-great-grandmother. "I've got my first murder!" she said. "I've been promoted to Detective Sergeant."

"Go girl," Dottie said.

"Go Mum," Dora said.

Eden glanced at her watch. She needed to be on her way. "You get gone. If Eric," Dottie said of her son, "can't take the girls, I'll call a taxi."

Detective Inspector Guido Black wasn't your typical copper. It wasn't that he was Morse or Lindley posh, far from it, although he wasn't urban working class either. The son of a bank manager and a housewife, and educated at a very minor public school, his roots lay somewhere in between. His choice of career, not an obvious one for someone of his background, was made young. The story was known throughout the force:

In the classroom, a teacher addressed his class, a clear blackboard behind him, a piece of chalk in hand. "Does anyone know the name of the last man hanged in England?" he asked. Despite the rows of boys sitting behind wooden desks only one hand went up. That of ten-year-old Guido Black. "Yes, Black?"

"My grandad. Davy Storey. And he didn't do it neither."

Every eye in the classroom was on him. "Your grandfather was very unfortunate then," his teacher said. "And the word is either not neither."

Black told this story at his interview.

"I wasn't aware Davy Storey's conviction had been overturned," the head of the interviewing panel said.

"I'm confident it will be one day, sir."

"What makes you so sure he didn't do it, son? He confessed, didn't he?"

"With respect, sir, in those days that didn't mean a lot – and no, he didn't. His accomplice did, but he didn't. I don't believe either of them killed the victim."

"Why?"

"My mother saw the victim alive at the window when they drove away. They'd left her in the back of the car."

"I've read the case. Nobody said this at the time."

"She was told her dad was away on business, then that he'd died. She didn't find out the truth until she was a young adult. She wrote to the Home Secretary, every Home Secretary, newspaper editors, you name it – but no one believed her. She was barely six at the time, and his kid. Without more than a child's hazy memory, my grandad's going down in history as the last man in England to drop."

"Why apply to join the police force? To use our resources to clear your grandad's name?"

"I won't lie, it would certainly make gaining access to the records easier, sir, but no. It's the old story – believing I can make a difference. The evidence against my grandad was strong: the history of criminality, the feud with the victim, arranging to meet the victim in a remote location, the last to see him alive, the confession. Yet I truly believe Davy Storey was innocent of murder. Not because he's my grandfather, but because I believe my mother a credible witness despite the time lag – and there were always holes in the case against him. If it's taught me one thing, it's not to take anything at face value. This must make me some use to the force."

The interviewing panel considered him, and called him back:

"The police force has had to take a strong look at itself," the head of the interviewing panel said. "We recognise that in *the past we might not have done as good a job as we should have done, although many, such as myself, believe we did a better job than we're credited for. We also acknowledge some of our past mistakes were down to Groupthink, leading to the dismissal of contrary view points. The police force recognises it needs to change with the times. We need officers who challenge more and kowtow less. We like your attitude. We're prepared to make you an offer, son – but one piece of advice. Don't strut around like you're the only one here who wants to do a good job. It isn't fair and it won't win you any friends."*

Eden had heard of officers refusing to discuss their cases with Guido Black, least they spent the next week justifying their conclusions to him. Some refused to work with him – thinking him a fanatic obsessed with righting a non-existent wrong, or just plain anti-police. Conversely, others sung his praise. She wondered, as she walked towards a police interview room, how she would find him.

She turned the corner and there was the man himself. Apart from the matchstick sticking out of his mouth – his equivalent of Nicotine – he was fairly innocuous looking. He was of average height, wore his hair short and was clean-shaven. Perched on his nose were round gold-rimmed spectacles. He wore a dull dark suit and tie, and his shirt was buttoned up to the top button. A pale blue pullover brightened the prosaic outfit. When he saw Eden, he broke into a large smile and extended his hand towards her. His face was so expressive, kind and open that Eden's first thought was that he could almost have been a counsellor, or a Minister of the cloth.

"Guido Black, delighted to meet you, Eden," he said, avoiding all formality. "Welcome to murder."

She smiled and returned his handshake. His ease was contagious. The apprehension she'd felt walking along the corridor suddenly vanished. "We've dragged you here on false pretences, I'm afraid," he continued. "The husband's confessed – the usual sordid domestic tragedy." He gave a sigh at lives ruined in a moment of madness. Eden couldn't help but be disappointed. Nobody wanted anybody to die at the hands of another, but it was so easy to go unnoticed in the force, difficult to make a mark. Here had been an opportunity for her to stand out. She hoped her face didn't give away her feelings. She hesitated, unsure what to do next. She was still technically under his command but he hadn't given any. Was she still required? Even a confession came with a mountain of paperwork. She sighed. "I was looking forward to working with you, sir. Maybe another time."

He scowled. "You're not getting away that easily, Detective Sergeant." Here it came. The mountain of paperwork. "There's been another murder."

Her eyes widened in surprise. "In the Vale of Tye?"

"The village of Osborne Tye, to be precise. An unmarried middle-aged male was found at home with significant head injuries, from which he later died. Apart from a gang of burglars operating in the area, there aren't any obvious suspects. I'd like your help on it, starting now. I'll drive."

He waited until they were both in the car and belted up, to say: "Know why I asked for you by name?" She gave a nervous shake of her head. She hadn't realised he had. "Your answer to the 'How would you best describe yourself?' on your promotion application. 'Bloody-minded'." He glanced at her, laughing. "Most people put a bit more. I wrote about four sides."

"Bloody-minded, teetotal, single mum, with an eye for detail. Unusual upbringing, bit of..." she said.

"You had me on Bloody-minded," he said. "File's on the back seat. You'd better have a read through before we arrive."

She reached over and picked it up. The murder victim was fifty-three-year-old Stafford Mills. He died after being struck across the side of the head by a heavy object. He'd been discovered in his front room by a Mrs Brenda Munro, one of three live-in staff members, bleeding heavily from the head, but still alive. She'd remained with the victim. Her husband, Hector, had called the ambulance. The paramedics attended the scene within ten minutes. They declared Mills dead and alerted the police to a suspicious death. During the time the paramedics were at the property, Mrs Bridget White, the third live-in staff member and sister of Mrs Brenda Munro, was found unconscious by the back door and taken to hospital, where she remained. The preliminary interviews with Mr and Mrs Munro had revealed that a number of people had visited Fenn Farmhouse during the morning. Some to view a pair of silver candlesticks the deceased was selling on Craigslist. By all accounts the meetings were stormy. The visitors all left before the attack. The presence of only one silver candlestick at the scene, and the spate of burglaries in the area, suggested a botched burglary.

"Damn and blast it," Black said, swinging round a bend in the road to find his way blocked by a squad car. Eden lowered her window to show her badge to a police officer standing a few yards from the car blocking the road. With an embarrassed look he scuttled over to move his vehicle. "Oooh er, there's a strong country smell out here," Eden said, quickly raising her window and wafting her fingers under her nose.

They continued along a country road, reaching Fenn Farmhouse a couple of hundred yards later. The property was cordoned off by a combination of police tape and vehicles. SOCA had taken over, making negotiating the drive impossible. Black left his car at the top of the drive. There they suited and booted up, and traipsed down the drive, dog teams on either side. At the front door they pulled shoe covers over their police wellies and ducked under the bright yellow crisscrossed tape emblazoned MURDER INVESTIGATION – NO ENTRY. A uniformed Detective Sergeant met them.

"The body's still where it was found, sir," she explained, "first door on the left." She pointed along the inner hall. "Prof Prichard is inside."

"Are Mr and Mrs Munro still here?" Black asked.

"Waiting in the kitchen, sir. He's holding it together, but she's pretty cut up."

"Can't say I blame her," Black said to Eden, as they walked towards the murder scene.

They stood shoulder to shoulder, just inside the room, to survey it before going further. On one side of a long, ceiling-high bookshelf, SOCA were taking wide-angle shots of an ordinary sitting room. This part of the room appeared undisturbed: there weren't any indents in the carpet suggesting furniture had been moved. The deep three-piece suite still had all its cushions in place. The rugs were unrucked. The ornaments still in place. The pictures on the walls, straight. The plastic runner leading from door to fireplace was unmarked and undisturbed. They could even make out vacuuming marks across the carpets. Not so the area to their left – a little self-contained library up on decking. Here a hefty leather chair lay on its side, next to books knocked from the shelves. The curtains were drawn and face down in a pool of blood, lay the body of a man – pieces of string emanating from him to the many surrounding blood splats. The Pathologist, Prof Matthew Prichard, was on his haunches by the body, gripping a solid silver candlestick in a gloved hand. The candlestick was blood free. He ignored their approach, busy comparing the wound on Stafford Mills' shattered skull with the bottom edge of the candlestick. This done, he looked up. His terse expression mellowed upon seeing Eden, and his twinkling eyes lingered on her for longer than protocol demanded. He tore his gaze from her to her superior officer and said, "Guido." His eyes returned to Eden. "I don't believe I've had the pleasure."

"Matthew, allow me to introduce my new Detective Sergeant, Eden Hudson. Eden's helping me with this one," Black said.

Prichard grinned. "Another one with an unconventional first name," he said, with a tilt of the head towards Black.

"My mum was going through her river goddess phase," Eden replied, without a hint of humour. "I got off lightly. My sister's Belah, but we call her Leah."

Matthew liked her. A down-to-earth girl with a hint of directness, he thought. A counter balance to Guido.

"What have we got, Matthew?" Black said.

"Blunt trauma to the side of the head causing a massive intracranial haematoma," he said. "Single blow from above, sharp corner impact. I'm pretty confident he was looking down when hit, probably at his phone – we found it halfway across the room," he motioned to where the phone had been recovered. "Screen shattered but still working. The blow came from this angle." He windmilled his right arm to show the trajectory of the blow. "It was the angle and sharpness of the corner which did the damage. He took next to no preventative action. He never saw it coming."

Black looked at the candlestick in Prichard's hand. "That the murder weapon?"

"Too clean," Prichard said, "but the impact radius area is a perfect match, making its missing twin the smoking gun."

"He was murdered in the library with a candlestick?" Black said. "Bit Cluedo isn't it?"

"Isn't one of the live-in staff a Mrs White?" Eden said.

"Well, that's that, then," Black said. "It was Mrs White in the library with the candlestick. Two murders solved in less than one day – we'll be getting our Christmas bonus early." He used a stepping plate to cross the room to the window. It had been pulled shut, but was unlocked. He had a quick glance out of the window. "You finished here, Matt?" he asked.

"All done," he said.

Hector Munro was exactly ten years older than his late employer, Stafford Mills, but his wife Brenda was the same age. Their photographs taken, their clothes removed for analysis, the couple sat next to each other at the kitchen table, dressed in police overalls. A young female police officer was there for support. Hector Munro was grim faced, but composed. His wife though, was quite distressed. Her eyes were red, her nose too. It looked sore. She sipped from a glass of water, and clutched a paper handkerchief, continuously dabbing her eyes and nose until the handkerchief disintegrated, forcing her to clumsily discard it in a wastepaper bin by her side, and pull another one from a box on the table. Her refusal to loosen her grip on her husband's hand, meant the support officer had to steady the tissue box each and every time another tissue was ripped from it. Eden and Black took their places across the table.

"Mrs Munro," Black said, "I understand you found Mr Mills?"

She nodded and said, in a barely audible voice, "It was horrible. At first, I thought he'd had a fall and banged his head. That he'd tripped or something."

"I'm terribly sorry this has happened to you, Mrs Munro, but I'm afraid I'll need you to tell me exactly what happened," Black said.

"He'd wanted his lunch brought up. He was a very particular man about things like that," Brenda Munro said.

"About everything, more like," her husband said.

"He always had a cheese and tomato sandwich for lunch and a glass of orange juice. Everything had to be prepared fresh. Cheese freshly grated, tomato freshly sliced. The bread, always white, had to be cut from an unsliced loaf, crusts cut off. Buttered. Margarine wasn't allowed in the house. It's why we have a larder – to keep the cheese and butter at the right consistency. Not too hard and not too soft. Like I said, he was very particular, Mr Mills. Took me ten minutes to prepare, all told. I brought a tray up to him. I knocked on the door and said I had his lunch. He shouted back for me to leave it outside, and I did. On the table by the door."

"Was that usual?" Black said.

"If he was occupied with some business of his own, on the phone or something, it was."

"Was it usual for him to eat his lunch in that room?" Eden asked. "Why not use the dining room next door?"

"He took his breakfast and dinner in the dining room, but if he ate lunch at home, it would usually be in there. In his library as he called it," Brenda said.

"It's where he did most of his business. He'd spend hours in there," Hector added.

"What happened after you left him the tray, Mrs Munro?" Black asked, his tone soft and patient.

"I came back here, and the three of us – that's Hector, me and my sister, Bridget – had our lunch. We always finish lunch with a cup of coffee, which we make fresh in the percolator. That done, Hector decided to go up the track for some manure."

"For my vegetable beds," Hector said. "The old farmer's got a pile in the next field. Sells it for twenty pence a bag, but lets us have some for nothing."

"We smelt it," Eden said.

"Bridget took herself up the lane at the back to pick crab apples," Brenda said. "For jelly. She took the dog with her, more's the pity. She'd have warned us there was someone prowling around." She lowered her head, fighting back the tears. The policewoman on her other side put her arm around her.

"In your own time, Mrs Munro," Eden said.

"After I'd cleared up here and loaded the dishwasher and the like, I went to get the tray, but it was still where I'd left it. Nothing had been touched. That's when I started to get worried. I knocked on the door, asking if everything was alright, but he didn't answer or come to the door. I thought he must have gone out, but the door was locked. He'd do that now and then if he was in and didn't want to be disturbed, but he never locked it behind him when he went out. I had a look through the keyhole. The key was in the lock. He had to be inside. I decided to go outside to have a look through the window, but the curtains were drawn. I thought that very peculiar, given the time.

"By now I was panicking. I'd've called Hector, but he never has his phone on, so there wasn't much point. I tried to calm myself down, told myself he'd probably nodded off, but I had this bad feeling. I can't explain it. I felt I'd better check on him, just in case. I wasn't sure what to do, really. Getting the police out seemed a bit excessive, but it wasn't like him to sleep so heavily in the day. I dithered a bit then remembered that thing you see on films. You know, where they push a piece of paper under the door? I used the newspaper, and the knife from Stafford's lunch to push the key out. It worked! I heard it fall. The doors are so old and warped, the newspaper easily came out with the key still on it." She looked across the table at Eden and Black. "I'd just put the key in the lock when I heard Hector come back. I called out to him."

"I came straight in," Hector took up the story. "She said she was worried about Stafford. He'd locked himself in and wasn't coming to the door. Something wasn't right. I said he'd most likely fallen asleep, but we both agreed it was best to make sure, even if we got our heads bitten off for it."

"Hector went in first," Brenda said.

"I knew straight away something was wrong," Hector said. "There was a chair overturned."

"I saw his feet first," Brenda said, burying her head in her hand. "He was face down, and the blood, the blood. It was all around his head. I said to Hector: 'He's had a fall and hit his head.' We all know how they can bleed. Hector went to call an ambulance and I went over to Stafford. I held his hand, so he'd know I was there and said help was on its way. I asked him what on earth happened. Had he tripped? He groaned something. I got as close as I could, but all I could hear was him groaning. He was too far gone for words. He'd stopped by the time Hector got back."

"The ambulance man formally pronounced him dead and said it looked suspicious," Hector said. "I couldn't believe my ears. 'This isn't an accident?' I said. The paramedic pointed to the angle of the body, and started on about blood splatters."

Beside him, his wife straightened herself up. "When I heard him use those words, I turned to this man," she rested her hand on her husband's chest, "and I said: 'Hector – it's happened. The burglars have finally killed someone'."

"I take it you know about the burglaries, Detective Inspector?" Hector said.

Black knew nothing more than the reference to the same in his initial report. He nodded.

"It's been going on for months," Brenda said. "None of us know when we leave our homes that we won't come back to find them turned over."

"It goes quiet for while, then starts again," Hector said. "We keep being told it's most probably a gang from

London. They come up for the day, select a property, and strike when they think no one's home."

"The local police set up a meeting. Everyone came from all round. We said we didn't feel safe in our own homes. What if one of us came home and disturbed them? That was weeks back, but nothing's changed. The police never seem to arrest anyone. There's been letters to the paper about it," Brenda said, suddenly becoming quite angry. "This would never have happened if you lot had done your job."

"Brenda," her husband said.

"Sorry," she said, crumbling in on herself. "I'm a bag of nerves. With this, and my sister…" The support officer gave her hand a squeeze.

"You have nothing to apologise for, Mrs Munro," Black said. "I'm sorry this has happened to you."

"I warned Stafford about selling that silver," Hector said. "You know they're targeting the area, I told him. But he wouldn't listen. Said he'd done it for years, and he could look after himself."

"Did he sell much online?" Eden said.

"He makes his money buying old houses, doing them up and selling them," Hector said. "This online stuff started as a hobby, until he started making money at it. What he liked most of all was not having to give someone a cut."

"Did buyers often come to the house?" Eden said.

"Wasn't unusual," Hector said.

"They pay in cash?" Eden said.

"Some must have. He never seemed to be short of it," Hector said.

"The Craigslist advert specifies two candlesticks, yet we've only found one," Eden said.

"He was definitely selling a pair, dear," Brenda said. "Bridget and I polished them last night."

Black leaned forward. "I believe, that on top of everything else you've been through, Mrs Munro, your sister has been taken to hospital following a fall."

"I found her concussed on the back doorstep," Hector said.

"Someone had to tell her about Stafford," Brenda said. "I was too upset, so Hector went to find her."

"When I didn't find her indoors," Hector said, "I went outside to have a look for her. The three of us live in a small cottage in the grounds. Thought she was most likely there, but she was face first on the back doorstep, blood pouring from her head. 'Christ,' I said to myself. 'Not another one.' Thank God the ambulance was still here."

"They were fantastic," Brenda said. "Really calm. You can imagine the state I was in. They explained I couldn't go with her, with Stafford's death looking suspicious, that I had to stay behind and not change my clothes or anything. I was really upset, but they promised me they'd take excellent care of her and she'd be okay."

"The ambulance man didn't seem to think she'd been attacked too, thank God," Hector said. "Said from the look of things, she'd tripped and hit her head. The washing basket was by her feet on its side, the washing on the line. We found a bowl of crab apples on the table. We think she went inside with the fruit, then back out again to put the washing out, but somehow or other managed to trip herself up on her way back. It's not the first time we've found her out cold."

"She wasn't very steady on her feet," Brenda said.

"Why was that, Mrs Munro?" Eden said. Mrs Bridget White was only fifty-one.

"My sister's an alcoholic," Brenda said. "She has falls all the time. We found her at the bottom of the stairs once. The doctor said her being drunk saved her. Made her nice and floppy."

"And Mr Mills tolerated this?" Black said.

"Stafford knew I wouldn't abandon her. They bumped along quite happily," Brenda said. "It's why we stayed as long as we have. Where else could I have looked after her and still had a job?"

"Mr Mills wasn't married, was he?" Eden asked.

"No, but he was with Corrine a long time. They split up only last month," Brenda said.

"Corrine?" Eden said.

"Corrine Beechwood. They were together for years. I thought they'd marry. I was quite upset when they split up," Brenda said.

"Does she live near here?" Eden said.

"Oh yes," Brenda said. "The next village."

"Can we return to the attack on Mr Mills?" Black said. "The window to the part of the room he was found in was closed, but unlocked, yet the other window was locked. Are the windows normally kept locked?"

"As a rule, yes, but Stafford was always opening and closing windows," Hector said. "He was a bit of a fresh air freak. He slept with his window open most nights, even in winter."

"Did the advert for the candlesticks get a good response?" Black said.

"Can't say it did. Only three people responded and one of them never showed," Hector said. "Knowing Stafford, he asked way too much."

"I understand a number of people called here this morning, and some of the meetings were stormy?" Black said.

"I can only tell you what I personally witnessed," Hector said. "The first visitor this morning was Eddie Edwards. His appointment was at 10.00…"

Hector Munro calmly recited the morning's events. When done, the two officers got to their feet. "Thank you very much for your assistance," Black said. "I'm afraid I'll almost certainly need to speak to you again at some stage, but I'll leave you for now. Do you have anywhere to stay tonight?"

"We have a little caravan near here," Brenda said. "We'll go there."

"I hope your sister makes a speedy recovery, Mrs Munro," Eden said.

It was already growing dark. Black decided to leave his walk around Fenn Farmhouse until the following day.

"Get yourself home now," he said to Eden. "See you first thing tomorrow."

3

"A generation goes, and a generation comes, but the Earth remains forever."

"Excuse me, sir?" asked the young police officer on sentry duty. It was first light and the young constable, coming to the end of an overnight shift, was struggling to keep awake. The appearance of the Senior Investigating Officer had forced him to jump to attention.

"Osborne Tye's in the Domesday Book, Constable," Detective Inspector Guido Black said. He was dressed, as usual, in a dull dark suit, his top button done up, his tie in a Windsor knot, enlivened by a pullover. Today's colour, British racing green. "How much skulduggery do you think it's seen in that time?"

"Quite a bit, sir."

"Quite a bit," Black repeated.

Behind its police cordons, Fenn Farmhouse was deserted. The wind had died down taking with it the "country smell". That should make the dogs' jobs easier, Black thought. To get the lay of the land, he positioned himself on the country road and faced the gate. He saw the hawthorn hedge to his right, and the larch and oaks to his left. He looked along the drive. It cut a straight line between the tree-lined boundary and the front lawn until splitting in two, a fork continuing to the double-garage immediately ahead, another making a right angle to cross in front of the house before continuing around the far corner.

Before he walked it, Black moved to the start of the bridle path which skirted the tree-lined boundary. On the other side of the path were yet more trees and beyond them, a stubbly hill enveloped in the morning mist, and then farmland. He returned to the gate and started to walk down the drive towards the garage. He stopped at the window of the murder scene, its curtains drawn against voyeurs, and turned his back to the window. The room looked out onto the larch and oak trees and the hill beyond them. Had the killer approached the farmhouse from this direction, skirting along the brow of the hill concealed by the thicket of trees, to lie in wait until the coast was clear? It wouldn't take long to get from there to the window. If Mills had his back to the window, or was asleep, or in the other half of the room behind the shelves, or somewhere else, with the window unlocked, or even open, the killer would be inside in a flash – quickly, quietly, unnoticed. Then again, it wasn't out of the question that Mills knew his killer and let him or her in. Through the front door if the meeting wasn't a secret, or the window if it was.

Black continued on his way. He glanced at the room's second window, but its curtains were also drawn. A side-door, secured to the wall by a cabin hook and eye, opened onto a tiled passage leading to the inner hall. Black made a note in his day book to ask Hector if this door was usually locked or unlocked during the day. Next came the dining room, its curtains drawn. The garage's concertina doors were two-thirds open, revealing forensics dabbing for prints, Stafford Mills' Jaguar, having already been taken by forensics. He judged from the garage's position to the house – it jutted out beyond the farmhouse's rear wall by about three or four feet – that it was newer than the farmhouse. Its construction reduced access to the back garden, from where he stood, to an area precisely one and a half paving slabs in width. Black stood on the first slab. He couldn't see much of the back garden from this location, nor did he believe anybody outside his direct line of vision could see him. He continued into the back garden. Behind the garage was a two-storey brick building with a corrugated steel roof and a wooden stable door. He looked around. The narrow path he stood on widened and continued past the outhouse and down the garden. This was laid out to lawns, dotted with fruit trees and flowerbeds. A whirligig stood motionless, yesterday's washing hanging limply from it, put out before the murder and forgotten, now damp with morning dew. Standing alone, away from the main house, on the opposite side of the garden, was a smaller property, converted from a barn. He crossed to it. Inside was a kitchen and a front room, and upstairs two bedrooms and a bathroom. This was the cottage the Munros lived in with Bridget White.

Black turned to face the house. Beyond the conservatory built onto the dining room, was a patio with the usual garden furniture and pots, which the back door led straight onto. Next came the first of the L-shaped kitchen's two windows. The second was around the corner. He crossed the patio to the drive running down that side of the house to peer along it, seeing, as he did, the second of the two kitchen windows, and the side door by which Ocado had left the previous day's shopping. Beyond that was the cloakroom window. The drive continued to and across the front of the house, but also behind him to the end of the garden. Here, another barn, recently converted into three terrace cottages, awaited holiday bookings. On the ground floor alone, there were any number of ways in and out, and hidey-holes everywhere he looked, not to mention upstairs windows. Shimmying up a ladder in broad daylight was audacious, but he'd seen more audacious than that in his career. With no CCTV in the immediate vicinity and, he suspected, a dearth of forensics, this was going to be a difficult nut to crack.

He returned to the outhouse behind the garage and went inside. The floor underneath his feet was concrete, and the ceiling above his head a mass of cobwebs. The place stank of booze. Two officers were searching through logs.

"Anything?" Black asked.

"Nothing out of the ordinary, sir," one of the young officers said. "We've yet to have a look up there." Black followed his officer's gaze to a wooden mezzanine floor. Two ladders led to it: one, a shiny new police ladder, and the other the building's own rickety-looking wooden one. Had the assailant used this to access the property, he wondered. Returning it afterwards seemed a big risk for little pay off. Nonetheless, he ordered it to be removed for fingerprinting. His eyes scanned the mezzanine – he saw bedding and a few bulging plastic bags, stacked against the wall.

He left the outhouse to take a walk around the perimeter of the property. The thicket of larch and oak trees continued to and along the rear boundary, as did the bridle path which had begun at the road outside. He quickly checked its route on the Ordnance Survey – the bridle path continued along the rear of the property, all the way to the village of Osborne Tye. He returned to the main road at the front, to walk along the bridal path. The dense tangle of ivy, brambles and other undergrowth growing over and between the trees made it nigh-on impossible for anyone on the path to get a good view of the property on his right, or vice versa. On his other side was farmland.

Black walked till he drew level with the end of the garden. Here the path veered right and continued to the village. He didn't go any further, but stood to look along its length. On his left was drilled farmland and on his right, a wooden fence marking the rear of Fenn Farmhouse. He used its gate to return to the back garden. After a quick shufti of the greenhouse (plants in pots on shelves) he went to the holiday cottages. Through the window of one he saw empty, flatpack furniture in boxes leaning against the wall, next to mattresses still in their plastic.

He returned to the front of the house once again, positioning himself on the front lawn. He took in the property's blue-tiled roof, its old uneven red-brick walls, the two large windows on either side of the stepped porch, and the three windows on the upper floor. Everything taken in which needed to be, he walked crisply across the lawn, jumping deftly over the flowerbed and landing on the drive. At the front steps, he replaced his police wellies for shoes, over which he slipped a pair of elasticated shoe covers.

At first glance, the hall didn't offer many obvious hiding places. A second look around, though, revealed more. The tread of the wooden stairs was carpeted but the remainder, from handrail and balusters to the baseboard, was painted in white gloss, which effectively camouflaged a cupboard built into the stairs. He went over to it and gave its white handle a tug. A door opened with a click, revealing a small space holding a vacuum cleaner, a floor polisher, various cleaning materials, some pictures leaning against the wall and other knick-knacks. He couldn't immediately see anything disturbed. What a splendid place to play hide and seek, he thought. "Get forensics to search in here," he said to a uniformed officer.

In the long, narrow inner hallway he opened the door to the murder scene.

The room was still and empty. Virtually everything once in it had been removed for forensic analysis. A circular police stepping plate remained inside the door. Black picked it up and took it with him to the sitting room section of the room. He made sure not to step on the cards littering the floor, marking the positions of the removed items: comfy chair, leather-backed chair, small round coffee table. He looked over to the door, and from there to the bookshelf dividing the room. Its solid back was decorated in the same wallpaper as the rest of the sitting room.

He crossed to the decking. The panelled bookshelves were devoid of the books which had lined them on the day of the murder. In their place, cards read: book; book; book. He looked over his shoulder to the door. The attacker couldn't have entered that way if Stafford Mills had been in the room, unless invited in or he was a very deep sleeper or drugged. He pictured one scenario: Stafford Mills slipping out of the room, maybe to the cloakroom opposite. The attacker entering. Stafford Mills returning. But how had that worked? Mills was sitting down and likely looking at his phone, when hit from behind. Had a trapped, panic-stricken burglar sneaked up on him from behind? Possibly. Just as possibly, though, this was a pre-planned job and the killer had hidden, waiting for the moment to strike.

Black climbed the wooden steps to the library, and from the stepping plate, looked down on a white outline, crisscrossed with string leading to a halo of bloodstains, circled in ink. The gory cats-cradle of murder.

He returned to the inner hall, his footsteps echoing across its tiles. Overhead his team were hard at work. He looked in on the dining room. It looked undisturbed. It was about two-thirds of the size of the front room. Place settings at the table and condiments and cereal packets on a cabinet pushed against a wall, confirmed its regular use. Its window had been found closed and secured. A stag's head above a dark cabinet marked the end of the inner hallway. He opened a door to his right. This took him into a small utility room with hooks and coats and shoes and the back door. After this came the L-shaped kitchen. It was well-equipped and large enough to hold both the kitchen table and a central breakfast bar. The dishwasher was half-full, but the fridge half-empty.

He looked out of the window into the garden and could not see either the outhouse or the garage. He went to the back door and stepped outside to the spot where Hector Munro had found his sister-in-law, unconscious and wrapped around the laundry basket. From here he could see the outhouse, and most of the back garden, but not into the kitchen, nor around either corner. He went over to the whirligig where, on the morning of the murder, Bridget had hung up and taken down two loads of washing. The spot afforded an excellent vantage point. Had she really tripped after putting out the washing, or been drawn to investigate something and attacked for it?

Black drove himself back to the police station.

4

As her boss circumnavigated Fenn Farmhouse, Eden's first priority that morning was a visit to the home of the deceased's ex-girlfriend, Corrine Beechwood. Eden drove herself there, parking outside the suspect's semi-detached house. At forty-three, Corrine was nearly ten years younger than the late Stafford Mills. She came to the door looking as though she hadn't slept for a month. She barely glanced at the badge in Eden Hudson's hand.

"Mrs Corrine Beechwood?" Eden asked.

"If you're here to tell me Stafford's dead, don't bother – phone's been ringing off the hook."

"I'm Detective Sergeant Hudson, Mrs Beechwood. I need to ask you some questions, I'm afraid. May I please come in?"

Corrine shrugged and stepped aside.

In the living room, Eden waited for Corrine to slump into an armchair, before pulling a chair closer. "When was the last time you saw Stafford Mills alive, Mrs Beechwood?"

"Not since we split up."

"Which was?"

"Best part of five weeks past."

"Had you been together for long?"

"If you consider seven years long, yeah."

"Would you mind telling me why you split up?"

Corrine shifted uncomfortably in her seat, blinking rapidly, unconsciously undoing the plastic clasp securing her hair to the top of her head, which fell about her shoulders until swept back up, twisted, and re-secured with the plastic grip. She inhaled a couple of times, steadying her nerves.

"I know it's hard, Mrs Beechwood," Eden said.

"Do you?" She lowered her eyes to the ground. When she looked up her eyes were brimming with tears. "I'd been on my own for two years when I met him," she said. "This place, a big mortgage, and my daughter, was all I got from twelve years of marriage. He was my knight in shining armour, so I thought. But he'd never commit. Says everything, doesn't it? We didn't even live together. That was down to him. Last month was my birthday. I didn't want a lot of fuss, but he insisted we do something. We ended up going to a restaurant with my daughter, Stacey, and her boyfriend. Stacey was convinced Stafford was going to pop the question. We had a lovely night. Great food, champagne flowed. A birthday cake appeared and everyone sung me happy birthday, staff included. Everything but a proposal. Stacey's boyfriend was the designated driver and at the end of the evening, we all piled into his car, Stafford in the passenger seat, me and Stacey in the back. Stacey can be a bit pushy at the best of times, even without the drink.

We hadn't got far when she blurted out: 'When you going to make my Mum an honest woman then, Stafford?' He looked round and through me, like I wasn't there, and said he hadn't given it a thought. Hadn't given it a thought! It was like a dagger to my heart." She looked away, her anguish written all over her face.

"Stacey just wouldn't let it go. She just doesn't know when to shut up sometimes. 'Well, give it some thought,' she said. 'It's been seven years, for God's sake!' I told her that was enough. 'If I ever do get hitched,' Stafford suddenly announced, 'I'll want a prenup – don't want her running off with my money.' Well, Stacey blew her top. 'Who the hell is this her? The dog's mother?' she said. 'This 'her' young lady, is whoever I marry. I never said anything about that person being your mum,' he said. Seven years we'd been together and that's how much I meant to him. It was all I could do to stop myself breaking down. I told Stacey's boyfriend to stop the car and let me out, but he wouldn't hear of it – insisted on taking me to my door. Stafford and Stacey were at each other's throats the whole way. 'I've worked hard for what I've got,' he said. 'What, buying houses up cheap when their owners fall behind with the mortgage, you mean?' Stacey said. 'That hard work, is it? But Mum slogging her guts out in the factory and getting next to nothing for it, that's easy.' I told them both to shut up, and they did. I didn't even say goodbye to Stafford. Just ran in. He rang the next day. To see if I was 'still sulking.'" She made speech marks in the air. "I asked him if he even wanted me in his life. We had the usual 'where is this going?' conversation. He said things were okay for him, and I said, well they weren't for me. Can't say which of us slammed the phone down. Couple of days later

Bridget White arrived in a taxi with my stuff. There wasn't even a note."

"Has there been any communication between you since then?"

"No."

"Mrs Beechwood, I have to ask where were you yesterday between twelve thirty and two p.m.?"

"I work shifts. I spent the morning cooking and freezing my meals for the week, then left for work at a quarter to twelve."

"Where do you work?"

"Cranford's bakery supplies. They've a factory in the middle of nowhere. They supply the trade. Means I never buy bread or cakes, but I don't lose weight neither."

"What time did your shift start and finish?"

"Half-past twelve – it takes me less than thirty minutes to get there, but I like to be early. We were short staffed. Didn't get off till gone six."

Eden felt like a journalist when she said, "Corrine, how did you feel about the relationship ending the way it did?"

"I know you have a job to do, love, but is that really necessary?"

"I'm sorry – yes."

"I knew he was a hard man, but I loved him and thought he loved me. But he didn't." She spoke the words matter-of-factly, though there was bitter disappointment behind them. Eden's heart went out to her. If it had been allowed, she'd've given her a hug.

"It wasn't me," Corrine said. "If I'd wanted to kill him, I'd've done it the day he sent Bridget round with my stuff in a cardboard box, not weeks later on my way to work." She lowered her head and kicked the carpet. "Dunno. Somewhere inside me, thought we'd patch things up. But now we can't."

5

The Vale of Tye police HQ was a large, modern, circular building, located on the ring road leading into the region's second largest city: Sylham. Triple glazing and thick walls kept the roar of traffic outside.

In an interview room, Detective Inspector Black and Detective Sergeant Hudson started a series of interviews, beginning with Eddie Edwards. "Shocking news, this," Eddie said. "Everyone I've spoken to says it's burglars."

"Mr Edwards, we've been unable to find a match for the name and date of birth you've given us," Black said. "Moreover, the registered owner of your address isn't Eddie Edwards, but a Captain Jeremy Havelock – a man whose LinkedIn's mugshot looks an awful lot like you." A computer screen on a stand stood to one side of the table. On it appeared Eddie Edwards' own photograph. "I'm showing the suspect exhibit SM725, the LinkedIn photograph of Jeremy Havelock," Black said. "Are we to take it you and Captain Jeremy Havelock are one and the same, sir, or do you have an identical twin with a different surname?"

"Captain Jeremy Havelock and Eddie Edwards are one and the same," Jeremy Havelock said. "Apologies for any confusion. Stupid of me not to have said."

"May we ask why you have two names?" Eden asked.

"Ah. I'm thinking of changing my name to Eddie Edwards," he said. "New life, new name, sort of thing. Wanted to try it on first, if you get my drift."

Guido Black leant back in his chair and took in the captain. This one's going to have an answer for everything, he thought.

"Do you have other names you're trying on for size that we should know about, sir?" Eden said.

"Only Eddie Edwards, Detective Sergeant," Jeremy Havelock said. "Should've said straight away. Stupid of me"

"What do you do for a living, sir?" Eden said.

"I'm a professional gambler."

"Your LinkedIn Profile says you're a family man, yet you live in a one-bedroom flat, sir," she said.

"My wife and I are having a trial separation. What of it?"

Black leaned forward and rested his chin on his knuckles for a few moments. "How should we address you? Mr Edwards or Captain Havelock?" he said.

"Jeremy."

"Jeremy, in your statement you claim you were at the farmhouse to buy a pair of candlesticks, but lost your rag when Stafford Mills told you he'd sold them."

"That's right."

"Bit excessive, isn't it, storming out yelling – 'Don't think this is over'?" Black said.

"I'd come a long way."

"Why do you think Stafford Mills told Hector Munro to show you in, if he'd already sold the candlesticks?"

"Because he hadn't sold them," Jeremy Havelock said. "Oldest trick in the book. Get the price up by pretending you've an offer on the table. I wasn't buying it. Told him he'd wasted my time. We ended up arguing."

"Did he threaten you?" Eden asked.

The captain hesitated. "No."

"You were pretty cross when you left, by all accounts," Black said. "Were you so angry that you returned and confronted him?"

"I'd come some way with genuine intents, and I wasn't pleased, but we're only talking about candlesticks. I sat fuming in a lay-by over his rudeness, then went for a run. That did the trick. Calmed me down nicely. Nothing like a bit of nature for putting things in perspective."

Aidan Stanton was the next to be interviewed. He was thirty-three years of age, and he lived in Osborne Tye with his fiancée, Jenna Nesbitt.

"What do you do for a living, Mr Stanton?" Black said.

"I run a music website, selling and renting anything to do with music. I also place self-employed music teachers and musicians. I used to have a music store on the high street, but this is more profitable, so when the lease came up, I let it go."

"Where do you store the equipment?" Eden said.

"Rent a couple of storerooms in Sylham."

"You visited Fenn Farmhouse yesterday morning, in the hours before Stafford Mills was killed. Could you tell me why?" Black said.

"Happy to," Aidan said. "Stafford and I sing in the local choir, just so know you. A few weeks back, he and I got talking about the burglaries. You know about them?" Black nodded. "I mentioned I was thinking of beefing up our home security. He said someone at his London club had recommended a security firm they'd used, and did I want details? I wasn't sure. Sounded a bit expensive, but it doesn't hurt to call, and I took the number. Their quote was quite reasonable and we went with them. After all, they had been recommended by someone who'd used them. I wasn't there the day the young man came to fit the new system, Jen can tell you more, but to cut a long story short, the very same evening, we were broken into. Jen thinks she disturbed whoever did it, but even so, we lost cash and a canteen of silver cutlery. She rang me in a terrible state, poor girl. I was on the train from London. I told her to call the police and got home just as they arrived. I say they, it was actually one police officer. He took one look at our new alarm system and said it was designed for potting sheds, not houses. He asked how much we paid, and Jenna said she'd given the fitter one hundred and fifty pounds cash for twenty percent off. According to this police officer, we'd have done a lot better hanging onto our money as we could have picked one up for twenty quid. Twenty quid!" he repeated indignantly. "They'd taken much more than that in cash.

"Jen gave him the fitter's number, but it was unobtainable. One of those unregistered pay-as-you-go numbers. Jen gave them a description, and they dusted for prints, but neither of us held out a lot of hope. Jen blamed herself, but I blamed Stafford Mills. He gave us the bloody number after all! I wanted to go straight round, but Jen persuaded me to wait for the police to do their bit. 'You know what he's like,' she said. 'He'll end up suing you for libel if you're not careful.' Saturday morning just gone, as I still hadn't heard, I called the police for an update. They'd drawn a blank. No match on the prints or the description. They had however got hold of Stafford. Turns out, the security firm hadn't been recommended by somebody at his swanky London club, as he'd said, but by a barista selling coffee from the back of a bike, who'd made him the perfect mocha, and who hadn't as such recommended the firm, but rather given Stafford his son's business card with the words – 'He's just starting out, needs a leg up.'"

"Stafford Mills admitted this to your local police force?" Eden said.

"Apparently," Aidan said. "He also told the officer that naturally he hadn't liked to engage the young man's services himself, not knowing him from Adam, but had wanted to do the barista a favour as he'd made such a good mocha. I'm not normally an aggressive man, but I hit the roof. It's all Jen could do to stop me going straight round and throttling him there and then." He rolled his eyes. "Possibly not the most tactful thing to say in a murder investigation. I was speaking metaphorically you understand. Jen called the farmhouse and spoke to Hector. He said Stafford was out and he didn't know when he'd be back. Whether that was true, I don't know. She left a message, but Stafford didn't return it. I was there yesterday to confront him."

"And how did that go, sir?" Eden said.

"He said he couldn't see that I had much to be angry about. They'd only taken some cutlery, hadn't they? That's what he said."

Aidan Stanton threw himself back in his chair in exasperation, almost immediately throwing himself forward to lean across the desk again, his arms folded. "I told him our being burgled would affect our insurance premium, and he said he couldn't see how that was any concern of his. As far as he was concerned, it was our fault. We hadn't done any research and we'd gone with the cheapest quote. I was speechless." Aidan leaned even further across the desk, getting as close as he could to the officers, and pointing at both in turn. "Do you know what he said next? Had the barista's son been okay, he'd have used him himself. Now he had to find someone else. I thought it better I leave. He was alive and smug, when I left him. I didn't see or speak to him again."

"Where did you go after you left Fenn Farmhouse?" Eden asked.

"Jen and I went home. I stayed there, working on a composition of my own to calm myself down. I hadn't realised Jenna had gone out again, until she rang me from the Speckled Hen with the news."

"Of Stafford Mills' death?" Eden said.

"Yes," Aidan said. "She was speaking so quickly, I could barely follow what she was saying. The poor girl was more worried about the argument I'd had with Stafford than anything else. I told her to calm down. There was nothing to worry about on that score. The police were too intelligent to think I'd smash a man's head in over such a silly thing. Besides which, I was at home at the time."

Jenna Nesbitt was three years younger than her fiancé. The couple's nuptials were in a few months. "I didn't want to go to Stafford's yesterday," she explained. "I don't like him. Didn't like, I should say. He gave me the creeps. Aidan insisted I go. Strength in numbers, he said. Total waste of time that turned out to be. Told him it would be. He left angrier than he arrived."

"Can you tell me more about the alarm fitter?" Black said.

"I called the number on the business card Stafford gave us," she said. "A youngish sounding man answered. He said he was more than happy to help. His quote was quite competitive. He'd had a cancellation for four o'clock Monday, or it would be another month. That wasn't the problem for me, I don't work Mondays. I go in Saturdays instead. He arrived on time and everything. He was quite young, but he seemed to know his stuff. Knowing next to nothing about such things, I let him get on with it. I thought he'd be longer, but after about ten minutes he said it was all set up and ready to go. It didn't look much. Just a single hub in the hall by the door, and a couple of remote-control fobs. He reassured me that everything was wireless nowadays, and the hub had an operating range of one hundred and twenty-five metres, which, in a house the size of ours, was more than sufficient. He gave a little demo. It was very loud. He said we shouldn't need to do anything else, but if we did, the instructions were in the box and very easy to understand. And if I still had a problem, to give him a call. I went to pay on my card, but he said it was twenty percent off for cash! Bit naughty, but hey, you don't look a gift horse in the mouth, do you? I had just enough on me and got a receipt. It wasn't till after he'd gone that I had a proper look at the paperwork. I couldn't see where it said the fob's range was a hundred and twenty-five metres. I had to go to my spin class and left it out for Aidan to look at when he got back. We were burgled the same evening. Thankfully, they didn't get a lot. Think I must've disturbed them when I came back from spin."

"What happened to the alarm fitter's business card, Stafford Mills gave you?" Eden said.

"The policeman who came to the house asked the same," she said. "I looked everywhere for that. Turned the place upside down. Never found it. I think he must have slipped it into his pocket and taken it with him. I had his number on my phone, but they couldn't trace it."

"On the day Stafford Mills was attacked, you and Mr Stanton left Fenn Farmhouse together, yet you later returned," Eden said. "Why was that, Miss Nesbitt?"

"I wanted a cigarette," Jenna said. "Aidan thinks I gave up yonks back – it's ridiculous really – I'm a grown woman, but he makes such a fuss, I end up sneaking off for a secret smoke. I didn't actually go to the house until I heard the siren. I went to the bridle path at the back. When I heard the ambulance at the farmhouse, naturally I went to have a look. I was halfway down the garden, when Hector started shouting. I ran as fast as I could. I got to the back door the same time as the paramedics. Bridget was just lying there, not moving. She must've tripped over the washing basket and knocked herself out. It's not the first time. I really thought she was dead." She looked at the ceiling and touched her breast bone, and said, "She wasn't, thank God. Hector looked terrible. Kept saying: 'Not her too.' 'What do you mean, Hector?' I asked and he told me Stafford was dead and they were waiting for the murder unit. It sounded like something from CSI. I had to sit down there and then.

Old Hector and I ended up sitting on the lawn. Shouldn't've been surprised really. It was only a matter of time."

"What was Miss Nesbitt?" Eden asked.

"Those burglars killing someone in their own home." She paused to let the point sink in. "Poor Hector didn't know how he was going to tell Brenda that Bridget had only gone and knocked herself out as well. You know with her already being so shaken up about Stafford."

"I believe the paramedics asked you to remain at the scene, yet you didn't Miss Nesbitt?" Eden asked.

"I needed a stiff drink after that. Also I had to call Aidan to tell him about Stafford and I can't get any reception at Fenn Farmhouse. I'll level with you. I was really worried about that stupid argument he'd had with Stafford, but when I got through to him all he said was: 'Well that explains all the sirens.' He told me not to worry, just to come straight home, which I did. After that stiff drink. You can't think Aidan did it. It was just a stupid argument," she said, looking back and forth between the two imploringly. "I have a horrible feeling the burglars drove past me the evening we were burgled," she said. "A black Ford Focus passed me as I turned into our Close. I didn't really get a good look but I think there was more than one person inside. The man who fitted the alarm was quite stocky with tattoos, and his head was shaved. I'm pretty sure I'd recognise him if I saw him again. I don't think he was in the car. That's probably why I dismissed it. It didn't seem much at the time, but the more I think about it, the more I think it was them. I should have said something sooner, shouldn't I? It didn't seem important."

"Better late than never," Eden said. "Registration number?"

"Couldn't say, sorry," Jenna Nesbitt said. "I'm rubbish with stuff like that. It was a black Ford Focus. I know because I used to have one."

"Approximately when was this?" Eden said.

"Spin finishes at quarter to the hour, and then I have to drive back. I'd say just before nine at night."

"That gives us something to go on," Black said.

"Have I helped?" She came across as genuine.

"Every piece of information helps," Black said.

"Stafford was a bit thick putting those candlesticks on Craigslist with all the break-ins there've been," she said. "Hector said he'd warned him, but he knew better, which doesn't surprise me in the least. You might as well know. Stafford wasn't well liked. He didn't treat people right. Look what he did to me and Aidan! I think it most likely he surprised burglars, but if it turns out it was someone with a grudge who did it, can't say I'd be surprised."

"Who's next?" Black asked Eden, after Jenna Nesbitt was shown out of the room.

"The third visitor to Fenn Farmhouse yesterday morning," she replied. "Mr Tim Smith."

Tim Smith showed none of the nerves or hesitancy of those interviewed thus far, rather the opposite. "What you do for a living, Mr Smith?" Eden asked.

"I'm an independent auditor for clinical research papers. Someone coshed him and left him for dead, did they?" he added, glibly. Eden found this ghoulish excitement distasteful, but Black didn't bat an eyelid. Probably seen it a hundred times, she thought.

"Can I ask how you know so much about the crime, sir?" she asked. "Our press release only said he was found with significant head injuries."

"And that you'd launched a murder enquiry," he replied, a hint of excitement in his voice. She really didn't like this man.

"Could you answer Detective Sergeant Hudson's question, Mr Smith," Black said.

"I was having a beer in the village local, speculating with the landlord and the other imbibers on the number of police cars suddenly descending on the village from all quarters when this girl came bombing in, waving her arms around. She was breathless and bright red in the face. She could hardly talk at first. The landlord poured her a brandy and she calmed down enough to tell us that Stafford Mills had been found with his head smashed in and the police were treating it as murder. I nearly fell off my stool. I'd just left him, and he was all too alive then. The landlord poured me a brandy and one for himself and asked her if she was sure of her facts. The girl said absolutely. She'd just come from Fenn Farmhouse. Place was swarming with police officers. She was convinced it was burglars. Struck a popular chord with the locals." He shook his head in bewilderment. "It can't have happened long after I left. Still can't take it in. Bit shellshocked, to tell the truth."

Eden was starting to wonder if what she'd taken for ghoulish excitement was really shock.

"Why did you visit Fenn Farmhouse yesterday, Mr Smith?" Black said.

"My sister and her husband both turn fifty this year, as well as celebrating their silver wedding anniversary. Naturally my mind turned to presents. I was surfing the net, as they say, and came across a pair of antique silver candlesticks dated 1750 on Craigslist. What could be better? The ad gave viewing slots and I made one for yesterday. I got this book from the library to know what to look for. It gave all manner of advice, testing with a magnet, checking that the date on the sprocket matched the hallmark. I made notes and brought them with me. I arrived slightly early on purpose. The book said to do that. Stafford Mills answered the door himself and took me into his front room. He'd turned part of the room into a little library for himself. I thought to myself, now here's a clever fellow. The candlesticks were there, on a table. I asked if I could take a closer look and he told me to be his guest. I checked for all the things the book said to. I didn't have to check my notes, but I noticed him grinning to himself. He'd worked out I was a rank amateur. To try and make myself look genuine, I commented on the tear fluting around the base, and he asked did I want them or not. I did, and made what I thought was a lowish offer. He said he'd accept it for cash. I said I didn't have that amount on me in cash, but I could go to the bank and come back. He said he hadn't time for all that and I could have them if I paid the money straight into his bank account. I couldn't see that was a problem, he clearly had the candlesticks, and we shook on it."

Tim Smith's evidence flatly contradicted that given by Jeremy Havelock. "Mr Smith," Black said. "When you made an offer to buy the candlesticks, Mr Mills didn't say anything about having received an earlier offer?"

"No," Tim Smith said. "Quite the contrary. Appeared eager for a sale. I got the distinct impression I was making him late for something. Maybe the earlier offer was withdrawn?" he suggested.

"Maybe it was, sir. Please continue," Black said.

"I only had his Craigslist ID: Fenny1, and asked for his details to set up the payment. He gave his name. Stafford Mills. I had to ask him to repeat it. 'Stafford Mills,' he said, adding that Stafford was his mother's maiden name and spelling it out for me. I'd heard him the first time. The reason I'd asked him to repeat his name again was because I was flabbergasted." Almost in an instant, Tim Smith's mood changed. It was as though he'd fallen in to a deep despondency, which consumed him so entirely he forgot where he was. Eden wanted to chivvy him along, but with Black motionless, silently scrutinising him, she held back. After a few more minutes, he said, "You see – Stafford Mills is the man I hold responsible for the death of my daughter."

Eden shot Black a brief, surprised look. He didn't reciprocate. On the surface he remained as composed as ever, but she noticed his eyes narrowing.

"Mr Smith, I'm going to have to ask you to explain yourself," Black said.

"Very well then," he said, brushing his thick hair back from his eyes. "The Tim Smith you see before you is a lonely, childless widower, but it wasn't always so. Fifteen years ago, I had a wife, Jayne and a daughter, Sarah. My Sarah was the sweetest gentlest girl," he said, sadly. "When she was sixteen she started a job in a house in London as a housekeeper. Jayne and I were naturally concerned when we learned her new employer was an older unmarried man, but as girls of her age do, she brushed our concerns aside. Our worst fears were confirmed only when we read her diary after her death. Everything was in there – her love for an older, unnamed man, her delight when her feelings were reciprocated, her trepidation, but also happiness at learning of her pregnancy, her heartbreak and despair when he denied paternity and ended the relationship. She opted for an abortion, as many girls in her position safely do, but she was the one in a million. She had an adverse reaction to the anaesthetic, the first time she'd ever had one, and died.

"Although she didn't identify Stafford Mills by name, Jayne and I were left in no doubt as to who was responsible. I wanted to know how he could live with himself, but my calls weren't answered, nor my letters. I went to the inquest to confront him, but he didn't show and couldn't be forced to. I turned up on his doorstep – in those days he still lived in London – but a woman answered the door, insisting he'd moved. She wouldn't say where to and threatened me with the police if I called again. Jayne told me to stop it. We had to try and move on with our lives or we'd go mad, she said. Easier said than done, Detective Inspector. For all her apparent show of strength, she never recovered from Sarah's death. She fell into a deep depression and one day I found her dead in bed. Her heart had simply stopped. She died of a broken heart. This, too, I lay at Mills' feet."

Eden didn't take her eyes from Tim Smith. He wasn't glib or bloodthirsty, he was heartbroken.

"You didn't recognise him when he came to the door?" Black asked.

"Yesterday was the first time I set eyes on the man."

"After you realised who it was, what happened?" Black gently probed.

"When it had properly sunk in, I told him my name. 'The T stands for Tim,' I said. 'Tim Smith.' He looked blank. 'I'm Sarah Smith's dad. 'And who might Sarah Smith be?' he wanted to know." Tim Smith teared up. "He'd forgotten her. All these years I imagined his remorse, regret. But he couldn't even remember the girl's name. 'The young girl you got pregnant and dumped,' I told him. 'The one who ended up having an abortion and dying.' That's when the penny dropped. 'Oh yes, her, yes, now I remember,' he said. 'That was all very unfortunate. You surely don't blame me for that? It was a medical blunder, man.' I exploded. It's the closest I've ever come to physical violence, Detective Inspector. If I'd stayed, I'd have ended up pushing him through the window. I told him what I thought of him and removed myself from the situation." He buried his face in his hands. "I'm sorry," he said. "This has brought so much back. You think it gets easier with time, but it doesn't. It gets worse."

"Would you like a break, sir?" Eden asked.

He shook his head. "I want to get on with it."

"Where did you go after you left the Speckled Hen?" Black asked.

"I didn't. The minute I heard he was dead, I knew I'd end up in a room like this having this conversation with someone like you. I booked a room there, and told the police where they could find me."

"Did you see one or two candlesticks?" Black said.

"Two. He was selling a pair."

Black rummaged under the desk and picked up the candlestick found at the farmhouse. It was now in a clear forensics bag. He set it in front of Tim Smith. "Is this one of the pair of candlesticks you saw yesterday?"

Tim Smith picked up the bag and studied the candlestick closely, turning it around in his hand. "It looks identical," he said, placing it back on the desk. "But I'm no expert."

"Mr Smith, I'm sorry for your loss, I really am, but do you seriously expect us to believe that despite your presence in the vicinity, you played no part in the murder of a man who had done you such a wrong and with whom you'd just argued?" Black said.

"I assure you my story will check out. That man was alive and well when I left."

"Did you return to the farmhouse again yesterday?" Black said.

"I did not, Detective Inspector," Mr Smith said. "As the landlord will tell you, I didn't leave the Speckled Hen. I wonder if you could kindly do me a favour? In my desire to get out of Fenn Farmhouse I nearly knocked some poor lady off her feet, and was unnecessarily abrupt to some poor gentleman. Could you please pass on my apologies, if you'd be so kind?"

Tim Smith's place in the interview room was taken by forty-six-year-old divorcee, Mme Sylvie Laurent.

"What do you do for a living, Mme Laurent?" Eden asked.

"Since my son, Pierre, was born, I haven't been able to commit myself to anything more than part-time casual work. Now he's older, and doesn't need me as much, I'm retraining as an interior designer."

"The late Stafford Mills was your son's father?" Black said.

"He was, yes," she said. "Pierre was conceived during a brief relationship, which Stafford refused to believe was an accident. He accused me of trying to trick him into marriage, as I was getting on in years and desperate. We nearly ended up in court, but eventually he agreed to pay his son's school fees. As you can probably tell from my accent, I grew up in France. After Pierre was born, I returned there and eventually married. Unfortunately the marriage floundered, and I returned to live here. In the hope that a relationship would develop between father and son, I sent Pierre to a school less than an hour's drive away from his father's house. Unfortunately he showed no interest in his son. Pierre is nearly fourteen and his father hasn't once communicated with him. I believed things would stay like this – until last month, when something extraordinary happened.

"I was at Trowchester for the day for a display of medieval tapestries at the Cathedral. All part of the textile designer thing," she added. "I went for a wander afterwards, but ended up getting completely lost. I had to be at the bus station for four and was starting to panic. I don't have much by way of a sense of direction, I'm afraid. I saw this man across the street from me, walking away. I crossed and ran towards him, calling out to get his attention. He spun around. It was Stafford. I saw Pierre in him. I didn't know what to say. I was so surprised.

"It was he who spoke first. 'Sylvie Bignold?' I explained it was Sylvie Laurent now. 'Good Lord. Imagine bumping into you,' he said. I felt the same way. He asked how I was and I said I was well, so too was his son. Seeing him again after all that time, and with so little animosity on his side, confused me. He asked me if I was married, and I told him I was divorced. A son needs his father. I could not allow the opportunity to slip. I put aside those cruel words he'd said to me when I told him I was pregnant. He'd mellowed, as we all do with time. I asked if he'd like to see a photograph of Pierre, and he said he would. 'See how much of you is in him,' I said. 'He's small for his age, but wiry and tough.' Stafford laughed and said he was the same at that age. 'I would like you to meet him,' I said. He smiled and said he'd like that as well. I explained I had a bus to catch and asked for his number. He became quite maudlin, and begged me not to rush off. I told him I had to. He took a hold of my hand and said, 'I never had any more kids, Sylvie, and can't see I ever will. Pierre is my only child. Will he see me?' 'It's half term next week,' I said. 'Let me speak to him.' It ended up with me agreeing to have lunch with him after Pierre went back to school. He pointed me towards the bus station. I didn't look over my shoulder, but I believe he remained there for while. On the journey back, I kept thinking how attentive he'd been, and how at ease we'd been with each other. It was as though no time had passed at all, and we'd parted without any ill-feeling." She smiled wistfully to herself as she said this. In Eden's view, Sylvie Laurent hadn't only been transported back to the moment she'd bumped into Stafford Mills in Trowchester, but to fourteen years ago, when still a young woman, head over heels in love.

"I won't lie," Sylvie said. "I was ecstatic that he'd invited me to lunch. I wanted to see him again. I couldn't help myself. Maybe I was flattering myself, but I came away with the impression that he wanted more than just his son back in his life. Not that it matters now." She stared down at her hands, as though admiring her perfectly painted nails.

She rallied and looked up. "There was only one problem with all of this. My son. It was all very well his father and I patching up our differences, but neither of us could force a reconciliation. Pierre is stubborn; he takes after his father in that. When I called Pierre and said his father wanted to meet him, he made it clear he didn't want to see him and put the phone down. I left him to calm down, and when I picked him up for half-term, he had. We had a long talk over the break. 'He is your father,' I said, 'and nothing can change that.'

"He reluctantly agreed to meet Stafford, but on strict conditions. He didn't want to be alone with him, until he got to know him better. He also wanted his father to pay for his school skiing trip. I've never been able to afford to pay for him to do much of anything. Stafford pays the school fees, and something towards Pierre's keep over the holidays, but nothing else. The poor child's only been on a single school trip the whole time he's been at that school. I know Pierre intended it as a sign of goodwill, but I was concerned his father would think we were out to get what we could. I told Pierre we wouldn't make it a condition, but if the moment was right, I'd test the water. This brings us to yesterday.

"As we'd arranged, I dropped Pierre off at school for the start of term, and drove to Stafford's house. I won't pretend. I chose my outfit with care. I wanted him to notice me, but not make it too obvious. I think I'm still attractive for my age. Nice and slim." She gently tapped the sides of her legs. "I wore jeggings, and a tight top. I wanted to look casual, yet alluring – but not desperate. I knew he likes heels and I wore kitten heels. I bought them especially." Her mood changed. "I expected him to have done well for himself, but so well? He'd given his own son next to nothing, yet lived in a lovely country place. My mood wasn't helped when the door was opened by a member of staff. He could afford staff, yet give his son nothing." She stopped to compose herself.

"I went to the cloakroom as much to calm down as anything. I reminded myself of his kindness the week before, and that people change. When I eventually saw him, it was all rather surreal. He'd obviously just argued with someone and was clearly angry, but, and I say this with complete honesty, the moment he saw me he instantly calmed down. We exchanged pleasantries, as though the unpleasantness I'd just witnessed, hadn't happened. This gave me the confidence to say that his son was interested in meeting him, but was understandably nervous. 'It might help if you could see your way to making him a token of goodwill,' I said. I suggested the skiing trip. 'Pierre so badly wants to go,' I said, 'but my resources can't stretch to it. It would mean so much to him. You'd be doing something you don't have to do, that's not something he'd forget.'

"That is all I said, I promise you, but it was enough. He went red in the face and said no one in their right mind could consider a skiing trip a token, and was I taking the piss? He didn't raise his voice, rather he hissed the words at me. I reminded him we were talking about his son. He accused me of selling access – of selling my son's love. I tried to reason with him, but he wouldn't listen. He said my sex were all the same – out for what we could get. I begged him to calm down and see reason. I might have touched his arm to placate him, but nothing to warrant him physically attacking me. It's a wonder I wasn't injured!"

"Yet you didn't call the police Mme Laurent?" Eden said.

"Pierre is everything to me. I didn't want to jeopardise any future relationship with his father. The argument was as much my fault as his. My timing was terrible. Stafford was still hot around the collar after his earlier argument, and in truth, so was I. Age had mellowed him. I'd seen the change myself. Allowing things to cool down was the best course. My intention was to ring him and apologise, if I'd offended him. But things turned out very differently."

"Where did you go after you left?" Black asked.

"Straight home. I was more shaken than I looked, I can tell you. I filled the car up on the way back. I needed to talk things over with someone, and popped in to see my neighbour. She's quite old and frail, but she gives good advice. Her home help was there as well, and we sat around a table having a girly chat. I'd just got home when one of your officers rang with the news."

"How did that make you feel?" Black said.

"Shocked, and if I'm truthful, sad. Now there isn't a chance of Pierre and his dad having a relationship."

"Mme Laurent, can you see, that to some people, the timing's a bit fanciful to say the least," Black said. "You bump into your son's dad in the street, after the best part of fourteen years. He's a changed man. He invites you to lunch. You argue. An hour or so later he's murdered."

"It's what happened," she replied. "I had nothing to do with it. My neighbour and her home help will confirm I was with them. What reason would I have to kill Stafford?"

"Will Pierre benefit from his father's death financially?" Eden said.

She stared back, blinking rapidly before replying. "I don't know. I really don't. I very much doubt it, given his past treatment of his son."

"Stafford Mills was selling candlesticks on the day he was killed. Did you happen to see them in the room?" Black said.

"I didn't, but I wasn't looking. I really wasn't in the room long enough to notice much."

"Was there a window open?" Eden asked.

"I can't say."

"During your visit to the cloakroom, did you open the window?" Black said.

"I was there only to splash my face," she said.

"Thank you for your time and information, Mme Laurent," Black said. "I'm sorry this has happened."

She got to her feet, hesitated, and sat down again, glancing between Eden and Black. "Do you know what happened yet? Pierre is asking. The only thing we've been told officially is that Stafford was found with head injuries."

"We're still awaiting the result of the post-mortem," Black said.

"Did he say anything in his final moments? Make mention of his son? Is there anything I can tell Pierre to make this better?"

Eden was starting to feel rather sorry for Sylvie Laurent. "With those injuries, Mme Laurent, he wouldn't have been aware of much," she said.

6

———

"Afternoon sir," the guard at the security gate said, lifting the barrier to allow Black through. Black gave a nod in the guard's direction and Eden returned her badge to her pocket. The aircraft hangar laboratory ahead, clad in tubular metal beams and banks of dark windows, glittered in the afternoon sun.

The white and grey autopsy room took up much of the ground floor. Evenly spaced potted plants leaned towards the little natural light able to filter through the room's opaque windows. By the door, a skeleton perched on a circular stand, its bony hand pointing to the slogan on its T-shirt: *Winter Is Coming*. Overhead, extractor fans valiantly tried to suck the smell of blood from the air.

"Tell me about it," Black told the skeleton.

Four of the room's five stainless-steel dissection tables remained spic and span, beneath wooden slabs. On these, rested trays neatly laid out with autopsy equipment. Pathologist Matthew Prichard, dressed in a white overall and mask, stood by the fifth table. Its wooden slab, jutting out from the head of the table, was covered in an array of bloodied dissection equipment.

"Perfect timing. We've just stitched him up," Prichard said.

Black and Eden joined him at the autopsy table where lay the body of Stafford Mills. Neatly stitched wounds ran the length of his chest, and around his skull. "Whose body are we looking at, Matthew?" Black said. He hadn't asked in order to satisfy himself; he knew this was Stafford Mills. He'd asked for the official records of the case – another case, the case of Hawthorne unspoken, but always present.

Eden had still been on the beat when the story went from family tragedy to a media goldmine. The facts: samples taken from two young female friends killed in a car crash, were mislabelled and their bodies given to the wrong families. One was cremated, ashes scattered, the other interred in another family's tomb. The mistake came to light and the families were informed, whereupon half the prison population demanded an immediate retrial. This might have been the end of it, had not an ill-judged, flippant private email of the Detective Superintendent in charge of the review, querying whether this was as big a deal as the families claimed, been forwarded to a Sunday paper.

"Two long-serving staff members identified him as Stafford Mills," Prichard began. "The dental records support this, as do our initial tests on the hair and saliva samples taken from Stafford Mills' hairbrush and toothbrush."

"Cause of death?" Black said.

"Confirmed as acute subdural haematoma – single blow to the rear side of the head." He used a pointer to indicate a wound on the right side of the skull towards the back. "The sharp corner of the candlestick caught the side of his head."

He used his fingers to make an arrow, moving his hands forwards and backwards, to mimic a sharp corner impacting the head. "The blow cracked his skull. Upon impact, he fell frontwards, landing on his face, breaking his nose and knocking himself out, if the blow hadn't already done that. He was taken unawares, there's no evidence of defensive action." He pointed to the wounds and bruises on the face, talking to future students of anatomy as much as the two officers in the room. "With head injuries the real damage is invisible. Blows to the head tear the blood vessels on the brain's surface, leading to a build-up of blood and cerebrospinal fluid in the intracranial space. The pressure builds and builds, the individual slips into unconsciousness, becomes comatose and without surgery to alleviate the pressure, dies. How quickly this happens varies from individual to individual. Some people lapse into unconsciousness within minutes, others potter around feeling a bit dazed for hours afterwards, then drop down dead. With fatal head injuries, there's always the possibility the victim was alive for some time after the injuries happened, but unable to raise help. We can discount that with Mills here. He was almost certainly looking at his phone when struck from behind. Forensics confirm he last logged in at 12.57. The Munro's call to the paramedics was timed at 13.07. We're talking a quick bleed."

Eden noted the time of the attack at 12.57. "Brenda Munro says he groaned," she said.

"More likely air leaving the body."

"Male or female assailant?" Black asked.

Prichard shook his head. "Difficult to say. It was the angle of the blow which killed him, not the force behind it. Also the fact of his sitting down. Here, our killer got lucky. Stafford Mills was exactly six foot tall, making smashing him over the head a challenge for anyone. His last meal was the toast and marmalade he'd eaten for breakfast. No drugs or alcohol in the blood. For a man in his early fifties, he was in pretty good shape. He had very little body fat, or muscle wastage. He didn't smoke and his heart and lungs were in good shape. All in all, I'd have expected him to last another thirty or forty years, had somebody not coshed him across his head."

"We certain the missing candlestick was the murder weapon?" Black said, with a glance towards the silver candlestick standing aloof in its evidence bag away from the scattered and bloodied tools of Prichard's trade. Prichard reached across to pick the bag up, and held the candle's square base next to the deceased's skull, just above the fatal wound. "The corner, and the impact site are a precise match," he said. "Blood sprayed outwards, backwards and sideways, but primarily in the direction of the window. The murderer probably escaped the brunt of the showers, but no one can escape tell-tale blood splatter completely."

7

The Speckled Hen on Osborne Tye's main street had begun life three centuries earlier as a coaching inn and the old stone archway at the building's side, which once led to stables, still remained, although it now took customers to a car park and a beer garden. Black drove under it and after parking, Eden and he took a look around. They walked through the sheltered beer garden to a fence and a gate at the rear of the public house. This led to the bridle path. Take a left, and in a little over five minutes, they'd be at Fenn Farmhouse. They returned to the building.

A middle-aged man came to the door. He glanced at their police badges and said, "Been expecting a visit. Come in."

Black liked what he saw: exposed red brick, wooden beams, oak furniture. He surreptitiously reached over to a table. It slightly wobbled. A fire was laid but not lit in an enormous stone fireplace. There was real ale in its pumps, and a food menu of scotch eggs and pork pies. His girlfriend, Chloe, preferred wine bars and gastro pubs. But this was his type of place.

"Could you confirm your name and date of birth, sir?" Eden asked the publican.

"Harry Sykes. I'm the landlord." His date of birth made him fifty-five.

"How long have you been the landlord of the Speckled Hen, Mr Sykes?" Eden continued.

"Going on twenty-five years," he said. "First there was me and Mrs Sykes number one. Then there was me and Mrs Sykes number two. Now there's just me."

"Do you recall a man arriving here before midday, Monday seventeenth. Monday just gone? He wouldn't have been a local," Black said.

"You mean the day Stafford Mills got done in?"

"Yes," Black said.

"I do. I hadn't been long open when he came in. The place was dead. Don't know why I bother opening during the week sometimes, particularly lunchtimes with daytime drinking frowned upon and villages like ours turning into dormitories for commuters. Running a pub's a thankless task in this day and age. He sat there," he pointed to a stool at the bar, "and ordered a pint. He was a bit peculiar. I don't mean in an odd, eccentric way, I mean he came across as a bit shaky, but trying not to show it. I asked if he was okay and he said he was, then just as quick said he wasn't. I got his whole life story. Bad business, his girl dying like that. You know about that?" he asked. "About Stafford Mills and his daughter?"

"Yes, sir," Eden said.

"I had to leave him to his sorrows. I could hear the phone ringing at the back, and I had a barrel needed changing. I was quite glad of the excuse to get away, tell the truth. I left him at the bar. There's bells over the doors if someone comes in, or goes out, and the till was empty. Said to yell if he needed anything. Was on the phone longer than I thought and then I had a problem changing the barrel. I was away for the best part of twenty minutes in the end, with one thing and the other. Half expected him to have had another pint on me and scarpered, but it didn't look like he'd moved. His glass was empty though and he ordered another pint and a pie. He'd obviously got what he needed to say off his chest and he sat quietly reading the paper. A few others came in, giving me a bit of business. I heard an ambulance go by, thought nothing of it, then all these police cars roared past. Couldn't hear nowt but sirens. We went outside, but no one knew anything. We'd just about traipsed back indoors when young Jenna Nesbitt come bolting in. Through the back door, same as you did. She was in a terrible state, gabbling on about Stafford being murdered, Brenda and Hector finding him in a pool of blood, head caved in. I couldn't believe my ears. This is Osborne Tye. People come here to grow old, not get murdered. I asked if she was sure he'd been murdered? She said she was one hundred percent positive. She'd only just come from there, hadn't she? Said he'd been hit with a heavy instrument and stuff had been taken. She folded her arms like this…" he folded his across his chest,"…and said: 'We all knew this would happen, Harry, let's face it.'"

"What do you believe Jenna meant by her words?" Eden asked.

"Those burglars did for Stafford," he said. "Don't know how many burglaries there's been here and abouts.

The police never seem to arrest anyone." Harry Sykes reached across the bar and picked up the morning's editions of well-known national newspapers. He lined them up along the bar, folding his arms across his chest, triumphantly. It was the first time Black and Eden had seen the morning's headlines:

Burglars Kill Man In Own Home!
The police are working on the theory that the death of property tycoon Mr Stafford Mills, 57, is linked to burglaries in the area.

Did East European Crime Gang Kill Man?
The police have been unable to rule out the possibility that a European crime syndicate are behind the murder of property developer, Stafford Mills (59) brutally murdered in his own home.

Was Stafford Slain For Stolen Silver?
The police have confirmed valuable silver is missing from the home of the forty-nine-year-old businessman murdered in Osborne Tye on Monday.

Eden and Black glanced at each other briefly. "Just how old was Stafford?" Harry Sykes asked.

"Fifty-three, sir," Eden said. "We're aware of the burglaries, but it's too early to say whether there's a connection between them and the death of Mr Mills."

"How did Mr Smith react to the news of Stafford Mills' death?" Black asked.

"Mr Smith?"

"Mr Smith is the man who was sat there and told you about his daughter," Eden said.

"I weren't really paying him a lot attention," Harry Sykes said. "Reckon he was pretty shaken up. Don't really blame him. Remember him asking for a brandy."

"The bridle path at the rear runs all the way to Fenn Farmhouse, doesn't it?" Black said.

"It does."

"Could Mr Smith have got from here to Fenn Farmhouse and back in the time you were away from the bar?" Black said.

"On foot it's just about possible, but he'd have been pushing it. More likely if he did, he was on a bike or a moped or something, but I haven't heard of one being handed in."

"When you returned to the bar did Mr Smith look out of breath, dishevelled or more agitated than when you left him?" Eden said.

"Not noticeably."

"Was he wearing the same clothes he'd arrived in?" Black asked.

"Normally I'd say 'haven't a clue', but your Mr Smith was what my first missus would've called a dandy. He stood out like a sore thumb. So that's a yes."

"Do you have CCTV either inside or out?" Black said.

Harry Sykes shook his head. "Me and my regulars don't care to be spied on by Russians."

"Has anybody been in here trying to sell a candlestick or anything else since the crime occurred?" Eden said.

"No," he said abruptly. "Wouldn't dare. I've run this place for over twenty-five years, without a run-in with the police, as your records will show. I've had people trying to fence, steal, sell drugs, sell themselves, you name it. I don't put up with nothing like that. Why should I risk my livelihood? I can spot a bad 'un." He tapped the side of his nose. "Someone I don't like the look of, I keep my eye on them. One false move and they're out. Anyone came in here trying to sell something dodgy, they wouldn't do it twice. Local thugs know it and keep away."

"One last question, Mr Sykes," Black said. "What was your opinion of the late Stafford Mills?"

"Never knew what mood he was going to be in. He was better if he had Corrine, his lady friend, with him. She was always alright, but not him!" He rolled his eyes. "Sometimes he'd be okay, other times what I call a PIA customer. Pain in the arse. Haven't done hot food since he told the chef how to cook a steak. That said, he'd be okay if you saw him in the street. Not standoffish like some. And he usually had enough money on him."

8

At twenty-four, Philip 'Pilot' Philpott was the youngest officer on the team, and possibly the heaviest. It was day three of the murder investigation, and he took his place alongside the rest of the team in the incident room. Black was on his feet, a laptop open on the table in front of him, a photograph of the deceased in better days on a screen on the wall behind him.

"Stafford Mills, fifty-three years of age, owner and resident of..." Black pressed the curser and the photograph of Stafford Mills became Fenn Farmhouse. "...Fenn Farmhouse, Osborne Tye, Vale of Tye. He was attacked at home in this room."

The blueprint of the ground floor of the farmhouse came up, the crime scene edged in red, the position of the body marked by a white outline. "Stafford Mills was a fairly wealthy man, mostly self-made from property. We understand he also bought and sold stuff online, a hobby he took quite seriously. I'm getting the feel of a competitive man, quite an arrogant and abrupt person. He occasionally kept large sums of cash in the house, but if he had a stash of cash at home when he died, we haven't found it."

Next on the screen was an aerial photograph of Fenn Farmhouse and the village of Osborne Tye. "Fenn Farmhouse is separated from the village by farmland, which surrounds it." He used the cursor to point out the hill at one side of the property, and the flat fields at its rear and other side. "The property fronts the main road between Osborne Tye and Burnley Tye. A bridle path runs from the main road, along the property's western boundary, between it and the hill, and along the rear of the property to Osborne Tye, effectively running parallel to the road. By road, the distance between Fenn Farmhouse and Osborne Tye is only two to three minutes. Longer on foot. We're talking a country location here, making our job all the harder. There aren't going to be many CCTV opportunities. The property's surrounded by trees and hedges. We only have one camera on Osborne Tye's high street, and a couple in local shops, but none in the local pub."

"We're not going to get any images from the camera on the high Street, sir," Pilot said, "it's broken. This is happening more and more. Cash-strapped local authorities haven't the money for repairs. Some are even turning their cameras off to make savings."

"Making our CCTV opportunities even more limited," Black said. He called up a photograph taken from just outside the crime scene. "The room faces west overlooking the side of the house. For those of you who haven't yet visited the scene, the bridle path I spoke of is behind those trees. An intruder approaching around the base of the small hill that you can see over the trees, would be nicely hidden from the property. If they lay flat, they're lost between the brow of the hill and trees. It takes seconds to sprint to the window."

He called up the blueprint of the ground floor again, enlarging the murder scene until it filled the screen. "Stafford Mills was attacked and died in this room, which is divided by a large book shelf, running two-thirds of the width of the room." Black pointed to the bookshelf dividing the room, and then at each of the two windows. "A number of scenarios present themselves. Stafford Mills wasn't in the room when the intruder entered. Stafford Mills was in this part of the room," he highlighted the sitting-room area, "and the intruder entered by this window," he pointed to the library window, "or vice versa, although that scenario is less likely as that window was locked. "Alternative scenarios: Stafford Mills wasn't in the room and the intruder entered by the door. Stafford Mills invited them in. Someone else let them in. We can't rule out an accomplice." The blue-print of the library was replaced with a photograph of a pair of silver candlesticks. "He was selling these silver candlesticks on Craigslist and one was used to kill him. We've yet to recover the murder weapon, but its twin was left at the scene.

"The setup at the farmhouse was a bit odd. The deceased was unmarried. He had been in a long-term relationship, but this ended in the weeks prior to his death. He employed a married couple as live-in housekeepers, Hector and Brenda Munro. They live in a small converted barn on site along with Mrs Munro's sister, Bridget White." Photographs of all three appeared. "This arrangement's apparently been going on for years, and suited everyone. The Munros claim to have found Stafford Mills barely conscious. Brenda stayed with him when Hector called the ambulance. This call was logged at 13.07. The paramedics arrived at 13.21 and pronounced Stafford Mills dead. The pathologist tells us the attack most likely occurred as the deceased logged into his phone, meaning he was struck at 12.57."

He let them all take in this information, then continued: "To complicate matters further, after the paramedics arrived, Hector Munro discovered his sister-in-law, Bridget White, unconscious on the back doorstep. We haven't as yet been able to establish what happened. Mrs White is unfortunately alcohol dependent, and this isn't the first time such a thing has happened. The paramedic team already at the property took her to hospital. She's due to be discharged later today. We've searched the property and its grounds three times, yet little has come to light. We've no unidentified fingerprints, or footprints, discarded clothing, nor the murder weapon – all highly indicative of an attacker wearing protective clothing – suggesting something was preplanned that day, whether burglary or murder or something else entirely. The exterior of the library window was substantially wiped of prints and the interior partially wiped. Forensics have found traces of paint stripper on the exterior, but not the interior. The killer did leave us a short trail of blood from the body to just before the window, when the dripping candlestick was bagged. We're still waiting on hair, fibre and blood splatter analysis.

"So much for the crime. Let's turn to those suspects we know about. In addition to Hector, Brenda and Bridget, a number of individuals called at the house that morning, some, but not all, about candlesticks the suspect was selling. First to show was Captain Jeremy Havelock, although he introduced himself at the door as Eddie Edwards." Havelock's photograph appeared on the screen. "Havelock made an online candlestick viewing slot in the name of

Eddie Edwards. He claims he travelled some way, only to be informed by the deceased on arrival that the candlesticks were sold and if he wanted them, he had to make a higher offer. This so infuriated him that it caused an argument, overheard by witnesses. He maintains he didn't see the deceased again. We don't as yet have his full movements for the rest of the day. His abrupt departure was witnessed by the next at the scene – Aidan Stanton and Jenna Nesbitt, a local couple. Aidan and Jenna called unannounced and uninvited to confront the deceased over a so-called security expert he'd recommended, whose incompetence they claim led to a burglary at their home."

"I spoke to the local investigating officer," Eden said. "He confirmed the alarm system fitted was wholly inappropriate for the property and also that Stafford Mills admitted recommending an alarm fitter as a favour to a man who'd made him the perfect mocha one day in London. Claimed to remember nothing of the man, other than the coffee, and hailing him when he'd cycled past pulling a coffee machine. He thought it might have been somewhere around Fulham."

"I take it we haven't located the barista or his alarm fitting son?" Judy McDermott, the Detective Superintendent overseeing the case, asked.

"Neither," Black said. "It's too early to say if the alarm fitter is connected to the recent spate of burglaries in the area, but you have to wonder. All indications are of a London gang targeting property in the vicinity. We can't rule out the possibility of this being a botched burglary. That's certainly the consensus amongst the locals. Miss Nesbitt remained in the hall, while her fiancé spoke to the deceased. Another conversation which ended badly. Jenna Nesbitt was alone in the hall for a while. Both claim to have gone straight home after their visit. Aidan claims he stayed at home, and was still there when he learned of the murder. Jenna, on the other hand, went out shortly afterwards claiming she went to have a cigarette on the bridle path at the rear of the farmhouse, and was there when she heard sirens and went to investigate, explaining her presence at the property. Jenna now claims she may have seen the burglar's car on the night she and Aidan were burgled. She can't say any more than that it was a dark Ford Focus – the same make of car driven by Jeremy Havelock, incidentally."

Tim Smith's photograph replaced Jenna's. "Next at Fenn Farmhouse was Mr Tim Smith, arriving after Aidan Stanton and Jenna Nesbitt had left. He says Stafford Mills answered the door to him, and took him through to look at the candlesticks. Hector Munro has confirmed he didn't show him in, but did show him out. Mr Smith claims he wanted the candlesticks for his sister and brother-in-law's fiftieth birthdays and twenty-fifth wedding anniversary. Tim Smith arrived at the property almost an hour after Jeremy Havelock, yet says the candlesticks were still for sale, and he made an offer for them, which was accepted. Having only the seller's Craigslist ID, he asked for his details only to learn that Craigslist seller Fenny1 was Stafford Mills, the man he held responsible for the death of his daughter."

"He didn't recognise him?" Judy McDermott asked.

"Says he had no idea it was the same man. Claimed they'd never met. This meeting also ended badly, as you can imagine. From there, Tim Smith went to the Speckled Hen public house on the high street of Osborne Tye and was still there when news of Stafford Mills' death broke. The publican left Mr Smith alone in the pub for a short while, giving Smith just long enough to return to the farmhouse, hit Stafford Mills and get back. If we're honest, this scenario is problematic. The lack of forensics suggests a premeditated attack, yet for Tim Smith to be our killer, he must have left and returned to a pub he couldn't have anticipated would be empty. Also we haven't found the clothes he must have changed in and out of, nor the wheels he must have had to get there and back in such a short time.

"This brings us to the last visitor we know about: Sylvie Laurent. Mme Laurent is the mother of the deceased's thirteen-and-three-quarter-year-old son, Pierre. The couple didn't marry and she described the relationship as brief. The deceased pays his son's school fees under a voluntary court order. According to Mme Laurent the deceased had never shown any interest in meeting his son until a month ago when they bumped into each other in Trowchester on a day trip. She couldn't give a precise location, and will need to be taken back there to retrace her steps. We might have some CCTV opportunities here. As Mme Laurent tells it, she chatted briefly with the deceased, who showed an interest in finally meeting his only child. She described the meeting as amicable and finishing with an invitation to join Stafford Mills for lunch – her reason for being at his house that day.

"Mme Laurent witnessed Tim Smith's angry departure. She claims Stafford Mills initially appeared quite happy to see her, but that his mood changed suddenly and he physically ejected her from the room – a claim supported by Hector Munro. She left at a little after midday, the best part of an hour before he was attacked. She's provided us with her movements afterwards. Pilot, how are you getting on, checking these stories out?" he asked.

"I've allocated a team member to each suspect," Pilot said. "We're going through everything line by line. There's a huge amount to do. We'll get there, but not fast."

"I telephoned Pierre Laurent's school, sir," Eden said. "His mum dropped him off when she said. They ring the bell for lunch at 12.45 and he was one of the first in. When questioned, he said he spent the time in between gaming on his PlayStation, which is on its way here. I also called Corrine Beechwood's factory. They confirmed she was there for her shift that day, which straddled the time of the attack."

"We have one other line of enquiry which may or may not be significant," Black said. "A week before the murder, a man calling himself Leslie Gallagher rang the landline of Fenn Farmhouse and spoke to Hector Munro, asking for an appointment to see the candlesticks. Leslie Gallagher failed to show up. Needless to say, the number Leslie Gallagher called from was withheld."

"Did you say he called the landline, sir?" Pilot asked.

"I did."

"The Craigslist advert doesn't contain a phone number," Pilot said. "It only gives the address after the appointment's made."

"My goodness me," Judy said. "We really are following a number of enquiries. Besides surprising an intruder, any other motives spring out at you, Guido?"

"Virtually every visitor to the house argued with the deceased," Black said. "Only Tim Smith has any credible reason for murder, but he has an alibi unless we can break it. Also we have to ask why he'd announce his presence in the area if he was there to kill Stafford Mills after so many years? I've still to speak to Stafford Mills' lawyer about his will, but unless his son Pierre is a beneficiary, I can't see what reason Mme Laurent would have for murdering her son's father, other than anger. Not to mention her alibi. Likewise, unless the live-in staff benefit enormously from the will, or had a huge falling out with the deceased, I can't see any motives there. We're still awaiting forensics on their clothes. That just leaves the spurned girlfriend…"

"The spurned girlfriend with an alibi, sir," Eden said.

"…and Captain Jeremy Havelock, a man with something to conceal… and local couple, Aidan and Jenna. Their beef with Stafford Mills seems a bit trivial for murder, but we only have their word that's what the argument was about."

9

The mobile home park where the Munros kept their caravan was a short drive from Osborne Tye. Outside the caravan, Black and Eden slammed their respective car doors, triggering a furious barking from inside.

"Will you shush down, Dandelion," Brenda Munro yelled, as her husband opened the door, the dog in his arms.

"Sorry to disturb you," Eden said, "but we've a few more questions for you."

Brenda and Hector glanced at each other. "We're supposed to be picking Bridget up from the hospital in half an hour," Brenda said.

"We've arranged for your sister to be collected and brought here, Mrs Munro," Eden said.

"Well, you'd best come in then," Hector said, stepping aside. "We'll do all we can to help. It's a dreadful businesses, this. Dreadful."

The caravan was warm and snug and filled with the smell of baking. Newly baked scones cooled on a tray. "Let me make us a nice cup of tea," Brenda said. She stayed on her feet, busying herself putting the kettle on, dropping some teabags into a teapot, putting the scones on a plate. Her husband invited the two police officers to take a seat at the kitchen table, but they remained standing.

"After you, please," Black said to Brenda. She left the tea brewing and sat down next to Hector. She was the more nervy of the two, crinkling her dress up and releasing it. Eden noticed how Hector continuously looked over to his wife, his concern evident.

"How long did you work for Mr Mills?" Black asked.

"Me, from before I married," Brenda Munro said. "I worked for his parents before him. When Cybil had to go into a home, he moved back to the area and asked me to housekeep for him. I said I was engaged to marry and he said that wouldn't be a problem, he needed a gardener."

"I was working as a jobbing gardener-come-odd-job man at the time," Hector said.

"My sister didn't live with us then," Brenda Munro continued. "She only moved in after she lost her husband, Ronnie. That's when all this drinking started. Her losing him so young. We've tried everything to get her to stop but nothing's worked."

"It's true what they say, if someone won't help themselves, there's nothing anyone else can do," Hector said.

"Did it work, living on top of the man you worked for?" Black said.

"It sounds a bit Downton, but it wasn't like that. It worked," Hector explained. "Stafford needed someone to look after him and his home. He didn't have one jot of interest in doing anything himself. I don't remember him ever making so much as a cup of tea. No doubt my wife would accuse me of the same." The tension in the room lightened.

"Brenda and I did what was needed without being asked," Hector went on. "He wasn't always looking over our shoulders, like some. We mostly kept out of each other's way. In exchange, he paid us a good wage, and let us live in our own place at a greatly reduced rent. My wife and I speak as we find, and he was all right to us."

"Is there anything about the late Stafford Mills we should know about?" Eden said.

The couple exchanged a glance. "Stafford wasn't a criminal," Hector said slowly, "but he didn't like paying for things much."

"He was a thief?" Black said.

"Nothing like that, no, but if he could find a reason to complain and get a bit knocked off the bill, he would. That kind of thing. It got a bit embarrassing on occasions," Hector said.

"Tax was a big bugbear of his," Brenda said. "He'd have done anything to get out of paying it. I once said to him: 'Nobody likes paying tax, but if we want schools and hospitals...' He came out with the usual 'I don't have kids argument. There wasn't any point arguing further with him, and that was the end of that."

"But he did have a child," Eden said. "Pierre."

"He didn't have a lot to do with him, dear. Out of sight, out of mind," Brenda said.

"Those candlesticks he was selling, he did a lot of that," Hector said. "Made quite a bit, if he was to be believed. We never asked if he declared it, but I'd be surprised if he did. Think most of it was cash in hand. He was certainly never short of the stuff. Had wads of it."

"You make him sound like a middle-class Arthur Daley," Eden said.

"In some ways he was," Hector said.

"Where did he keep all this cash?" Eden asked.

"On him. Hidden about the place," Hector said.

"He put quite a lot of it into Bridget's bank account," Brenda said. "He'd get her to take it out later and hand it over. For a long time he rented out a house he'd bought in her name. He kept the rent, obviously. We only got to hear of it after it was sold. He was gloating about not having to pay tax on the rent he took in or the profit he made when he sold it, because the Revenue thought it was Bridget's home. Hector had to tell him to cut it out. That was a step too far."

"We couldn't have him dragging Bridget into it," Hector said. "When she's been drinking, she'd sign anything put in front of her and not remember. He was taking advantage and we had to put a stop to it. She could have gone to jail for that. Far as we know, it never happened again."

"Was he okay about that?" Eden said.

"It was a while back, wasn't it, Hector?" Brenda said. Hector nodded. "He never mentioned it again. If he held it against us, he never said."

"He couldn't really risk us opening our mouths," Hector said.

"How well did you know Corrine Beechwood?" Eden asked.

"They were together a long time," Brenda said. "They never lived together – he'd never have that – but she was at the house a fair bit, though he spent more time at hers than she did here. She never threw her weight around. I was upset for her when they split up, but not altogether surprised."

"Why not?" Eden asked.

"He'd never commit. He could be quite nasty to her. Putting her down and stuff. And I don't think he was faithful to her, although I can't prove it," Brenda said.

"Have you seen Mrs Beechwood since the split?" Eden continued.

The Munros shook their heads. "Stafford got me to pack her stuff," Brenda said. "He wanted me to take it to her, but I wouldn't have known what to say to her. Bridget went in the end."

"It seems from what you've said that Stafford Mills rarely mentioned his son?" Black said.

"To be honest with you, the only time he ever talked about Pierre was to complain about how much the boy cost him," Hector said. "Brenda and I haven't been blessed with children, and it wasn't something we could comment on much."

"Did he say anything about reconnecting with the boy?" Black said.

"Not to us, but then he wouldn't, not stuff like that," Brenda said. "Might have said something to Bridget. She got on okay with Stafford. He had a soft spot for her, used to tell her all sorts of things, if she's to be believed."

"Not that she can remember half of it," Hector murmured.

"Do you know of anyone who might have reason to kill Stafford Mills?" Black said.

"We've racked our brains," Brenda said. "Haven't we?" Her husband nodded. "Stafford could be a right pain, but not enough to warrant someone murdering him. We're still of the mind he disturbed a burglar. Hector warned him against putting the candlesticks on Craigslist, with all the burglaries there's been."

"He was a stubborn man," Hector said. "Not one to take advice."

"Is there anything else either of you have remembered, which might be of help to the investigation?" Eden said. "However small."

"Brenda thinks she heard a car," Hector said.

"Pulling to a stop outside when we were having our lunch," Brenda said. "It started the dog off, not that that takes much. I thought it might be the Sally Army come for the bag of clothes I'd left out the night before. I didn't hear any more and the dog quietened down. No one came to the door. Thought nothing of it."

"Noise carries in the country," Hector said. "We can't always tell where it's coming from when we're at the back of the house."

"Did your sister join you for lunch, Mrs Munro?" Eden asked.

"She'd had a fry-up for her breakfast, and didn't want anything much," Brenda replied. "She hung the washing up. She can manage stuff like that, a bit of light housework. She had a coffee with us, before disappearing off to pick her crab apples. Didn't see her again until Hector found her unconscious on the back doorstep. She must've tripped over the basket. Dread to think how long she'd lain there."

"I'm sorry to ask you this," Black said. "But when you last saw your sister, was she sober?"

Hector and Brenda shook their heads sadly in unison. "She's usually all right 'til mid-morning, then she starts drinking," Hector said. "The outhouse. That's where she usually went. She had bottles hidden there, as if we didn't know."

"We've tried everything, even had her hospitalised," Brenda said. "But you know how it is with people like that. Unless they admit they need help, it's hopeless. We're fighting an uphill battle with my sister."

"And losing," Hector said.

Eden ran into the small living room. There wasn't anything for breakfast. Dixie was curled up in an armchair, feet tucked underneath her, sipping from a mug. She quickly covered it with her hand when she saw her young daughter, but its fumes filled the room. "It's just tea, darling," Dixie said. "You know how much mummy needs her tea in the morning."

"I know, Mummy," Eden said.

When had she become a party to the lies?

"We're hungry."

"Well, make yourself breakfast."

"There isn't anything."

"Well, go next door then. Mrs Goodson will have something. She always does. She's so fucking wonderful."

Eden forced herself back to the moment. Hector was telling them that the day before Stafford was murdered, Ocado had delivered exactly the same order they delivered the day Stafford died.

"They'd been the day before with the exact same stuff. Bridget forgot and put the order in again," he said.

"Did the deceased have any brothers or sisters that you know of? Nephews or nieces?" Eden asked.

"A brother, Martin," Brenda said. "They had a falling out years back. I haven't the faintest idea if Martin married or had children. I don't even know if he's still alive."

"What did the brothers fall out over?" Eden asked.

"Martin caused a fatal accident, and Stafford got caught up in it," she said. She looked angry. "I never thought him the type to do something like that. You think you know someone." She looked down.

Black unwrapped a telescope, unearthed by the search team in some undergrowth close to the farmhouse, but wiped of prints. "We found this close to Fenn Farmhouse," Black said. "Have either of you seen it before?"

Hector leaned across the table to study the object. "Looks like Stafford's," he said. "He got one when he got interested in stargazing. Soon got bored. Last time I saw it, it was gathering dust on a shelf in the garage. If you don't find a telescope there, then that's his all right."

Outside, a car tooted its horn, waking the dog from her slumbers under the table. She bolted to the door, bristling and barking. Eden got to her feet. Out of the window she saw an unmarked police car pulling up beside Black's car. It had two police officers in the front, and Bridget White in the back.

"It's your sister, Mrs Munro," she said.

Brenda went outside to greet her, narrowly avoiding being tripped up by Dandelion, overcome with excitement.

"You'll be wanting to speak with her, no doubt," Hector said. "Just so you're aware, she has blackouts. The little she can remember is disjointed. Don't expect her to make much sense." He also went outside, leaving Eden and Black inside.

"Dixie was hallucinating by the end," Eden said.

"Dixie?"

"My mum. Became impossible to tell if she was lying, seeing things, or telling us something that happened twenty years back. Don't think even she knew."

They heard footsteps stomping up the steps, and then Bridget's accusing voice: "Thought you were coming to collect me?"

"We couldn't, Bridget," Hector explained. "The police had more questions for us. They're here now, wanting to talk to you, too."

"Me?" Bridget said, stepping inside the caravan, dog in her arms. "I don't know anything."

Hector and Brenda followed her inside and shut the door. "I'll make a fresh brew," Brenda said, and started doing just that.

"I'm Detective Inspector Guido Black and this is my colleague, Detective Sergeant Hudson," Black said. "I hope you're feeling better, Mrs White."

"Still got a bit of a headache on me," she said, collapsing wearily into a seat at the table. "Doctors say it'll pass. They packed me off with some tablets for the pain meanwhile."

At the kitchen counter, Brenda looked rather alarmed at these words, but said nothing. After waiting for Bridget to add five teaspoons of sugar to her mug of tea, Black said, "Your brother-in-law found you unconscious outside the back door, I believe."

"If you say so. Can't imagine how I came to be there," Bridget said, taking a mouthful of her heavily sweetened tea.

"Hector found you next to the washing basket. You most likely tripped and knocked your head," Brenda said.

"Bloody stupid place to leave a washing basket," Bridget snarled. "Could've been killed."

"What can you remember of the day before yesterday?" Black said.

"Waking up in the hospital, and the nurses saying I'd had a fall, then this policewoman coming in and sitting down on the end of my bed telling me Stafford was dead. She asked me if I'd seen anything, and I said such as what? She told me he'd been attacked and they were looking for the person who did it."

"See how well you can remember stuff, when you haven't been drinking, Bridget?" Hector said.

She glowered at her brother-in-law for a few moments before turning back to Black and Eden. "You're not even

100

safe in your own home any more," she said. "I saw them, you know."

The Munros exchanged a glance, as did Eden and Black. No one had expected this.

"You saw them?" Black asked

"The burglars who killed Stafford!" she said. "Saw them with my own eyes. They were loading our car, with our things. I saw them. They loaded our car and drove off in it." The Munros exchanged another startled glance. "Dandelion set off after them, and they took her too!"

"Bridget, none of that could've happened. You must have dreamt it," Hector said.

She spun round. "Don't you patronise me, Hector Munro."

Her sister gave a sigh, and crossed to take her sister's hand. "Bridget, Hector's right. The farmhouse wasn't burgled. Our car's right outside the caravan, and Dandelion is right there," she pointed at the dog lying under the table.

"I thought you were coming to collect me from the hospital?" Bridget said crossly. "I waited and waited."

"We couldn't, Bridget," Brenda said again. "You know we would've if we could."

"Mrs White, is it possible the car you saw being loaded and driven away was Stafford Mills' Jaguar?" Black asked.

"Oh, I can't remember. A car's a car to me."

"Can you remember when you saw this?" Eden said.

"Not really. It was daylight."

"Did this happen recently or a while back?" Eden asked.

Bridget White pondered. "You know, I haven't a clue, dear. Everything seems an age ago now. Even breakfast."

"Mrs White, do you remember if you saw Stafford Mills on the morning of the seventeenth?" Eden said.

"I'm not sure I can. I have an awful bad head," Bridget said, raising her hand to her head and leaving it there. "What day are we talking about again?"

"The day before yesterday, Bridget," Brenda said. "Monday. I'd washed the Union Jack tea-towels and you put them out and said the garden looked like the Queen's Jubilee with that lot on the line." She spoke slowly and patiently, well practiced at providing her sister with memory aids.

A confused look crossed Bridget White's face. "I don't remember that." She turned to address Black and Eden. "I knocked my head, you know. That can affect memory."

"You're doing very well, Bridget," Black said.

"What did you want to know again?" Bridget asked.

"Did you see Stafford Mills the day you banged your head? The day the garden looked like the Queen's Jubilee," Black said.

She frowned as she thought back. "Let me see." After a while, in her head some penny dropped. She looked triumphant. "I did! I remember now. I was outside and he said, 'Hello Bridget.' Then he started laughing. I asked what was so funny and he said, 'Someone's been a bit naughty.'"

"He said what?" Black said.

"Someone's been a bit naughty."

"Did he say anything else?" Eden asked. Bridget closed her eyes in thought. After a few minutes her sister touched her arm. "I'm thinking," she snapped. "Don't want to get muddled up." When she opened her eyes, it was clear she'd remembered something. She leaned forward conspiratorially. "He wanted me to help him, but not say."

"What did he want you to help him with?" Black asked.

"He had to go in. Said he'd tell all later."

"Can you remember what time this was?" Eden said.

"No, dear. Never wear a watch, you see."

"Are you sure this happened on the day he died?" Eden said.

"Which day was that, again?" she asked.

"The day before yesterday," her sister said. "The day you put the Union Jack tea-towels out to dry. The day you banged your head."

"I can't say for certain, but he had his new Barbour on," Bridget said. "Made a change to see him in something else."

"He only bought that about four weeks ago," Brenda said.

"Did you see Stafford Mills again?" Black said.

She looked quite sad. "Not that I can remember."

"Mrs White, can you remember anything else from that morning? Something out of the ordinary? Anybody loitering? A parked car? A sound you can't quite place?" Eden asked.

Bridget White shook her head and grimaced in pain, raising her hands to her temple.

"If you don't mind, Detective Inspector," Brenda said. "I think that's enough for now. My sister needs to rest."

Black and Eden got to their feet. "Thank you, Mrs White, Mr Munro, Mrs Munro. You've been very patient and helpful," Black said.

Hector Munro walked with them to the car, leaving his wife indoors with her sister. As they left the caravan, they heard Bridget White say: "Don't know why they asked me all that stuff. If they'd caught those burglars when they should have, Stafford'd still be alive. You're not even safe in your own home any more."

When they reached the car, Eden said: "Just to clarify, Mr Munro, has the farmhouse ever been burgled, or your car stolen?"

He shook his head. "No, nor has Dandelion ever been dog-napped. Thank God. Don't know what my poor wife would do without her. My sister-in-law's getting more and more confused, I'm sorry to say. The doctors say the alcohol is damaging her brain. She has night-terrors. She's on tablets for them."

"Did Mr Mills ever drive your car?" Eden asked.

"Quite a bit, if his needed filling up, or he wasn't going far and couldn't be bothered to get it out of the garage."

"Mr Munro, your wife said Bridget was all right until she started drinking mid-morning. Can we take from that, that if she really saw the things she said, they must have occurred before that time?"

"I'd concentrate on the *if she really* part of that question, Detective Sergeant. But yes, basically."

10

Eden drove herself to the regional Ocado warehouse. She was there to interview the supermarket delivery driver who'd called at the property on the morning of the killing. She spoke to him in a small, cramped back office. The interview didn't take long and revealed little. The delivery to Fenn Farmhouse was on his morning's list. He knew the property, having been there the day before. He had no idea what the order consisted of. No – the green boxes left by the back door weren't unusually heavy. The delivery was one of many he had that day. His job was to get to and away from a delivery as soon as he could – and as safely, he added quickly. This wasn't always easy, he wanted her to know. Had he passed anybody on the driveway? Might have. Couldn't say for sure. Had he seen anybody at the property? Only the man who'd directed him to the back door. Delivery made, he left. He had other deliveries. From Fenn Farmhouse he went straight to his next delivery, five miles away and from there to the next one. He wasn't at Fenn Farmhouse for more than five minutes. He'd checked.

Eden left the warehouse clutching a printout of the shopping orders delivered to Fenn Farmhouse the day of and the day prior to Stafford Mills' death. In her car she looked over the lists. The orders were identical. Any home economics teacher would have been proud – all the food groups were covered. It was a perfectly standard supermarket shop.

She drove next to the Royal Mail sorting office, showing her badge to the man behind the reception desk. The nod and raised finger told her she was expected. He picked up the receiver and called the staffroom. "Tell Vaz there's a young lady to see him." After a pause and an, "Okey dokey," he replaced the receiver, got to his feet and motioning towards the doors leading to the main building, said, "If you'd be so kind."

Eden was escorted up a flight of stairs and along a dreary corridor to a small room, where the postman who'd delivered the post to Fenn Farmhouse on the morning of the murder, waited. Vaz Banks appeared perfectly relaxed. He lounged back in a chair, tilted slightly backwards, his hands clasped behind his head, one leg crossed over the other, right ankle resting on left knee. The room overlooked the main factory floor and even though the windows were double glazed, the noise still filtered through. Eden went to the window to draw the blinds.

Vaz groaned. "Couldn't we leave them open?" he said. Eden knew his type – a relisher of attention.

"'Fraid not," she said. "Your fifteen minutes of fame will have to wait, Mr Banks."

"Call me Vaz, love, please," he said.

"My name is Detective Sergeant Hudson, if you don't mind, Mr Banks."

"Sorry, love, I mean Detective Sergeant. But everyone calls me Vaz. Keep calling me Mr Banks, I won't know who you're talking to."

"Vaz, you were at Fenn Farmhouse only hours before Stafford Mills was killed," she said.

"I know! What about that then? Fucking hell! Sorry, love, I mean Detective Sergeant. Rude word." He gave a pretend grovel. She'd heard way worse and carried on. "Could you please tell me what you can remember of that day?"

"I had a parcel for Brenda. Hector was signing for it when this man came bombing towards us, crashing about, yelling his head off. Hector didn't have a clue who he was. I was genuinely worried things might turn nasty, and decided to stick around like, but to us he was okay. Kept calling Hector squire." Vaz nearly fell off his seat laughing. "Squire! Who the fuck talks like that?" Vaz flinched and, raising his hands as though in prayer, apologised for his language. "My missus is always picking me up on it," he said. "Now we've got a kiddie on the way, I've got to learn to mind my tongue. Can't keep f…ing this and that, can I?" He giggled.

"What happened next?" Eden said.

"Oh, yeah, sorry," Vaz said. "Squire left – still haven't a clue who he was – and Hector signed for the parcel. I was nearly at the van when what sounded like a right barney kicked off from somewhere indoors. Could hear Stafford yelling from where I was. Hector and I went in to see what was going on. It was only the lady who'd arrived with me, wasn't it? Couldn't help but notice her. For an older woman, she weren't bad looking. Great figure. I don't know what happened, but I heard a scream, and next thing she was on the floor.

"The way I see it – Stafford must've pushed her. Can't see any other way it could've happened." Vaz used his arms to demonstrate taking someone by their upper arms, and pushing them away. "Me and Hector ran over to help her. I don't care what happened, that was bang out of order." He was pointing in indignation. "I'm no angel. I've got a temper on me, but I would never do something like that to a woman. She's half his size! Bang out of order. Hector didn't know where to put himself. I was all for calling the police, but she wouldn't have it. Turns out Stafford's her kid's dad!" He gave a bemused head shake. "That was the last time I was at the place. I can't vouch for his mental state, but Stafford Mills was alive and well when I left."

"What did you do after leaving the farmhouse?"

"Called me Missus to tell her what happened, then finished me round. Took forever. I only ended up getting stuck behind a flock of sheep, didn't I? Our customers don't like when their post's later than usual, and make a point of waiting around to say so, making me even more late." He grinned and shook his head. "When I was finally done, I grabbed a bite and hotfooted it back to the depot."

"Where were you when you learned about Stafford Mills' death?"

"At the depot. There was me, telling everyone about the bargy over at Stafford's place, when me line-manager came over, yelling that Mills had been cudgelled. Now, I ain't never heard that word before, and said to him: 'What's cudgelled mean, then?' He prodded me in the chest, and said, 'It means he's been done in, mate. Murdered by a person or persons unknown. At about the same time you say,' he emphasised the word say, 'you were eating your sausage sarnies!' I got the piss taken out of me after that, I can tell you."

Eden silently studied him. He grinned. "They were pretending like I done it! But I never," he added quickly, lurching forward, the smile vanished.

"Where did you eat your lunch?"

"In the van."

"And where was the van?"

"I parked in a lay-by."

"Where?"

He looked up to the ceiling before answering. "On High Lane," he said, glumly.

"High Lane's only a few minutes from Fenn Farmhouse," Eden said. "Did anybody see you?"

"Dunno. Might have done. You can't think I done it. Why would I kill him? Rough him up a bit maybe, but not kill him."

"How long was it between your leaving Fenn Farmhouse and arriving here at the depot?" Eden said.

"All in all, best part of two hours." This took him past the attack on Stafford Mills.

"Were you in the van the whole time?" Eden said.

"I have to get out to push the letters through the door."

"Apart from that."

He looked embarrassed. "I might have had a slash."

"You ate your lunch during or after your round?"

"I was hungry," he said indignantly. "Me missus had made me sausage sarnies. She puts mustard in them. The smell was driving me nuts."

"I'm not from Human Resources," she said. "I don't care where or when you ate your lunch, I'm after the chronology of events."

He slumped in his chair. "During my round."

"Vaz, are you aware there have been a number of break-ins in the area?"

"What of it?"

"Did you know about them?"

"Of course. Everyone around here does. I've had to give statements a couple of times about what I saw on my rounds, which is nothing. You're not trying to pin them on me as well?" His legs had long since been uncrossed, his arms no longer relaxed behind his head. In the course of the interview, he'd moved from lounging backwards, ankle of right-foot resting on knee of left leg, to slumping more and more forward. Now he was positively hunched. How are you enjoying your fifteen minutes of fame now, Vaz? Eden thought.

"Mr Smith made mention of silver candlesticks when you were there, didn't he?"

"You think I went back to help myself and he caught me and I biffed him one? Come off it," Vaz said. "Just cos I'm working class, drive a van and call at a few big houses, doesn't mean I'm a burglar." Involuntarily he put out his arms, keeping them bent at the elbow, and turned his palms up. "Wish I'd've insisted on a lawyer being here now."

Eden got to her feet. "I don't think I have any more questions, Vaz."

"Mr Banks if you don't mind."

"We'll be in touch if we have any more questions, Mr Banks."

11

The Coroner's Court inquest into the death of Stafford Mills opened on the fourth day after his death. After receiving evidence confirming the identity of the deceased, along with his time and place of death, the inquest was immediately adjourned to allow the police to make further investigations; the body was to remain in the morgue until further notice.

As the inquest opened and closed, Guido Black asked his team, gathered in the incident room, if any of them had anything else to report.

"We're still ploughing through email and text histories," Pilot said from the head of the table. "Nothing much yet, but we'll keep looking. Nobody's been on Tor or the Dark Net on any of the devices we've recovered. Everyone's story checks out thus far. Tim Smith did have a daughter who died during a routine operation. It seems she did briefly work for a Stafford Mills in London. Mills was asked to give evidence at the Inquest, but refused. Tim Smith's sister and brother-in-law do both turn fifty this year, and are celebrating their twenty-fifth anniversary to boot. His search history shows he searched for silver candlesticks, ending up on Craigslist. He wouldn't have known the seller's name from the Craigslist advert."

"The deceased was registered as the father of Sylvie Laurent's son, Pierre," Eden said. "We took Sylvie back to Trowchester. She led us to the street where she thinks she bumped into the deceased. There isn't any CCTV of the area, but she was in Trowchester that day and did visit the Cathedral. The deceased was the sole director and shareholder of a property company renovating a house in Trowchester and was also there that day. His car was clocked and his phone pinged. It's quite possible their paths crossed. It wasn't difficult finding out about Stafford's link with the area. A name search brought up his company director's entry at Companies House. From that I got the name of the company: Mills Luxury Homes, and from that the house in Trowchester. That said, there isn't anything in her search history showing she did this."

"Anything else of significance?" Black said.

"Only that Jenna Nesbitt received a call from Fenn Farmhouse a week before Mills died," Eden said. "She's friends with the Munros and Bridget White, so it probably has an innocent explanation but she didn't mention it when we spoke to her. I'm going to pay her a visit tomorrow."

"We took a look at Stafford Mills' brother, Martin," Pilot said. "Looks like he caused a fatal accident about fifteen years ago."

A newspaper report appeared on the overhead screen:

Martin Mills was today convicted by a unanimous verdict of causing the death of teenager Russell Dye by reckless driving. The defendant and Russell's parents broke down in tears at the verdict. Sentence was deferred for a month for psychiatric reports.

"He served time for it. I've asked archiving to dig the old file out," Pilot continued. "We have an address in Brighton for him. A flat. The local force've been round, left messages on his answerphone – we can't find a mobile phone for him, only a landline – pushed a note under his door, but to no avail. They've been unable to make contact. A neighbour of his says he's away but doesn't know where."

"Probably doesn't even know his brother's dead. Declare him a person of interest to the investigation," Black said. "How's door-to-door getting on?"

"They've taken statements from two-thirds of Osborne Tye's residents," Eden said. "Everyone they've spoken to knew the deceased, didn't think a lot of him, and either has an alibi for the time of the attack, or no rational motive for murder, or both."

"Our forensics on this one is lamentable," Black said. "Brenda Munro's clothes were pretty blood-soaked, but without the blood spatter consistent with her being behind the attack. We've taken the clothes everybody wore on the day and they're all negative for Stafford's blood. We haven't any unexplained fingerprints, footprints, or the murder weapon. The ladder we took from the outhouse hasn't revealed anything. We still can't explain the telescope found in the grounds, the different cloths used to wipe the window, why the window was wiped at all given the lack of prints found at the scene, or why only one of the candlesticks was taken. This lack of forensics points to a preplanned job, but whether that job was a burglary or a murder, only time will tell."

12

Law firm Thompson & Co LLP, went back to 1843 and the days of its founding father, the venerable Thompson Thompson, Solicitor. Over a century and a half later, his firm was one of the largest law firms in the region, with its offices taking up the ground and first floors of a modern, out-of-town office development.

Badge in hand, Black crossed a Reception large enough to house lesser law firms. Its floor was tiled in the company's navy blue and white. Its furniture upholstered similarly. To one side of a long, highly polished reception desk hung a glass panel on which was etched *T&Co LLP*, and on the other, a long list of the firm's many Members. As Black approached, a smart receptionist, also in navy and white, said into a headpiece, "The police are here, Janice."

Stafford Mills' solicitor wasn't quite what Black had expected. Janice Burnett was plump, and wore clothes that were slightly too tight. She had a short brown bob, which mimicked the movement of her head. Black put her at between forty and fifty years old.

"I've booked us a meeting room," she said, pausing by a door just along from Reception, clutching two fat files and a will packet. She broke into a large grin. "This is the part where I normally apologise for our meeting rooms being a bit like police interview rooms."

For a woman who dealt in death, Black found her remarkably cheery. But then, who was he to talk? She allowed him to enter first and waited for him to sit down before squeezing herself into a seat between the wall and the table. Across from him, she rested her hands on the files and the will packet. Black looked around. He saw a window, carpet, a wall photograph of a country path meandering up and over a river, and a computer on the desk. Nothing more. "This is nothing like a police interview room, I can assure you," he said, taking out his notepad and pen.

"I've had clients commit suicide, die in freak accidents, succumb to tropical diseases, or million-to-one genetic conditions," she said. "I even had one drop dead in front of me, thirty seconds after signing his will. As his own son put it: dying as efficiently as he lived. But this is my only murder. I suppose you'd like to know who gets the loot?"

"It might help with our enquiries," he said.

"I'm not sure it will." She held up the long brown envelope containing the will. "This is Stafford's will. I can tell you what it says without reading it. After expenses, and one small bequest, the estate of the late Stafford Mills is to be divided evenly between the hospice which nursed his mother in her final illness, and UKIP."

Black looked up, his pen poised above his notepad. "UKIP? The political party?"

"Oh yes. Had this happened a few years ago, I'd say your suspect was a five foot eight, middle-aged male with grey temples and one testicle."

Black made a mental note of her Nigel Farage joke. Something occurred to him. "Given they were all but wiped out in the last election, what happens to the legacy if they disappear completely?"

"Their share falls back into the remainder of the estate."

"Who's the bequest to?"

"Hector and Brenda Munro. Three months' salary in lieu of notice, tax-free, and enough to replace their car with the latest version of the same or similar model."

Black made a note. "Nothing for his son, Pierre?"

She shook her head. "The cost of Pierre's education is covered by a trust fund Stafford set up in accordance with the voluntary agreement he reached with Pierre's mother, and sealed by the court. When I took initial will instructions," she touched the file by her side, "I asked if he wished to leave the boy anything. He said no. I asked again when I sent him the draft will for approval, and again, when he called in here to execute his will. On each occasion he was adamant that he was paying for his son's private education to the age of eighteen, and as such had met any legal and moral duty to a boy whose birth he had no say in. These sentiments are recorded in the file, and also in a clause specifically added to the will, to defeat any estate claims by Pierre, or his mother on her son's behalf. The reason we made the trust fund more generous than it need be, is primarily to stop any such claim dead in its tracks."

"If a claim was brought nonetheless, would it stand a chance?"

"Stafford Mills asked me the same question when this will was drawn up, and then I said categorically not. However, since then, the law on this subject has been challenged. You may have read about a daughter successfully claiming a share of her late mother's estate, despite being excluded from it by a lawfully executed will. The daughter brought a claim for reasonable financial provision against her mother's estate under the Inheritance Act 1975. Her initial claim was successful for various reasons, one being the estate had come originally from the claimant's father, who had always intended her to benefit after his wife, her mother's, death. Both she and the charities originally benefiting, appealed. The daughter because she felt the amount awarded was insufficient, the charities for the opposite reason. The Supreme Court has upheld the original award, disappointing both parties. The case was unique on its facts and shouldn't be taken as a precedent. Unfortunately neither the 1975 act, nor the latest ruling, provides much clarification on what factors should be taken into account in deciding if an adult child is deserving or undeserving of reasonable maintenance from their deceased parents' estate. If I was drawing up this will today," she rested her fingers on the will packet, "I would advise Stafford that the chances of his son bringing a successful claim against the estate is still unlikely, but the odds are less against it than they were. It could go either way, but even if Pierre did receive an award, no court would overturn the entire will."

Bit shaky, committing murder on the basis of an expensive law case not certain to succeed, Black thought. "Did Thomson and Co advise on the trust fund?"

She nodded and her bob nodded with her. "I drafted it with advice from a colleague in the family. Stafford resented having to make any financial provision for the boy. Initially, he wanted to drag Sylvie Laurent through the courts, until we explained that because the child was his, and he was a wealthy man, he would have to make some provision, and far better to do so consensually than lose a long and expensive court battle. They agreed out of court in the end. The settlement covers school fees and clothing mostly. Pierre's mother, Sylvie Laurent, receives a small amount of maintenance to cover the holidays. Everything stops when Pierre turns eighteen."

"The deceased hadn't been in touch about changing his will?" Black asked.

Janice looked surprised. "No."

"We have information to suggest he wanted to build a relationship with his son."

"Funny what time will do," she said.

He was en route to his car when the station called. "Hector Munro's on the line, sir, insisting on talking to you."

"Put him through," Black said, climbing into the driver's seat and closing the door behind him. "Mr Munro?" he said.

"That you, Detective Inspector?" Hector Munro said.

"It is, Mr Munro."

"It's about those people who called at the farmhouse the day Stafford died. I was convinced I knew one of them, but I couldn't think from where. I didn't like to say nowt, in case I was wrong. I've been racking my brains ever since.

Then it hit me. There's a photograph on the wall of the breakfast room you should take a look at, Detective Inspector."

13

A bemused Guido Black faced Jeremy Havelock in the interview room, wondering whether the captain was deliberately trying to frustrate his investigation or was just an idiot.

He picked up a framed photograph taken from the breakfast room of the farmhouse. "I'm showing the suspect exhibit DFTH789," he said. "Captain Havelock, this is a picture of your army regiment taken twenty-eight years ago." He used his finger to indicate a uniformed individual on the second row. "This I believe is you, Captain Havelock? Am I right?"

"You are, sir."

He moved his finger along the back row, pausing above an officer's head. "This, I believe, is the late Stafford Mills."

The captain peered at the photograph and said, "It is. Good Lord! Thought there was something vaguely familiar about him."

"In the entire time you were in that room together, neither of you recognised the other, despite your five years together in the London Regiment?"

"It was a while back. People change."

"Did you both flunk army facial recognition training, Captain?"

Jeremy Havelock scowled but otherwise held himself together.

"Captain, did you make the Craigslist appointment under a false name because you wouldn't have got across the front doorstep using your own?"

"No."

"Captain, I'm having problems with your story. Let's wind back. Why did you visit Stafford Mills on the day of his death?"

"To view a pair of candlesticks."

"And what did you argue about?"

"Him wasting my time."

"Where did you go after you left Fenn Farmhouse?"

"Pulled up outside Osborne Tye and went for a run."

Guido Black resisted the temptation to roll his eyes. "Captain Havelock, make it easier on yourself and start telling the truth. You and the late Stafford Mills are both recognisably the same people you were when that photograph was taken. What were you doing at Fenn Farmhouse? Why did you use a false name? What did you really argue about?"

Jeremy Havelock gripped the armrests and ran his hands along them. "Okay, okay," he said after a few moments. "I was there to look at the candlesticks. I didn't know he was the seller, the ad doesn't give a name. I recognised him the minute I arrived, and he me. That's why I was so pissed off when he expected me to beat the higher offer – not even match it. 'Come on, Stafford,' I said. 'We go way back. There is such a thing as loyalty to the regiment.' He told me to better the offer or get out. I lost it. Hurt, I guess."

"Why didn't you tell me this earlier?"

"Thought I'd come across as a bit pathetic." He watched himself clasping the polished armrest between the index finger and thumb of his left hand and run it to the end and back again. He looked up.

"How many silver candlesticks do you already own, Captain?" Black said.

"None. They were to start off my silver collection."

"Were they really, sir," Black said.

Eden pushed open the door to Jenna Nesbitt's hairdressing salon. Jenna was in the reception, no more than a small desk and three chairs, an A7 page-a-day diary open in front of her, making a customer an appointment. In the main salon, a girl with shoulder-length pink hair stood behind one of two black leather chairs facing large mirrors, trimming her female customer's hair. When Jenna saw Eden she blinked a couple of times before turning her attention back to her customer. Eden waited for Jenna's lady to leave, before saying, "Can I have a word, please, Miss Nesbitt?"

Jenna led Eden through the salon to a door at the end of a dogleg holding the sinks. Eden felt two pairs of eyes trained on her. The chatty conviviality she'd pushed open the door to had vanished, leaving only the clipping of scissors to cut across the tense atmosphere. Jenna opened the door. It led to a store room. She let Eden go in first and, after shutting them in, leaned against the door, arms folded.

"A call was made from the landline at Fenn Farmhouse to your mobile phone, five days before the murder of Stafford Mills, Miss Nesbitt," Eden said. "Shortly after the call was logged, another call was made, this time from your mobile phone to Fenn Farmhouse. Can you tell me what the calls were about?"

Jenna looked disconcerted and began running her hands repeatedly through her hair, and blinking quickly. Eden knew better than to take Jenna's nervousness as a sign of guilt. Being caught up in a murder investigation was nerve racking for anyone.

"Not off the top of my head, I can't," Jenna said.

"Might someone else have used your phone?" Eden asked.

"No, I always have my phone on me. Can I check the diary at the desk? I use it for myself, as well as here."

"Go ahead."

At the reception desk, Jenna flicked back through the diary. Each page was divided into two columns. Jenna's name always topped the left-hand column. The name of two different women, alternately topped the right-hand column, making the girl in the salon today, Amy. Jenna stopped at the day in question and ran her finger down the list of entries. She frowned, and turned to the next page, and again ran her finger down the list of entries. With a

128

palpable sigh of relief, she gave the page a slap, and turned the diary around to face Eden, pointing out an appointment made for eleven-thirty the day after the exchange of calls. The appointee was Bridget White.

"Don't know why I went blank," Jenna said. "Nerves. I always do Bridget's hair, and Brenda's and Hector's. Bridget always picks eleven-thirty," she said, flicking back through the pages to an earlier appointment made six weeks earlier for Bridget, also at eleven-thirty. "Any earlier and she'd still be sleeping off the night before, any later and she'll be good for nothing. That sounds awful I know, but I can't think of another way of putting it. She called to check when her next appointment was for. I checked and called her back."

"Did you also cut Stafford Mills' hair?"

"No fear," she said quickly. "I went out of my way to avoid him."

Eden slowly turned the diary's pages. Jenna Nesbit had scribbled notes to herself below her list of appointments for the day: card for mum, milk, book MOT, cat jabs, RENT, Aidan's choir practice. On the day they'd reported the burglary, she'd written: *Alarm Man – keep morning free. Spin class 7.45.*

"Do you rent the salon?" Eden asked.

"I rent the room from a landlord, the other girls rent a chair from me."

"Who's your landlord?" Eden asked.

"I'd need to look it up. He lives in London. It's not Stafford Mills, if that's what you're thinking – thank God."

"Maybe you could show me out, Miss Nesbitt?" Eden said.

Jenna looked a bit surprised by the request, the door was an arm stretch away from Eden, but she went over to it anyway and held it open. Eden paused outside, indicating that she'd like Jenna to join her. She did, pulling the door to behind her.

"One last question, Miss Nesbitt. If you went out of your way to avoid Stafford Mills, why go for a smoke so close to his house?"

The hands went to the hair again, and the rapid blinking resumed. Jenna raised herself on the balls of her feet and lowered herself again. After an awkward pause, she said, "Aidan wouldn't think to look for me there, for that reason, but I never saw Stafford there. Not ever."

"Can I see your cigarettes?" Eden asked.

She shook her head. "I've given up."

14

B lack and his girlfriend, Chloe Joyce, were going out
to dinner that evening to celebrate some anniversary
or another. He wasn't quite sure what anniversary – they
seemed to celebrate one every few weeks, but at least he was
on time for once. He let himself in. Chloe heard him and
came downstairs in a silk dressing gown. She greeted him
with a kiss.

"I'm nearly ready," she said. "Just got to finish
dressing."

He pushed her against the door, slipping his hand
under her silk dressing gown. "Let's give whatever it is we're
celebrating a miss and stay home," he said, trying to kiss
her. She pushed him away and told him to behave.

"Everyone from school's going," she said.

Great, he thought.

"It's five years since we opened. I did tell you."

"You probably did," he said releasing her. "I'd better let you finish getting ready, then."

She left him to go upstairs, with a vague "won't be long!" shouted over her shoulder. He wandered into the front room to wait. On the corner table he saw a plastic bag of cotton wool balls, a string bag of marbles, a container of tennis balls, a Christmas ornament, a packet of dried peas and three woven wicker balls in a plastic wrapper, labelled: three woven wicker balls. Chloe taught preschoolers at the local Montessori school and Black was getting used to coming across such eclectic piles. Deciding a class project on spherical objects lay behind the collection, he searched through his pockets for the bag of Maltesers he remembered buying, but not eating. He found them in an inside pocket and deposited them on the table. He heard her coming down the stairs.

"Ready, Guido," she called out.

He went into the hall. She was a vision in purple silk. "You look beautiful," he said. "I'm a lucky man."

"I'm sorry about tonight," she said.

"It'll be fine," he said. "With any luck, your deputy head will get as sozzled as last time."

"Only hope he doesn't serenade us with *My Yiddish Mother* again."

In her own house, Eden Hudson wasn't so happy. The washing machine had refused to start that morning, and she'd returned home to discover her stepdad, Eric, had been unable to fix it, her daughter, Dora, had dropped her laptop, and Eric's van wasn't likely to pass its MOT. Eric's severe arthritis prevented him from working, leaving her salary and a few benefits to support three adults and one child. The mortgage alone left their finances stretched at the end of the month. It didn't matter how many times she stared at her bank balance, there wasn't the money for another washing machine – even a second-hand one – a laptop, and a van. Brilliant, she thought.

"I have to have a laptop for school," Dora said for the umpteenth time. Eden ignored her. "Mum!"

"Well, maybe you shouldn't have dropped yours then?"

"It slipped!"

She couldn't expect Eric or Dottie to lug the family's washing to the launderette on top of everything else they did for her. The pay rise which came with the promotion wouldn't be in her account till the end of the month, and then wouldn't do much more than pay off her overdraft. They'd have to rent a washing machine. How much would that end up costing? What choice was there? In the meantime, she'd have to visit the launderette after work. Brilliant. She curled the noodles of her chicken pad thai around her fork and looked at her daughter. "Don't keep telling me you have to have a laptop for school."

"But I do." Dixie's alcoholism had put Eden off alcohol for life, but at moments such as this one, she saw the attraction.

"Mum!" Dora said again.

"How did it slip?"

Dora shrugged.

"Dora?"

"I don't know."

"You'll have to use the laptops in the school library until I can get you another one."

"You have to book them," Dora said indignantly.

"Well, book one then."

Her daughter teared up. "It's not fair. It slipped."

"Dora, we're not made of money." She carried her plate over to the sink. "I'll get you another one as soon as I can, but for now you'll have to use the school's. I'm sorry, but that's just how it is."

Dora left the kitchen unimpressed, to stomp upstairs.

Dottie joined Eden in the kitchen. "I'd become a lap dancer, but I'm seventy-six, fat, and waiting for a new hip," she said.

"I'd become a lap dancer, but I can't afford the implants," Eden said looking down at her chest.

"What's a lap dancer?" Dora said, reappearing from nowhere.

15

E den Hudson and Guido Black set off nice and early to visit the flat Stafford Mills' brother Martin owned in Brighton.

"Thanks for driving," Guido said, "I imbibed more than I intended to last night. Still got a bit of a sore head. Useful, you being teetotal."

Isn't it, she thought. At least the early start meant she avoided Dora and her whining for a new laptop. "I've added the Postman, Vaz Banks, to the list of possible suspects," she said. "He was close by, with no alibi to speak of."

"Motive?"

"Robbery," she suggested. "Tim Smith was sounding off about the candlesticks when he was there. Might be part of the gang or acting on impulse. Jenna Nesbitt's explanation for the phone calls to and from Fenn Farmhouse checks out, but I'm not convinced she was on the bridle path for a smoke, or even that she's a smoker."

Due to the early start, it was still fairly early when they arrived at the leafy residential area where Martin Mills lived. His flat was on the second floor of the purpose-built block. Their counterparts in the local force still hadn't been able to contact him. At the top of the stairs Eden rang his landline. The phone inside the flat rang unanswered. Once it stopped, Black gave the door a sharp rap and called out: "Police." No one came. He knocked and called out a couple more times without success. A young woman, no older than twenty, appeared at a neighbouring flat, cradling a toddler in her left arm, which she gently bounced.

Eden showed her badge and said, "I'm Detective Sergeant Hudson, and this is Detective Inspector Black. Would you mind telling me your name, love?"

"Melinka Patellma," she said.

"Is this your flat?"

"I rent it from the Council. If you're here for Martin, he isn't there. He had to go away for a bit. He didn't say where."

"Is that like him?" Eden said.

"Not at all. I've never known him go away. He hardly ever goes out, 'cept to buy food. He's the type that keeps himself to himself. I'm one of the few he ever speaks to. I hope nothing's wrong. He's a lovely, lovely man. Always asks after the little one, buys him things," she jiggled the child up and down again and he gurgled in delight.

"When was the last time you saw Mr Mills, Melinka?" Eden asked.

"About a month ago. I collect his post from the foyer, what there is of it, and feed his cat. He left masses of cat food – floor-to-ceiling – but he's been gone so long it's nearly all gone. I'm on my own. I can't afford to feed someone else's cat. Can you take her with you? It's really weird I haven't heard from him. Hope he's okay."

"He didn't give any indication where he was going?" Eden said.

"Nothing. Just that he had to go away and would I look after the cat."

"Did he leave a contact number?" Black asked.

She shook her head. "He doesn't have a mobile. He doesn't even have Internet. Says he doesn't need it."

"Does he work?" Black asked.

"Not that I could see. If he does, it's from home."

"Could you let us in to Mr Mills' flat please, Melinka?" Eden said.

Melinka glanced at the badge in Eden's hand. Eden wondered if they'd have to end up getting a warrant and breaking the door down, but Melinka darted back into her own flat, with a, "One sec." She re-emerged with a solitary key on a key ring. She left her own door on the catch and followed the officers inside Martin's flat.

A narrow hallway with a door off to a small bathroom opened into the flat's main room. Upon the sound of an opening door, the cat appeared, and ran over to them to meow and wrap herself around their legs. Eden picked her up. "Is there a cat basket we can put her in?" she asked, stroking her. Melinka raised a finger, meaning yes, and went to the kitchen to fetch it.

"What's your name?" Eden asked the cat, attempting to read the disc on the animal's collar. "Betty Boop,"

Melinka said from the kitchen doorway, swinging a metal cat basket from her right hand. Eden carried the cat over to her. Melinka put down her child and held the cat basket open.

"Sorry about this, Betty B," Eden said, attempting to place the cat inside. Claws and splayed limbs forced Black to run to the bathroom for a towel to wrap the animal in. Eventually humans overcame cat, and the basket and its furious contents were left by the door.

"Who's the lady in the photograph?" Eden asked, gesturing towards a framed photograph on top of a wooden cabinet of a woman in fancy dress. "Did he say?"

"He said it was his mother," Melinda said, picking up her grizzling child. "He wants his nap," she said. "Will you be needing me any more?"

"Thank you for everything, Melinka. We can take it from here," Eden said.

The flat door pushed to, the two police officers gloved up, to make a rudimentary search. "You start out here," Black said, "I'll take the bedroom."

The flat was stuffy and smelt of cat, forcing Eden to the window. It overlooked the rear garden, and beyond that, across the rooftops, the sea. She threw it open. Fresh sea air poured in. To the sound of the sea and squalling gulls away in the distance, she set to work.

The room was furnished basically, and on a strictly needs-only basis. Two armchairs faced the TV, one worn from use, the other barely touched. The smallest of a nest of tables stood by the armchair. On it were a couple of remote controls, some biros and a placemat. The TV and DVD player stood on the second of the tables, surrounded by piles of box sets. The third table sat by the door, where Martin's post waited, letters in one pile, magazines in another. Model planes filled a glass-fronted cabinet. A magazine rack was stuffed with magazines. Eden picked up a letter from the pile. It was an old bank statement, revealing that Martin received Disability Allowance and a small top-up income from share dividends. His income, though meagre, exceeded his few outgoings, which didn't include either rent or a mortgage. Lucky him, she thought.

She opened the most recent statement. This was interesting, she thought. It showed a large credit from Barclay Stockbrokers, followed by a large cash withdrawal. Enough to fill a suitcase. All done shortly before he'd gone away. Was he being blackmailed? She put the statement down to look through the rest of the post, but it didn't contain anything of interest. She wandered into the kitchen. Other than the fish fingers, frozen peas and sliced bread in the icebox, the fridge was empty. The remains of a bag of dry cat food stood in the corner alongside cat litter and feeding bowls. Tea bags, cans of baked beans and tuna fish were the only things in the cupboards. She went to find Black.

The main bedroom held a bed (stripped bare), a chest (its empty drawers pulled out by Black), and a virtually empty wardrobe, its doors open. A door led to a box room where Black was standing, his back to her, framed by the door. She joined him. A trestle table and a chair stood in the middle of the box room. On the table lay a half-constructed Hercules fighter jet and, on the floor by the chair, a model plane box.

"He retreated here, to this life, after he came out of prison," Black said. "He spent his days watching box-sets and building his models. Only in this way was he able to cut himself off from his past."

"The model's half-finished," Eden said. "Not even put away or covered."

"He left expecting to come back."

Black slapped the door frame a couple of times, then turned and walked away. Eden gazed into the room. "What a lonely life," she said.

She followed him into the main room and showed him the bank statements.

"Interesting," he said. "But they don't tell us where he is. Come on, let's go. We'll drop the cat off at the local station on the way. They can take her to the RSPCA."

"Think I'm going to hang onto her 'til Martin Mills turns up, if that's all right," Eden said, picking up the cage. "It'll take my kid's mind off wanting a new laptop, with any luck."

They were roaring down the dual carriageway, with Eden again at the wheel, and an All Points Bulletin issued for Martin Mills. Over the noise of the cat mewling angrily in its cage on the backseat, they discussed possible reasons for the share sale and large cash withdrawal immediately preceding Martin's disappearance. Then the station rang.

16

Once again, Captain Jeremy Havelock faced Black across a desk in a police interviewing room. Eden was also present, as was the captain's solicitor.

"Your online history makes interesting reading, Captain," Black said.

"How so, Detective Inspector?"

"You owe a great deal of money."

"I told you – I make my living gambling," the captain explained. "I'm a professional gambler. I calculate the odds of a card falling using a series of algorithms. I wrote the program myself. Sometimes I lose, mostly I win. This time I lost. Nobody wins every time. I think of it in similar terms to investing in blue-chip shares. The market goes down, yes, but overall it goes up more."

"Yes, but with the stock market, you still have your shares, if you can sit it out. In gambling, what do you have left at the end of a bad day? Nothing but debt."

"We could talk on the subject for hours, and many do, Detective Inspector. I'm a professional gambler. That's what I do."

"A professional gambler who's had a run of bad luck, it appears."

"I'll win my money back and more, don't you worry, copper."

"Were you at Fenn Farmhouse to ask Stafford Mills for money?"

"Why would I ask Stafford Mills for money?"

"Because you haven't got any."

"If I'd wanted money, I'd've gone to a bank, not a man I hadn't spoken to for decades."

"You've spent a lot of time online researching overseas bank accounts," Black said.

"My wife and I have separated. I don't want her getting the whole lot. I fail to see how this impacts on this enquiry."

"Let me propose a scenario," Black said. "You made a big gambling loss, with a tight settlement deadline that you're not going to be able to meet. Your wife throwing you out and filing for divorce didn't help. A solution presents itself – a new life. But new lives costs money, the stuff you haven't got. But your old mucker, Stafford Mills, does. Why not ask him for help? But wait. Can't just turn up out of the blue asking for money. Have to butter him up a bit first. But to do that, you had to get through the door without him smelling a rat. But how?

"Then you saw the Craigslist advert. That would get you inside – just so long as you used a false name and remembered to be surprised at the identity of the seller. What happened once you were alone with him? Come clean straight away, did you, or did you tell him about this wonderful scheme you had for making money and did he want in? Whatever you said, can't've worked very well, judging by what happened. What did happen, Jeremy? Did he insult you? Belittle you? Laugh? Did he make you so angry you felt compelled to return and have it out with him? Did things get out of hand? Is that what happened, Captain? If it was, say so, and I'll approach the Crown Prosecution Service for a plea bargain."

"I didn't kill him," Jeremy Havelock said.

Jeremy Havelock's solicitor spoke for the first time: "Detective Inspector, how did my client know the seller's identity? I've seen the Craigslist entry. There's no identifying information in it. The address only appears when the appointment's made."

Black didn't as yet have an answer for that.

"All you've got on my client," continued the solicitor, "is a string of bad luck. Do you have any questions for him based on facts or is my client free to leave?"

"For the time being," Black said. "It might help your client's case if he was slightly more forthcoming."

17

Days passed, then more, spent mostly staring at computer screens, or on phones, or following up some lead or other. Always the same questions: did the main suspect's stories check out? Was there any connection between any of them not already known about? Were they where they said they were, doing what they said they did, in the days leading up to, and the hours after, the attack on Stafford Mills?

The next breakthrough was Pilot's own. Eden and Black stood by his desk as he said, "Leslie Gallagher had an appointment at Fenn Farmhouse on the morning of the murder, but never showed up. Hector Munro says Leslie Gallagher telephoned the landline four days before the murder, asking to make an appointment to look at the candlesticks he'd seen on Craigslist, but the ad didn't contain a telephone number. I went through the other calls made to the farmhouse that day with Hector and he recognised all of them but one. That number I traced to a private London club. A private London club listing both

Leslie Gallagher and Stafford Mills as members. They didn't want to let on they had internal CCTV until I threatened them with a warrant, and they coughed this up."

On his screen, CCTV images of a flagstoned entrance foyer appeared. "We're just inside the club's door," Pilot said. The camera caught only the lower portion of a flight of stairs and a phone box behind a glass door. The images reminded Black of his boarding school days. Cold and utilitarian. Probably offered the club's members some nostalgia. Various people walked in and out of shot, up and down the stairs.

"Keep your eye on the phone box," Pilot instructed. It stood empty and unused. "We're two and a half minutes away from Leslie Gallagher calling the farmhouse." Two pairs of legs appeared, descending the stairwell, both belonging to men. The stairs were wide enough to allow the men to walk down them side-by-side. Gradually more and more of their bodies came into view. By the bottom of the stairs, the men were completely visible, revealing one as Stafford Mills. He was deep in conversation with the other. Upon seeing him, Black and Eden gave a start.

"The other one's Leslie Gallagher, sir," Pilot said, tapping the screen just above the second of the two men. The two stopped by the phone box and Leslie Gallagher stepped inside, leaving Stafford Mills outside. He turned his back to the cubicle as though keeping guard. In the phone box, Leslie Gallagher made a brief call, after which he replaced the receiver and stepped back into the foyer. Stafford Mills thanked him and the two shook hands, followed up with a grateful back slap from Stafford Mill. He waited at the bottom of the stairs as Leslie Gallagher returned upstairs. After raising his hand in appreciation, Stafford Mills turned and left the club by the back door.

"Stafford Mills was behind the call?" Black said.

"Leslie Gallagher's got some explaining to do," Eden said.

"Speaking to him tomorrow," Pilot said.

"You're only as good as your last job, Pilot," Black said. "And that was a good job. Eden, get everyone together."

Within ten minutes the team had gathered to watch the CCTV recording taken in the club. Black gave everyone a few minutes for the new information to sink in.

"Until Pilot's spoken to Leslie Gallagher," he said, "we can only speculate as to the reason for the call. Let's review the rest of the evidence to date."

He used the cursor to call up the suspects' photographs as he came to them. "Captain Jeremy Havelock's hiding something, but whether that something is murder, we can't yet say. He argued with the deceased on the day of his death, and doesn't have an alibi. Money or some old grudge are possible motives. Tim Smith's backstory checks out, giving him a motive. His possible absence from the empty pub provided a very narrow window of opportunity, but again, we need to ask why he waited so long and was so obvious about it if it was him? And where are the forensics? And how could he have ensured the pub would be empty?

"Sylvie Laurent's alibi mostly stacks up – we have her filling her car and she did visit her neighbours when she said she did, although we haven't any CCTV from the garage to her door. We haven't found anything disproving this chance meeting with Stafford Mills in Trowchester. It's not out of the question for her to have doubled back on herself on the day of the murder, but for that to work, her neighbour and the carer would have to be wrong about the time she arrived. Given her son doesn't inherit under his dad's will, I can't see she has much of a motive.

"Neither Aidan Stanton nor Jenna Nesbitt have an alibi and we only have their word for what the argument was about. Jenna Nesbitt was alone in the hallway for part of the time, allowing her to leave a window or door open, and she was in the vicinity when the attack happened. Corrine Beechwood was the deceased's long-term girlfriend. They split up a few weeks before his death. I can't see any real motive there unless they met up and argued. Anyway, her alibi stacks up.

"We can't rule out burglars. The gang operating in the area have gone to ground since the murder. Postman Vaz Banks was at the property when Tim Smith mentioned the candlesticks. He's a local man and he knows the area. He hasn't an alibi. It's possible he's part of the gang or got greedy.

"That just leaves the live-in staff," Black continued. Photographs of the three appeared in a row. He began with Bridget White. "Bridget White, an alcoholic, sister of Brenda Munro, found unconscious on the back doorstep around the time of the crime. We don't know how she came to be there. There isn't any direct evidence to suggest she was attacked, and she has a history of falls. She was one of the last people to have seen the victim alive, claiming he'd referred to somebody as having been naughty, and promising to share a secret with her. Our problem is her reliability."

Eden was open about her family history. "For those of you who don't know," she said, "my Mum drank. By the end, her memory had gone. She was hallucinating. It got harder and harder to separate fact from fiction, past from present. Her consultant said alcohol damages the brain in a way not dissimilar to Alzheimers."

Black moved on to Brenda and Hector Munro. "They've worked for the deceased for years. I can't find any motive, in fact the opposite. They've lost their jobs and their home. Mrs Munro in particular is very shaken by events. She was already suffering from depression over her sister before all this. Realistically, none of the three make likely murderers, but we can't discount an argument we don't know about."

The next photograph was Martin Mills, taken when he was a younger man. "This is the only photograph we have of the deceased's brother, Martin Mills. He hasn't been at his flat for over a month. We don't know where he currently is."

"I've flagged his only debit card, but nothing," Eden said.

"What more do we know about the deceased?" Black said.

"He wasn't in business with anyone else, meaning no cheated business partners," Pilot said. "Now and then he'd make his contractors wait a bit for their money, but always coughed up in the end, usually in cash. Can't find any secret gambling or drinking or swindling innocents out of their life's savings. If he could get out paying for something he would, but that seems to have been the worst of it. He was no saint, but no criminal mastermind neither."

"Someone might have been after the rumoured stash of money," Eden said. "He was a middle-class wheeler and dealer, let's not forget."

Meeting over, Black returned to his office and closed the door. He sat down and stretched his legs out in front of him, ankles crossed, hands behind his head – perfect thinking repose. He gave a sigh. He believed the work his team were doing in their dutiful questioning of the residents of Osborne Tye, and their trawling through the minutiae of Stafford Mills' life for buried secrets, excellent. However, he didn't believe it would produce results. He remained convinced the murderer came from one of two groups:

The so-far unidentified gang behind the burglaries; or

Those at Fenn Farmhouse that fateful morning, whose faces were moving across his screen.

18

Pilot picked up his bag from under his desk and threw it over his shoulder, ready for the off, when Stafford Mills' phone began ringing from inside his desk drawer. He dropped his bag to the floor and, moving as quickly as his large frame allowed, opened the drawer to retrieve the phone. He was too late. The call went to voicemail, the number emblazoned across the screen as *unidentified*.

He put on a pair of plastic forensics gloves from his drawer, removed the phone from its storage bag and listened to the message. "It's Money Brokers here, Mr Mills," a young-sounding male voice said. "We've had an offer for the silver cutlery. We're just closing up for the night. Give us a call back tomorrow if you don't mind."

Pilot sat down abruptly. Silver cutlery? Wasn't it silver cutlery that had been nicked from Aidan Stanton and Jenna Nesbitt's place after their burglar alarm failed to go off? Hadn't Stafford Mills recommended the alarm fitter? Pilot immediately returned the call but it was too late, the shop was closed. He didn't leave a message. He replaced the mobile phone in its plastic bag, took off the gloves and sat back down at his computer. There he called up details of the Stanton/Nesbitt burglary, while, on his laptop, he visited Money Brokers' webpage:

Money Brokers invites you to shop for a range of upmarket jewellery, watches and antiques. (All items are pre-owned unless stated otherwise.)

It was a pawn shop. He scrolled down the various links to *Silver (Antique)*. A click on the link produced a multitude of silver pieces. Jewellery, hairbrushes, mirrors, candlesticks, napkin rings, art deco items, cutlery and condiments whizzed by in a shiny silver blur. Whenever a candlestick appeared, he stopped to take a longer look, on the look out for the murder weapon. Realising he was still only on page five of seventy, he decided to concentrate only on canteens of silver cutlery. This reduced the entries to two dozen. Only one was of any interest:

Set of six knives, six forks, silver, 1882, together with original leather case, slight scuffing on case corners only. Competitive price. Owner wants a quick sale.

He magnified the image. Six antique silver knives and forks lay inside a silk-lined case, each in its own individual slot. He compared the description of the silver for sale on Money Brokers to the young couple's description of their stolen silver. Same number of knives and forks. Same date. Same leather case. Same silk lining. Hmm, he thought, noticing Money Brokers had a retail shop in Slyham town centre.

The shop opened at eight a.m.. Pilot walked through its doors at five past. He showed his badge to a man at the till.

The young man had thick, dark, shoulder-length hair and a massive beard, through which Pilot saw a young buck, like himself.

"I'm Detective Constable Philip Philpott," he said. "Last night someone from here called a Mr Stafford Mills about some cutlery."

"That was me," the young man said, hesitantly.

"Could you tell me your name, sir?" Pilot said.

"Ian Vaizey."

"Mr Vaizey, I'm sorry to have to inform you that Stafford Mills was murdered last month, on Monday the seventeenth."

Ian Vaizey looked visibly shocked. "You're kidding!"

"'Fraid not," Pilot said.

Ian looked around for somewhere to sit, alighting on a stool by the till, pulling it towards himself and abruptly sitting down. "I knew someone'd been murdered, I didn't realise…"

"You rang Mr Mills about some cutlery of his you had for sale. Could you tell me how your company came to be selling cutlery for Mr Mills?"

"He brought it in himself. Said it was a family antique. It was nice stuff. Old. Solid silver. Good nick. Ticked all the boxes. At first he only wanted a loan on it, but just as quickly changed his mind and instructed me to put it on our For Sale board. Someone made an offer yesterday."

"Did you take ID?"

"Had to. He didn't have an account with us. We always take ID first time round in case the items later turn out to be stolen."

"They were stolen, as a matter of fact."

"You're kidding? His ID checked out."

"I'll need to have a look at that."

"No probs." Ian called up the e-file on his computer screen.

Pilot studied the identification produced by Stafford Mills. He'd need to compare it with the originals, but at this distance it looked like Stafford Mills' photographic driving licence and credit card. The file also gave a description of the items lodged by the customer and the date they were brought in to the shop. Two days after the burglary at Aidan and Jenna's home, he noted. "The man in this photograph is the same man who came in with the cutlery?" he asked.

"Yeah, that's him all right," Ian said.

"Can I see the cutlery?"

"It's in our warehouse."

"I'll need an address."

Ian Vaizey nodded and handed Pilot a card giving the location of the warehouse. "I'll tell them you're coming," he said.

"No, don't do that," Pilot said, just in case someone was in on it with Stafford Mills and got rid of the cutlery before he got to it. "You've had no contact from Mr Mills since he came in with the silver?"

"I haven't. Let me see if anyone else did." Ian lowered his head over the keyboard and tapped. His nerves showed slightly, causing him to shake as he typed, but he kept them in check. After a while, he looked up from the screen, shaking his head. "Nothing."

Pilot thanked him for his time and left. Inside his car, he arranged for a uniformed officer to collect the cutlery from the warehouse, and set off for London.

Whilst Pilot battled the M25, Black, Eden and Judy McDermott gathered at a table in the police café. Eden fed Judy's baby, Ollie, his bottle. "I haven't done this for years," she said, smiling.

On the table was a clear plastic bag containing a rectangular leather-cased box, secured with an eye and hook. Wearing gloves, Black removed and opened the box, revealing a canteen of solid silver cutlery. "Only fingerprints on the lid are from the employees of Money Brokers. None from Mills, even though he handled it, meaning he wiped it before bringing it in. Only fingerprints on the inside are from Aidan Stanton and Jenna Nesbitt."

"Why would a wealthy man like Stafford Mills nick his neighbour's cutlery?" Judy asked.

"Was Mills part of the burglary gang, you reckon?" Eden said.

"If he was, we need to ask why? He didn't need the money," Black said.

"The thrill?" Judy suggested.

"So now he's Raffles," Black said.

"Makes you wonder about Bridget White's burglar dream," Eden said. "I'm wondering if the farmhouse was a drop-off? Might explain why no one's been picked-up with anything on them."

"Surely the Munros would've suspected?" Judy said.

"Those two know how to keep kept their mouths shut," Eden said.

"Stafford drove their car from time to time," Black said.

"The gang behind the burglaries are professional," Judy said. "They never leave a trace, yet Stafford waltzed into a local shop with stuff stolen from a neighbour? It doesn't make any sense."

Judy's point was a good one, to which neither Black or Eden had a possible explanation. The discussion was suspended when three full English breakfasts were set down in front of them, along with fresh toast and tea. Black was the first to tuck in. He enjoyed being able to eat a meal without it first being photographed and posted on Instagram by Chloe.

"Let's you and me take another look through the evidence after lunch, Guido," Judy said, cutting her breakfast into bite-sized pieces to enable her to eat it with one hand, whilst gently rocking her son with the other.

19

In Stafford Mills' private London club, Pilot was shown into the panelled bar. The unmanned circular bar cut across a corner of the room. The rest was given up to tables and chairs, each unoccupied, except for one solitary figure sitting by himself at a table by a bay window, a pot of tea in front of him, his legs crossed under the table. He tapped one foot angrily.

"The police are here, Mr Gallagher," the club secretary announced, before discreetly withdrawing, pulling the door closed behind him and hanging on it a *Private Function – Do Not Disturb* sign.

Leslie Gallagher didn't bother looking over. Pilot crossed from the bar to the bay window. His footsteps carried in the silence. Gallagher made no attempt to get to his feet, nor offer a handshake, even as Pilot reached his table, badge in hand.

"Expected you hours ago," he eventually snarled, still staring out of the window, down onto Regent's Park. "Tea's gone cold and, thanks to you, all the staff are downstairs and I can't even get a fresh pot."

"I'm sorry if you've been inconvenienced, Mr Gallagher," Pilot, who wasn't that late, said, taking a seat. "Traffic."

"Just because I'm a member of a private club, doesn't mean I'm Bertie Wooster with nothing to do all day but play the fool."

Pilot had no intention of apologising again. He took out his notepad and opened it at a clean page. "You called Stafford Mills' home telephone a few days before his death…"

Leslie Gallagher finally turned to look at him. He thrust his pointed finger under Pilot's noise. "Stafford's the reason I waited. It's a shocking business. Want to see it cleared up."

"As I was saying, sir, you called Stafford Mills' home telephone a few days before his death from the phone in the lobby here, claiming to be a prospective buyer of some candlesticks he was selling. We know Mr Mills was present when you made the call."

"What of it?"

"Why did you make the call?"

Leslie Gallagher lent forward, leaving his legs crossed under the table, forcing him into an uncomfortable-looking twist. "Because Stafford asked me to."

"Why did he ask you to do that?"

"None of my damn business. A gentleman doesn't stick his nose into another chap's business. He asked me to call Hector and pretend to be interested in some candlesticks he had up for sale. Didn't enquire why. He'd have done the same for me had I asked." An uncomfortable silence descended.

"Has Stafford Mills ever asked you for a similar favour?"

"A few times, over the years."

"Along the same lines?"

"Pretty much."

"Did he ever ask anyone else here the same type of favour?"

"Wouldn't have a clue. They wouldn't let on if he had. Any more damn-fool questions?"

Pilot emerged from the club, surprised he'd escaped without being called a pleb. He'd got as far as opening his car door, when his phone rang. It was the station. "You still in London?" "Yeah."

"Get your arse over to West Brompton sharpish. We've got new information."

A video recording of Fenn Farmhouse had been made in the hours immediately following the murder, beginning on the road leading to Fenn Farmhouse. The recording continued along the drive and into the garage. The camera swept around, recording the contents. Black re-played it. He was looking for the telescope. It wasn't logged as having been removed from the garage, and shouldn't be there. It wasn't, making the one recovered from the grounds, Stafford Mills' own.

Black skipped through the tour of the property's garden, restarting the recording in the inner hallway, the side door behind the camera, dining room and utility room doors on the left, the murder scene, main hall, stairs and the front door, on the right. The camera made a 180° panorama sweep from left to right. Judy froze the picture.

"The killer can't have swanned in through the side door," she said. "It's insanely risky. There are doors everywhere, and the stairs. There's even a cupboard under the stairs. Anyone could've appeared from anywhere."

"Killer could've taken their time, staked out the property, realised there were only four people there, including his target," Black speculated. "Saw Bridget leave, then Hector, and Brenda busy in the kitchen."

They started the recording up again. The camera moved along the hallway and into the room where Stafford Mills was slain. Although the body was gone, a white outline of it remained, illuminated against the polished wooden decking by the sun filtering through chinks in the drawn curtains. The room was still eerily beautiful. "Even you must concede, the killer can't have waltzed through the door if Mills was in the room," Judy said.

"Not through the door, no," Black said, "but let's not forget the library window was found unlocked. If Mills was in one part of the room," Black moved the cursor to the sitting room area, "and our killer climbed in through the window in the other part of the room," he zoomed in on the library window, "it's possible he or she did so without being heard."

Judy pressed play. The camera left the library and passed the dividing shelf and into the sitting room. Halfway through another 180° panoramic shot, Judy suddenly jerked forward and froze the image. When she started the recording again, it was to zoom in on a chest of drawers under the sitting room window. The dark heavy chest was one of the few remaining pieces of furniture in the room. "Dudley Dennington," she said.

Black shot her a sideways look. Impressed and surprised by her knowledge of the antique trade. "That's what those chests are called, are they?" he asked.

"Dudley Dennington was a petty criminal, Guido, when I was still on the beat. He was getting on when I knew him. One of the last to meet your grandad. Never thought him capable of murder. Well, our Dudley had a chest like that one there," she pointed at the piece of furniture. "And good use he made of it, too."

Aidan Stanton seemed surprised to find Eden at the door, but invited her in happily enough. He'd just closed the front door behind her when, from upstairs, a disembodied voice called, "Who is it?"

"It's that nice lady police officer, Jen," he called back.

Jenna Nesbitt scuttled across the hall and appeared at the top of the stairs, her eyes falling on the cutlery-box-shaped police evidence bag in Eden's hand. She quickly descended, keeping her eyes glued on the bag.

"Is that our cutlery?" she asked at the bottom of the stairs.

"Is it?" Aidan said.

"Can we go through? I have a few questions for you," Eden said.

The three went into the living room. The young couple sat down beside each other on their sofa, while Eden moved a chair and sat down facing them. She removed the canteen of cutlery from its police evidence bag.

"You were right," Aidan said to Jenna, looking impressed.

"I could tell from the shape," she replied.

Eden opened the leather cutlery box. "Is this the canteen you reported stolen?"

"It most certainly is," Aidan said. "Where was it?"

"Have you got the burglars?" Jenna asked.

"We haven't made any arrests yet, Miss Nesbitt," Eden said. "The cutlery was advertised for sale online. We have a positive identification on the person who put them up for sale – Stafford Mills."

"What!" Aidan said. He glanced at Jenna, but her eyes remained firmly focused on the cutlery. "What in the name of God was he doing with our cutlery?"

"That, as yet, we haven't been able to establish," Eden said.

"Was he in on the burglaries?" Aidan asked. "I'd put nothing past him."

"We haven't anything conclusively linking him to the burglaries," Eden said

"Other than our cutlery," Aidan said.

"Miss Nesbitt, do you have any thoughts on how the deceased came to be in possession of your stolen cutlery?" she asked.

Jenna Nesbitt's eyes narrowed. She tore them away from the cutlery and looked directly into Eden's eyes. "He set us up."

"Who?" Eden asked.

"Stafford Mills," Jenna replied. "It all makes sense now. That alarm fitter was one of his mates most likely."

"Why did the deceased want your cutlery so much?" Eden asked.

"Don't suppose he did," Jenna said. "He wanted to screw us around."

"Why?" Eden said. The couple glanced at each other, but neither spoke. "Was there some personal animosity between you?"

Jenna Nesbitt leaned forward: "Yes."

Aidan also leaned forward. "Personal animosity would be putting it too strongly, but there was some ill-feeling."

"Aidan is being his usual nice self," Jenna said. "Stafford Mills was as jealous as hell of our happiness."

"Could you elaborate?" Eden said.

"He didn't get that I wanted Aidan, not him. He fancied himself as sugar daddy. But money isn't everything, is it?"

Eden put all thoughts of her broken washing machine, daughter's smashed laptop, overdraft and the van's looming MOT to the back of her mind, and said, "Do you share Miss Nesbitt's view, Mr Stanton?"

"It was as clear as day. Couldn't take his eyes off her," he said. Beside him, his girlfriend squirmed in her seat. "All this leering got a bit much for us in the end, and I told him to cut it out. She's my girlfriend, not yours, I said. Or words to that effect."

"When was this?"

"Weeks back. He went incommunicado for a bit. Then we met at choir practice, and he acted as if nothing had happened. I did likewise. Didn't need to labour the point."

Jenna Nesbitt glowered. "He set us up," she repeated. "He was pretending he was alright about things and he wasn't. His ego had taken a big hit."

"Why didn't you mention this earlier?" Eden said.

"Nothing to mention," Aidan said.

"Nothing to mention?" Eden said. "You had an argument with a man on the morning of his death, who you'd also argued with earlier…"

"We didn't argue," Aidan said, quite calmly. "I told him to stop ogling my girlfriend. She wasn't interested."

"And that didn't make you suspect his motives in recommending an alarm fitter?" Eden said.

"Not for a minute," Aidan said. "Maybe I'm just naive like that."

Jenna Nesbitt leaned forward. "Now look here," she said. "Don't you start pointing the finger at us. We're the victims here. We're the ones done over by a so-called friend."

In South London, the door of a four-bedroomed, hall-entrance, terraced house was answered by sixty-seven-year-old Jean Janes. Pilot showed her his badge. "I'm Detective

Constable Philip Philpott, Mrs Janes. I understand you've reported your lodger missing."

"This place is much too big for just me," Jean Janes said, leading Pilot into the kitchen. "Please sit down," she waved towards the table and chairs. Pilot pulled a chair out but waited for her to sit down, before he did. He opened his notepad on the kitchen table.

"I let rooms as much for the company as the money," Jean said. "Although I can't pretend it doesn't come in useful. Can I make you a cup of tea, dear?" He raised his hand in a negative gesture, and gave a little shake of his head.

"I have two tenants at the moment," she continued, "a young lady in one room, and Martin in the other. They're nice rooms, *ensuite*. I could get a lot more if I wanted, but I'd rather have someone nice in my house than a rich banker, thank you very much. The young lady's been renting a while now, but Martin's only been with me a short while. I wouldn't dream of calling the police ordinarily. But he's been so ill!"

Pilot looked up from his notes. "Martin Mills is ill?"

She nodded furiously. "He's got cancer, didn't you know? Of course you didn't. Stupid old woman!" She banged her forehead with her fist.

"Don't you apologise, Mrs Janes. Now, please tell me everything."

"He's being treated at the Royal Marsden. That's why he was staying here. It's only a couple of tube stops away. He actually lives on the South East coast. He was totally upfront about everything. Said the doctors told him he needed chemo but it would make him ill, and was that a problem for me? I said – not a bit of it. If you can't help another human being in their hour of need, what's the point of being alive? I lost my dear husband to cancer. I knew what to expect."

She dabbed her eyes with a tissue removed from her sleeve, keeping it crunched up in her hand. "The chemo made Martin so ill. He lost all his hair. I knew he would, having been there before. I hardly let anyone in, in case they had a cold or a virus. They won't let you leave after chemo, unless you have someone with you, and I went with him to the hospital. I couldn't very well let him go alone, could I? I had to insist, he wouldn't have asked; he wasn't the type. He kept apologising. 'Martin,' I told him, 'I want to help. I want to be useful.' Am I speaking too quickly? My husband used to say, slow down woman, I can't listen that fast."

"I have every word, Mrs Janes." Pilot patted his notepad with his biro.

"It wasn't too bad to start with. We used the tube, but then he got so ill, I drove him. I don't know if that's what's behind it."

"Behind what, Mrs Jane?"

"Him not coming back. His treatment isn't finished, you see. He's only halfway through. His doctors told him to have a break and let his platelets recover and he decided to take himself away. Couldn't blame him. I assumed he was going home, but he didn't say and I didn't ask. I dropped him at Victoria Coach Station. Now when was it, exactly?" She stopped to ponder, eventually getting to her feet to look at a calendar on the wall. She turned back a page and pointed to a day on which she had written: Run Martin to Victoria.

Pilot thought back. The day she'd taken Martin to the coach station was the day before Stafford Mills was murdered.

"He had an open return," Jean said. "He was going to call me to pick him up but he never did. I haven't heard from him since I dropped him at the coach station. All his stuff's in his room, not that there was much. I've had lodgers do a bunk before, plenty. Stay for the night, go out the next morning with a cheery wave, and an I'll see you this evening Mrs Janes, then up I go to have a tidy and all their stuff's gone. They'd just wanted a place to lay their head for a night. But Martin wasn't like that. He was too considerate. You couldn't ask for a nicer man. And then there's the money. No one leaves that much money behind." Pilot waited for Jean Janes to explain. "He turned up with two suitcases, you see. One had his clothes and stuff, and the other was full of cash. He showed me. I said, 'Martin, you have to put that in the bank.' He couldn't see it. The way he saw it, only the two of us knew it was there, him and me, and the money was to pay the rent, and in a way I was welcome to it. I told him he was silly. He didn't even know me."

"Where's the money now, Mrs Janes?" Pilot asked.

"Where he left it. In a suitcase under the bed. I'd prefer you to take it with you, if you don't mind. My grandson calls me Nanny Worrywart, but I'd rather call you out and find Martin didn't like it here, but didn't like to say, than find out later something happened to him and no one bothered to check up on him. He hasn't got anybody else."

"Please don't be embarrassed about reporting your concerns to us," Pilot said. "We'd rather be called out over nothing, than not called out over something. We're talking about a seriously ill man who's gone missing. You absolutely did the right thing calling us."

"It isn't just that," she said. She scraped her chair behind her and got up from the table. Across the kitchen, she picked up two letters from inside the porcelain letter tray on the windowsill and returned with them. The letters, in brown A5 envelopes, were addressed to Martin Mills and franked by the Royal Marsden hospital. They'd been opened.

"I opened them," Jean Janes admitted. "I know I shouldn't, but when the second one came I didn't know what else to do. I was that worried." She clumsily pulled out a letter from one of the two envelopes and held it out to Pilot. It was Martin Mills' next appointment. "He missed the first and they sent this." Pilot read the second hospital letter. The letter said he'd missed his appointment, and contained another one, stressing the urgency of his attending.

"He should have started treatment again by now," she said. "I don't understand it. He's so sensible. I thought he wanted to get better. Where is he?"

The chest identical to the one once owned by Dudley Dennington was still in place in the sitting room at Fenn Farmhouse, under the window. Judy pulled out the chest's top drawer as far as it went. It was empty. She left it like that, and lowered herself until eye-level with the drawer, studying each side in turn. Black did likewise.

"Fan of *Flog It*, are you, ma'am?" a young constable cheekily asked from the door.

Black shot the young constable a disapproving glance but Judy replied, her eyes still on the drawer, "As a matter of fact my husband and I are fans, but at the moment I'm more interested in why the interior of this drawer is considerably smaller than the exterior," she replied.

The young constable peered in. "Help me with this, will you, Guido?" Judy asked, taking one side of the drawer. With Black holding the other side, they carried the empty drawer over to the centre of the room and put it on the floor. A distinct thud could be heard as they did. Black tipped the drawer on to its side and there was the thud heard again. Black turned the drawer face down.

"Allow me," the young constable said, holding out an electric screwdriver.

It took the removal of all six screws to finally separate the wooden base from the rest of the drawer, revealing the drawer did indeed have a false bottom on which rested a plastic bag.

"I knew it," Judy said.

Black peered inside the bag and, with a grin, tipped it upside down. Plastic money bags containing wads of cash fell out, along with a pair of leather gloves and a small notebook, secured with an elasticated strip.

"Good old Dudley," Judy said.

"There must be thousands there," the uniformed officer said, staring at the cash.

"Bag it up and get it counted," Black ordered, slipping the notepad into a small plastic bag and pocketing it. "Bedtime reading," he said, giving his pocket a pat.

To avoid hitting his head, Simon Pigott – the consultant treating Martin Mills – ducked under the door as he

169

entered the windowless consulting room where Pilot waited. His height, fair hair and blue-eyes led Pilot to suspect that the consultant's ancestors had arrived on a longboat. Pigott made no attempt to disguise his irritation at the police's insistence on a meeting.

"I can't tell you anything which will breach my patient's privacy," he said.

"I appreciate that, sir, but Martin Mills is a person of interest in a murder investigation and we need to locate him."

Simon Pigott looked slightly surprised.

"He's gone missing," Pilot continued. "Reported by his landlady. She told us all about his ongoing cancer treatment here." Pilot took out the hospital letters. Pigott did no more than glance at them. "Did he attend his last appointment?"

Simon Pigott considered his reply. "If a patient who hasn't formally declined any further treatment fails to present for treatment, we send four chasing letters, copied to their GPs, after which, if they still haven't presented for treatment, we desist. Experience tells us there's no point continuing, although we leave their file open. We can't force treatment on someone. As it's already in the post I can tell you that we sent Martin Mills his third letter by first class post today."

"How long has he got if he doesn't re-start chemo soon?"

Simon Pigott mellowed slightly. "I can't discuss individual cases, but suffice to say, cancer is a cluster of fast-dividing cells, which causes all manner of problems if it gets into the lymphatic system. Chemo kills fast-dividing cells. The more there are of them, the more it's got its work cut out. The disease quickly builds up a resistance if chemotherapy ends halfway through."

"Is his treatment to buy time or cure him?"

Simon Pigott got to his feet. "That I can't answer. If you'll excuse me, officer. I have to pick my daughter up." He paused at the door. "If you do locate Martin Mills, please impress upon him the importance of recommencing treatment as soon as possible. There is now some urgency."

20

Sustained by black coffee and digestive biscuits, Black read Stafford Mills' notepad at his kitchen table. Its tiny handwritten entries filled the book. It covered the last year. Later discovered in the drawer was a bag of other notepads covering earlier years. Reading them, Black decided, was a job for others in his team.

Stafford Mills recorded his financial deals in code. The code wasn't difficult to translate: PR = price received; PP = price paid; PD = profit declared; LD = loss declared. Often the letters C or B appeared, indicating, Black presumed, cash or bitcoin. It was an aide memoir of the deceased's wheelings and dealings over many a year, the frequency and volume of which made remembering them impossible. Black wasn't surprised to learn that the figures contained in the notebook didn't correspond with those on Mills' bank statements and tax returns. He'd've been surprised if they had. He imagined Stafford Mills alone in his library, whisky by his side, flicking back through these pages, revelling in getting one over on the Inland Revenue.

If Stafford Mills was involved in the burglaries, he hadn't recorded it here. But would he have been so stupid as to do so, given the penalties? Black put down the notebook. He'd spent most of the night on it, and what had he learned? That Stafford Mills bought for less and sold for more than he told the Revenue, helped the buyers of his houses reduce stamp duty in exchange for a cut, and paid his contractors in cash to avoid NI contributions. It wasn't legal, but was hardly criminal underworld stuff. One entry in the notebook though, might provide the motive for murder.

The entries made by the deceased in the days running up to his death, suggested a number of big cash sales with a total value exceeding the sum retrieved from the drawer by four and a half thousand pounds. Where was the money? It wasn't anywhere at Fenn Farmhouse or in the bank, in either of his accounts, or in the account set up for Bridget White. Had the killer stolen it? How had they known about it? There wasn't any evidence of torture. Why was so much cash left behind? If Mills had caught the thief red-handed, why was his body found where it was? Why not by the chest? Was there another hidey-hole somewhere? More questions. Black flicked through the remaining pages. Every page from then on was blank, until the back of the book where, on the notepad's last page but one, Black found a list of Stafford Mills' various passwords. He obviously didn't like to store them on his devices. They were all different. Sensible man, Black thought. On the very last page Mills' had scrawled something lengthwise. Black turned the notepad on its side to read the entry.

Fireworks H H!!!!

After the entry, Mills had drawn an exploding firework. There was a date afterwards – a few days before his murder.

Black returned the notepad to the plastic bag, and polished off the last digestive in the packet, pouring the last crumbs down his throat. It was very late and he needed sleep. He went to bed rueing the coffee he'd drunk.

21

Overnight, the investigation's webpage was updated: Martin Mills was named as a person of interest to the investigation;

His most recent photograph was added;

He was invited to contact a member of the team as a matter of urgency, as was any member of the public with information on his whereabouts;

A photograph of the canteen of cutlery recovered from Money Brokers was uploaded;

That it had been stolen from a property in Osborne Tye and recovered from a property in Slyham was made public with a request for information on its whereabouts between given dates;

Any member of the public who had bought or sold something from the deceased in the months prior to his death was invited to get in touch; as was any member of the public able to provide further information on the initials HH.

Eden's morning began with a read through of the morning's media coverage of the enquiry:

Did Murder Victim Have Secret Life of Crime?

Did Gang Kill Stafford To Silence Him?

Murdered Man's Brother's Done a Runner!

Murder Victim's Brother Has Killed Before!

Brothers' Blood Feud...

And so it begins, she thought. No matter how the case turned out, this was what people would remember. Oh well, if she was going to work on murder, she'd have to get used to it, however much it piqued her sense of justice. Just as long as it gets the phone ringing, she thought, just as her phone rang.

She reached over to it:

"Hudson."

She listened in silence, not quite able to believe her ears. She couldn't have been more surprised if the caller had rung to tell of bodies buried behind Fenn Farmhouse.

"I'll be right there, sir," she said, replacing the receiver. She waited a few moments for the news to sink in, before getting to her feet, raising her hands in the air, and saying out loud, "For God's Sake."

At the rear of the factory, at the end of an aisle, balding but beardless warehouse manager, Stuart Beard, with Eden in

178

his wake, stopped and put his hand up. She was to go no further. As a forklift truck, gigantic packets of self-raising flour in its forks, rumbled by, Eden looked up nervously. Ceiling-high shelves crammed with industrial-scale baking supplies loomed over her on either side. She, a woman of average height, felt like a hobbit.

"All clear," Stuart said, as the forklift disappeared through the delivery bay doors.

The aroma of many things savoury and many things sweet, which had engulfed them in the warehouse, accompanied them into Stuart Beard's cluttered office. He cleared a chair for her by throwing files and papers on to the floor, then sombrely took a seat behind his desk, hands resting in front of him, eye contact made.

"We've totally screwed up. On behalf of Cranford's Bakery Supplies I can't apologise enough," he said. "It's not company policy to obstruct or mislead the police in any way. I've informed head office. There'll be an enquiry. Can't apologise enough." As he spoke he made slicing movements through the air with his hands.

"Cranford's are now saying that Corrine Beechwood wasn't here at the time of Stafford Mills' murder, having previously said she was. Is that correct?" Eden said. As she spoke the first sentence, Stuart Beard shook his head. When she said the last sentence, he nodded gravely.

"Her shift for the morning of the seventeenth started at 12.30 all right, but she wasn't here for then. I know – I saw her arrive. Let me wind back. I've just got back from my hols. I don't know about you, but I'm never sure going on holiday is worth the aggro of getting everything up-to-date. My last day was Monday the seventeenth. On top of everything else, I was short a staff member. Ended up making a delivery myself. I was stressed out enough without that, I can tell you. Time I got back here, everyone had left for the night. I ended up staying till midnight to get my desk straight. Had to leave for the airport at three-thirty a.m the next day.

"I left with the delivery at half-past one in the afternoon. I was out back, getting the van ready, when Corrine waltzed passed me, half an hour late. She'd snuck round the side, knowing the camera there's been vandalised, so no one would hear her coming in late. You've got to understand, we've got people on different shifts, people moving around stations. If I hadn't seen her arrive, she'd likely have slipped in, sidled up next to someone and carried on, like she'd just been sent over from a different station or something, and chances are no one'd've known. 'Stead of which, she walked straight into me."

"I thought from the information provided that your staff had to key in and out?" Eden said.

"They do. I'll come to that in a mo if you don't mind. Corrine couldn't believe her eyes when she saw me. Neither could I. I was furious. Said – 'Where the hell have you been? Your shift started half an hour ago.' She looked embarrassed. Said she was sorry. Got her shifts confused. What kind of excuse is that? I'd've gone ballistic, but I didn't have time. She started on about I should be in her shoes and see how I liked it. I just walked off and left her, intending to deal with her later. Only, when I got back, first thing I heard was her ex had been murdered. Even I'm not that heartless."

"You missed the coverage, Mr Beard?"

"Knew nothing about it. Listened to an audiobook on the delivery. Went to bed late. Got up crack of dawn.

Didn't have time to catch up with the news. I visited my brother and his family in France. They live in the middle of nowhere. All their news is French. I never married, so yes, somehow I missed the coverage. Didn't know anything about it until Sue told me."

"Sue Blakeney? The lady I spoke to here?" Eden said. "The lady who confirmed Corrine Beechwood's alibi?"

"One and the same," Stuart Beard said. "First thing I wanted to know was: when did it happen? And here our confusion starts. Sue's very words were, 'Day you went on holiday.' But it wasn't. I went on holiday in the early hours of Tuesday the eighteenth. Not Monday the seventeenth. She meant the day I went on holiday from here. Excuse me for saying so, but a man wouldn't have put it like that. Had she said: 'your last day in work', I'd've known she was talking about the Monday and we'd have been having this conversation a lot sooner. I didn't really want to know too much, it's all a bit sordid for me. I got he'd been attacked the day I went on holiday, at home, and that Corrine wasn't in the frame. That was more than enough for me. I didn't want to know any more and left it like that.

"This morning I bump into Sue in the car park and she was still going on about it. 'Still haven't got anyone for it,' she said. 'Good job Corrine's shift that Monday was the time it was.' I wanted to know why so. Sue said cos otherwise she'd've been in the frame wouldn't she? I stopped in my tracks. 'What has Corrine's shift that Monday got to do with anything?' I asked her. She looked at me like I'd crawled out from under something and said, 'That was the day Stafford was killed. Monday, the seventeenth.' 'He was killed on the seventeenth?' I said, reminding her that she'd said Stafford Mills was murdered the day I went on holiday, and I hadn't gone on holiday on the seventeenth, I'd gone on the eighteenth. She rolled her eyes and snapped did it really matter if he'd been killed the day I went on holiday or the day after? She couldn't see why it mattered. Corrine was here for her shift and that's what mattered. 'No she wasn't,' I said. 'Not for the start of it, she wasn't. She was late. Please don't tell me we've told the police she was here when she wasn't?' That's when it all came out. I dragged her in here and made her tell me exactly what happened." He lowered his head briefly and tapped his fingers on the desk. "Sue didn't mean to mislead you, I give you my word. She's devastated…"

"Mr Beard, please just tell me what happened after I rang and asked Cranford's to confirm Corrine Beechwood's alibi for the time of the attack on Stafford Mills," Eden said.

"To go back to your question, yes we do key in and out here. The first thing Sue did, after your station called, was to check the time Corrine keyed in. Only Corrine had forgotten to key in or, to be precise, she'd forgotten to key out the night before. It happens. Sue thought nothing of it. It's not uncommon. We all do it from time to time. Sue then checked the time Corrine's shift was meant to start, and who else was on around the same time. The first couple of people she asked, remembered seeing Corrine. The shift-managers that day both saw her. They'd changed halfway through the shift so they would have done. She turned up ten minutes before the changeover. You've seen how big the warehouse is," he said. "It's why I took you through it, so you'd see. People work different shifts. They come and go. If a line is short, someone goes over to help out. I'm not making excuses, just trying to explain."

He shook his head ruefully. "I told Sue straight: 'Sue,' I said, 'you've misled the police in a murder enquiry! She got defensive: 'I asked. People saw her. She was here.' Then she started on about Corrine never being late. Which is true, I've never known her be late, which in my opinion makes what happened even more suspicious. Truth is, Detective Sergeant, Sue didn't want to land Corrine in it. She should have asked around until she found someone who definitely saw Corrine arrive at midday when she said. But she didn't. She'd heard all she wanted to and didn't dig any deeper. In her heart of hearts, she couldn't believe her mate capable of such a thing. Least she had the decency to cry. Had to send her home. I rang you straight away. Can't apologise enough."

Eden could see how it happened. The factory was big and busy, some shifts straddled each other, others overlapped. She'd asked for CCTV from the start only to be told the cameras were mostly for show. She mentioned this to Stuart Beard.

"It's an expensive system to maintain," he said. "Head office decided cameras alone was enough to put staff off nicking stuff. However, there are cameras on the delivery vans."

He turned his computer screen to face Eden. On it were images of the wholesaler's car park, taken according to the day and time displayed in yellow across the bottom, shortly after Stafford Mills was attacked. There was little activity other than occasional shots of Stuart Beard coming and going as he loaded the van. Then, approximately thirty minutes after her ex-boyfriend was attacked, Corrine Beechwood came into shot, running, flustered, across the car park.

22

In the Munro's caravan, Black shared the discovery about Leslie Gallagher and the phone call. "Can you think of any reason why Stafford Mills got Leslie Gallagher to make that appointment?"

Hector and Brenda Munro exchanged a puzzled glance. "Not sure we can help you there, Detective Inspector," Hector said. "Only thing I can think of is he wanted to disappear off somewhere without us knowing he'd gone."

"None of you heard him go out?" Black asked.

The couple shook their heads. "We didn't," Hector said. "Might you have, Bridget?"

He looked over to his sister-in-law, sitting up in bed, a blanket pulled around her despite being fully clothed and under the bed clothes. Dandelion lay at her feet. Bridget White shivered as though cold, and sweated as though hot. Black realised she was in alcohol withdrawal. He noticed she clutched a bowl.

"If I did, I don't remember," she said, flinching as if in pain

"Nothing about him surprises us any more," Brenda said. "I've just this minute come off the phone to Jenna. Is it right that Stafford got someone to pinch their silver?"

"I can confirm Stafford Mills asked a local shop to sell the silver stolen from Aidan and Jenna," Black said. "How he came to be in possession of it, we haven't as yet established."

"Was he in with the burglars, you reckon?" Hector said.

"I can't comment on that at this stage, sir," Black said.

"Jenna's convinced Stafford was behind it, because he was jealous of her and Aidan. She's a pretty girl, let's face it," Brenda said, as her sister gave out a loud groan.

Black glanced over to her. She was rake-thin and looked terrible. He could only hope she got through this and stayed off the booze permanently. Now, that would be a result.

"Do any of you know what the letters HH mean? We think it might be shorthand for a place, or possibly a person?"

The Munros looked at each other blankly. "Sorry," Hector said. "Can't help you there."

"Mrs White?"

Bridget slowly and painfully shook her head, whispering, "No, sorry."

"Did any of you know that the chest under the window in the living room had a secret drawer?" Black asked.

186

"Did it really?" Hector said. "Him and his secrets."

"The chest had a secret drawer?" Brenda said. "Where?"

"The top drawer had a secret bottom," Black said.

"Good heavens," Brenda said. "The number of times I've dusted that thing."

From the small bed, Bridget raised her head and said, "I knew."

"Mrs White, do you feel up for a short walk," Black said.

The little dog jumped to her feet and off the bed on mention of the word walk and ran over to the cupboard containing her lead. Bridget meanwhile slowly swung her legs around and onto the floor. A few moments passed and she painfully struggled to her feet, still clutching a blanket around her. "There's nothing I'd like better," she said.

Once out of the caravan, Black slowed his pace to match Bridget's steps. They walked slowly to the edge of the caravan park, she clutching a water bottle and a plastic bag in case she was sick. There they stood in silence, side-by-side, looking across the neighbouring field, at a herd of cows lying down, Dandelion frolicking on her lead.

"All right?" Black gently asked her.

"I feel slightly better outside," she said. "Fresh air and all."

"It's going to rain," Black said, glancing up at the mass of grey clouds speeding towards them, snuffing out the light.

"I haven't had a drink for forty-eight hours," Bridget said. "Stafford's murder was a wake-up call. Not being able to help you or Brenda was disgraceful. Had to pull myself together. Hope I can make it this time. I feel like shit. I can't tell you. But I have to do it. I have to." She took a sip of water and spat it out.

"Tell me about the drawer, Bridget."

"He used it to hide cash and other bits and bobs he didn't want Corrine or the taxman knowing about. Sometimes he had so much cash in there, he put it into my account and got me to take it out again later on. He held onto the card. We'd've been out on our ears if I'd said no. Where would we have gone? We haven't a bean between us. Even a sad old soak like me knows what side her bread is buttered, Detective Inspector."

"Mrs White, is it possible the farmhouse was used as a drop-off by the gang? I'm wondering if your burglar dream actually came from something you saw. If not the day Stafford died, then another time maybe?"

Bridget smiled indulgently and placed her hand on Black's arm. "Detective Inspector, Stafford Mills was no angel. But I can't see him as a burglar or a fence. He wasn't that stupid or desperate. He'd have gone down for a long time for something like that. He most likely had Jenna and Aidan's place turned over to teach Aidan a lesson for standing up to him. He didn't like that."

"You picked a bowl of crab apples on the bridle path on the day Stafford died. Did you see anybody else there?" Black asked. "Someone you knew from the village?" He was thinking in particular of Jenna Nesbitt.

"I can't remember picking apples," she said. "I'm best at remembering bits of things or things that made an impression on me."

Emotional memory, Black thought. "Did Stafford have many friends?" he asked.

"I don't think he had any. He knew a lot of people, sang in the choir, club in London, but the only people who visited regularly were Corrine or her lot, till that ended."

"What about Brenda and Hector? They have a lot of friends?"

"Not really. Never have. Keep themselves to themselves. Particularly him. Ronnie and me, we were always going out. Not them. She used to when she was younger, before she married Hector. When we were young, we were out every night, danced the night away we did. You might not think it now, but Brenda and Bridget Besthorpe were something to look at back then. We were the toast of the town. Broke a few hearts. Had ours broken back. But time moves on, and here we are."

The sky had grown darker and it started to spit. They turned back. Bridget zipped up her raincoat and put up the hood. Black, who hadn't a coat with him, could do no more than raise his collar and lower his head against the shower. Dandelion was unperturbed.

"Did you know Stafford's brother, Martin?" he asked as they trudged back.

"Oh, don't," she said. "Broke his poor mother's heart that business did. None of us could believe it. Ronnie was still alive then. He tried to help, but Martin wouldn't have it. Wouldn't see any of us – even..." She stopped and frowned, a confused look on her face. Black followed her gaze to a nearby caravan where a couple watched the detective between their curtains. This kind of thing annoyed him. It was an invasion of his witnesses privacy and left them disconcerted and upset. The couple realised they'd been seen and jumped back out of sight, curtains flickering behind them.

Black glanced at Bridget. She looked quite sad. It was raining heavily now, and Black took her by the arm. "The gawping will stop eventually, Bridget," he said, softly steering her back to her own caravan. "You'd be amazed how quickly people forget. You were saying Martin turned his back on all of you even..."

"Even his mother. Ronnie said it was an awful shame he wouldn't let any of us help. An awful shame. He didn't do it, you know. Martin." They'd reached the caravan. She stopped and looked at Black, her face framed by the hood of her coat. Dandelion pawed at the door to get in.

"You'd better go in before you catch your death," he said.

Rather than going in, she continued to study him silently, her eyes narrowing. Her hands shook continuously. "Mrs White?" Black said. "Is everything all right?"

"We weren't outside when Stafford said that stuff about someone being naughty. We were in the hall, and he was putting his new Barbour on. I can see him doing it. He was laughing. I asked what was so funny and he said – 'Someone's been a bit naughty.' I can still hear him saying it now."

"Can you remember anything else?"

She closed her eyes, clearly trying to remember more. But nothing else came and she opened them again and shook her head, regretting it immediately judging by the look of pain on her face. "No, sorry," she mumbled.

"Do you remember when this happened? The day? The month?"

She teared up and looked down. Black wondered if she was going to be sick but she wasn't. She looked up again. "The 'when' part of my memory's gone, Detective Inspector. The doctors say it'll never come back."

"Bridget, you've been enormously helpful," Black said.

"Have I?"

He looked at her and she looked back, rain dripping from her hood, bedraggled, vulnerable, neither young nor old, and willing to do anything she could to help. He hoped from the bottom of his heart she'd conquer her demons. "Enormously." He took out his business card and handed it to her. "Call me on this number, day or night if anything comes to mind."

He returned to his car and threw his drenched jacket on the back seat. He was soaked through. He turned the heating on to full blast, wrung his pullover out and gnawed at a matchstick for comfort. Was Stafford Mills behind the burglary at Jenna and Aidan's place or did he get hold of the cutlery some other way? Why risk jail selling it locally? Why get Leslie Gallagher to make that appointment? Why had he argued with so many people on the morning of his death? And what were so many old acquaintances doing there? Why did Jenna go back to the farmhouse? What was Jeremy Havelock really there for? Where was Stafford Mills for the missing forty or so minutes? Who was this someone who'd been 'naughty'? Was Stafford a blackmailer? Is that why Martin Mills withdrew so much money? And where was Martin Mills anyway? And why did everybody swear he was innocent? And why was one candlestick left behind? And where was the other one? And the forensics? And why pinch a telescope? Why not arrive with a pair of binoculars? And what or who was HH? And why was he sitting in a car talking to himself?

23

"Why did you lie about where you were when Stafford Mills was killed?" Eden asked Corrine Beechwood in a station interview room.

"Because I didn't have an alibi."

"Where were you?"

"On the abandoned viaduct outside town. Stafford and I used to walk it at weekends. I hadn't slept. I've hardly had a wink since the split. Things keep whirring around my head. I needed fresh air if I was going to get through my shift. There's a bench up there. Thought I had plenty of time. I just sat there trying to get my head around things. You know how we blame ourselves. The time just went. Next thing I'm late for work. Really late! There's no quick way of getting down all those steps. Traffic didn't help. Went in the side way hoping I'd got away with it, but would you believe it, Stuart Beard was there. Trying to explain anything to him is pointless. Said I was sorry and left it like that. I hadn't been there long when one of the other ladies put her arm around me and led me off the floor to tell me about Stafford. I was good for nothing after that and went home."

"Did anybody see you at the viaduct?"

"I doubt it. Not many people go up there, even at weekends. That's what Stafford liked about it. I don't remember seeing anyone." She looked about, clearly highly anguished. "I didn't kill Stafford. I wasn't angry it ended. I was numb. I know I should've been straight with you, but things looked bad. He'd dumped me and next thing he's murdered and I don't have an alibi. I panicked. Had to be that day I was late, didn't it? First time in fifteen years." The panic mounted in her voice. "You can't charge me with murder! Perverting the course of justice, or whatever it is, but not murder! I don't deserve that – I don't deserve any of this. I'm a decent woman who makes rubbish choices is all. I'm not the first woman to do that."

You're certainly not, Corrine, Eden thought. She had a hunch Corrine's story would check out. "Mrs Beechwood, have you heard of Automatic Number Plate Recognition? If you'd been straight with us from day one, we could've checked out your story without the need for any of this. I'll need the precise route you took that day to and from the viaduct. We can use a map if it helps. After that you're free to go."

"That it? Aren't you going to charge me?"

"That's not my decision, Mrs Beechwood. Let's start at the beginning. What time did you leave home on the seventeenth?"

24

That night, Eden was woken from a deep sleep by her phone. She'd worked late catching up on paperwork and hadn't got to bed until midnight. Though still more asleep than awake, she reached over to answer the call before it woke the rest of the house. It was the station. It took a while for the news to sink in.

"I'm on my way," she said, falling out of bed. It was six forty-five a.m.. There was barely time to splash her face, dress, discover the biscuit tin was empty and scrawl a hurried note to Dottie:

Had to go in – Dora has spelling 2day – book on top of fridge – we need biscuits! xxx

before rushing out of the door.

A traveller journeying from the direction of Fenn Farmhouse towards Osborne Tye would pass a small park on their left, before reaching the village itself. The park was St. Osborne's Gardens and it lay next to a sports field.

195

It was still dark when Eden arrived there. She parked up on the verge outside and took a look around. The gardens and the sports field were bordered by a hedge and a wire fence, in that order. From the road an entrance led into the park and another, further along, to the sports field. At the rear, directly across the park from the front entrance, a gate led to the bridle path. Over the years, individuals too lazy to stroll over to the official entrances/exits had added one of their own by stamping down the fence and ripping a hole in the hedge behind the sports field.

About half way between the two, a caretaker's shed was covered by a forensics tent. Parked outside it, alongside police vehicles, was a truck. There was Black, with two uniformed police officers and a young man wrapped in a blanket, shaking uncontrollably. That had to be twenty-seven-year-old Andy Slater, the park's caretaker, Eden thought, taking the footpath to cross over to them. She knew only that Andy Slater (local, married, couple of kids, no previous) had found the body in the shed.

"This is Detective Sergeant Eden Hudson, Mr Slater," Black said as she reached them. "Mr Slater found the body in there," he nodded towards the tent, "under some tarpaulin, Detective Sergeant."

"I'm sorry, sir," she said to Andy, "coming across a dead body is an unpleasant experience for anybody."

"Can't stop shaking," the young caretaker said. "Dunno what's wrong with me."

Black gave Andy Slater's arm a reassuring pat. "Shock. You wouldn't be human, man, if you took it in your stride."

"Mr Slater has just informed us that he mowed the lawn yesterday and came back today to touch up the lines on the playing field," Black said.

Andy Slater pulled the blanket closer to him. "It's my boy's birthday today. We've got him a new bike. Hid it at my parents. That's why I got here so early," he explained. "Wanted to get cracking at first light so's I could give him his bike before he went to school. I'm in charge of all the parks and schools around here."

Eden knew of many a colleague who would have interrupted Andy Slater brusquely by now, urging him to get to the point quicker, particularly as Black had heard this already. But Guido Black rarely interrupted. He allowed people to talk. Partly from politeness and partly on the lookout for contradictions.

"I go from park to park and keep the mower with me." Eden's eyes followed his over to his truck where she saw a sit-on lawn mower. "But the striping machine and the paint and stuff, I keep in there," he said of the hut. "First thing I notice is the padlock's missing. I let you lot in to search after the murder of that Stafford Mills, and I locked up afterwards. The padlock was definitely on then. Thought there'd been a break-in and we'd been done over. I gave the door a push. We're meant to report things like that and call the police, but if I waited for them to show up my kid would have turned eighteen. No offence like." He raised his hand in a conciliatory gesture and gave a half-grin, half-grimace. "When nothing happened, I gave it a kick, but it didn't budge. I had a closer look and realised the bolt had been drawn across from the inside. Oh, yeah, I thought – some tramp's dossed down for the night. I hammered on the door and yelled at whoever it was to get out, but nothing happened. Thought, I'm not having this. I went to the truck for my punch bag." He moved his head in the direction of a punchbag on the grass near by. "I'm an amateur boxer," he added. "I put it against the door and put my shoulder to it. Whoever was inside hadn't done a good job securing the lock. Only took a couple of smashes for the lock to give and I was in.

"I stayed outside – you've got to give them an escape route – punch bag at the ready, yelling: 'Where are you? Let's be having you.' There was this eerie silence and this horrible smell. Something had to be up for something to smell that rank. I shone my torch around, but couldn't see anything out of place, then I noticed a bundle in the corner under some tarpaulin. I figured whoever it was, was most likely dead, given the smell, but I had to make sure. I used a stick to lift the tarpaulin out of the way. He was curled up like a baby. I gave him a couple of gentle prods to get him to stir. Nothing nasty or anything, just a gentle tap. I didn't want to get too close. Said: 'You can't stay here, mate, you need to be on your way.' He didn't move. I couldn't tell if he was breathing and checked for a pulse. He was as cold and dead as a dodo. That smell was him decomposing. Poor bugger."

Andy Slater abruptly sat down on the grass. A police officer quickly poured him a cup of milky sweet tea from a thermos flask. He took it and drank.

"When was the last time you were in the shed?" Eden said.

"When you lot searched it. Haven't been here since. Haven't needed to."

"When was the search?" Black asked Eden. She checked.

"The nineteenth, sir."

Andy Slater looked up at them from the grass, his legs sprawled out in front of him. "Know the worst thing? Missing my kid's face when he got his bike."

Eden and Black donned the usual protective clothing and stepped through the canvas entrance. The shed appeared standard for its type: wooden, rectangular, windowless, pitched roof. Inside, Matthew Prichard squatted by a body of a man in middle age. The dead man was skeletal, his dark hair thinning and flecked through with grey. As Matthew Prichard looked over, his grim face softened at the sight of Eden. Black took a moment to look around the shed. He saw a line-making machine next to cans of paint, hedge cutters, what looked like a broken strimmer and various other gardening and maintenance implements. His eyes alighted on a shelf lined with more paint tins, paint brushes, sandpapers, various cloths and paint remover.

"What have we got, Matt?" he asked.

Matthew got to his feet. "Death occurred within the last few weeks. The cold snap we just had preserved the body."

Eden and Black glanced at each other. The shed had been searched by their team since then. How could they not have found the body, Black thought crossly.

"At first glance, I'd say the death was natural," Matthew Prichard continued. "Most likely a heart attack." He showed them a wallet found on the body, now in a police evidence bag. "This is either Martin Mills, or someone with his wallet. Having autopsied Stafford Mills, I'm going for the former."

It was Black's turn to squat by the body. The two men weren't identical twins, far from it. They weren't the same height or weight, and this man was clearly very unwell when he died. Nonetheless, the brotherly resemblance and the wallet told him Matthew was right, this was Martin Mills. What the hell was he doing here? He got up. "How soon can you carry out the post-mortem, Matthew?"

"Soon as I get him back to the lab."

They left the Professor inside with the body and made their way over to their cars. "He was here to visit his brother," Eden said. "Arrived late. Didn't want to wake the house. Decided to overnight in the shed. Fell asleep. Never woke up."

"Another visitor from Stafford Mills' past," Black said. "What I want to know is why the search team missed his body."

"Screw up?" she ventured. "Didn't look under the tarpaulin?"

Black did not look very pleased. "Call the station. I want to know how he travelled from London to Osborne Tye and when. Then I want you to go to London. I'm going to pay another visit to the Munros and Bridget White..." He stopped talking, distracted by something. They'd reached the entrance, but he was making no attempt to go to his car. Instead he peered across Eden's shoulder, scowling, and focusing intensely on something behind her. She turned her head to follow his gaze to a dead tree on the verge outside the park. Like him, she noticed flies buzzing around the tree trunk.

"Will you look at that," he said.

"It's suddenly got warm out," Eden said. "When you think how cold it's been. It's brought everything out. The cat chased a butterfly yesterday." She frowned. "Suppose we'll have to keep her now. Dora'll be happy."

Black wasn't listening. His eyes were firmly on the tree. A look she hadn't seen before crossed his face. She watched him advance on the tree, putting the gloves he'd just ripped off, back on. The flies, she noticed, were hovering by a knothole halfway up the trunk. Black swatted them away and, after removing his jacket, thrust his right arm into the knothole. With the knothole at his chest height, he managed this easily. By now Matthew Prichard had joined them, as intrigued as everyone else. Surrounded by a group of police and forensic officers, Black wiggled his arm about, attempting to grasp something just out of reach. He strained and scowled with the effort. "Oh no you don't," he said. More wriggling followed.

"Gotcha!" Whatever he had hold of had become wedged and some effort was needed to get it out of the tree trunk.

"There ain't no flies on Black," he said, tugging a plastic bag out of the hole. He looked inside and grinned. "There may be flies on some of you guys, but there ain't no flies on Black."

He removed the bag's contents with his gloved hand and held it aloft: a candlestick, different only from the one found in the library at Fenn Farmhouse by its grime and the tarnish of its silver. Professor Prichard put his face up to it. "Blood on the bottom left corner, if I'm not mistaken," he said.

"Was Martin Mills in the shed lying low after killing his brother, only to die himself?" Eden wondered out loud.

25

B lack drove to the Munro's caravan, wondering how the two women in particular would take the news of Martin Mills' death.

"You've just this minute missed them," Hector explained after showing Black in. "They caught the eight twenty-five bus to Sylham. Getting a bit of retail therapy in. Is there anything I can help you with?"

Both men remained standing, just inside the door.

"Mr Munro, I'm sorry to break yet more bad news, but we've found a body we believe to be Martin Mills, not far from here."

Hector Munro steadied himself against a chair. "Not him, too," he said. "First Stafford, then his brother. What's going on?"

"The body was found in the caretaker's shed in St. Osborne's Gardens. We think he may have died in his sleep."

"Died in his sleep? From what? Hypothermia?"

"He had health problems," Black explained.

Hector tightened his grip on the back of the chair and stared at the ground, taking in the news. "My wife and her sister are going to be devastated." He looked up. "What was he doing in Osborne Tye?"

"That we still need to establish, sir."

"Was he down to see his brother, you reckon?" Hector said.

"It would seem logical. He hadn't been in touch?"

Hector shook his head. "Not with us. Brenda and Bridget would never have let him sleep in a shed! If he'd been in touch with Stafford, he never mentioned it. I never once heard him speak his brother's name in all the years I worked for him. Martin Mills didn't drive down, then?"

"Seems not. What makes you ask?"

"Anyone with a car would have slept in that, not a shed," Hector said. "Why didn't he come to the house, I wonder? Or call and say he was coming down?"

"Maybe he did," Black suggested. "In the weeks leading up to Stafford Mills' death, did he make or receive any calls you can't explain?"

"Not to the main line, which I answer. If Stafford spoke to him, he never said."

"Did Stafford receive any letters out of the ordinary? Appear unsettled or rattled by anything?"

"Not that I can think of."

Black showed Hector a photograph of Martin Mills, taken after his death. "Did you see this man in the days before Stafford's death?"

Hector raised his glasses to study the picture. "No, can't say as I did. That him, then? The brother?"

"Yes, Mr Munro," Black said. "That's Martin Mills, photographed after his death."

"You'll be wanting to speak to my wife and sister-in-law, I take it, Detective Inspector?"

"We will, yes."

"I'm telling you now, if they knew Martin was around, they wouldn't have let him go without saying hello."

26

Pilot took the wheel, allowing Eden to call home. She spoke to Dottie. "I'm en route to London. Not sure when I'll get back," she explained. "Dora get off okay?"

"We practised spelling over porridge," Dottie said. "Twenty out of twenty. Went off to school as happy as Larry. Don't worry about getting back late, she's having her tea at her friend's. Where's the laundry? I went to get it and it wasn't there."

"In the boot. I meant to take it to the launderette yesterday, but ran out of time. I'll take it tonight."

"Don't bother. Eric cut Mrs McNulty's hedge for her and she's letting us use hers 'til we get a new one."

"That's something. Dottie I've got to go — my McBreakfast's getting cold. See you later."

"That your mum?" Pilot asked, when she came off the phone.

"Step-granny," she replied. "My stepdad's mum."

Eric pulled a bottle out of a packet of cornflakes. "What this?" he asked Dixie. "I don't know." "You don't know? I suppose it wasn't you who hid a bottle of whisky in a cereal packet?" "I don't know how it got there. Stop shouting at me." "One of the kids put it there, did they, Dixie?" "Stop shouting." "What if they'd found it?" Eden and Leah watched the scene unfold in silence, empty cereal bowls in front of them. Leah started to cry. Eric left the packet of cereal next to the half-empty bottle and went to the table. He picked Leah up in one arm and Eden in the other. He'd reached the front door when Dixie caught up with them. She pummelled his back. "No," she said. She took a hold of Eden and tried to pull her from Eric's arms. "She's not even yours." Eden kicked out at her mother. "No!" she yelled with such ferocity that Dixie let go, stunned. "I'll send mum round for their stuff," Eric said, from the other side of the front door.

To this day Eden still saw her mother slumped down on all fours, in tears, as they left.

"He took us straight to Dottie's and there we stayed," Eden said. "We'd've ended up in care otherwise."

"Your real dad drink too?"

"No idea. Don't know who or where he is. Eric's my dad."

"It's great you look out for each other." After a reflective pause, he said, "Who are we off to see again?"

"Plashet Willoughby, Sotheby's head of English and Continental silver sales."

"Mrs Willoughby may know a thing or two about silver, but is she an Advanced Dungeons and Dragons Grand Master?" he wanted to know.

"Probably. Her type usually are," Eden replied, wondering what an Advanced Dungeons and Dragons Grand Master was, but unwilling to ask, lest Pilot spend the rest of the journey telling her. She'd finished off her breakfast burger and was feeling a lot better for it. She'd taken a slurp of coffee when Pilot said, "Women can be Grand Masters too. Haylee Smith's one."

"Haylee Smith? The goth?"

"I don't mind that. Goth's are cute."

"You and Mace split up?" she asked innocently. "When did this happen?"

"I haven't split up with Mace," he said. The answer was hurried and defensive. "I'm just saying that Haylee Smith happens to be an Advanced Dungeons and Dragons Grand Master."

"I'll bear that in mind if I ever need one," Eden said.

"Why's the boot full of your laundry?" he asked.

"We can't really afford where we live, but there's no alternative at the moment. Leaves things a bit tight. My kid dropping her laptop and the washing machine blowing up at the same time as Eric needing a new van is one big bill too many."

"I might be able to help," he said. "Leave it with me. How do you think I should play it?"

Eden glanced at him. "Play what?"

"Me and Haylee and Mace. I'm not really a two-woman guy, but Haylee's more into the same things as me. And she's my height."

"You asking me if you should finish with Mace?"

"Let's not be too hasty," he replied.

"Then, you're asking me how to juggle two girlfriends so you can make your mind up, without pissing them both off?"

"That's more like it."

The office of Plashet Willoughby, Sotheby's head of English and Continental silver sales, was bright and spacious, its furniture a mixture of ultra-modern and antique. Posters announcing silver sales over the years adorned the walls. Perfume filled the air. The lady herself wore a knee-length dark woollen dress, a pale pink pashmina fastened by an antique silver brooch thrown nonchalantly around her shoulders. Eden felt dowdy in comparison. Even Pilot felt scruffy.

Plashet directed them to a circular glass table under a bay window. The window looked down on the chaos of London, but its triple glazing kept the room quiet. Silver miniatures dotted the bay windowsill. Somehow Plashet managed to close the blinds without disturbing any of them. She pulled up a seat and joined Eden and Pilot. "How can I help?"

Eden took the candlestick recovered from the murder scene, now in its clear police evidence bag, and placed it on the table as Pilot called up the Craigslist's ad on his laptop and turned the screen to face her: "Does this ad describe that candlestick?" he asked.

A fine pair …

"It says pair," Plashet observed, looking up from Pilot's laptop.

"The other's with forensics," Eden said.

Plashet returned to the entry:

A fine pair of George III antique silver candlesticks (1750 Sheffield). Tapering stems and square shaped bases, nicely fluted. Height 12 inches (30.5cm), base 5.25 inches (14cm). GDP £7000 (Seven thousand pounds sterling).

After reading the ad through a couple of times, she said, "One mo," and got up to cross the room to take a hardback book from a bookshelf. "I still find it easier to look things up in books than online," she said, returning to her seat, book in hand. She flicked through the pages, leaving it open on the table when she reached a page of hallmarks. After studying the candlestick for some time, she used a magnifying glass to compare its hallmark with those on the page. Her detailed examination finished, she returned the bagged candlestick to the table and rested the magnifying glass on the open page.

"Except for the price – yes," she said, answering Pilot's question.

Eden and Pilot glanced at each other, both a bit disappointed that the build up had led to an anti-climax. "No way are they worth seven thousand pounds," she continued. "A dealer would try for two and a half thousand and take one and a half. Silver everywhere is down at the moment. Precious metals are an inflation hedge and their price won't pick up significantly until inflation kicks off again."

"A line of enquiry we're following is that someone went to a lot of trouble for those particular candlesticks. Over and above common-or-garden burglary," Pilot said, leaning back in Plashet's ridiculously comfy chair, one leg crossed over the other, wondering if he could stay there for the rest of his life. "Is there anything about these particular sticks which might make them a motive for murder?"

"Murder? Good heavens. Everything has a value, but there's nothing massively unique about these to increase the figure I've put on them. Perhaps something along the lines of a 'Dear Jo, here are those candlesticks you like so much, Napoleon' letter would add considerably to their value, but without that they look pretty ordinary to me. There's a big crime memorabilia market, but that's after the event not before. If you'd like a second opinion, I can call in a colleague, or ring my counterparts at Bonhams or the London Auction Rooms?"

"That won't be necessary, Mrs Willoughby," Eden said. "I'd like you to take a look at something else for me, if you don't mind." From another bag she took out the canteen of cutlery stolen from Aidan Stanton and Jenna Nesbitt, and recovered from Money Brokers. "These were stolen from a residential property in the days preceding the murder we're investigating and put up for sale. What can you tell me about them?"

Plashet spent a few moments studying them. Her verdict: "Canteen of silver cutlery. Twelve pieces, six of each. German silver marks, crown and moon, 800 grade silver, dated 1882. Pieces nicely decorated with a garland of harebells. Produced by the cartload for the homes of the aspiring middle class."

"Nothing to connect them with the candlesticks?" Eden said.

"Different eras, different objects, different silver, different makers," Plashet said. "I'm sorry I'm not being much help."

"On the contrary, Ms Willoughby, you've been extremely enlightening," Eden replied.

The two thanked her and left. They had one more job to do, before returning homewards.

"Oh look at me crying," Martin Mills' London landlady said, dabbing her eyes. "I hardly knew the man. Since I lost my husband anything sets me off." Eden pressed a cup of tea into Jean Janes' hands and sat beside her.

"Did Martin ever mention his brother, Stafford?" Pilot said.

"I didn't know he had a brother. He didn't seem to have anyone. No one rang to ask after him. Even with him so ill. He never talked about himself. He was a very private person." She started to cry again. "I can't bear to think of anyone being unhappy. My husband used to say I want everybody to be happy but not everyone can be, that's not how life is."

"Did Martin ever talk about his past?" Eden said.

"No, he didn't. I asked if he had a lady friend and he said he didn't. I asked if there was anyone he'd ever been close to – I'm a bit nosy like that. He said he was a confirmed bachelor. I don't think he was gay though. Didn't get that impression."

"He was once involved in a serious car crash," Pilot said. "Did he ever talk about it?"

"A car crash? I didn't know he could drive. He didn't have a car. I'm sure of it."

"Mrs Janes, you knew Martin Mills and were one of the last people to see him alive," Eden said. "As there are no

213

family members, can I ask you to formally identify the body for us? If you'd rather not, please say."

Mrs Janes appeared a bit startled. "You want me to come with you now, dear?"

"We'll send a car around in the morning, Mrs Janes, if that's all right with you."

27

Jean Janes arrived at the morgue the next morning in an unmarked police car, accompanied by her daughter and a policewoman from the Metropolitan Police. Pilot met her by the entrance and led her inside.

By a trolley, a forensics officer pulled back the sheet covering the body of Martin Mills. She ensured only his face was revealed, leaving the rest of the body, and its autopsy scars, hidden by the sheet. Nonetheless, when Jean Janes saw him she gave a little jolt and raised her hand to her mouth, saying, "Oh."

The policewoman put her arm around her. "Can you confirm this is your lodger, Martin Mills?" she asked.

Jean nodded sadly. "That's Martin, all right." The police officer gave her a cuddle.

"I'm all right, dear," she said, patting the police-woman's hand. "His suffering's over."

Professor Matthew Prichard and Guido Black waited for Jean Janes to be escorted out of the room by Pilot before entering it. The Professor uncovered Martin Mills' body in its entirety.

"He had stage three colorectal cancer. The tumour shows evidence of shrinkage following chemotherapy. Cause of death confirmed as myocardial infarction. Significantly, whoever bolted the shed wasn't Martin Mills."

"It was bolted from the inside."

"Not by Martin Mills. The body was interfered with after death. To be precise someone attempted to strangle him," Prichard said.

"After death?"

Prichard nodded. Black leaned back on his heels to take in the information.

"Was he moved?" he asked.

"I can't say definitively, but unlikely. There's only one set of lividity marks along the side he was lying on, so probably not. That said, he wouldn't have been difficult to move, he weighed next to nothing. He was as light as a feather. A child could have picked him up. I'm certain about the strangulation though. See the faint bruising around the neck?"

"I do," Black said, peering down at the body, raising his glasses to his forehead and screwing his eyes up.

"The hyoid bone was fractured." Prichard called up images of his autopsy on a computer screen and, after magnifying the required image, used the cursor to pinpoint the precise point where the tiny U-shaped hyoid bone had snapped. "A ligature was applied from behind. Something soft: a pair of tights, scarf, necktie, cravat. Almost no pressure was used. Being dead, he didn't put up much of a fight. That's why we didn't spot the bruising straight away. Precisely how long he'd been dead before he was strangled, I can't say, but if we assume the attacker strangled him not realising he was already dead, it can't have been very long. He wasn't in *rigor mortis*. He was found on his left side, his back to the wall, covered by a sheet of tarpaulin as though he'd covered himself and drifted off to sleep. The attacker can't have strangled him when he was in that position – insufficient space – therefore he was put into the position after death. When attacked, he was standing, leaning against or between something, or sitting."

"How can he have been, if he was already dead? He'd've fallen over the minute they touched him, surely?"

"Not necessarily so. Please take a seat, Detective Inspector," Prichard invited, sweeping one hand in the direction of a nearby chair, and using his other to remove his tie in a single movement at the same time.

Black sat down as Prichard moved behind him. "Lower your head as though asleep on a plane, your back supported by the seat, and relax," he instructed. Black did. He felt the loop of a soft silk tie drop over his head and gently tighten around his neck. His hands instinctively went to his throat.

"You're dead, Guido."

He lowered them again.

"Relax as much as you can. Trust me – I'm a doctor."

Black relaxed his neck, chest and shoulder muscles. Prichard, tightening his tie a little more, said, "From this position, I could snap your neck bones in two with one sharp tug." He stopped tightening. "You haven't fallen over, and there's no reason to suppose Martin did just because some fellow gently slipped a ligature around his neck. I'd say we have a killer who's stealthy, slow and meticulous. Couldn't risk waking the victim he assumed asleep." The tie was removed. "One tug's all it took."

Black's mind turned to the benches in the park. Some backed on to the tree-lined footpath behind the hedge and fence – the hedge and fence with more than one way through. He pictured Martin Mills sitting on a bench as night fell, his heart failing, his head slumping forward. He imagined a face peering out from that tree-lined footpath, checking the lay of the land, finding the park deserted, seizing the moment. He pictured a shadow slipping stealthily into the park under cover of darkness, creeping over to its victim, gently, slowly, deliberately placing a ligature around his neck and pulling. But why? "Was our assailant male or female?" he asked.

"With the lack of force needed, could be either."

"When did he die?" Black said.

"A few hours or days either side of his brother. Doubt I'll be able to get closer than that. There's something else." He went over and opened a tall metal cabinet leaning against the wall. It contained a pair of shoes and a heavy overcoat. "These were what he was wearing when found, but they're not his. The clothes he had on underneath were his, but not the overcoat or the shoes. They're much too big. I ran a match-check and guess what? Looks like Martin Mills was wearing his brother Stafford's shoes and coat when he died."

In the station, the team gathered in the incident room to watch the result of the post-mortem. Detective

218

Superintendent Judy McDermott watched from home video link. Black gave them time to take in Matthew Prichard's comments. Under Martin Mills' picture appeared: *Body found Osborne Gardens (Park). Cause of death: Heart Attack. Post-death strangulation. Body moved? Body concealed.* Under the photograph of the murder weapon was added: *recovered from tree trunk in vicinity of same park.*

Black got to his feet to speak. "What was Martin Mills doing in Osborne Tye? If our information is correct, he only knew three people there. Bridget White, Brenda Munro and Stafford Mills. I've still to speak to Brenda and Bridget, but Hector Munro's adamant that none of them had a clue Martin was in the area. Let's assume they didn't. Question is, why was he there? If he wanted to speak to his brother, why not just telephone or even write? Why turn up in person? Was he expected or was he there to doorstep his brother? The missing murder weapon was found close by. Are we to infer from this that Martin was involved in his brother's death? Is that why he swapped his coat and shoes for those of his brother? We know he withdrew a great deal of cash before he left Brighton, which he left in his London lodgings. Possibly it was intended to cover the rent as he couldn't have known how long his treatment would go on for. Equally possible is that some of it was intended for other purposes. We need to consider if he was being paid by someone to kill Stafford, or being blackmailed, possibly by Stafford." He looked in Eden's direction. "How did forensics get on? Anything?"

"Nothing of significance on the coat and shoes he was wearing," Eden said, "and the tarpaulin he was found under was already in the shed."

"Victoria Coach Station confirmed Martin Mills was on the coach to Sylham on the morning of Sunday the sixteenth, confirming Jean Janes' statement that she last saw him there," Pilot said. "Sylham's the closest drop-off point to Osborne Tye. The coach's tracking wasn't on, but it left on time and even allowing for traffic delays it would have arrived in Sylham by lunchtime. Sylham's a good twenty miles from Osborne Tye. He doesn't seem to have been on the connecting bus, and we've drawn a blank on hire cars or taxis. He might have walked or hitched. A couple reported driving past a man walking towards Osborne Tye matching Martin Mills' description, but the times don't match. If he did walk, it would've taken some time – we're talking about a very ill man. Nonetheless, I can't see him arriving that late. He had half a day to get there. Can't see why he wouldn't have gone to the door, unless he lost his nerve or something."

"We need to fill the gap in his timeline," Black said.

"He must have been at the farmhouse at some stage to have got hold of his brother's clothes," Judy said. "How did he get them? Was he inside?"

"The Munros mentioned putting some clothes out for charity," Eden reminded them. "Maybe Martin helped himself? Weather was pretty rubbish wasn't it?"

"Persistent showers most of the day, carrying on overnight," Pilot said. "Anyone outside for long, would've got pretty damp and miserable."

"Okay we need to confirm the coat and shoes Martin was found in are the same ones Brenda Munro put out," Black said. "If they are, that puts him outside, if they're not, that puts him inside. We still don't know where Stafford was for part of the morning. Was he meeting his brother somewhere? It would explain Martin's presence in the area."

"If Stafford was blackmailing Martin, it might explain why Martin killed him, but not who then tried to kill Martin," Eden said. "Or vice versa."

"You know, I'm not sure either brother's behind this," Judy said. "There's a gaping hole in Martin's timeline, and Stafford's. Martin could have easily turned up at the farmhouse at the wrong time and seen something."

"And fled the scene, followed by the murderer, who caught up with him in the park, where Martin ran out of puff, sat down and died, only the killer thought he'd fainted, strangled him and put him in that shed," Eden said.

"Martin Mills was the unluckiest man on earth," Pilot said.

"There is an alternative scenario," Black said. "Martin was persuaded to kill his brother by someone who then silenced him."

A knock on the door, and a note handed to Black, ended the meeting.

28

B lack drove to the caravan park with a heavy heart. Dandelion yapped to announce his arrival and drew Hector Munro, first to the window, then the door. Black stepped in sombrely, clutching a holdall containing the overcoat and shoes taken from Martin Mills' body. He looked around but couldn't see Bridget White. "Is your sister here, Mrs Munro?" he asked.

"Having her hair done, dear," she said, on her feet. "She shouldn't be too long."

"She's enjoying a new lease of life," Hector said. "How can we help you, Detective Inspector?"

"Let's all take a seat, if we could," Black said, motioning towards a table.

Brenda Munro was the first to sit down. The expression on her face was one of fatalism. The Detective's presence and his tone could only mean more bad news. Her husband sat next to her and took her hands in his. Black sat down last.

"No doubt your husband has told you, Mrs Munro, that the body of Martin Mills was found in St Osborne Gardens yesterday. We know he travelled from London to Sylham on the coach the day before Stafford met his death, but we don't know where he went from there except that he ended up in Osborne Tye. Do you have any information which might help us?"

She shook her head. "I couldn't believe it when Hector told me. What on earth was he doing in Osborne Tye? Why didn't he let us know he was coming? He could have stayed here, rather than sleeping in a shed."

Black took out the posthumous photograph of Martin Mills. Brenda turned her head away. "It's been a while since you saw Martin Mills, Mrs Munro. It's possible you passed him in the street without realising it?"

"I don't need to see that," she said. "I'd know Martin anywhere."

Black reached down to the holdall and removed the bagged shoes and coat. "Can you confirm these were the clothes you put out for collection?"

"I can, yes," Brenda said. "Why?"

"Martin Mills was found wearing them," Black said.

"Well, I'm glad he got something of Stafford's," Brenda replied curtly.

"There is no easy way to tell you this, I'm afraid," he said. Hector gripped Brenda's hand tighter. "Although Martin Mills died of a heart attack, an attempt was made after death to strangle him."

"What are you saying, Detective Inspector?" Hector said, as his wife's hand went to her mouth in shock.

"Somebody strangled Martin Mills, presumably not realising he was already dead," Black explained.

Hector looked as astonished as his wife looked horrified. She jumped to her feet with a gurgled cry. "Martin was strangled?"

"I'm afraid so," Black said.

"That's horrible," Hector said, lowering his head.

He remained in his seat, gripping the edge of the table, while Brenda crossed to the sink to drench a cloth in cold water. Nobody spoke as she rung it out and pressed it to her face, holding it there.

"Who would want to hurt Martin?" she said, the cloth pressed to her cheek. "Martin was as gentle as a lamb."

Black narrowed his eyes. There it was again. Martin was as gentle as a lamb. Martin was such a dear man. A lovely man. Innocent. This, the same Martin convicted of causing death by reckless driving while under the influence and fleeing the scene. The same Martin estranged from his brother for decades.

"This business has been very hard on my wife, Detective Inspector," Hector said, his voice lowered. "First Stafford, now this. We've lost our jobs, and our home. On top of everything her sister's put her through over the years."

Brenda let the cloth drop. She splashed her face with cold water and spent a few moments composing herself, then wiped her face and returned to the table. "I'm sorry," she said. "It was such a shock, that's all."

"You have nothing to apologise for, Mrs Munro," Black said. "It might be as simple as Martin stumbling onto something, and ending up cornered in the park where the exertion killed him. He wasn't in good health."

"The burglars killed two people that day," Hector said. "Hope they're proud of themselves."

"At this stage, we simply don't know. You can't think of anyone who'd wish Martin ill?"

"The only person to wish Martin ill was Stafford," a voice said from the door. They looked over. Bridget White had arrived without anyone noticing. "It's high time you told him, Brenda."

29

"So here you are once again, Captain," Eden said to Jeremy Havelock across a desk in the interview room.

"Why am I here?" the captain asked.

"You know why."

"If I knew, I wouldn't have asked." He raised his hands. "Hands up to doing 62 miles an hour in a 40 limit, but that doesn't explain why I'm here. I passed a breathalyser."

"Let's cut to the chase, Captain," Eden said. "£4,500 in cash is missing from Fenn Farmhouse. The same sum was found in a holdall in your boot."

"Mills had £4,500 in cash lying about the place? Man was a bigger fool than I took for him for."

"The money, Captain – where did it come from?"

"Won it gambling," he said. "I'm a professional gambler."

"Where and with whom?"

"We meet every eight weeks in a hotel room. We don't give our real names and we play for cash. I'm Barry. The others are Larry, Gary, Harry, Lenny and Dusty. We suggested Busty but she didn't see the funny side." He grinned. Eden didn't.

"I'll need the name of the hotel, sir."

"Never knew it. Used the back door. Cheap, not very cheerful. Could've been a boarding house."

"Where was it? Street and town."

"Can't help you there either, I'm afraid. Get picked up at the roadside and dropped back."

"By?"

"Whoever turns up. Lenny this time," the captain replied.

"What car does Lenny drive?"

"Can't remember the make or the number."

"Or the route to the hotel, I'm guessing?"

"'Fraid not. Slept the whole way. There and back."

"How do the others get in touch?"

"Text me the next game," he said.

"Can I see the text?" Eden said.

"Lost my phone, didn't I? Bloody nuisance."

"This all looks mighty suspicious, Captain Havelock."

"This all looks mighty circumstantial," the captain said, using his fingertips to slowly push himself up. "If Mills' fingerprints were on the money, you'd have said." He leaned closer, a smug look on his face. Eden watched him for a few moments without speaking. The captain was right. The notes taken from the car were negative for Stafford Mills' fingerprints. If the money had come from the farmhouse, Mills had used gloves.

30

"Cybil Mills was the most beautiful woman I ever saw – and she wasn't young when I worked for her," Brenda Munro said. "The boys adored her, competing for her affection. Years before I knew her, she'd met Pablo Picasso on holiday. Ischia, I think she said. He wanted Cybil as his mistress, but she'd have none of it. She said he followed her around for weeks, begging, but she held firm. Eventually he gave up, but painted a plate for her as a parting gift. She showed it to us once. Didn't look much. Just a yellow plate with a blue squiggle which she said was a blue Jasmine. Could've fooled me. But the artist's signature was clear enough – Pablo Picasso. There was a photograph as well. Her with him and the plate. It was definitely him." Black leaned forward in his seat. Brenda smiled. "Even I know what Picasso looked like."

"After Martin's trial Stafford thought he should get the plate," Bridget said, "but Cybil felt Martin would need it more, when he got back out. Although she tried not to show it, Martin was her favourite. She and Stafford had this big row but she insisted. She never gave up on Martin." Bridget still looked far from well. She appeared nauseous and shook continuously, constantly sipping water, but she was lucid and calm and from what Black could tell, still off the drink. "She never believed he did it," Bridget added. Here it comes again, Black thought. "She always believed Martin's drink was spiked. That's what we think too. He wasn't the type to do something like that."

"He left the scene of the accident," Black reminded her.

"He didn't know there'd been an accident until they told him," Bridget said. "Anyway, when Cybil's will was read, she'd left Martin the Picasso."

"Stafford was furious," Brenda said. "He wanted to contest the will, but his lawyer told him he'd be wasting his money. He didn't stop shouting for weeks."

"Stafford never forgot it," Bridget said. "It's why Martin was *persona non grata*."

"Do either of you know what happened to the plate?" Black said.

Both sisters shook their heads. "Martin most likely sold it when he came out of jail," Bridget said.

"Is the photograph about?" Black asked.

Bridget snorted in derision, and Brenda said, "Like Stafford would have had that in the house. I don't know what became of it."

"I reckon it's with the plate," Bridget said.

31

G uido Black joined Eden and Captain Havelock in the interview room, where he mimicked the captain by leaning back in his seat and lowering his voice. "Since the start of this investigation, I've asked myself the same question: Is Jeremy Havelock lying to buy time or because he's a murderer?"

The captain said nothing.

The note handed to Black at the end of the meeting, had informed him that Jeremy Havelock had been caught speeding with four and a half thousand pounds in cash in a holdall in his boot. He'd left Eden to interview the Captain, returning to the station keen to hear Havelock's explanation for the money. Instead he'd found Pilot waiting for him, and insisting they speak. "You're never going to believe this, sir," he'd said.

Captain Jeremy Havelock remained calm. It was as though he was detached from the proceedings. He'd pushed his chair back and crossed one leg over the other. His fingers tapped the arm rest. Black picked up a buff-coloured file Pilot had finally received from archiving.

"This, Captain, is the police file of Martin Mills' trial for causing death by dangerous driving. He was convicted on your testimony. You placed him behind the wheel." The finger rapping stopped and the legs uncrossed.

"Who was really at the wheel the night of the accident, Captain Havelock?" Black said.

"Martin Mills."

"Sir, over the years I've crossed swords with many a drunk driver," Black said. "Far too many of whom do their time, get into another car and do it again. Drunk drivers are, without exception, arrogant, conceited individuals, indifferent to everyone but themselves. Martin Mills wasn't arrogant or conceited. You told me yourself he was desperately shy. Desperately shy men do not get into cars tanked up and drive like maniacs. Who was at the wheel that night, Captain? No more lies."

"Martin Mills."

"No more lies mean something different to you than the rest of us, sir?" Eden said. She could feel herself getting annoyed. "I'm not sure you grasp the gravity of the situation, Captain Havelock. Years after testifying at the trial which sent Martin Mills to jail, you turn up at Stafford Mills' house out of the blue, calling yourself a different name. You and he have a blazing argument hours before he's murdered. We find money's missing – same amount as we later find in your boot. To add insult to injury, Martin

Mills, the man you originally helped convict, turns up dead, meaning the case against him can't now be reopened."

"It was Stafford Mills behind the wheel, wasn't it?" Black said.

"Stafford was elsewhere that night."

"So you said at the trial, but you lied, didn't you? That's why you turned up like a bad penny after all those years, Captain. You wanted money for your continued silence," Black said.

Jeremy Havelock's demeanour had visibly changed. He was no longer brash and slightly irritated, but instead closed in and monosyllabic. Black and Eden had seen this a hundred times. It was a sign of guilt. But for what?

"Stafford tell you to get lost, did he?" Black said. "That why you flew off the handle? When you doubled back was it to try and reason some more or to kill him? Did you always intend to take the money, or did you find it after you smashed his head in?"

The captain looked at the ceiling and closed his eyes. He was in the crosshairs and when suspects were in such dire straits they did one of two things. They replied "No comment" to every question from then on, or they said:

"I want a deal."

"You want to plea-bargain, sir?" Eden said.

"Yes. But not for killing Stafford. I didn't kill him." Beads of sweat appeared on Jeremy Havelock's upper lip. He wiped them away.

"The only deal on the table, Captain," Black said, "is you being charged with the murder of Stafford Mills and the attempted murder of Martin Mills, if you don't start telling the truth."

"All right, all right," Jeremy Havelock said, raising his arms in despair, sweat soaking his shirt. "Late one evening, when we were in the London Regiment – that's Stafford, Martin and me – Stafford took a pool car out for a spin. I jumped in and he dropped me outside the base to visit my girlfriend. My married girlfriend. After I'd done there, I walked back to base. Next thing Stafford's shaking me awake, jabbering he's fucked up, and I'm to say Martin was driving. He'd only overtaken on a blind bend, forcing another vehicle into a ditch. 'Did you stop? Go back!' I said. Course he hadn't. He was drunk. I only learned later an eighteen year-old kid died that night. The stupid, fucking idiot."

Jeremy Havelock buried his head in his hands. "He wanted me to pretend it was Martin driving, and Martin who'd dropped me off. He also wanted me to give him an alibi by saying we met up and spent the night drinking. I told him straight I wasn't interested. Why the hell should I help frame Martin? He picked me up by the scruff of the neck and told me that unless I wanted everyone to know I was screwing an officer's wife, I fucking would. He had photographs of us. He shoved one under my nose. I was a married officer. I'd've been court-martialled and divorced, and likely hospitalised by her husband. I did what he wanted. Martin didn't stand a chance. He'd returned the car to barracks and signed it in after Stafford had telephoned him saying he had to get the car back but had had too much to drink. Martin was a good sort who didn't want to see his brother on a charge. His kindness and discretion did for him. No one could say for certain who'd taken the car out. No one saw Martin leave the barracks –

they weren't as strict about signing people in and out like they are now. Didn't have ANPR in those days. Tracing calls was nigh-on impossible. It was our word against his. Two against one. I stuck to my story: Martin was driving when I got out of the car; and Stafford was never in the car. Martin was convicted, court marshalled and sentenced to five years in jail. I heard he served four. The worst thing was the betrayal. I couldn't look at him across the courtroom." He looked up to the ceiling again, blinking away tears. Like your life had been destroyed, Eden thought. "Stafford was always jealous of Martin. Don't know why. Think it was because the ladies liked him more."

"You've told us about the stick Stafford Mills used, but did he also use a carrot?" Black asked.

"How do you mean?"

"Did money pass hands for your testimony?" Black said.

The captain hesitated. "A little," he said. He looked back and forth between the detectives. "Imagine how I feel?" He looked down. "The poor bastard's dead and I can't ever make it up to him."

"How did you find out where Stafford Mills was now living?" Black said.

"From a mate in military intelligence."

"He also tell you about the candlesticks Stafford was selling?" Eden asked.

"Not about the candlesticks per se, but he told me Stafford was a regular on Craigslist and gave me Stafford's seller ID. I couldn't see how that would help, I wouldn't get past the front door. He said Stafford had live-in staff.

'Well, Stafford would,' I said, 'but what of it?' He said: 'Don't you see? Stafford's not likely to keep lackeys and answer the door himself, is he? Pretend you're there to buy something.' I went straight into Craigslist for his area and saw he was selling a pair of candlesticks. It was a godsend. I made the appointment and turned up. Walked straight in. Put him on the hop, I can tell you. He wasn't pleased about it, seeing me after all that time, to put it mildly. I got straight to the point. Told him we were going to clear his brother's name."

"If you wanted to clear his brother's name so much, Captain," Eden said. "Why not walk into a police station?"

"Wanted him to confess."

"Why?" Eden said.

"Police mightn't've believed me. Nor might a jury. Trials can go either way. Mills was the type who'd snatch at a chance. If he thought he'd get a lesser sentence for coming forward, he would. He belittled me, goaded me, threatened me, said it was my word against his. All the usual, hoping I'd back down. I made it clear, it wouldn't work this time. Told him never underestimate a man with nothing to lose. He wasn't going to squirm his way out of it. He had twenty-four hours to change his mind or else."

Black sat back in his chair and folded his arms, wondering if truth telling was alien to Jeremy Havelock's personality. Eden was more direct than her boss. "I'm having trouble getting my head around this, sir," she said. "You were prepared to go to jail for perjury for a clear conscience?"

"Is it so incredible?" Jeremy Havelock replied. "Put it this way. I'm a middle-aged man with arrhythmia and a wife who doesn't like him. Doctors say I could go on another thirty years, or drop dead tomorrow. None of us can turn the clock back, but I had the chance to right the worst wrong I'd ever done."

"Stafford Mills might have got credit for confessing, but he was still looking at a lengthy stretch," Eden continued "I'd've thought him more likely to hire expensive lawyers and deny everything, than offer to clear his brother's name."

"He threatened to," Jeremy Havelock said, "but it was all bull. He'd have got twice as long if he went to a jury and they convicted him, which they would have done with my testimony. Given a few days to mull things over, he'd've come round. That's what I was really doing there. Should have come clean straight away, but I didn't want to incriminate myself. I expected you to have found Stafford's killer by now."

"Let me propose an alternative scenario, Captain," Black said. "You're a middle-aged man, heavily in debt to some scumbags, with few options left. Your visit to Fenn Farmhouse was less a crisis of conscience, and more a crisis of debt. You demanded money in exchange for your continued silence, but Stafford Mills knew all too well that you couldn't dob him in, without dobbing yourself in and called your bluff." Captain Havelock looked as though he wanted to say something, but Black continued. "Did he tell you to get lost? Threaten to call the police and have you charged with blackmail? Or worse – did he offer you a lot less than you needed? If that's what happened, Captain Havelock, just say so, man."

"I didn't kill him. Stafford Mills was alive when I left."

"He was found alive, Captain," Eden pointed out.

"I meant alive and well."

"We found the murder weapon concealed by a road we know you drove along. A couple of hundred yards away from where Martin Mills was found. Had you and him hatched some plot?" Eden said.

"No! I haven't set eyes on Martin since the trial."

"Was he in the park waiting for you to tell him how it went? Was it you who strangled him and put him in that shed?" she said.

"Why the hell would I do that?" Sweat poured from every pore. He took out a handkerchief to wipe his face. He visibly shook and started hyperventilating.

"You'd persuaded him to kill his brother but didn't trust him to keep his mouth shut?" Eden said. "You didn't want to split the money with him? You were only meant to talk to Stafford, not smash his head in, and Martin was horrified." She went in for the kill. "Killing is easier second time round, so I'm given to understand."

"Stafford gave me the money you found in the boot," Jeremy Havelock burst out. "I told him I'd perjured myself for him, and the little he'd paid back then wasn't enough, I wanted more. He told me to fuck off. I told him he had twenty-four hours. He said I wouldn't dare. I said: 'Try me.' He was laughing when I left the room, but when I got to the car I found a plastic bag by the wheel full of bagged up notes and him at the window. He shot me the filthiest look and mouthed: 'Now fuck off.' Someone must have come in because he looked over his shoulder and vanished. I didn't hang around. That was the last time I set eyes on Stafford Mills. I swear it. What Martin was doing in Osborne Tye, I can't imagine, but it wasn't anything to do with me."

Black pictured the scene: Stafford Mills deciding in a trice to pay off Jeremy Havelock. Donning gloves, furiously filling a plastic bag with money from the secret drawer. Hurling it out of the window, mouthing obscenities, Aidan Stanton bursting in, all guns blazing. Stafford closing the window, but not having time to lock it.

He placed his hands flat on the desk, pushed himself up and walked crisply to the door, opening it and addressing one of his team, "Please show Captain Jeremy Havelock to the cells." He turned back to him. "Later today, you'll be formally charged with perjury, blackmail and obstructing the police in the course of their investigations. You're entitled to have your lawyer present if you wish."

"Please, I've lost everything," Jeremy Havelock said.

"No, sir," Eden said. "Martin Mills lost everything."

32

Eden looked through Martin Mills' personal belongings, which had been collected from his Brighton flat and London room. Everything from Brighton fitted easily into two boxes, the contents of the room he hired in London, not even that (the suitcase of money having been transferred to the police safe). From the Brighton box she removed the photograph of his mother she'd seen in the flat. It was still in its silver frame. She turned it over and opened the back. It held only the one picture. She closed it again and returned it to the collection. None of the boxes held anything extraordinary and certainly nothing like a yellow and blue plate with *Pablo Picasso* scrawled along the rim. The only item of interest was a do-it-yourself will unopened and still in its plastic wrapper, which she found in the bottom of the London box. She showed it to Pilot. He picked up his phone and called Jean Janes.

"Sorry to bother you again, Mrs Janes," he said, "but did Martin ever say if he'd made a will?"

"Funny you should say that," she replied. "We got talking about that very subject over dinner one evening. He said he didn't have a will and should probably make one, with him being so ill. I said my husband and I had ours done by a local firm of solicitors and they were quite reasonable, but I'd seen do-it-yourself ones for sale in the shops, and did he want me to pick him one up to be getting on with? He said that would be very kind. I got him one the next time I was on the high street. Can't say if he ever got around to writing it."

"Thank you, Mrs Janes," he said.

As Pilot spoke with Jean Janes, Eden googled Yellow Plate/Blue Jasmine/Pablo Picasso. Despite numerous entries, and there were pages and pages on Picasso ceramics alone, none related to a yellow plate with a blue Jasmine flower in its centre. In his Blue Period he seemed to have painted anything and everything blue except for a flower on a yellow plate. Had the sisters been mistaken? Their story was detailed and consistent. This usually meant accuracy.

She gave Plashet Willoughby at Sotheby's a call. "Ceramics isn't really my department," Plashet said. "Let me scroll through our database, see what pops up. Bear with me a mo." She chatted as she scrolled. "Picasso ceramics rarely come up – most are with the family." She paused, reading. "We haven't anything catalogued which could be your plate, either on the market or with a private collector or a gallery. That isn't to say it doesn't exist, only that it's not catalogued."

"Excuse my ignorance, but meaning what?" Eden said.

"It could still exist. Undiscovered Picassos turn up rarely, but it happens from time to time. He was prolific, and we know he had an eye for the ladies. I wouldn't discount it out of hand. Then again, people make mistakes, forgeries abound, and ceramics break easily."

"We have two witnesses both claiming to have seen the plate and a photograph of Picasso holding it."

"That's interesting."

"Say we find it, how much might it be worth?"

"I'd find it first," she said. "Then bring it here for us to value. Even if we can establish authenticity, condition is almost as important."

"Okay, understood. Genuine and in good condition. How much approximately?"

"Based on our last auction, we can't be talking less than a six-figure sum," Plashet said.

Eden stood in the open door of Martin Mills' Brighton flat and took a look around. A lot had changed since she'd last stood there. The pictures were gone from the walls, leaving grubby rectangular marks. The shelves were empty, so too the cabinet, its doors open. Even the TV was gone. She slowly walked through the flat, escorted by two uniformed officers from the local force: Bobby and Rob. At the kitchen door, her way blocked by units emptied and removed from the walls, she asked, "What's under the kitchen floor?" Rob stamped his foot on the Lino. "Concrete."

"We'll start in the box room," Eden said, putting the mask dangling under her chin over her mouth and nose.

The trestle table where Martin Mills had once built his model planes leaned folded up against a wall, its chair, also folded up, pushed beside it. The models had been removed, leaving only the furniture in the room. Bobby produced a lino cutter and squatting by the furthest wall, shoved it between the carpeted floor and the skirting board, then dragged it along the wall, cutting through the carpet with a ripping noise. Stopping a few times to shake her arm out, she continued to the end of the wall.

"That should be enough," Rob said, taking hold of the corner of the carpet and yanking it away from the floor, whereupon both carpet and underlay instantly disintegrated into plumes of billowing dust. With a deft jump over the rump of carpet, Eden went to the window and threw it open. Fresh air flooded the room. Behind her, Bobby ran the lino cutter width ways across the room, between the carpet and the wooden floorboards underneath, cutting one from the other. This allowed Rob to gently roll the carpet back.

Eden's phone buzzed in the next room. She left her colleagues removing the carpet and went to answer it. It was Dora on WhatsApp. Her daughter's excited face appeared on the screen. "I teached Betty Boop a trick," she squealed.

"You taught Betty Boop a trick – and why aren't you at school?"

"I am."

"You've taken the cat to school? Why?"

"To show my friends."

How had nobody noticed Dora leaving the house that morning with the cat? Had Eric and Dottie both lost their minds? Overnight? Her heart missed a beat. If she couldn't trust them look after Dora, what was she going to do? There had to be a rational explanation. "Dora, why is Betty Boop at school?"

"To show her. When will you be home?" Dora asked. "I want to show you the trick." Eden glanced at her watch. It was already past one o'clock. She had no idea what time she was going to get away, then there was the journey home. "I don't know. I'm in Brighton. I should be back in time to tuck you up," she said.

"But I want to show you the trick," Dora said.

"You can show me tonight or tomorrow."

"She'll have forgotten it by then. I'll show you now." The phone was trained on the cat, who Eden was relieved to see was on a lead. "Betty, sit!" Dora said. Betty didn't.

"Dora, I haven't time for this, I'm at work. Call Eric to pick her up. You can't keep her at school all day, she'll be scared. I have to go. I'll see you later. Promise me you'll call Eric?"

"He's already coming. Betty, sit." The cat rolled over.

"Find a cat box to put her in. I have to go. See you later. Love you."

Her heart was still beating fast when she got back to Rob and Bobby. "Anything?" she asked them. The two were squatting in the middle of the room, staring at the floor. She joined them and saw they were looking down on a small square door with a wooden handle, cut into the floorboards.

They all put on their forensics gloves. Rob pulled the handle and opened the door. He used a spotlight to look inside the exposed cubbyhole.

"Ah ha," he said, reaching inside and retrieving a fairly large tin box. Bobby unfolded the trestle table, whereupon the tin box was placed onto it. Rob used a screwdriver to prise open the lock.

They opened the lid, revealing towelling. Underneath that lay a brown paper parcel, thin and rectangular in shape. Bobby picked it up and the bubble wrap under the brown paper went pop. Underneath the rectangular parcel was more towelling. Eden pulled it back to reveal a circular parcel, also wrapped in brown paper and bubble wrap. This she left where it was. Bobby gently removed the brown paper and bubble wrap from the rectangular parcel, discovering a framed photograph of a man. All three stared at it. The man was unmistakably Pablo Picasso in his older days. He was sitting on a rocky shore, his arms around a young woman, a plate in her hand. Eden held it up to have a better look, Rob and Bobby on either side of her. "Stone me," she said. "The ladies were right."

Rob reached towards the circular parcel, but Eden stopped him. She slipped the picture frame back inside the bubble wrap and its brown paper, and returned it to the box, tucking the towelling around it and shutting the tin box. "Please arrange for this to be taken to Sotheby's with a police escort, and given into the custody of Plashet Willoughby" she said. "And for God's sake don't anyone drop it! Ceramics break easy."

"Never got Picasso, meself," Rob mused.

"Well, unless you've got a couple of hundred thousand lying around, my friend, you don't need to," she said.

Eden left Rob to carry the box to the car, Bobby walking ahead, to fend off any possible attackers. She shone a torch around the cubbyhole to search for anything left behind – photographs, letters – but it was empty.

She was still in the flat when her phone rang again. It was Eric.

"It's bring-your-pet-to-school day," he told her. "And before you start blogging about your maternal failures on badmothers.com, none of us knew until her little friend turned up with a rabbit. The van's scraped through its MOT, by the way. Only needs new tyres and exhaust. The garage just called. Time we've paid for that, there should be just enough for a new washing machine or a laptop for Dora. Which should we go for?"

She was about to say washing machine, definitely washing machine, when she heard him say, "Will you be quiet."

She'd assume he was addressing the cat.

33

"Well, that throws the case wide open," Black said, after Eden telephoned him the news. "Both brothers worth a mint. Maybe Janice Burnett is right – we should be looking at UKIP."

He'd just decided to give Stafford Mills' solicitor, Janice Burnett, a call, when she called him.

"I've just been on your webpage," she said. "I think I can help you with the HH thing."

"Can we return to that?" he said. "I need to run something by you." He told her about the discovery of Martin Mills' body.

"Blimey. They're going down like ninepins," Janice said, "and it's not even winter."

"Confidentially," he added, "we're treating the death as suspicious. Martin Mills died of natural causes, but an attempt was made to strangle him after death."

"How horrid," Janice said. "Why on earth would anybody do that?"

"We have a number of theories."

"Do you know if Martin Mills made a will? I ask because if he died intestate, it might affect Stafford's estate,"Janice said.

"He didn't leave a will."

"Is there anything in his estate of value?"

"There is – if the Picasso we found under his floorboards is the real thing," Black said.

He could almost hear Janice sitting bolt upright. "Good Lord. Did Martin have a family do you know?"

"He didn't. Stafford Mills was his nearest relative."

"In that case I need to ask, which of the two died first? Stafford or Martin?"

"What difference does it make?"

"Quite a lot. As Martin didn't make a will, the intestacy rules will kick in. Intestate estates pass to the closest relatives living at the time of death. Spouses and offspring first, grandkids next, siblings after that, then their kids, etcetera. To put it simply, Martin dying before Stafford, makes Stafford his closest living relative at the time of death, and Martin's estate therefore falls into Stafford's, to be distributed in accordance with Stafford's will, as he too is now dead. Martin dying after Stafford, though, makes Stafford's son, Pierre Laurent, Martin's closest living relative at the time of his death and so Martin's estate would go to him."

Now it was Black's turn to sit bolt upright. "Even though Pierre's illegitimate?"

"Makes no difference under the laws of intestacy."

"And if we can't determine who died first?" Black said. "What then?"

"The presumption is that the youngest died last, and the oldest first. For example, if a husband and wife both die in a plane crash, and the wife is the youngest, her husband will be treated as having died before her, and his estate will leapfrog to her beneficiaries under her will or intestacy. In this case, Stafford was the oldest, and Martin the youngest, therefore the presumption will be made that Martin outlived Stafford, unless you can prove otherwise."

"Meaning Pierre Laurent gets the Picasso?"

"Basically, yes. I'd appreciate it if you could keep me informed. In the meantime I'd better not wind up Stafford's estate until we know one way or the other." Black heard what sounded like the playful clapping of hands down the phone line. "Oh, this is exciting," Janice said. "Selling old ladies premium bonds is normally as exciting as my day gets."

A thought occurred to Black. "Janice," he said, "did you draw up a will for Cybil Mills – Stafford and Martin's mother?"

"Before my time, but Thompson and Thomson might well have. Shall I get archives to dig out what files we've got for a Cybil Mills?"

"Please." He was about to end the call, when he remembered she'd called him. "You were going to tell me about HH?"

"So I was," she said. "Yesterday I had to tell the son of one of my deceased clients that there wasn't as much in the estate as they'd anticipated. The very words he used were:

253

'Can't say I'm surprised. Dad blew our inheritance at the Hollywood Hilton.' I believe the pun was intended. I asked what the Hollywood Hilton was, having never heard of it. It transpires the sleazy hotel his dad was found dead in was also known colloquially as the Hollywood Hilton."

It's a sleazy hotel, Black thought. Of course. *Fireworks. HH!!!!*

"Would you like its real name?" Janice asked.

34

"Bit of a dump," Pilot said, pulling to a stop outside the Broadway Mount Hotel.

"It averages 4.5 on Trip Advisor," Eden said, undoing her seatbelt.

"That'll be the free Wi-Fi," Pilot said.

A peeling roadside billboard reading: *Broadway Mount Hotel. Rooms from the hour. Discretion assured. Free Wi-Fi* had directed them to a slip road off the main road and from there to the hotel in front of them.

The Broadway Mount Hotel was set out as though a US motel. Wings radiated from a central building, creating an incomplete hexagonal. No wing was higher than three storeys, and each room therein could be directly accessed from the car park, via exterior steel stairs in the case of the upper storeys. A small sign over a set of revolving doors in the central block directed those who needed it, to the reception.

Eden led the way in and out of the revolving doors, spilling out into a small reception, moments before Pilot. They caught sight of themselves on the screen above the reception desk, where a middle-aged man in a checked shirt ignored them in favour of something more interesting on his laptop. Behind him was a closed door. Three vending machines serving hot dogs, hot and cold drinks, and condoms, stood in a row just inside the revolving doors. At the desk Eden showed her badge. The receptionist didn't even bother looking up. "Fifty pounds a day, twenty for an hour. We take cash, cards, contactless…"

Only when Pilot held his badge over the laptop did the receptionist stop talking and look up.

"I'm Detective Philip Philpott, this is Detective Sergeant Eden Hudson," Pilot said. "Could you tell us your name, sir?"

"Keith Richards. Easy to remember," he said. "And yes, my parents did meet at a Stones concert."

"Are you the hotel's owner, sir?" Eden said.

"The manager. A company in London owns it."

"Do you recognise this gentleman?" Pilot put a photograph of the late Stafford Mills down on the desk. Keith Richards picked the photograph up and looked closely at it. A glimmer of recognition flickered across his face. He dropped the photograph on the desk. "Can't say."

Pilot motioned to the camera above the desk. "How long do you keep your CCTV images for?"

"One week only, and the only camera is in here."

"We'll need your CCTV, card and Wi-Fi records for the last month," Pilot said.

"You having a laugh? I start giving up stuff like that, we'll go bankrupt."

"We're investigating a serious incident, sir," Eden said. "It'll take only a couple of hours to get a warrant."

"What say you take another gander at the photograph, sir?" Pilot suggested, handing it back to him.

"Hold your horses," Keith Richards snapped. "I'll have to call head office for the okay." He snatched his phone up from the desk and disappeared through the door behind him. Pilot raised a knowing eyebrow at Eden, who grinned. They heard a noise behind them and turned to see a man following a woman through the revolving doors into the reception.

"You take contactless?" the man asked.

Beside him, his bored-looking companion vaped on an electronic cigarette, smoke billowing out from her nose as though she was a steam train. Eden held her badge up. The results were dramatic. The woman choked and almost dropped her vaporiser. She turned on her heels, dived into the revolving doors and was gone, her gentleman friend not far behind her, leaving in their wake a trail of smoke and spinning doors. This time Eden raised the eyebrow, and Pilot grinned.

Keith Richards reappeared. He shot a glance through the revolving doors at the two scampering away across the car park and scowled. "Give me another butchers," he said.

Outside, car doors slammed, an engine started up and tires screeched. Inside, Pilot pushed the photograph of Stafford Mills across the desk. Keith picked it up and looked at it for longer than necessary. "Now I come to think about it, he was here. Only the once, mind."

"Can you remember when that was, sir?" Eden asked.

"Thursday 13th September. I was just about off home at the end of a marathon back-to-backer – five to five – when he showed up, calling himself Mr Smith and wanting a room for two hours. Paid in cash."

"What time of day was this?" Eden said.

"Early evening. He took one of the rooms off the car park."

"Was he alone?" Pilot said.

"In here he was. Only got a shufty of her when I went to my car. He was giving her a hard time. She was crying and stuff, and he was getting angry. I went over to see if everything was okay. She said it was. I asked her again, to make sure, and he said: 'She's told you she is.' He was a real arse-hole. I needed to be sure so I asked again. She sort of pulled herself together and said she was. She wasn't, but she said she was, so what could I do? He put his hands on her shoulders and steered her inside room fifty-one. It's one of the downstairs ones. To the left. That's the only time I've ever seen either of them here, and that's the God honest truth."

"Would you be able to identify her?" Eden asked.

"God, yes," he said. "Wouldn't forget her in a hurry. Pretty little thing. Gap between her front teeth. Stood out like a sore thumb compared to the usual skanks we get in here."

On his tablet, Pilot opened an App containing photographs of the principal female suspects: Sylvie Laurent, Bridget White, Jenna Nesbitt, Corrine Beechwood, and Brenda Munro, interwoven with photographs of other randomly selected women, ranging in age from twenty to sixty.

"Sir, my colleague is going to show you a collection of photographs and I'd like you to tell us if the woman you saw here with that man on the day in question," Eden pointed to Stafford Mills' photograph, lying on the desk, "is one of them."

Pilot handed his tablet to Keith Richards and moved with Eden behind the desk to stand on either side of him. Keith skimmed through the photographs, using his right index finger to slide them across the screen, one after the other. One caused him to pause. He stayed with the picture for a while, after which he absentmindedly scrolled through a few more, until evidently deciding he didn't need to see any more and returning to the photograph which had first caught his eye. He used his thumb and index finger to enlarge it on the screen. He nodded to himself and tapped the screen with a finger. "That's your girl."

"You sure?" Pilot said.

"Unfortunately for her, I am. Hope I haven't got her into trouble."

"Thank you, Mr Richards," Eden said. "If we hold a formal identity parade, you'll be required to attend the station, but that's all for now."

From his desk at the station, Guido Black called Martin Mills' hospital consultant, Simon Pigott, at the Royal Marsden Hospital. With Mr Pigott's duty-of-patient confidentiality ended by his patient's death, Black found him much more approachable and open than had Pilot.

"Had Martin Mills continued with his treatment, what was the likely outcome?" was Black's first question.

"The primary cancer was in his bowel, and he had secondaries. The cancer was very aggressive. There's no certainty in life, but the likelihood of his still being alive in five years was at best twenty percent – but, realistically, less than five percent – with one caveat. Modern cancer treatment is being revolutionised by a new treatment called immunotherapy."

"I've heard of it," Black said.

"It offers the best hope we currently have against this disease, particularly when combined with our current treatments. Cancer tricks the body's immune system into thinking it's harmless until it's too late. Immunotherapy helps the body's own immune system to identify and destroy cancer in its earliest stages, sometimes later. Immunotherapy is coming, and it's coming quite quickly for a medical treatment, but we're still not out of the woods. Medicine often promises more than it can deliver. The treatment brings with it side-effects, occasionally fatal, and it's still a bit of a lottery who will and won't respond to it, although that's changing as our knowledge grows and our diagnostic tests improve. Across the planet there are immunotherapy drug trials aplenty. The specific type of bowel cancer Martin Mills was suffering from wasn't amongst the group of cancers being targeted for immunotherapy trials in the UK, but there is a trial currently ongoing in the US combining genetic profiling and tailor-made immunotherapy. Martin was prepared to give it a try and asked if he could get on it. I rang the hospital and got a yes. I explained that the national health service would not cover the cost, which would be down to him, although he could undergo treatment here, under their supervision. Martin was fully aware that the cost of participation was a hundred thousand pounds minimum and more likely three or four hundred thousand, for an experimental drug treatment which might not work and might even kill him more quickly. He understood that even if he did respond, he'd still need chemo and might be on drugs for the rest of his life. He was an intelligent man. He understood the consequences and wished to proceed nonetheless."

Hope springs eternal, Black thought.

"He went off to raise the money," Simon Pigott continued. "When he didn't come back, I assumed he'd been unable to raise the capital required, or he'd had a change of heart, and decided not to continue with treatment."

35

J enna Nesbitt was in her salon along with Meg. Meg's own hair had changed colour since Eden had last visited the salon. It was pink no longer, but metallic silver. Both hairdressers were colouring their respective customer's hair. All four ladies in the salon looked over when the door opened and Eden stepped in. Meg grinned broadly; Jenna froze.

"I need you to come with me, Miss Nesbitt," Eden said.

"I can't, I have a customer."

"Now, please, Miss Nesbitt," Eden said.

The customers exchanged astonished glances. Meg, now as panic-stricken as Jenna, reached out and touched Jenna's arm. "I'll finish your lady, Jen, no worries," she said, her eyes fixed on Eden.

"Let me get my stuff," Jenna mumbled, shuffling her way to the room at the back. Eden had taken the precaution of stationing an officer out back, but she needn't have for

Jenna quickly reappeared holding her coat and handbag and trying not to cry. The expression on her face was one of resignation and fear. When she reached the front door, Meg called out, "Should I call Aidan?"

Jenna spun around and with a raised hand, said, "No! Don't, please."

"Okay," Meg said hesitantly. "What about your mum?" Jenna dissolved into tears. Eden steered her, hands on shoulders, sobbing to the car.

"We've been given information that you visited the Broadway Mount Hotel with Stafford Mills four days before he was murdered," Guido Black said in the interview room. The interview was being conducted under caution and the duty solicitor was also present.

"I never did," Jenna Nesbitt said.

"We have a witness who places you there, Miss Nesbitt," Eden said.

"Your witness is wrong."

"We can arrange an identity parade," Eden said.

Jenna looked across to her lawyer, who nodded. She buried her face in her hands, all bravado draining away.

"We know you didn't want to be there, Jenna," Black said. "So why were you?"

Eden poured Jenna a glass of water and passed it to her. The room fell silent as she took a drink. Her next words were so low as to be almost inaudible.

"Jenna, I'm sorry but I have to ask you to repeat that and to speak up," Black said.

"He made me," she said.

"Stafford Mills forced you to the hotel against your will?" Black said.

"Not exactly forced," she said.

"What exactly then?" Black's tone was low and gentle. Jenna started playing with her hair. She wrapped it around her hands, then unwrapped it, and started again, even putting it in her mouth. "Jenna, please answer my question," he said.

"I needed the money. If I'd thought for a second…"

"You had sex with Stafford Mills for money?" Eden said.

"No," Jenna said. "I'm not a slut. He made me."

"How?" Eden said. "We talking blackmail?"

"Yes, blackmail," Jenna said.

"I'm afraid we'll need more, Jenna," Eden said.

Jenna looked up to the ceiling, blinking back tears. "We weren't burgled. I made it up and he found out." She brought her head so far forward, her hair almost obscured her face.

"Let's start there, Jenna." Black said. "You weren't burgled."

"I never called the alarm fitter," she said, "the one Stafford recommended. I really, really wanted the Grange for our wedding reception, but we didn't have the deposit, and they wouldn't hold it. Aidan didn't see why it mattered, but it mattered to me. I was only going to pawn the silver and use the money as a down payment. It was a victimless crime."

"You were going to pawn the canteen of silver cutlery you reported stolen during a burglary at your house?" Eden said.

"Yes. I was going use the money as a down payment," Jenna said, "then redeem it and get it back."

"How would you have explained its return?" Eden asked.

"I don't know. I'd've thought of something." She looked back and forth between the two officers. "I saw the alarm in a charity shop for a fiver. That got me thinking about all the burglaries there'd been and I had an idea. I'd stage a burglary at ours and blame it on a shonky alarm system. I thought it would look a bit sus if all they took was a cutlery box and some cash, so I pretended to come home early and disturb them."

"And the story about passing a black Ford Focus the same night?" Black said.

"Made it up," she admitted. "There was one parked outside Stafford's when we were there. I was trying to deflect suspicion onto whoever it was."

"You provided a number you said was the alarm fitters?" Eden said.

"It was an old one of mine, a phone I picked up years back in a supermarket. I chucked the card Stafford gave Aidan. It was the only one Stafford had, so he said. I had it all planned. It wasn't 'til afterwards, I started thinking of all the ways it could backfire. Stafford getting his head smashed in wasn't one of them. When that happened, all I could do was lie and hope you didn't find out."

"So all that about the alarm fitter being the son of a barista Stafford Mills wanted to do a favour for because he'd enjoyed the coffee so much, wasn't true?" Eden said.

"Stafford must've made it up on the spur when the police called him," she suggested.

"Jenna, have you any idea how much time and resources we have spent trying to track down the alarm fitter and the bicycling barista?" Black said.

"I'm sorry," she said. "I panicked. Okay. I'll accept a caution without argument. Pay a fine. Now, before I leave."

"How did Stafford Mills learn the truth?" Black said.

"I gave the cutlery to Bridget to hide 'til I could pawn it. She wouldn't say nothing, even if she could remember. But Stafford saw me pass her something then her hide it in the outhouse. He waited 'til she was out of the way then went to have a look. He claims he was worried I was passing her drugs to hide, like I'm into them. Anyway, next thing, he's hearing from Brenda and Hector that me and Aidan have been done over and silver cutlery taken, and Aidan's baying for his blood because the new alarm failed and he recommended the fitter. Didn't take him long to put two and two together. That call from Fenn Farmhouse you asked about, that was him not Bridget. Said he knew I'd been a naughty girl, but not to worry, he wouldn't tell as long as I was nice to him. What was I meant to do? Everyone would know I was a liar and a thief. Aidan, my mum and dad – everyone. Osborne Tye's tiny. Everyone knows everyone." She buried her face in her hands. "I begged him not to make me do it, but he said he'd lied to my fiancé and the police for me. Said I'd done the crime, and I had to do the time… That hour I spent with him was the worst of my life. I'll never forgive myself. I still feel dirty. I can't get him off me." She brushed herself. "I've showered and showered, but he's still on me."

Jenna was the someone who'd *'been a bit naughty'* Black realised. "But he didn't return the silver?" he said.

Her head hung low again, and her hair fell over her face. She shook her head. "No. Said he'd hang onto it a while longer if I didn't mind. I said I did mind, quite a lot, to which his only comment was that I wasn't in a position to dictate terms. Nothing I said would budge him. When Aidan said he was going to have it out with him, I was frantic. Said we should forget it, just claim on the insurance, but he was having none of it. I was terrified Stafford was going to grass me up to Aidan. But he didn't. Having too much fun wasn't he? And now I discover he'd only put the bloody silver up

for sale and was just pretending he still had it, so I'd put out for him. What did he have to lose? Even if I'd seen it up for sale there wasn't much I could do about it was there? I could hardly go to the police."

"Why did you return to Fenn Farmhouse that morning?" Eden said.

"I had to speak to him. Stop it going any further. But it was too late. Bridget was out cold. Stafford was dead. Hector was frantic and jabbering on about burglars, and how it could as easily have been me with my head smashed in as Stafford. After all that I had to have a drink."

"Jenna were you behind the attack on Stafford Mills?" Black said.

She was horrified. "No! What would have been the point? We'd already…"

"To stop him demanding a repeat performance," Black said.

"He was already dead when I got there. I didn't get further than the back garden. You have to believe me."

"If you want us to believe you, you should have told us the truth from the start," Eden said.

"I couldn't. I just couldn't. The whole thing's humiliating enough. I didn't have an alibi. Oh, God. This is a nightmare. I can't believe this is happening."

"Does your fiancé know what you've just told us?" Eden said.

"God, no," she said. "I'd die if he found out. You're not going to tell him?" She looked and sounded close to hysteria. "Please don't. Please." She looked at her lawyer. "They can't tell him. They can't."

"I'm afraid they can," she said.

"You must see, Jenna, that what you've just shared with us, not only gives you a motive for wanting Stafford Mills dead, but it also gives your fiancé a motive."

"I don't see how."

Black leaned forward. He spoke slowly and softly. "If he found out about Stafford blackmailing you, and what followed?"

"Aidan doesn't know."

"What makes you so certain? Eden said. "For all you know, you and Stafford might have been spotted at the hotel, or you might've given yourself away somehow, or Stafford Mills might not have kept his mouth shut when Aidan was with him."

"Aidan knew and didn't say? No way. He'd've said something."

"Did the two of you plot and carry out his murder together?" Black said.

"No." Her voice was urgent, her eyes panic stricken, her glance darting between Eden and Black. "I don't know who killed Stafford, but it wasn't me or Aidan."

"I'm afraid we'll need to detain you until after we've interviewed your fiancé," Black said. Jenna dissolved into tears. "Please make Jenna as comfortable as possible, Detective Sergeant."

It gave Guido Black no pleasure to inform Aidan Stanton of Jenna Nesbitt's confession. He spoke concisely but precisely, breaking down the salient points, watching and waiting for a reaction. If Aidan Stanton knew before he'd stepped into the room what Guido Black was telling him now, he concealed it well. His face became more and more anguished as he struggled to comprehend what he was hearing. "There wasn't a break-in?"

"No, sir, there wasn't," Black said.

Aidan removed his glasses and bowed his head, covering his eyes with his hand. "Why didn't she say anything? Why didn't she just tell me?" Slowly he put his glasses back on, tipping his head back, his eyes closed, a hand resting on his forehead. "I need time to take this in," he said. Black gave him the time he needed. When he eventually opened his eyes, he rested his crossed arms on the table. His eyes met Black's gaze.

"I knew things weren't right." His voice nearly broke and he clenched his fists tightly. "She's been so edgy, distracted, jumping down my throat. That's not Jenna. I put it down to Mills getting murdered just before the wedding. All brides want everything just right, even I know that. One of the guests being murdered casts a pall over things."

"Stafford was on the guest list?" Eden said.

"I invited everyone in the choir. Jenna didn't want me to invite him. Neither did I, to tell the truth, but I could hardly invite everyone else and not him." He looked up to the ceiling again. "Why didn't she just tell me? Why let it get so far?" He looked away. "Stafford must've been laughing his socks off. There's me banging on about our alarm system and all the time he's thinking: You haven't a clue, Stanton!"

"Mr Stanton, did you know any of what I've just told you before today?" Black said.

The look on Aidan Stanton's face changed from dumbfounded to anger as he took in the meaning. "If you're going to start asking questions like that, Detective Inspector, I'm entitled to have a lawyer present."

The interview resumed with the duty solicitor present.

"Had your fiancée, Jenna Nesbitt, confessed to having had sexual intercourse with Stafford Mills at the Broadway Mount Hotel, before you visited Fenn Farmhouse on the morning of Stafford Mills' murder?" Black asked.

"First I heard of it was from you," Aidan replied.

"Mr Stanton, did you, either alone, or with an accomplice, attack Stafford Mills in his home?"

Aidan Stanton got to his feet and threw his glasses on the table in exasperation, causing them to crack. He was in tears and his voice repeatedly broke as he spoke. "Can you imagine how humiliating it is to be dragged in here and told by some copper that the woman I love has lied and lied? Can either of you begin to imagine what that's like for me?" He looked between them. Neither spoke. "No?" he said. "Well, I hope you never do."

He remained standing, his fists on the table, head forward, quietly sobbing. Eden opened the drawer under the table and removed from it a small packet of tissues which she pushed across the table. "Thank you," Aidan Stanton mumbled, shakily taking out a tissue and using it to blow his nose, then another to wipe his eyes. He sat down again and inhaled a couple of times. "I'm sorry," he said. "I know you have a job to do."

"Detective Inspector, I think my client needs a break," his lawyer said.

"I want to continue," Aidan Stanton said, his composure only partly recovered. He spoke slowly and softly. "Everything I've told you is true. I went home and stayed there. I didn't go back to the farmhouse, and I didn't attack Stafford Mills. Even if I had known what you've just told me, I wouldn't have killed him. I might've threatened to, but I'd never have done it. I'm not the type. No point. Wouldn't've turned the clock back. Wouldn't've made things any better."

"You're free to go, Mr Stanton, for the time being," Black said. "If you decide to go on any trips, please let us know."

Aidan got to his feet, his cracked glasses wonky across his nose. "Please don't tell me you've charged Jenna with murder? Jenna wouldn't hurt a fly. Literally – I have to release them."

Jenna Nesbitt waited in another room. She looked up through red, tear-soaked eyes as Eden entered. "Have you told him?"

"Your confession? Yes. He's waiting for you in the front reception. You can leave by the back door, if you'd prefer."

Eden admired Jenna's reply. "I'll leave through the front, thank you."

"Follow me, please."

Eden escorted Jenna to the door leading to reception. She reached out to open it, leaving her hand on the handle, as she said, "Sure you wouldn't rather use the back?"

"Can't avoid him forever." Jenna hesitated and took a deep breath. "Ready as I'll ever be." Eden opened the door and Jenna stepped through it.

There were two police officers on reception duty, both behind a desk. One was answering a call, via a head set, the other typing. Aidan Stanton was sitting on a bench along one wall, one leg across the other. As Jenna nervously emerged into the reception, with Eden behind her, he turned his head towards them. Jenna froze, her knees buckling beneath her. Eden bent down and put her arms around Jenna's shoulders, one eye on Aidan. He was on his feet and calmly walking towards them. When he reached them Eden got to her feet and withdrew, to allow Aidan to take over. He wrapped his arms around his girlfriend and pulled her towards him.

"Oh God, Aidan, I'm so sorry, I never meant it to get so far," she said. "I didn't know what else to do. I couldn't tell you what I'd done. I couldn't. He was dead. I didn't have an alibi. It just got worse and worse." The scene was watched by those there in silence. "Can you ever forgive me?"

"You made a mistake, love," he said.

"Quite a big one."

"A whopper."

"Wouldn't blame you if you never spoke to me again."

"What would that achieve except making us both miserable?"

She looked up at him. "I have to come back tomorrow morning."

"I'll be with you," he said, getting to his feet and helping her to hers.

"Everyone's going to know everything. It'll be all over the papers. Oh, God!" she said.

"So what if it is? You haven't killed anyone."

"I haven't!" She looked around to each of the officers in turn to ensure they'd heard her.

"Things get too much, we can move, change our names. Invoke our legal right to be forgotten and get Google to delete their data on us. Everyone's entitled to a second chance," he said. "Come on, let's get you home." He led her by the hand towards the exit.

"I didn't kill him," she repeated, looking over her shoulder at Eden. "I didn't."

Afterwards, in the incident room, Eden and Black re-watched the interviews with Aidan Stanton and Jenna Nesbitt, and the couple's reunion in the police reception. "Stanton seems genuinely taken aback, but he could just be a good actor," Black said.

"He's had plenty of time to rehearse," Eden said. "They both have."

36

B lack pushed open his front door at the end of a long and trying day. He dropped his keys into the pot on the hall table and called out, "Chloe? You home?"

He heard the strangest reply. It sounded almost as if his girlfriend had turned into a cockerel. He walked down the hall towards the kitchen with a growing feeling of trepidation. This was something to do with that school, he knew it. He timidly pushed open the kitchen door and peered inside. It was empty. The back door lay open and from the garden came the noise again: *Cockerdoodledoo.* "Chloe?" he called again.

"Here," a disembodied voice called from the garden.

He stepped through the door to have his worst fears confirmed. Chloe was on the back lawn holding a cockerel in a metal cage. His neighbours were at the fence between the two gardens, looking alarmed. He knew how they felt. As he walked over to his girlfriend, he gave them an embarrassed shrug.

"How's the case going?" she asked, giving him a quick peck on the cheek.

"My list of suspects grows longer daily." He glanced at the bird in the cage.

"Jamie Marsden brought him in," Chloe said by way of explanation.

"Did Jamie forget to take him home again?" Black asked.

"For the project," she continued.

The project, if he remembered correctly, was for the children to bring in an example of everyday objects in the shape of a ball. He'd contributed a bag of Maltesers he'd found in a jacket pocket, with strict instructions they weren't to be eaten as he couldn't be sure how long they'd been there. "I appreciate Montessori encourage lateral thinking but…" he pointed to the bird, "…it's not even nearly ball-shaped. I'm not sure it even counts as an object."

She stopped him with a gentle squeeze on his arm. "Jamie and his brother went to the field behind the golf club for golf balls for the project," she explained. "His brother heard something overhead. They looked up and saw a box up a tree. It was really high up. They got it down and found him inside. Whoever put him there made air-holes, but no water. They wanted him to suffer." She teared up. "Why are people so cruel, Guido?"

He put his arms around her. "If you want to know about cruelty love, just do my job for a day."

"He really perked up after we gave him some food and water."

"Glad to hear it, but why is it still here?"

278

"I didn't like to leave him alone after what he's been through."

"Isn't there an animal charity it can go to?"

"They're overwhelmed, Guido. He needs tender loving care until we find him a new home."

He glanced over her shoulder to the neighbours, still looking over the fence, still unnerved. She followed his gaze. "He's only staying for a few days," she said to them. "Don't worry, I'll take him in at night. Foxes."

The neighbours didn't look convinced, but wandered off towards their house. Chloe put the cage down and opened it, gently helping the bird out. She held her mobile and knelt on the ground to video the cockerel pecking the ground. So now he's going to have his own Instagram page, Black thought. "What should we call him?" she asked, looking up.

"How about – Don't Get Comfortable," he replied, stalking off. At the back door it crowed again. "I thought they only did that at sunrise?" he said.

"He's disorientated."

"What's for dinner?"

She was still videoing the bird. "I got some chicken out of the freezer this morning, but I've gone off the idea," she said. "Thought I might have cheese on toast."

37

The team's morning began with a video-conference to Sotheby's, where Plashet Willoughby was joined by Sotheby's senior Picasso specialist, John Bolton, the Picasso plate propped up on a table beside them. Although both were doing their best to appear calm, the atmosphere was charged. Black wasn't in the best of moods. The rooster had woken him up at some ungodly hour which the rooster clearly considered civilised but which Black did not. He'd told Chloe the blanket over the cage wasn't thick enough. He struggled to hide his yawns.

"It's a Picasso," announced John Bolton, touching the plate.

"With what degree of certainty?" Black asked.

"The style and signature alone put it at more than 90%. With the provenance of the photograph and story behind it, we're talking close to a hundred percent. We asked the V&A to date the photograph. It was taken and developed in the early 1950s. This is really very exciting for us. Picasso ceramics come up so rarely, the majority are still with the family."

Pilot asked the question on everyone's mind: "How much is it worth?"

"At auction, £400,000 easily," John Bolton said. "Could even go as high as £600,000 or more. I have a list of private buyers. It's a beautiful piece with a lovely back story. Please allow us to sell it."

"That isn't our decision, sir," Eden said.

"Can I at least suggest we safeguard it for the time being?" John Bolton said.

"I'll have to check with my superiors," Black said, "but it makes sense."

"Out of interest – who does it belong to?" Plashet Willoughby asked.

"That, Ms Willoughby, is the ten-million-dollar question," Black said.

"I've dug the will of Cybil Mills out of the file in storage," Stafford Mills' solicitor Janice Burnett said. "Looks like that Picasso is genuine. She left it to Martin on condition that if he were ever to sell, Stafford had first refusal."

So that's what he was doing in the area, Black thought. He was there to offer Stafford the Picasso to cover the cost of his treatment. So, he wasn't being blackmailed. The money in the suitcase under the bed was just to cover his London expenses, nothing more.

"Do you know as yet the order of the brothers' deaths?" Janice asked. "It'll make a tremendous difference to Stafford's estate if Martin died first."

"Not as yet," he said, "but as you're on the phone, can I pick your brains?"

"Shoot."

"Remember I mentioned that an attempt was made to murder Martin Mills after his death?"

"I do."

"Let's say Martin died after Stafford. Pierre was eating lunch when his father was attacked and can't be the attacker there, but what happens to Pierre's inheritance if I can prove Pierre was involved in the attack on Martin Mills?" Black said.

"The legal principle, as you know, is that no one can profit from their crimes," Janice said, "meaning no one convicted of murder or manslaughter can inherit their victim's estate, unless the manslaughter is by way of diminished responsibility, when it's down to the judge's discretion. The principle please remember, is that no one can profit directly from their crime. An individual convicted of attempted murder can still inherit their victim's estate, unless the victim subsequently dies of the injuries sustained during the attempted murder. If the victim happens to die of something else or as in Martin's case, was already dead, being party to the attack wouldn't in itself disbar them.

"Let me provide an infamous example by way of illustration – the Crown versus Roderick Newell and Mark Newell, 1994. Roderick Newell murdered his wealthy parents. His brother Mark Newell helped Roderick dispose of the bodies and destroy evidence after the murders, which he'd taken no part in. Mark Newell confessed his part and after serving his sentence, inherited his share of his parents' estate. He hadn't directly benefited from his crimes, those being for the benefit of his brother. Because Martin died naturally, even if Pierre was involved in the post-death attack, because he doesn't profit from that crime, even if he intended to, he would still inherit."

"What say Sylvie Laurent murdered Stafford with the sole intention of getting him out of the way to ensure the Picasso went to Pierre, and she did so before Martin died? Pierre surely can't inherit in those circumstances?"

"The principle only applies to killers themselves, not their offspring, unless the offspring are also convicted of murder or manslaughter," she explained. "If someone's prepared to kill a wealthy relative and go to gaol for it, it wouldn't necessarily prevent their kids from inheriting."

"Even if I can prove Pierre's mother murdered his father, Pierre could still inherit his uncle Martin's estate just so long as his mother murdered his father while his uncle was still alive?" Black said.

"Yes – if Pierre didn't take part in the murder. It may seem a travesty of justice, Detective Inspector, but it would be a greater travesty if the child was punished because of the actions of his or her parent."

The smell of his bacon butty and strong cup of coffee still lingering in the air, Black, energised by both, addressed the team from the head of the table.

"The suspects are now in this order," he said, scrolling through the photographs of the suspects as he named them. "The Munros and Bridget White still languish last, with Postman Vaz bottom from last and our anonymous burglars just above him. Tim Smith comes next, and above him Corrine Beechwood, having been overtaken at the hurdles by Aidan Stanton and his girlfriend Jenna Nesbitt – the new joint favourites for second place, making the new favourite for murderer, Mrs Sylvie Laurent, mother of the victim's son, Pierre."

On the screen Sylvie and Pierre's images appeared next to each other.

"She had every reason for wanting Stafford dead." Black said, immediately interrupted by various members of his team calling out:

"What about Martin?"

"How did Sylvie know he was dying?"

"Never had a family?"

"Hadn't made a will?"

"Was about to blow her son's inheritance on a drugs trial?"

"Why at Osborne Tye?"

"If I might be allowed to continue, ladies and gentlemen," Black said. "The problem, as you have pointed out, is that we have no evidence connecting Sylvie or Pierre with Martin Mills, other than her brief relationship with his brother years back. Sylvie and Pierre both have alibis for the time of the attacks and we have a complete lack of any forensic evidence linking them to either attack. Martin Mills didn't have a phone, nor was he on the Internet. Jean Janes maintains he didn't make or receive any calls while he was with her, didn't receive any visitors and only left the house accompanied by her. We've gone through the few calls made to his landline in Brighton and eliminated all of them. Martin Mills was virtually a recluse. That only leaves a face-to-face or the post."

"I haven't found any evidence of an ongoing correspondence with anyone," Eden said. "I got the local Brighton police to show his neighbour photographs of all our suspects. Says she's never seen any of them. Same with Jean Janes. Like you said, sir, he was a virtual recluse."

"The bigger question for me," Judy said, "is this. If the order of death's that important and Sylvie's behind things, why not wait a while before killing Martin Mills? Make sure he's seen alive after Stafford's death? Even if she'd somehow stumbled across him apparently sleeping, why strangle him? Why not just leave him?"

"Didn't realise how imprecise the timing of death can be?" Black suggested.

"Or maybe she stumbled across him," Pilot said, "and knew straight away he was dead, leaving her no choice but to strangle him and put him in the shed to try and make it look as though Stafford's killer had attacked him after killing Stafford?"

"I don't think we should dismiss the other suspects just yet," Eden said. "Neither Aidan Stanton nor Jenna Nesbitt have an alibi. We saw how angry she was when she realised Stafford had no intention of giving the stolen cutlery back and was just pretending he still had it to keep blackmailing her for sex. She could easily have seen it up for sale and snapped. Or him if he found out. Stafford's ex, Corrine Beechwood, doesn't have much of an alibi and lied. Jeremy Havelock hasn't stopped lying since day one and he also knew Martin Mills, giving him a reason for wanting Martin dead if the two had been acting in league."

"Martin might have got angry enough to smash his own brother's head in, if he'd refused to pay Martin what he needed for his treatment," Pilot said.

"If so, how did Martin end up being strangled and dumped in a shed in a park?" Black said.

"He escaped there but the trauma killed him and a weirdo found him," Pilot said.

"A passing weirdo strangled a man he found unresponsive on a park bench and put him in a shed, which he then locked from the inside?" Black said.

Everybody at the table turned to stare at Pilot. "What?" he said, raising his shoulders, arms and eyebrows at the same time. "It happens."

"I don't know about you lot, but I need another coffee," Black said.

A uniformed officer put her head around the door to announce Victoria Coach Station were on the phone asking to speak to Pilot.

"You lot won't believe this," he said upon his return. "The coach Martin Mills took from London only broke down halfway and a replacement sent."

"Thought there weren't any delays recorded?" Eden said.

"The coach's tracking didn't work, so they double checked their end. It was badly delayed and didn't get to Sylham till past midnight. Most of the other passengers would've had someone waiting for them, but not Martin. The driver can't be sure what he did, but with no buses or taxis around and no phone, I reckon he walked it."

"So the man that couple said they saw walking towards Osborne Ty, was him?" Eden said.

"Must've been. By my calculations, he'd've got there around six in the morning," Pilot said.

"With everyone asleep and the house in darkness," Judy mused. "He was too much of a gentleman to wake everyone up. Drenched to the skin, he helped himself to the dry coat and shoes left out for charity, and wandered off to kill time."

"Then what?" Eden said. "Stafford wasn't killed for hours."

"I reckon he found himself a bolt-hole and fell asleep," Pilot said. "I can sleep to midday on a day off, easy."

"Meaning we were right all along," Eden said. "He stumbled across the killer."

"Three scenarios come to mind," Black said. "Martin turned up at the door earlier than we thought and his brother told him to come back later, which he did. Martin waited in vain for his brother in a prearranged spot, and when he didn't show, he went to the house. Martin woke up about midday and went to the house. Any one of our scenarios has him there at roughly the same time as the killer."

"I've said it once, and I'll say it again," Pilot said. "Martin Mills was the unluckiest man on earth."

"If he was attacked because he saw something, that makes the order of deaths a red herring?" Judy asked.

"I think you and me need to have another chat with Sylvie Laurent, Eden," Black said.

38

The front room of Sylvie Laurent's small two-bedroom terrace house was one long showcase for her interior design skills. Its walls were painted in white with a hint of something or other. The floor was left uncarpeted, its original wooden floorboards varnished in stripes of different coloured varnishes. van Gogh sunflowers were painted over the white fireplace. A vase of the same image, complete with silk sunflowers, took centre place in an alcove. The yellow of the sunflowers was repeated in the silk cushions scattered over the furniture. The room's three armchairs were each a different design.

"We have a few more questions we need you to answer, Mme Laurent," Black said.

"I'm not sure I can add much," she replied.

"Stafford Mills had a brother, Martin," Black said.

"He was found dead in the park just down from Stafford's place, wasn't he?" she said.

"He was. Did Stafford ever talk about his brother Martin?" Eden asked.

"If he did, I can't remember him doing so. Stafford and I weren't together long."

"Did Stafford ever mention his mother bequeathing Martin an original Picasso?"

Sylvie shifted in her seat. "He didn't. I'm hardly likely to have forgotten that. Stafford and I split up years ago, remember. Had his brother actually inherited the piece when we were still together?"

"He inherited it nearly twenty years ago," Eden replied.

"How little I knew Stafford," she said.

"Are you *au fait* with the laws of intestacy, Mme Laurent?" Black said.

"The laws of what?"

"If a person dies without leaving a will, the laws of intestacy dictate what happens to that person's estate," Black said. "As Martin Mills died without leaving a will, his estate will belong to Stafford's beneficiaries under Stafford's will, but only if Martin died before his brother. If he died after Stafford, everything goes to Pierre." Black scrutinised Sylvie Laurent for any sign of emotion.

She stared back at him. When she eventually replied, she spoke slowly, almost leaving a space between each word. "Do I understand you? You suggest I killed my son's father to ensure he inherited this Picasso I knew nothing about until you arrived?"

"I'm not suggesting anything, Mme Laurent," Black said. "But it does provide a motive."

"Mme Laurent, we'll need to speak with your son," Eden said.

She got to her feet. "Now you imply my son is involved? First me, now him? How dare you? How dare you come into my home and accuse my son of murder? He's thirteen!" Thirteen touching fourteen, Eden thought. She and Black rose to their feet. This wasn't to intimidate her, but to show empathy.

"We'll visit him at school to put him at ease. A teacher will be present, and a solicitor," Eden said.

"Pierre was at school when his father was killed," Sylvie Laurent said.

"Still, we need to speak to him," Eden said.

"I insist on being present."

"I'm afraid that won't be possible," Black said.

"Do you have a solicitor you regularly use, Mme Laurent?" Eden said.

Sylvie slumped into the chair, and leant forward, bringing her head so low, she almost curled up in a ball, hugging her legs. "No," she whispered.

"Do you want us to arrange for a solicitor to be present when we speak to Pierre or do you wish to arrange this yourself?" Eden said.

She looked at both of them in turn, still bent, still clutching her legs. "Do you even have children?"

"I have a daughter," Eden said. "Nine going on twenty-seven."

Sylvie Laurent calmed down. "You don't both need to be there? You'll scare him. Just her," she said.

39

Pierre Laurent was a boarder at the private Southgreen school on the border between the Vale of Tye and the next county. At just before 10.30, Eden turned through its gates and into the school's extensive grounds. It felt to her as though she were arriving at a country hotel rather than at a school. Lawns stretched out on either side of the drive, became woodland, then lawns again. Here and there were various buildings described as Engineering Lab or Sound Studio. She could only laugh when she saw a sign pointing the way towards the school's obstacle course. Dora's school grounds consisted of a playground and a sports field.

The main school was housed in a substantial Edwardian building complete with a portico entrance, a two-tier balcony and a prominent bell tower, from which a bell tolled to announce the half-hour. Eden went inside the school's galleried hall. Chairs faced a stage and sturdy wooden columns supported the gallery from which doors led to schoolrooms. Netting stretched across the entire ceiling. There didn't seem to be anybody around. She was about to knock on a door when a woman appeared, identifying herself as the headmaster's secretary, there to escort Eden to the headmaster's office. The two women walked along a corridor, flanked by walls whose lower half was tiled and whose upper half was bedecked with portraits. "Former heads and pupils made good," Eden was informed.

In the office, two men rose to greet her. She already knew one as Kevin Calderstone, a local criminal solicitor. Although both men were in early middle-age, Kevin, tall and thin, was the physical opposite of Southgreen's headmaster, Malcolm Nixon. Kevin nodded a greeting and Eden reciprocated. Malcolm offered her a handshake and introduced himself, adding, "Kevin's just been telling me he went to school here."

"My claim to fame," Kevin replied. "Didn't have all that protective netting in the hall in my day. You went over the railings at your own risk."

"Would you mind waiting outside, Kevin?" Eden asked. "I'd like a word in private with Mr Nixon." Kevin Calderstone gave a nod, and shuffled out of the room.

"Sorry business, this," Malcolm Nixon said, and the two sat down.

"How long have you known Pierre Laurent?" she asked.

"I've been headmaster here for the last six years," he replied. "Pierre has only ever attended Southgreens. He started in the primary school, but that was before my time. Over the years, I've got to know the lad quite well. His father was obliged to pay for his education up to his eighteenth birthday. I'm led to believe his father's death won't change that. I'm hoping Pierre will join our sixth form. He's a bright lad."

"Did you ever meet his father?"

"Sadly not. He paid the school fees, nothing else."

"Was there any contact between him and Pierre that you are aware of?" Eden asked.

He shook his head. "To speak plainly, Detective Sergeant, Pierre's dad wasn't interested in his son. His mum, Sylvie, I know well. She visits regularly, and keeps in frequent touch with his teachers. She hasn't missed a sports day or a parents' evening. But his dad might as well have been dead, for all the interest he showed in his son. He refused a request for a contact number. Pierre doesn't know that."

"How much of a difference do you think his dad's death will make to him?" Eden said.

"To his day-to-day routine, none. How it will affect him emotionally, I can't say. Any dreams he nurtured of his dad wanting him in his life are extinguished now. Pierre isn't the first child I've come across in this situation. It comes with the territory, sadly. Some cope better than others on the surface. Deep down, Pierre's lost his dad. I lost my dad as a kid, but at least I have memories."

"I love you, I love you," Dixie shouted through the letterbox. "Why won't you open the door? Eden? Belah?" Her words were slurred, desperate, mixed with booze. Her young daughters, on the other side of the front door, didn't move. Eric and Dottie appeared in the hallway. "Eden, Leah, go upstairs now," Eric said. Dottie placed her hands on their heads, directing them towards and up the stairs. They went to their room obediently, but Eden didn't stay there. She slipped out and ran to the banisters and peered through them. The front door was open

now, blocked by Eric's frame. "You can't keep doing this, Dixie," he said. "Disappearing for months on end, turning up out of the blue like nothing's happened."

"I love them."

"Then leave them alone."

"How did Pierre learn of his father's death?" Eden asked.

"I told him myself. His mother rang me when the children were clearing their lunch things away. Thank God we have a no-phone-at-mealtimes rule," he said. "We called him out of the dining hall, poor kid. His housemistress, Linda Bagley, and I broke it to him in here. Ordinarily, I'd've waited for Sylvie to arrive, but the circumstances left me no alternative. I had to tell him before he heard it from somebody else." He muttered the word Internet under his breath.

"How did he take it?"

"Calmly at first. He asked what happened."

"How did you answer?"

"I have some training in this. Be honest without embellishment. Sugar coating's the worst thing, they'll inevitably find the truth out. I stuck to the facts. I said his dad had been found with head injuries, and had died. The poor kid just stared at me, trying to take it in. 'Did he hit his head?' he asked. Linda put her arm around him. 'He most likely did, love,' she said. Sylvie had told me the police were treating the death as suspicious. I decided, on balance, to withhold this until more was known of the circumstances. Pierre looked at us both in turn, as though one of us would say it wasn't true, then he dropped his phone and collapsed to his knees. Linda took him to one of the private rooms, and stayed with him until Sylvie arrived. She said he didn't stop shaking."

"Pierre didn't go home with his mother, did he?" Eden said. "He stayed on at school?"

"He insisted on staying. Sylvie didn't object. She thought he'd only dwell on it at home and I agreed. Sticking to his routine helped take his mind off things, I'm sure of it. We put him in his own room, to allow him to take himself away if things got too much for him."

"His father only paid the bare minimum, didn't he?"

"He paid the school fees, no more. Sylvie managed to scrape enough for him to go on a school trip to France a few years back, but that's the only school trip the poor kid's been on. We run extracurricular courses. When he wanted to take a media course, which Sylvie couldn't afford, the board dipped into the discretionary fund, but that's the only extra he's taken."

"Can we go back to the morning of his father's death?" Eden said. "What time did his mother drop him off?"

"Slightly earlier than usual, she said she had an appointment."

"You saw her arrive?"

"Had a brief word."

Although Pierre's PlayStation had shown he was gaming at school all morning, Eden still had to ask the question. "Is there any way he could've left the school and returned during the morning?"

"Only by the school bus or a taxi. You can see how secluded we are. We've handed over the CCTV from the entrances and exits." Eden had viewed it and seen Pierre arrive with his mother. There certainly weren't any images of his leaving again. "He was prompt down to lunch."

"Which was what time?"

"The gong goes at 12.45 precisely. About the time his dad was being attacked, I believe."

"Sylvie Laurent claims Pierre's father wanted to reconnect with his son," Eden said.

"She said the same to me," Malcolm said. "Some consolation for Pierre in the years to come."

Before visiting Pierre, Eden had a few words with his housemistress, Linda Bagley. She confirmed Malcolm Nixon's version of events. "Can you recall the first thing he said to his mother?" Eden asked.

"Asked her if she was all right," Linda said. "Poor Sylvie just threw her arms around him. 'Just as your dad was finally coming round,' she said. I left them alone after that."

Pierre's room was a fair size. It contained a single bed, a bedside table, a wardrobe, a chest of drawers, and a desk, where sat Pierre, his back to the door. There was a TV on the wall and a boy-sized Lego robot in one corner. Posters of gaming cartoon heroes covered the wall. Various components of a circuit board were scattered across his desk. Despite hollering: "Come in," in response to Malcolm Nixon's knock on the door, Pierre didn't look round when they entered, but continued to screw a piece into the circuit board with an electronic screwdriver, glancing now and then over to his laptop, where a young man and woman demonstrated the intricacies of the latest Raspberry Pie on

YouTube. Only when the assembly was completed, did he stop the YouTube video and swing round in his revolving chair. "Circuit boards are getting smaller and smaller, and faster and faster," he said, holding up the one he was working on for them to see. "I used to do stuff like this in the engineering lab, but no one knows what to say to me any more, since my dad died, so I do it here now."

"Pierre, this is Detective Sergeant Hudson. You and Mr Calderstone had a chat earlier," Pierre's headmaster said.

Sylvie Laurent's description of her son as small for his age, was accurate. Despite being nearly fourteen, the boy looked closer to twelve. He wasn't hugely tall, had no definite musculature and his fresh face was still immature and childish. His hormones hadn't yet kicked in, but when they did, he'd be a handsome young man, Eden decided. She could see his parents in him. She took her place between solicitor Kevin Calderstone and Malcolm Nixon. The interview would be recorded.

"Remember what you and me discussed, Pierre," Kevin said. "If you don't want to say anything, you don't have to. That can't be used against you. You're not an adult. Their rules don't apply to you."

Pierre shrugged. "I don't mind helping."

"How much do you know about your father's death, Pierre?" Eden asked.

"Quite a lot. I've been told stuff and there's masses online. I've made a scrapbook." He opened a folder on his laptop, which from what Eden could see as its pages fanned out across the screen, contained everything from newspaper articles to televised police interviews.

"And what have you learned from all of this?" Eden asked.

"Dad was attacked at home with a blunt instrument and died." As he spoke he constantly fiddled with the electronic screwdriver in his hands, turning it on and off.

"On the day your father died, what did you do after your mum dropped you back here?"

"Played Star Wars on my PlayStation." He screwed his face up. "Which you still haven't given back."

"I'll make sure we do," Eden said. "Did you ever meet your Uncle Martin – your dad's brother?"

He looked down at a screwdriver in his hands and turned it on. It whirred gently. He turned it off and looked up again. "I never did. Wish I had."

"Why so, Pierre?" Eden said.

"Well," he said, "one report I read said he was a recluse who spent whole days making model planes. I had to ask my teacher what recluse meant. The writer made out he can't have been all there, but I don't see why. I do that. Make models. Not model planes," the boy's eyes widened. "I make robots. Must of got that from him. Mum says sometimes children take after their parents' brothers and sisters more than their own parents."

"Your model-making is genetic is it, Pierre?" Malcolm asked.

"Could be," the grinning boy said. All of a sudden the smile disappeared. "It's funny him being found just down the road from my dad's place. He must have been there to see dad. Odd him being attacked as well." He turned back to the laptop and called up one of the online articles he'd saved to his scrapbook.

Was family dispute over will behind double deaths?

"I'm not sure about that," Pierre said thoughtfully, of the headline. "I mean, how could Dad and his brother kill each other and not be in the same place? Doesn't make any sense. Uncle Martin must've seen them."

"Seen who, Pierre?" Eden asked.

"The burglars who my dad surprised. The ones who killed him." He studied Eden silently. "If I was going to kill someone, I'd get a robot to do it. No clues, no mess. I'd program it to self-destruct if it was caught."

"Pierre wants to be a robotics engineer when he grows up," Malcolm said.

"Robots will be doing your jobs soon," Pierre said.

"The young lady and I have a few years left in us yet," Kevin said.

"She can't even nail whoever attacked my dad and uncle," he said, nodding towards Eden. "A robot would've had 'em in seconds."

"Not necessarily, Pierre," Malcolm said.

"They would of," the boy said indignantly. "Robots can fit clues together in micro-seconds." His face lit up as he spoke. "They can whizz through every murder ever, how it was carried out and why and stuff and use that to solve the one they're working on."

"Well, put it like that…" Eden said.

Pierre half-grinned. "People think me and mum did it because Uncle Martin was rich. But we didn't know. We didn't."

301

"Pierre, how do you feel about your father's death?" Eden said.

"You don't have to answer that, Pierre, if you don't want to," Kevin said.

"I don't mind. To start with I was sad. From what mum said, he'd changed his mind about us. But since he died, I've heard so much about him, I don't know how I feel any more."

"I don't think I have any more questions for you, Pierre," Eden said.

Eden quite liked young Pierre and left his school hoping Martin Mills had died after Stafford.

40

The reconstruction of the last known movements of Stafford Mills was intended to jog memories and help the murder team piece together what happened the morning he died. Guido Black wanted to test the suspects' stories, particularly their movements up to and after the attack. The reconstruction would take place over two days and would be repeated (and filmed) from various perspectives.

Black positioned himself on the front lawn of Fenn Farmhouse, Eden next to him, a cameraman next to her. Officers with cameras were positioned at the garage, on the road outside, and in various places throughout the property. Bridget White, still uncertain about her movements that morning, began near the front gate giving her a vantage point over the front and side of the farmhouse. Her sister and brother-in-law were inside.

"No one expects you to be word perfect," Black explained to the participants. "Just try your best."

The reconstruction began with a car appearing between the open gates, travelling along the drive, swinging right in front of the house, to eventually park around the corner, its driver to be let in by Hector Munro.

No sooner was the front door shut, than Aidan Stanton and Jenna Nesbitt acted out their arrival. They turned through the open gate and walked down the driveway hand-in-hand. Both were tense, she visibly shaking.

"Were you this slow on the day?" Black called out. "Thought you were in high dudgeon?" The couple mumbled apologies and returned to the gate to start their entrance again. Eden looked down and suppressed a grin. "The Oscar for best director goes to…" she mumbled. Black noticed her amusement but ignored it. Second time round, Aidan Stanton marched furiously down the driveway, half-dragging his reluctant fiancée behind him.

In the hallway, the trio repeated as much of the conversation of the day as they could remember, interrupted by Dandelion scampering along the hallway as fast as her short legs allowed. The little dog played her part to perfection, as she raced towards Jenna Nesbitt, tail wagging, only going slightly off script in her eagerness to greet in turn each of the police officers in the hall. The dog's presence lightened the foreboding atmosphere, and Jenna's smile at her appearance was genuine. She scooped the animal up in her arms and carried her over to a chair with a, "I think I've forgotten to bring your treat."

As Jeremy Havelock stormed out of the room, yelling and shouting, the officer playing Stafford Mills rushed over to the chest of drawers under the window. Having earlier practised, he found it quite easy to open the secret drawer. He quickly filled a plastic bag with pretend cash. He'd just managed to throw it out of the window to land beside Jeremy Havelock's car, when Aidan Stanton burst in ranting: "Why haven't you returned my calls?"

"Was Stafford Mills where I am now, when you entered, sir?" the officer asked.

"Yes, just there. Saw me and shut the window sharpish," Aidan said. "Didn't want anybody overhearing us, no doubt."

The officer looked back to the window. He could well imagine Stafford Mills forgetting to lock it, faced with the onslaught from Aidan Stanton.

Jeremy Havelock left the property accompanied by a young, lean policeman. "I want you to drive to the lay-by you say you stopped in, sir. Then you and me will go for that run you say you went on. I'm a cross-country runner, by the way," the officer added.

"It was more of a brisk walk than a run."

"Then you and me will go for a brisk walk, sir."

"Not sure I can remember where I stopped," Jeremy said.

"Well, that's what today is all about, sir, jogging memories. 'Scuse pun."

Their re-enactment over, Aidan and Jenna left accompanied by two police officers – one to shadow him for the rest of the morning, and the other her.

The supermarket delivery driver wasn't a natural. From his van, he stiffly opened and closed his mouth a few times as though a fish, but words failed him. Hector pointed him towards the side of the house, and after a very wooden nod, he promptly stalled. He managed to restart and move off, followed on foot by Hector. The driver was still self-consciously unloading shopping boxes when Hector reached him. "You were quicker on the morning," he said. "You were on your way by now." Hector's words spurred the driver into action and he jumped into his van and reversed away, only narrowly avoiding colliding with the wall. No one from the force accompanied him as he left the property, his alibi already verified.

Tim Smith pulled to a halt outside Fenn Farmhouse, briskly climbed the steps and grasped the brass door knocker, watched through the letterbox by the police officer playing Stafford Mills. Before Tim Smith brought the knocker down, he flung the door open as though about to step out, and said: "What the hell are you doing, man?"

"I'm here about the candlesticks."

"They're in me library. This way," 'Stafford Mills' turned abruptly to stride across the hall Tim Smith trailing after him.

Inside the library, the conversation followed the script provided by Tim Smith, while in the hall Hector Munro opened the door to Sylvie Laurent, with a glance towards Vaz Bank's post office van hurtling down the drive.

Vaz was a natural performer. He picked up his tablet from the passenger seat with a theatrical flourish and began tapping its screen indiscriminately, pretending to call up delivery details. When he felt sufficient time had passed, he climbed out of the van, tablet in hand, and sauntered to the back of his van as though no one else was present, let alone a police murder team.

Tim Smith emerged from the room on cue, dressed in the same pink trousers, purple jacket, striped shirt and polka-dot cravat, but this time he stopped by Sylvie Laurent.

"Again apologies for my behaviour the last time we met," he said, before neatly skirting around her to hurry over to Hector, where he placed his hands on Hector's shoulders. "I was frightfully rude to you the last time we met. I took everything out on you. Quite unforgivable. Please accept my heartfelt apologies."

"If we could try and stick to the script, sir," Black called out from the front lawn.

Sylvie Laurent gave a jolt when she saw the policeman playing Stafford Mills. He wasn't physically dissimilar to the man himself, being about the same age, colouring, height and build. He smiled to put her at ease. She took a breath and asked if everything was all right, just as she had on the morning.

At about the same time as Tim Smith turned towards Osborne Tye's high street, Corrine Beechwood left home for the viaduct, a police officer in the passenger seat.

A different policewoman accompanied Sylvie on her return journey, which included a stop at the garage and a visit to the neighbour.

Stafford Mills would be dead in less than an hour.

At the end of the first day, Black called his team together for a debrief. "Let's go in order," he said. "How does Captain Jeremy Havelock's story stack up?"

"Not particularly well," Havelock's shadow said. "Couldn't remember where he'd parked up for this power walk of his. First place he picked was impassable. Next place wasn't much better. Ended up, up to our eyeballs in mud. He kept saying he couldn't remember where he'd stopped, the countryside all looks the same. When we finally got started he was out of breath after less than five minutes. Had to keep stopping. And we weren't jogging – far from it."

"Jenna Nesbitt ," Black said to the next officer.

"Not sure her story rings true either," said the WPC who had escorted her. "Once she got back home she spent the whole time sorting and resorting wedding stuff, updating her wedding scrap book, so it was the same as her online one. Like it mattered. It was like she was saying – 'This is what I did for all that time. Honest.' She went out without a word to her boyfriend, which seems strange as he was only a couple of rooms away. I walked with her along the bridle path to the farm house gate. Didn't bother going any further. We know what happened next."

"Did you see anyone else on the lane?" Black asked.

"A young mother and her kids walking the dog. Took her number and gave her a call. She walks the dog there

308

twice a day, but can't be sure of the precise time she was there on the seventeenth as the baby often makes her late. She certainly doesn't remember seeing Jenna there that day, who she knows from the village. Jenna herself swears she didn't see anyone."

Black went through the rest of the team in turn:

"Aidan Stanton spent the rest of the morning at his piano working on his composition," Aidan's shadow said. "Didn't so much as get up, until Jenna rang from the pub. He's quite talented. And very polite. Kept asking if I wanted any refreshments."

"Tim Smith?" Black said.

"Didn't move from his spot. Drank a pint, told the publican his life story, ate a pie, read the paper."

"Mme Sylvie Laurent?" Black said.

"Took the route she said. Stopped at the service station to fill up, went to the neighbours. Exactly as we have on CCTV and ANPR. Her elderly neighbour and the home help were dead eager to discuss the events of the morning, but Sylvie was very subdued. Hardly said a word. May have been down to my presence."

"Postman Vaz Banks?" Black said.

Vaz's shadow grinned. "He swears he has a photographic memory which allows him to remember deliveries from months back, including the deliveries he made after he'd left Fenn Farmhouse on the seventeenth. Took me all over the place, pretending he had post for them. Even got out of the van and went to the letterboxes. Now and then he stopped to chat to the house owners. 'Number twelve had three letters and a postcard that day,' he'd say of an address, 'but their neighbour at number ten had diddly squat, as usual.' In between his last two deliveries, he pulled into this lay-by for his lunch. For authenticity his Missus had made him the same sarnies – organic pork sausage and French mustard. She'd made some for me as well. It would've been rude to refuse. After we'd polished them off, he finished his round and we went back to the sorting office, getting there pretty much the time we know he did. There wasn't a lot of traffic about so no witnesses to support or disprove his story. He was certainly close enough to Fenn Farmhouse to get there and back quite easily. He knows the area well, how to get about, where to hide bloody clothing, etcetera."

"Last but not least, Corrine Beechwood," Black said.

"She drove to the aqueduct and parked up. It's quite steep getting up there," said the chubby officer who'd shadowed Corrine during the reconstruction. "Halfway up the steps I had to get my breath back. More people should make the effort to go there. The view's lovely. We had a chat. She's still cut up about things. Still can't believe it's happened, so she says. I had to tell her when it was time to go to the factory."

"We've got her car travelling to the viaduct and from there to the factory," Eden said, "but nothing in between. Thing is, it's less than two and a half miles to Mills' place from the viaduct if she crossed the fields. It's a bit tight, but she could have run, twenty minutes each way, ten for the attack, or used a different vehicle or even a bike. I hate to say it, I feel for her, I really do, but she had the opportunity. If it was her," she added, "I doubt she went there with the intention of killing him. Just lost it."

Black now had a fairly accurate idea of the sequence of events that morning, and the time they'd taken to play out. Stafford Mills had just over an hour left to live. He sent

310

everybody home. In the morning they'd go through it again, step-by-step. This time the key players' parts would be taken by police officers, and the focus would be on the others in the house that morning: Hector and Brenda Munro and Bridget White. He wanted their timelines too.

Brenda Munro pretended to carry a full laundry basket downstairs to the kitchen, where she pretended to put the washing machine on before returning upstairs, securing Dandelion in the kitchen. With the upstairs untouched since the crime, she could do no more than pat the sheets, and run a duster over some surfaces. She looked over to the team awkwardly.

"You're all right," one of them said.

As her husband dealt with the various comings and goings of the morning as he had that fateful day, Brenda continued her chores by running the vacuum cleaner around the bedroom carpets and upstairs landing. Finished upstairs, and with the main house always left until the afternoon to avoid getting under her late employer's feet, she came downstairs to an empty hall. Jeremy Havelock, Aidan Stanton and Jenna Nesbitt having come and gone. She went to the kitchen where her sister was at the kitchen table, pretending to nurse a hangover, and her husband was making coffee.

"Ocado's been," Hector said, placing a mug of coffee in front of Bridget.

"Ocado came yesterday," Brenda said.

"And again today," he said, a glance in Bridget's direction.

Bridget still couldn't remember much of the morning of the seventeenth, but her sister and brother-in-law had assured her that the comment had annoyed her sufficiently to drive her outside for fresh air. Accordingly, she glowered at her brother-in-law and picked up her coffee, taking it outside with her through the back door. "When you've finished your coffee, the washing's nearly done. It'll need putting out, if you don't mind," Brenda said after her.

"We were sat here having our coffee," Brenda said, "when the front bell went."

"It was Vaz and that Frenchwoman," Hector said, as the front doorbell rang on cue. Hector got to his feet. "Best go let them in," he said, muttering something about Bill Murray in *Groundhog Day*.

"What did you do when Mr Munro went to the door?" Eden asked Brenda.

"Finished unpacking the delivery. Hector was right. They'd brought exactly the same as the day before." She rolled her eyes. "Time that took, the washing was done. Took it out and left it on the back doorstep for Bridget to hang up and put on the second load, tea-towels and the like. I'd just started making our lunch when Hector came back, full of the argument upstairs."

"You didn't hear anything of the commotion?" Eden said.

"No – but there's two doors between here and the hall, remember. And I had the radio on and the washing machine was going. Hector and I had our lunch and talked of nothing else. Bridget joined us for coffee. Still don't know where she'd been in between."

Bridget appeared through the back door. "I just had a walk around," she said. "Made me quite emotional."

"Did it help you to remember anything which might help us, Mrs White?" Eden said.

"No more than I've told you, dear," she replied.

The re-enactment now moved into its final stages: the attack on Stafford Mills. Hector, Brenda and Bridget stayed in the kitchen with Eden. The two doors separating it from the rest of the house closed, the radio on in the background, the empty washing machine churning through its cycle.

In the library, the police officer playing Stafford Mills ambled around. He sat down, stood up, reached for things to pick up and put down again. He took a book from a shelf and replaced it. He scratched his head a couple of times, pretended to cough and to sneeze. Black, positioned in the living room, on the other side of the long dividing bookshelf, heard everything. Roles reversed, the same thing happened. No one could make much noise on one side of the room, without someone on the other hearing it.

Black crossed to the steps leading up to the decking library. His colleague sat in one of the deep leather recliners, his back to the steps, facing the unlocked window. The base of the chair reached almost to the ground, only the short caster between it and the floor. Black removed his shoes and climbed the wooden steps as quietly as he could, but didn't get further than the second step before his colleague swung around.

As 'Stafford Mills' waited outside the door, Black crouched behind the solid recliner. The chair stood at an angle, concealing Black. 'Stafford Mills' returned to the room, pretending to speak into his phone. He looked up. "Wouldn't know you were there, Boss," he said, climbing up the steps to cross to the library window, where he sat in the chair Stafford Mills had last sat in. Face back in phone.

Black, in gloved hands and socked feet, gently slid across the decking. Only when at 'Stafford Mills', did he get to his feet and raise his arm. Only then did his victim look round and cry out – a yell of surprise, followed by groans of pain.

Black radioed Eden in the kitchen. "Didn't hear anything," she said.

Brenda Munro, tray in hand, knocked on the door. "Stafford, I have your lunch," she said. She left it a few moments before knocking again. "Leave it on the table, Brenda," a voice called out.

On her way to the kitchen, she opened the back door to call out, "Bridget, lunch is on the table."

Pretend lunch over, Bridget White, bowl in hand, strolled up the garden and through its back gate onto the bridle path at the rear. She was there to pick crab apples, accompanied by Dandelion and a police officer.

As Bridget made her way through the garden, Brenda busied herself in the kitchen, while just outside the garage door, Hector spread a tarpaulin over the boot of his car, on to which he threw a shovel and a reinforced gardening bag. As his sister-in-law advanced on the crab apple tree, and his wife pretended to take a load out of the washing machine, Hector turned right at the top of the drive, Black in the passenger seat. Once past the hill, he turned right again into a farm lane, at the corner of which a hand-painted sign announced:

Dung – 50p a bag – Help Yourself

Hector ignored the manure bagged up by a small table, on which was a smaller version of the roadside sign and an honesty box, and continued along the track.

"Why didn't you take the stuff back there?" Black asked.

"It wasn't there that day. The old farmer was going the sell it off and said I should help myself to what I wanted," Hector said.

He drove to the point where the lane petered out and became part of a ploughed field. Hector turned left into a track, for tractors and the like, running across the field. He continued along it, ploughed soil on either side, until he reached the point where the field ended and another began. This wasn't marked with a visible boundary, only by way of the field they were in being the higher of the two, and the furrows on both running in different directions. Hector parked and got out. Black, taking his cue from Hector, did likewise. Although not visible, the nearness of the dung heap was apparent from the smell. In the breeze, it wasn't pleasant, but wasn't overpowering. While Hector changed into his boots and took the shovel and bag from the boot, Black took a few steps forward and peered down into a concealed gully running between the two fields. And here was the dung heap.

"There's still some left," Hector said, climbing down and using the shovel as a walking stick. Black didn't join him, but used the time to look around. He couldn't see Fenn Farmhouse behind the hill. On the other side of the gully, two fields away and poking out beyond some trees, were the silage tanks of the farm which owned this farmland. Although he couldn't see it, he knew the remainder of the working farm was by those tanks. He walked back along the tractor track a bit and turned. Hector wasn't visible. He retraced his steps and jumped into the gully. It was deeper than he thought. He couldn't see much more than the car's roof, and some treetops. He used the shovel to help himself clamber back out, then held a hand down for Hector.

Back at the car he asked Hector: "How long were you down there?"

"Long enough to fill a bag. Ten, maybe fifteen minutes at most."

Ten to fifteen minutes, Black mused. Even ten minutes, plus five or so there and back, gave the killer more than enough time to arrive, strike and leave. He and Hector returned in silence to Fenn Farmhouse, lost in thought, parking outside the garage.

They used the side door to get back in, coming across Brenda on her knees staring through the keyhole of the front room, the untouched lunch tray still on the table by the door. "I'm worried about Stafford," she announced. "He's not touched his lunch."

"He's most likely gone out," Hector said.

"The door's locked from the inside. I can see the key. I've knocked and knocked and he's not answered. Hector, something's not right."

Hector went back outside. The curtains to the library window were drawn and the window closed. "Odd," he said, returning indoors.

In the kitchen, Bridget White left the bowl of freshly picked crab apples on the table. "They found the bowl there," she explained to the police officer shadowing her. "I must have got that far and gone out again to put out the washing." She picked up the bowl with both hands and put it back down on the table for effect. Then, Dandelion at her heels, she went to the back door. "Wouldn't surprise me if she tripped me up," she said of the little dog. She picked up the empty washing basket. "It was empty when they found me and the washing on the line. I must've tripped on my way back. Should I pretend to hang some washing up? I won't trip up this time. Promise."

Hector bent down to look through the keyhole but couldn't see past the key. "He's probably asleep," he said, "but we'd best be sure." The post was still piled on the chair by the front door and he helped himself to an A4 envelope, which he pushed under the door. He took out his penknife and used it to push the key from the lock. It fell onto the envelope with a gentle thud. Hector pulled the envelope and key slowly out from under the door. "Still can't believe it worked," he said to Black. "Good job there's that gap between the bottom of the door and the floor."

Brenda followed Hector in. "I saw him, over there," she said, pointing to the officer lying face down on the decking, precisely where the deceased had been found. "I saw blood, then him. It was horrible." She covered her face with her hands.

"Please carry on, Mrs Munro," Black said. "Take as long as you need."

"I got to him as quick as I could," she said, hurrying from the door to the body on the decking.

"And I went for an ambulance," Hector said, darting out of the room.

Brenda hesitated when she reached the top of the decking stairs, but forced herself on. Black watched her from the door. She knelt down next to the officer playing Stafford Mills and gently touched his head.

"Oh my God, Stafford, what happened?" she asked. She looked across to Black. "I thought I heard him moan or say something but I couldn't get it." She steadied herself on the floor with outstretched hands, and spoke into his ear. "Hector's gone for the ambulance, Stafford. What on earth happened? Did you fall?" She put her ear over his mouth to listen for a reply, eventually straightened herself up and still kneeling by the body, twisted around to address Black, who now stood at the bottom of the steps.

"I really thought he moaned," she said, "but he couldn't have. It was just air leaving the body. He was already dead. I kept stroking his head, told him to hold on, help was coming. Hector came back and said the ambulance was on its way. I told him it was too late for that. He'd gone."

She looked down at the officer playing the victim and over to Black again. "How could I ever have thought he was still alive? There was blood everywhere."

41

For the second time during the investigation, Eden was awoken from a deep sleep, not by her alarm or her daughter, but by her ringing bedside phone. On autopilot, she reached across to answer it. "What's happened this time?"

Black and Matthew Prichard had beaten her to it. Their cars were parked on the drive just inside the front gate of Fenn Farmhouse, along with as many SOCA vehicles as on the day Stafford Mills met his fate. She walked towards the house. Only a matter of days had passed since the reconstructions. That couldn't be a coincidence. She passed the house and continued towards the outhouse, passing a police car parked immediately before the garage, two uniformed officers on either side, a young male civilian sitting on the back seat. She nodded at the two officers, and gave the briefest of glances to the vehicle's sole occupant. He pulled a face, which was a cross between an embarrassed grin and a look of astonishment, as if he had no idea why he was there.

She ignored him and continued to the outhouse, where she suited up. Police tape stretched across its open door through which she saw Black and Prichard, their backs to the door. She joined them. At their feet lay the body of Bridget White. She was face down across the woodpile, arms spread out at her side, logs scattered all around.

"Poor girl," she said. "Just as she was getting her act together."

Matthew Prichard looked over to her. His eyes lingered.

"Did she fall?" Eden asked, looking from Bridget to the mezzanine floor above.

"She did. Whether by intention, accident or foul play will be very hard ever to establish," Matthew said. "Fell, jumped, pushed from behind, her injuries would be the same. I'm inclined to say accidental. We don't have any evidence to suggest she was suicidal, and pushing someone from up there," he motioned up to the mezzanine, "to down there," he nodded to the woodpile, "wouldn't guarantee death."

"It might with her liver," Eden said.

"She had five hundred pounds in cash in her jacket pocket, by the way," Matthew said.

"Matt, can I leave you to finish off here?" Black said.

"Of course, Guido."

"Eden, please have a chat with our friend in the car. I'd better visit the Munros," Black said sombrely.

320

Eden returned to the police car parked in front of the garage, where she spoke with one of the two officers. "Tom Hammond, twenty-three, self-employed vlogger. Here for a nose around," the policewoman said. "Claims he heard a scream, and an almighty crash and rushed in and found her. Stuck to his guns till we found this." She removed a camera from an evidence bag, whereupon Tom Hammond lunged at the door, attempting a breakout, only to be thwarted by the second officer promptly pushing him back inside and closing the door on him. This time Tom Hammond's escape route was blocked off and he slumped back in his seat.

Eden scrolled through his photographs. She began with the first photo he'd taken of the murder scene. Why did it show Bridget White buried under the logs, she asked herself. Had Matt removed that many? She closed her eyes. Matt hadn't moved them, the prat peering up at her helplessly had only thrown them out of the way to get a better photograph. She continued scrolling. Hammond had been there for a while. He'd taken shots from many angles: from a height, from the side. Full body. Here were close-ups of her head, and her upper torso. He'd even taken a selfie next to her body. Welcome to death in the modern age.

"He'd just started videoing the scene when Police Officer Linley found him," Eden was informed.

"How did he get in?"

"From the field over there," the policewoman pointed across to the house, in the direction of Osborne Tye. "It was still dark. Linley was the only one on patrol. She didn't hear any crash or scream."

"How long had she been on duty?"

"Less than an hour. We don't have anyone on overnights any more."

Eden tapped on the car window. Thomas Hammond rolled it down. "It's not what it looks like," he said.

"This is a restricted area. What were you doing here?"

"My job."

"Your job's taking photographs of severely injured people, rather than calling for help, is it?" Eden said.

"She was already dead, woman," he said defensively. "Dead and gone to her maker. What good would help have done her?"

"What made you so sure she was dead? Did you check for a pulse or were you too busy taking photographs?"

"She was dead!"

"Interfering with a body is a criminal offence, sir."

"I didn't interfere with the body."

"She was buried under logs when you found her – logs you moved to get a better picture. That's interfering with a body, Mr Hammond."

"I didn't like to leave her lying there. Not very dignified."

"And taking a selfie with her was?"

"Got a bit carried away. Hands up to that one."

"Tell me what happened. From the beginning."

The journalist rolled his eyes. "I already told her everything," he glanced towards the policewoman. "Ask her, woman – she wrote enough down."

"You and me are going to fall out, sir," Eden said. "You told my colleague you heard a scream and a crash and went to investigate. Did you?"

"No," he said. "I was there for a ladder and found her."

"What did you want with a ladder?"

"Shots of the inside. I needed them for a blog I'm writing on the murders. The curtains were drawn, all except for one upstairs. I figured there had to be a ladder somewhere or other, and went to find the outhouse I'd seen on Google maps. I was coming round the corner when I saw your girl on her rounds. I was surprised you still had anyone on duty. I hid up behind a corner and waited for her to go down the garden. Soon as she was out of sight, I ran to the outhouse, but I couldn't get in. The door was wedged from the inside. I had to put my shoulder to it to get it to open. I nearly tripped over the poor lady. There's me here for an interior shoot, and I find a body."

"Vloggers everywhere will know your name," Eden said.

"Don't be like that, woman."

"If you call me woman once more, sir, I'll arrest you for patronising a police officer."

"Sorry," he said disingenuously. "I'm just saying. I'll have you know I was pretty shaken up. It wasn't nice seeing someone like that."

"Didn't stop you going all David Bailey, though, did it?" Eden said. Hammond slumped back in his seat.

"The door was closed when you arrived?" she continued.

He nodded sullenly, clearly angry at Eden's attitude to him. "That a yes, sir?" His legs were crossed, as were his arms. He was sulking. "Sir?"

He shot her a disdainful look. "Yes, officer. The door was closed. Wedged closed by her body."

"Other than our officer, did you see anybody else in the vicinity at any time?"

"No. As God is my witness."

"Did you hear anything – raised voices, yelling, footsteps, anything?"

He shook his head. "Nothing. Just countryside noiscs. I'll accept a police caution," he added quickly.

"We'll need to hang on to your camera and your phone."

"Whoa there," he said. "You're welcome to the photographs, but not the phone. That's not fair."

"We're investigating a serious crime here, sir," Eden said. "What you think fair doesn't come into it."

"She was just some old lush who got drunk and fell off a ledge. If her boss hadn't been murdered here, nobody'd give a shit."

Eden felt fury rising inside her. She pushed her face into his. "Mrs White was a human being and how she lived her life is none of your business," she hissed. "You're under arrest for breaking and entering, interfering with a body, interfering with a possible crime scene and obstructing the police in the course of their enquiries. My colleague will read you your rights. You can call a lawyer from the station. You might want to call your other half while you're at it, and tell her you're going to be late home. Sir." She stormed off.

When Matthew Prichard joined her by her car, she was bent forward, her hands pressing on its roof. When she realised he was there, she looked over to him.

"I saw," he said.

"I shouldn't have lost it," she said. "I'm meant to be a police officer."

Matthew put his hand on her arm. "He's an arsehole."

"I can't go off like that every time I come across one of those," Eden said. "Won't have time for anything else."

He took his business card from his pocket and scribbled something on the reverse. "I'm a good listener," he said. "Give me a call if you want to talk. Or have a drink. Or dinner." He waited for her to take it. She did, although she wasn't sure what to say. He smiled and went to his car without another word.

42

Once again Black parked outside the Munro's small caravan. He stepped out of his car grim-faced and went to the door to announce his presence. Hector Munro answered, his wife, Brenda behind him, clutching a handkerchief to her face.

"Bridget's dead, isn't she? That's what you've come to tell us," she said.

"I'm terribly sorry, Mrs Munro," Black said. Was it his imagination, or was even the dog subdued? Maybe Chloe was right. Maybe they could sense human emotions.

Brenda staggered back inside and collapsed in a chair, burying her face in her hands. "Soon as we saw your face we knew," Hector said, letting Black in and closing the door. "We've not been able to get her on the phone. We called and called. Then you show."

Black walked daily through the valley of the shadow of death. There wasn't any death he hadn't seen – old, young, violent, tragic, lonely, attention-seeking, cruel beyond words, stupid, or pointless. The bodies, the names, the personal tragedies, were piled up in his memory. Over the years he'd become inured to death, but not to its tragedy. The day he became inured to the pain of death, its heartbreak, was the day to give up.

He took the chair Hector had pulled out for him. Hector himself moved to stand behind his sobbing wife, placing his hands on her shoulders. Experience had taught Black that the bereaved didn't want platitudes. They wanted facts. "She died from a fall," he said, taking Brenda's hands in his. "At the outhouse at Fenn Farmhouse. She was found this morning. We don't as yet know when she died."

"A fall? Like an accident?" Hector said.

"She fell from the mezzanine. How she came to fall, we may never be able to say for sure."

"What are you implying, Detective Inspector?" Hector said. "That she jumped or was pushed? For pity's sake, man, hasn't my wife been through enough?"

"I'm trying to be honest with you both, Mr Munro. Bridget died from a fall, and unfortunately, in such cases it's not always possible to establish the circumstances."

"What was she doing at Fenn Farmhouse?" Brenda said. "In the outhouse?"

"I was hoping you might help us with that one," Black said.

"That's where she used to do her drinking," Brenda said.

"Had she started again?" Black asked.

"Not that we were aware of," Brenda said. "Doesn't mean she hadn't."

"When did you last see your sister, Mrs Munro?"

"She went out last night. To meet friends, she said."

"What time was that?"

"I dropped her off at Osborne Tye," Hector said. "Said she'd make her own way back. It must have gone nine or half-past. I'd just come back from taking the dog out."

"Was this usual behaviour for her?" Black asked.

"Not unusual. Specially when she was still drinking," she said.

"She didn't say where she was going when she went out?" Black said.

"No," Brenda and Hector said together. Hector carried on: "Just that she couldn't stay cooped up here a minute longer."

"Was it unusual for her to stay out overnight?"

"She was a grown woman," Brenda said. "She had her phone on her. Hector woke up before me and realised she wasn't back and gave her a call, but she didn't answer."

"Thought she was asleep somewhere," Hector said. "It was still quite early."

"I started to worry when she still hadn't come back, and wasn't answering her phone. When you showed up I knew something bad had happened," Brenda said.

"I need to ask where you both were last night?"

"We were here, Detective Inspector," Hector said.

"In the last few days, had Bridget received any calls, letters, visitors?" Black said.

"Not that I can think of," Brenda said. "Can you, Hector?" She spoke slowly, as though it pained her to pronounce each word.

"Nothing as I can think of," her husband replied.

Black got to his feet. "Once again, I'm very sorry for your loss."

Hector walked with him to the door. There, Black said in a low voice, "Walk with me to my car, if you'd be so kind, Mr Munro." Hector nodded and stepped outside after the Detective Inspector, closing the caravan door behind him.

Only when at the car did Black say, "Your sister-in-law had five hundred pounds in cash on her when we found her. Might you know anything about that?"

"Bridget only had her disability allowance. When Stafford was still alive he gave her some cash now and then, but with him no longer around, I can't think where she'd get it. Wasn't me or Brenda, I can assure you. We haven't got that kind of money."

"Thank you, Mr Munro."

43

"D on't worry about it," Pilot told Eden in the station canteen over bacon sandwiches. "Matt's right. The guy's a complete arsehole. He'll be vlogging about his dead-body hell next."

"Like neither of us haven't seen worse. I shouldn't have lost it. He dug up some stuff," Eden said.

"You're allowed emotions. Shame about Bridget. You got to wonder about that."

"Matthew Prichard gave me his number," she said.

"Look at you."

"I don't know," she said. "Being a single mum on the murder squad's bad enough. Being a single mum on the murder squad and dating the pathologist?"

"I was bloody glad when my mum got a boyfriend," Pilot said. "Made a change to see her with a smile on her face. Haylee and I are meeting up Friday after work by the way," he threw in nonchalantly, grinning. "Unless another body turns up."

"Don't."

His phone beeped with a text. He scowled at the screen. Black had called a team meeting.

It began with a debrief:

"Bridget White's death coming only days after the reconstruction can't be a coincidence," Black said. "But how are the two connected? The reconstruction might well have unsettled her to the extent she went back on the booze – the mezzanine was her comfort zone – and somehow or other she fell. Another unsettling possibility, one we can't discount, is that the reconstruction jogged her memory enough for her to piece something together. She knew the names of the suspects. Wouldn't have taken much to find their address and get in touch, demanding a meet up. She was found with a lot of cash on her."

"You think she was blackmailing the killer, Boss?" Pilot said.

"Can't rule it out," Black replied.

"Foolish, foolish woman, if she was," Eden said.

"If, and until, we know one way or the other, we must work on the assumption she was there to meet Stafford's killer under cover of night."

"That rules out the botched burglary theory," Pilot said.

"Not necessarily. The gang could be local," Black said.

"Why leave the money behind?" Eden said.

"The killer was disturbed?" Black suggested.

His phone rang. The autopsy results were in.

Matthew Prichard addressed the team from the autopsy room. On the autopsy table behind him Bridget White's body was covered with a sheet.

"Bridget died from impact injuries," he said. "She had severe contusions and multiple injuries, causing internal bleeding. Her liver ruptured on impact. It was highly sclerotic. Her internal organs all indicated alcohol-related damage. She landed face down, whereupon the wood-pile collapsed on her." He lifted the sheet to show the room. The camera zoomed in to the body. Bridget's face and upper torso were black and blue.

"Her back, shoulders and buttocks are just as bad," he said, replacing the sheet. "As I feared, the extent of the bruising and nature of her injuries, internal and external, make it nigh on impossible to conclude if she jumped, slipped or was pushed. She had partially digested food in her stomach, and antidepressants in her blood. She died approximately five to six hours before she was found. There was no alcohol in her system."

44

A t her desk, Eden was about to begin making a series of calls when Dora texted.

Mum I'm in the school library by myself

All the better for getting on with things then, she texted back. She knew full well where this was going.

Mum. Laptop, Dora came back.

Eden rolled her eyes. She'd had a gutful the night before of her daughter's non-stop whinging about her woeful failure to replace the broken laptop. It had started the moment she'd got home. The only good thing to come out of poor Bridget's death was avoiding the morning school run, when inevitably it would have started again.

As soon as I can afford to, Eden texted in reply.

Thats not good enough, Dora texted sternly. *The situations intoilable*

The word's intolerable. Are you copying this from something?

This was too much for Dora. The texting was replaced by a call.

"What's up?" Eden said.

"I'm the only kid in school with no laptop."

"The Barnsley sisters don't have laptops."

"The Barnsley sisters!" Dora shrieked. "They're weird. They don't have a laptop cos they're weird."

"I might be able to get you one here."

"I don't want a stolen one. I want a new one. An Apple or ..."

"In your dreams, my love," Eden said. "I have to go, I'm at work. We'll talk about it later."

Finally able to get on, she telephoned Sylvie Laurent. "Mme Laurent, I need to know where you were last night."

"I was at home. Why?"

"All night?"

"Yes – all night."

"Do you have a witness?"

"I've slept alone since my marriage ended," Sylvie said. "My car was parked on the drive all night. Do you know the order of the deaths yet?"

"I beg your pardon?"

"I read up on those laws of intestacy your Detective Inspector spoke of. My Pierre will only get what's his if Martin died after his brother. I need to know who died first? Martin or Stafford? I need to know for my son. If

Pierre is entitled to his uncle's estate, it's only right he has it."

"We're still trying to establish Martin Mills' time of death."

"How can you not know? There must be tests you can do." Her voice had more than a tone of urgency to it.

"It's more complicated than on the telly," Eden said.

"How is it complicated? Martin died last. It's obvious," Sylvie said.

"How so, Mme Laurent?"

"Stafford disturbed burglars. Martin was there to speak to his brother and saw them. They went after him. He sat down to get his breath back and had a heart attack which they mistook for a faint. They killed the poor man somehow or other and put him in a shed."

"We're working on a number of theories," Eden replied wearily.

"When will you know?" Sylvie said. "It can't be that difficult. I've been patient enough."

Eden closed her eyes. Was the world conspiring against her today? "We might never," she replied calmly.

"Never?" Sylvie Laurent sounded as though she was about to explode. "What happens then?"

"As I understand it, the youngest is treated as having died last."

Sylvie Laurent sounded horrified. "If you lot can't get your act together, my Pierre won't get a penny?" More than a penny, Eden thought, distracted by the thought of what she could buy if she suddenly inherited a Picasso. She was brought down to earth by Sylvie saying, "How can that be fair?"

"You really need to speak to a lawyer, Mme Laurent, not a police sergeant."

"Oh you people." She slammed the phone down.

Eden took a deep breath, replaced the receiver, and picked it up again. She rang Corrine Beechwood, Jeremy Havelock, Tim Smith, Aidan Stanton and Jenna Nesbitt in turn. Each claimed to have spent the night in their own bed. Only Aidan Stanton and Jenna Nesbitt had anyone to support their story – each other.

Calls made, Eden wandered over to Pilot's desk to ask if he had any news.

"I do," he said, swivelling his seat round to face her, arms folded. "After you said your kid dropped her laptop, I had a word with the lady here who maintains our auction site. She and me are gaming buddies – she's a Grand Master," he added, with an impressed raise of an index finger. "She promised me first dibs if anything halfway decent came in – and it has. An Apple Notebook recovered from a raid. No one's claimed it in time. Said I could have it for fifty quid. New would set you back £750. It's still in its box. Don't think it's ever been used. Your kid'll be the coolest kid in class. What you think about that then?"

"She's not having it," Eden said. "She can have my old one. And thanks. Owe you."

"Think nothing of it. I've always liked kids," he said.

"Way your personal life's going, you'll have some of your own before long."

338

He looked sheepish. "Thanks for not grassing me up to Mace. I'm a one-woman man really, just me and Mace aren't getting along … "

The phone on Eden's desk began ringing.

Guido Black was closeted in Judy McDermott's office, called in to participate in a conference call with the Chief Constable.

"Black, what is going on?" the Chief Constable said, his voice booming around the office.

"Excuse me, sir?" Black said.

"We've got more bodies than an average episode of *Midsomer Murders*. I've just come off the phone to the Home Secretary's office. She's none too pleased. Got *Newsnight* on her back wanting to know if our failure to charge anyone was down to police incompetence or government cutbacks."

"We're doing our best, sir," Black said. "It's complicated."

"I need progress on this one, Black, not your Facebook status."

"The killer is proving elusive, sir," Black said. "There's a mountain of evidence to cut through. I appreciate you're coming under pressure, sir, but I don't need to remind you, Chief Constable, that leaning on lower ranks for results leads to round-shapes-in-square-hole convictions. None of us wants to go back to that."

"I'm not sure I care for your tone or your insinuations, Black."

"No offence intended, sir, I assure you. Apologies."

"Accepted."

"Grateful for the support, sir. As to our killer, I'm confident we're closing in."

A harassed Judy answered a knock on the door. "Unless you're here to confess, I don't want to know," she said to Eden and Pilot.

They glanced at each other. "Sylvie Laurent has walked into her local station and confessed to killing Stafford and Martin Mills," Eden said.

"In that order," Pilot added.

45

Black interviewed Sylvie Laurent alone, with the team watching on from another room. She'd declined legal representation. "After I filled the car, I returned to Stafford's house," she said.

"We haven't any CCTV of you turning back," Black said.

"I didn't use the main road," Sylvie replied. "I used the back lanes. There aren't any cameras there. I parked outside the village and walked to Fenn Farmhouse. No one was around. The window to the room I'd been in with him was open. The room was empty. I climbed in and waited for Stafford."

"Whereabouts in the room did you wait?"

She hesitated. "By the window. What does it matter? When he came back and found me waiting, he asked what did I think I was doing? I told him I wasn't going to let him treat us badly any more. He told me to get out. Said hateful things. The candlestick was within reach. I picked it up and hit him. I didn't plan it, it just happened. I couldn't help myself. I hit him and he fell down."

"Didn't he try to defend himself?"

"He'd turned his back."

"How many times did you hit him, Mme Laurent?" Black asked.

"I can't remember. Once, twice, three times. What does it matter?"

"Where did the blows strike?"

"I can't be sure. His head. It was his fault. He was so cruel, I lashed out. A blow landed and he fell down."

"You hit him at least once and he fell down?"

"Yes. I might have hit him again when he was on the ground. It's still a blur."

"Then what?" Black said.

"I climbed out of the window. I couldn't very well use the door, could I?" she said. "I ran down the garden to the back. I thought I hadn't been seen, but I hadn't reckoned on Martin Mills turning up. I stopped dead in my tracks when I saw him. He was just standing there, staring straight at me. At first I thought it was Stafford back from the dead, but it was a different man. He was looking at the candlestick. I still had hold of it. Blood was dripping from it. The look on his face – I'll never forget it. He turned and ran. He kept stopping to look over his shoulder. He had the start on me. I thought I wouldn't catch him, but at the park, he fell over. Poor man." She lowered her head. "I now realise he'd had a heart attack, but at the time I believed he'd tripped. I was in a blind panic. I had to make sure he was dead. What else was I meant to do? I was the one who strangled him and dragged his body to the hut. I left it there, and hid the candlestick. It's a miracle nobody saw me. I returned to my car, changed back and drove to my neighbour's house as though nothing had happened."

"How did you strangle Martin Mills?"

"I used his tie."

"He wasn't found with a tie."

"I took it with me."

"What did you do with it?"

"I don't remember."

"Did you do anything else?"

She paused. "Such as?"

"Did you do anything else to ensure he was dead?"

She hesitated. "I hit him with the candlestick to make sure."

"Where?"

"Where what?"

"Where on the body did you strike him, Mme Laurent?" Black said.

"Across his head."

"He wasn't found with head injuries."

"I couldn't bring myself to hit him with any strength."

"Was the shed locked or unlocked?" Black asked.

She studied him before answering. "I got inside, didn't I?"

"Yes, but did you break in or was the door unlocked?"

"I pushed at the door until it opened."

"Once inside, what did you do with the body?"

Again she studied him, but again he gave nothing away. "Left it under an old sheet. No – tarpaulin," she corrected herself. This didn't mean anything. The fact Martin Mills' body had been found under tarpaulin in a shed had appeared in at least one report online that Black knew of. "I prayed he'd be mistaken for a tramp who died of the cold. I secured the shed."

"How did you secure the shed?"

"I didn't. I just made it look as though I had."

"How did you dispose of the candlestick, Mme Laurent?"

Another pause as she collected her thoughts. "I hid it as best I could. It was quite big. I don't remember where. Everything's a blur. Killing Stafford was bad enough, but a man who had done nothing? It was a horrible, horrible thing to do."

"Yet you say you did it, Mme Laurent," Black said.

"I hate myself for it. I will take my guilt to my grave."

"When you returned to Fenn Farmhouse, did you do so intending to slay Stafford Mills?" Black asked.

"I returned to confront him for his cruelty. No more."

"Yet you'd changed outfits?"

"I thought you would ask me this. I feared no one would come to the door if they saw me arrive. Arriving on foot seemed the best answer, but my outfit wasn't suitable to trudge through fields and woods – therefore I changed."

And I thought Jeremy Havelock had an answer for everything, Black thought. "What did you change into?

"A tracksuit and trainers."

In the incident room Eden stood arms folded, shaking her head, while Pilot stormed around, rolled his eyes and waved his arms about in fury at Sylvie Laurent's 'confession'. Judy McDermott, more used to people explaining forensic evidence away, than the lack of it, sat at the far end of the table, her elbows rested on it, her face cupped in her hands, frowning in concentration.

"A mother bear will die protecting her cubs," she said.

"What did you do with the tracksuit and trainers afterwards?" Black asked Sylvie Laurent.

"I hurled them out of the window on my way home."

"One at a time?"

"You ask a lot of questions, Detective Inspector."

"Strange, that."

"I stuffed them in a shopping bag and dropped it out of the window. I couldn't say where exactly. Martin's tie was in there, too."

"Did you use any particular shopping bag?"

"A plastic supermarket bag."

"She's so lying!" Pilot said, arching his back and tearing at his hair in frustration. "The timing doesn't work, Stafford Mills was hit from above. Martin Mills wasn't on the ground when he was strangled. His body was carried not dragged. She can't even say where she hid the candlestick."

"Everything we've kept back," Eden said.

In exasperation, Pilot spun a complete 360°.

"We'll need you to return to the scene to retrace your movements," Black said. "See if we can gather any forensic evidence to support your story."

"Stafford's death was an accident. Manslaughter. His brother's death was a tragedy. I wish neither had happened." She banged her chest with her hand.

"Why are you confessing now, Mme Laurent?"

"I kept the truth from you to protect my son, but by continuing to lie, I only hurt him. It's time to tell the truth."

"Do you wish for a lawyer to be present when I charge you, Mme Laurent?" Black said.

She shook her head and said, very assertively, "I do not."

"Mme Sylvie Laurent, you are charged that on Monday the seventeenth of…"

By the time Black rejoined the team in the incident room, Pilot had worked himself into a frenzy. "She's a liar," he said. "Sir." He snatched Sylvie Laurent's phone from the table, and waved it in the air. "Soon as she came off the phone to Eden, she was checking out inheritance law. She knows full well he'll inherit even if she goes down."

"That doesn't mean she isn't telling the truth," Black said, taking a seat. "As she said herself, it gives her all the more reason to be honest."

"Where does poor Bridget White fit in?" Eden said.

"Not sure she does," Black said. He met Judy's eye. "What says you?"

"Had her confession matched halfway what we have, I'd be willing to believe her. But it doesn't. It's ludicrous. It's all over the place. There's gaps, memory lapses, key facts missing." She gave a sigh. "That said, we have a confession. I'll get Press to issue a statement to the effect, emphasising that our investigations are continuing and urging the public to come forward with any new information. In particular, the whereabouts of a plastic bag containing a tracksuit, muddy trainers and a tie."

"I'm going to re-interview the key suspects," Black announced. "One of them is keeping something from me. I can feel it in my bones."

46

The first one back in the interview room was Captain Jeremy Havelock, accompanied by his lawyer. "Let's go back to the morning of Monday the seventeenth – the day of Stafford Mills' death," Black said. "We don't know where Stafford Mills was for at least forty minutes. About the same time you say you were jogging. Any idea where he got himself?"

"Why would I?"

"There's a gap in your timeline straddling the same period."

"If you're suggesting I met up with him again, you're wrong. I didn't have any reason to kill Stafford. I had what I'd come for." He raised and lowered his hands.

"Let me propose an alternative, Captain Havelock," Black said. "Stafford Mills invited you to return later that morning intending to pay you off. You returned wanting more than he was prepared to offer, you argued, killed him and took off."

"I didn't."

"Bit of a coincidence Martin Mills showing up in Osborne Tye the same day you did."

"Where is this going, Detective Inspector?" Jeremy Havelock's lawyer asked.

"Captain Havelock, did you conspire with Martin Mills to kill Stafford Mills?"

"No! Why would I?"

"Revenge? Martin Mills was a wealthy man. He'd see you well rewarded."

"You've got the brothers confused, Detective Inspector. Martin Mills wasn't the revenge sort," Jeremy said.

"Perhaps you were only meant to talk to Stafford and report back to Martin, but things had escalated and Martin, man of principle as we know he was, couldn't be relied upon to keep his mouth shut?"

"I was at the farmhouse for money. Nothing else."

"Did you know Martin Mills owned a Picasso?" Black asked.

"Not 'til it was on the news. After his body turned up."

"Come now, Captain," Black said. "Martin Mills never boasted of scoring one over his brother?"

"You really didn't know Martin," he said. "To say Martin was private was an understatement."

"What about Stafford? He not say anything?"

"Stafford would never have wanted anyone to know Martin was set to inherit more than him."

"Again, Detective Inspector, where is this line of questioning leading? My client has already denied involvement."

"I'm wondering if your client, having killed Stafford Mills, decided to do the same to Martin to steal the Picasso hardly anyone else knew about?"

"A third party has confessed to the murder of Stafford Mills and the attempted murder of his brother," the solicitor said. "I must ask you to stop these outrageous accusations. My client has already denied involvement."

"Did you ever meet Mrs Bridget White, Captain Havelock?" Black asked.

"The lady found dead in the outhouse?" Jeremy asked.

"Mrs White lived at Fenn Farmhouse and was there on the morning Stafford Mills died and was also present during the reconstruction of the murder. It's quite possible Mrs White witnessed something on the morning of the murder, but either forgot or didn't realise its significance until the reconstruction jogged her memory," Black said.

"Now what are you insinuating, Detective Inspector?" Jeremy Havelock's solicitor asked.

"That rather than ring us, she approached the killer with a proposition, her silence for..." Black, interrupted by Jeremy Havelock quietly resting his fists on the table and getting to his feet.

His voice quavered as he spoke, his fists still on the table. "I'm a bad husband, a bad father, a bad friend, a bad army officer, a drunk, a liar, a cheat, a perjurer and a blackmailer. What I'm not is a killer. Singular or multiple."

"How did you feel when you learned Stafford Mills had blackmailed your fiancée into sex, Mr Stanton?" Black asked.

"Devastated. Still am." He looked around. "Was it in this very room you told me? Seems an age ago now. Jenna hasn't stopped crying."

"Was she in tears when she came back from the hotel that day?"

"Wasn't there. She was in the bath when I got back."

"Did you notice anything different about her behaviour that day?"

"She was upset. Explained it away as an elderly family friend dying."

"Where had you come back from, Mr Stanton?" Black said.

Aidan knew the police asked the same questions more than once, shaping them slightly differently each time. Give a man enough rope…

"I walked to choir practice, and waited, wondering where everyone else was. Eventually someone messaged to say choir practice was cancelled and didn't I know? As I was already there, I hung around, trying one of my own pieces out to test the acoustics, then went home. I couldn't have followed Jenna to the hotel that evening even if I'd suspected her, Detective Inspector. We only have the one car, see."

"How did Stafford Mills appear on the morning of his death?"

"More obnoxious and patronising than normal. Jenna said it was because he was on the back foot."

"We're missing forty minutes in Stafford Mills' timeline on the morning of his death, Mr Stanton. Might you be able to shed any light?"

"'Fraid not," he said. He knew where this was going. What had really passed in that room between himself and Stafford Mills? Had Stafford hinted about the hotel tryst? Or more? Boasted? Gloated? Ridiculed? Had Jenna broken down and confessed? Had he, Aidan Stanton, somehow learned the truth and become a killer?

"I know where you're going with this, Detective Inspector. I had no sane reason to kill Stafford Mills, until I sat in here and you gave me one, by which time he was already dead. He was alive when I left. I was at home when Stafford Mills was murdered, God strike me dead if I lie." God didn't and the conversation continued. "Jenna can't have either. She'd've been covered in blood, and she wasn't."

"When was the last time you saw Bridget White?"

"Heavens above," Aidan Stanton replied. "That's a good question. I haven't seen Bridget, Brenda or Hector since they moved into the caravan, although Jenna did her hair, I think. Sad about what happened. She was never going to make old bones, that one. Even so. We went to the caravan park to pay our respects when we heard. Jenna was devastated. All these deaths," he said, brushing his hair away from his eyes. "Whatever is happening to our lovely village?"

Tim Smith scowled at Guido Black. "My sister and brother-in-law claim two of your officers turned up on their doorstep demanding their passports and their marriage certificate. I appreciate you have a job to do, but a call first might have been nice."

"Please pass on my apologies for any distress caused, Mr Smith," Black said. "I've asked you here to touch base with you. Let's start with the candlesticks. Why pick them as a present, Mr Smith?"

"Why not? Two big birthdays, and one silver anniversary. Not much comes in pairs silver-wise but candlesticks and condiments. Candlesticks are nicer."

"Tell me again your movements on the morning of Stafford Mills' death, if you'd be so kind, Mr Smith," Black said.

"Where would you like me to start?"

"You can skip the breakfast and toothbrushing bit."

"My appointment was at eleven-thirty. I left home at just past the hour. The traffic was on my side as it turned out, and I was slightly early. I'd taken hold of the door knocker when the door swung open, nearly taking me with it. Mills was on the other side. I nearly fell on him. He demanded to know what the hell I was doing, or some such thing, and I said I was only trying to buy some candlesticks. I recall he stared at me for a bit." He pointed at Black. "Looking back, I think he saw something of Sarah in me. I didn't at the time, but now I do. He took me through to the candlesticks. I made a play of examining them. Nothing looked glaringly wrong. I made the offer. He accepted. I asked for his details and heard that name. No way were there two Stafford Mills in the world – no way!"

Tim Smith closed his eyes. "I'd waited so long, gone over and over in my mind what I'd say, if I got the chance…" He opened his eyes and leant forward. "I couldn't remember a word of it, dammit. Not a word. And there was so much I needed to get off my chest. He asked if I was going to pay up or just stand there gawping? That snapped me out of it. 'Have you ever lived in London?' I asked him. 'What kind of a question is that?' he said. I held my ground. I told him my daughter Sarah had once worked for a man called Stafford Mills, who'd abandoned her pregnant. He pressed his fingers into my chest and said, 'I don't know what your problem is. Do you want the fucking candlesticks or don't you?' I told him not to touch me. My daughter had died because of him. He told me to get out or he'd call the police." Tim Smith threw his head back, brushing his hair away from his face.

"Mr Smith, there were a number of other people coming and going from Fenn Farmhouse that morning. Before the morning of the seventeenth had you ever come across any of them?" Black said.

"Other than the poor lady I nearly knocked over, and the man I yelled at, I hadn't realised there were any others."

"You went straight to the Speckled Hen on the high street after leaving the farmhouse?" Black said.

"Straight there. Didn't pass Go or collect one hundred pounds."

"And you stayed there?"

"Not this again, Detective Inspector," he said wearily, running his hand through his hair, and again sweeping it back from his face. "I was in the pub when he was attacked. How could I have known the pub would be deserted? The barrel needed changing? I would have been covered in blood splatters. There would have been mud on the base of my shoes. There wasn't. You haven't any forensics linking me because it wasn't me."

"Mr Smith, did your daughter ever mention Stafford Mills' brother, Martin?" Black said.

"Would you like to see a photograph of her, Detective Inspector? My Sarah." Without another word he reached into his wallet and produced a photograph of himself sandwiched between two smiling woman, approximately a generation apart. "That's my Sarah," he said. "With me and her mum. Before you ask, yes there have been other relationships over the years. Some lasted longer than others. Didn't work out. No one's fault. Couldn't see beyond Jayne. A friend suggested online dating. Said I was a bit stuck in my ways for that, but the real reason is quite simple. I don't want to be happy without Sarah and Jayne. I want to stay unhappy. That way I'll never forget them. To answer your question – no, Sarah didn't ever mention a Martin Mills. She never referred to Stafford Mills by name, let alone his brothers or sisters. We weren't meant to know anything. Were they two of a kind? Stafford Mills and his brother?"

"In what sense?" Black said.

"The psychotic sense."

"You think Stafford Mills was a psychopath?"

"He didn't feel any guilt or remorse for what he'd done to Sarah, or Jayne. In my mind that makes him a psychopath."

"Do you believe in the death penalty, Mr Smith?"

He laughed. "Now there's a loaded question if I ever heard one. The answer is yes, I do, Detective Inspector, but only by due process of the law. I won't lie to you – whoever did this has my sympathy – but I'm not an anarchist."

"Martin Mills' body was discovered halfway between Stafford Mills' farmhouse and the Speckled Hen," Black said.

"So I heard. What of it?"

"It's possible Stafford Mills' killer was in league with someone and got a message to the accomplice that the deed was done, but there was a witness who needed to be dealt with," Black suggested.

"Detective Inspector, this is getting more and more absurd. If you're suggesting I was in league with the killer, may I remind you, you took my phone, my clothes, my shoes, my car, my computer – everything. How could anybody have messaged me without you finding out?"

"You might have more than one phone."

Tim Smith sank back into the chair. "Your search team can't be up to much if I did."

"Allow me to propose another scenario, Mr Smith," Black said. "You were the lookout. Martin Mills showed up at the wrong moment. You went after him. He was a very ill man. He couldn't outrun you. He sat down for breath. You strangled him. He didn't put up a fight and you returned to the pub without a mark on you."

Tim Smith stared back in amazement. "I don't know what to say any more, Detective Inspector. I really don't. How could I have been the lookout? I didn't leave the pub. I'm hardly likely to have staged an argument with Stafford Mills if I was to return as a look-out, now would I? Credit me with some common sense." He closed his eyes and inhaled a few times. "Detective Inspector – I've been as honest as I can with you. I know how it looks. Years after Mills did me a terrible injury, I turn up at his place, we argue, he's murdered. I wouldn't believe it myself, had it not happened to me, but it's the truth. Stafford Mills was alive when I left him. Am I glad he's dead? No, not really. I thought I would be, but I'm not. I haven't slept a whole night since. This whole thing has dredged up all sorts of memories I thought well buried. I keep seeing my Sarah and Jayne and hearing his voice: 'Oh, yes. Now I remember. That was all very unfortunate. Still, can't be helped...'"

Tim Smith looked up at the ceiling in despair. "My previous history with the victim and my presence in his house on the morning of his murder are terrible coincidences. Nothing more." He got to his feet. Black realised he was crying. "You can't imagine what this has been like for me all these years. Nobody can. If you want to speak to me again, Detective Inspector, you must do so in the presence of a lawyer."

Corrine Beechwood was accompanied by her lawyer.

"Mrs Beechwood, we still don't know where Stafford Mills was for part of the time you claim to have been at the viaduct," Black said. "Was he with you?"

"No comment," Corrine said.

"Mrs Beechwood, if you and Stafford met on the morning of his death, now is the time to tell us."

"No comment."

"If you and Stafford argued, now is the time to tell us."

"No comment."

"If you went to Fenn Farmhouse on the day of Stafford Mills' death, now is the time to tell us."

"No comment."

"If you struck him with that candlestick, now is the time to tell us."

This time she did no more than pointedly look away.

"Where were you on the morning of Stafford Mills' murder, Mrs Beechwood?" Black asked. "At a viaduct contemplating your future, or at your former boyfriend's home, in a violent struggle?"

"No comment."

In the interview room Jenna Nesbitt continuously clenched and unclenched her hands, staring down at them as if they could provide some solution to her private torment.

"Is there something you want to tell me, Miss Nesbitt?" Black said gently.

"I don't know why I'm here," she mumbled, looking up. "I thought that lady confessed."

"There are some irregularities in the timeline, and our investigations are continuing."

Jenna sighed audibly and lowered her head again. She replayed her boyfriend's words in her mind – 'Just tell the truth, Jen, or they'll trip you up.' She stretched out her hands and put them together as though in prayer, threading the fingers of one hand through the fingers of the other. Stop doing that, she thought, undoing them and gripping the armrests to steady herself. As she looked down, her hair fell about her face and she swept it away. She looked back up – a rabbit caught in headlights.

"I went back earlier than I said," she said.

Black sighed. "This is the second time you've changed your story, Jenna," he said.

She opened her mouth to speak, only to close it again. She let go of the chair and looked as though she was about to begin clenching and unclenching her hands again, then thought better of it, and clasped the chair rests instead. "I'm sorry."

"Go on," he said.

She looked down and up again, peering at him through her hair. "After we left that morning, Aidan and I went home, like we said, but I went straight out again. Aidan was playing the piano in the back and didn't hear me go. Stafford wouldn't give me the cutlery back. He said I wasn't going to get away that easily. He told me to meet him in the cottages round the back at eleven. The ones he'd just renovated."

"He told you this when?"

"At the hotel. Afterwards. I begged him, but he wouldn't budge. That's why he said nothing to Aidan when he went round."

"Was Stafford Mills waiting there for you?" Black said.

"I don't know. I never got there. I couldn't. I got as far as the greenhouse at the end of the garden, but my legs wouldn't go any further. It was worse than last time. I never thought he'd go through with it at the hotel, never mind make me do it again. I sat in the greenhouse. No one saw me through all the pots and cuttings. It was lovely and warm. I didn't know what to do. Call Stafford's bluff? Fess up to Aidan? I don't know how long I was there, I honestly don't, but I was still there when the ambulance arrived."

"Did you see anybody in the garden? On the path or the fields?" Black asked.

She shook her head. "You can't see the fields from there. I saw Bridget pass by with Dandelion. She must have sensed me because she tried to get in to say hello, but Bridget pulled her back. I don't think she saw me. I was still there when she came back. I'd decided to tell Aidan everything, when I heard the ambulance and went to see what was happening." She looked up through her hair again. "To tell the truth, I was hoping Stafford had had a heart attack or something. I don't mean I wanted him dead or anything," she added hurriedly, "just really, really sick."

"Jenna, when was the last time you saw or spoke to Bridget White?"

"I did her hair the day before she died. Some people are saying she jumped, but I don't see it myself," she said. "You don't have your hair done if you're going to top yourself, do you?"

"What do you believe happened to Bridget?"

"She fell. It was a tragic accident."

"Bridget was in possession of quite a lot of money – do you know how she might have acquired it?"

"She didn't say anything about money. She was excited because she'd been dry for the longest ever. She really thought she could do it this time. I was really happy for her. It was brilliant. I'd never seen her so happy, or so sober," she added. "That's what makes it so sad."

"We're working on the theory that Bridget White saw somebody at or near Fenn Farmhouse on the morning Stafford Mills died, which she initially dismissed or forgot until the reconstruction triggered her memory. It's possible she was at the outhouse that night to meet someone," Black said.

Jenna Nesbitt nearly fell off her seat. "Bridget was pushed? Oh my God! Brenda said she fell. Is that why you asked me about the money? Oh my God!" she repeated, then burst into tears. "After Aidan, she was my best friend. Aidan's right. We have to get away. Everything here's ruined."

47

B y a flowing river, as the morning sun rose from beyond a bank of trees, Guido Black leaned back in a canvas chair. He was there primarily to fish, but part of the pleasure for him was to see the sun slowly climb, heralded by the dawn chorus, its rays caught in the clear lapping water. This really was his favourite spot. The river, wide and straight, fringed with reeds, ran past his outstretched legs and curved away in the distance. A stick caught in the current rushed by, belying the river's stillness. Behind him, the riverbank, cut in two by a well-worn path, rose gently into a flat landscape. Above him, the solitary branch of the long dead tree he sat under, jutted out over the river, almost parallel with Black's cast fishing line. He loved it here, miles from anywhere, at this time of day. With only himself for company he could lose himself in his thoughts.

He closed his eyes. He heard only birds, insects, the running river, his breathing… and the sound of footsteps clomping along the river path. He glanced over his shoulder and gave a wry grin. "Thought I'd find you here," Chloe said, kissing the top of his head. "Your note helped." She was dressed in jeans, a wax jacket, patterned gardening boots and a tweed cap, and lugged a chill box.

"Very Glastonbury," he said.

She put the chill box on the bank and unfolded a second canvas chair, plonking herself next to him. "Thought you'd like breakfast before you go to work," she said, reaching for a thermos flask. Black tipped the remains of his lukewarm coffee away and refilled his mug as Chloe unwrapped a warm bread loaf from under its many layers of foil. Steam rose from it. She cut two thick slices, buttered them then sprinkled them liberally with chocolate sprinkles. Black helped himself to a slice. "Can I eat it or do you want to photograph it first?" he said, holding the slice of toast, chocolate and butter melting from it before his lips, poised to take a bite.

"Wouldn't mind a riverside shot of us first," she replied.

He'd got home so late and left so early, they hadn't seen each other the night before. "Shine even more sunshine onto my day, Loveliness, and tell me you've found a new home for the rooster?" he said. She took a mouthful of her hagelslag. He waited for her to finish, but she took another. "Chloe, I work shifts. We have neighbours."

She looked at him. "Fear not. Turns out our catering assistant lives on a farm and re-homes battery hens. She's promised to take him. In exchange, I'm going to show her how to use the iPad her daughter bought her. It lives in a drawer at the mo. I'm taking Red over to hers tonight. Thought I'd make him a special meal, as it's his last night."

Black grinned. "Is he really going to live on a farm, or are you trying to shield me from his real fate?"

Elsewhere, in a semi-detached house on a suburban street, Eden Hudson woke with a jolt and sat bolt upright.

"My God!" she said to herself. She fell more than jumped out of bed, pulling the clothes she'd worn the day before out of the laundry basket and throwing them on. She didn't have time for niceties. Why the hell hadn't she seen it earlier?

48

B lack walked into the incident room to hear a colleague ask Pilot how his date with Haylee had gone the evening before. Black's keen detective skills told him things hadn't gone well. There were many clues: the young detective groaning at the question, burying his face in his hands, shaking his head and replying: "It was worse than the worst disaster!" chief amongst them.

Black couldn't help but join the half-sympathetic, half-schadenfreude crowd gathered around Pilot's desk. Was he about to be regaled with some ludicrous tale of a deranged Uber driver or a flyaway market stall, he wondered. He looked around, vaguely wondering where Eden had got to, but putting it from his mind.

"I'll start at the start," Pilot said, sitting on his desk, his feet on his chair. "Mace went straight to Pilates from work, giving me time to shower and iron my shirt. I decided against aftershave."

"Best not on a first date," someone said.

"Then I put some on," he said. Glances were exchanged. "I left the flat in plenty of time, feeling pretty good about things. Bus turned up on time and on I got. You'll never guess what happened next?"

"George Clooney was on the bus and you introduced him to Haylee, cos you know she's a fan and now he's ditched Amal for her," a colleague suggested.

"If only. Mace was on the bus, wasn't she? My presence on the number thirty-two made her suspicious, given I'd told her I was going to my brothers and the thirty-two isn't the bus to his. 'Thought you were going to your brothers?' she said. These young city slicker types were sitting behind her. They grinned at me in a – You're so busted mate – way. Told her we were meeting in the pub. Get a few beers in before the match. Now, I thought Mace walked to Pilates, so I said: 'Thought you walked to Pilates?' It was a diversionary tactic much as anything. She didn't bat an eyelid. Said Pilates was cancelled, then she noticed my shirt. 'You can iron!' It felt like the whole bus was listening – I'm sure I heard the driver snigger. I jumped off at the next stop. The guys behind us got off too. Soon as the bus turned the corner, I was back at the stop. 'Enjoy your evening!' they yelled. I had to wait ages for the next bus. Wasn't sure Haylee would hang around that long, but I saw her through the pub window. She was at the bar. I straightened myself and heaved myself through the door, and who d'ya think I saw? And no, not George Clooney. It was Mace! With her tongue down some bloke's throat."

"Cripes!" another of those gathered around his desk said. "What did you do?"

"Legged it. I texted Haylee some excuse, but it was too late – she'd seen me. So that's over before it started. I'm no angel," he said. "But Mace's been going to Pilates for about a year. No wonder she's too tired all the time."

"You tried talking to her?"

"What's the point? She clearly likes her other bloke more than she likes me." He looked so dejected and miserable it was impossible not to feel sorry for him. A female colleague put her arms around him. "Bit unlucky you all ending up at the same place," she said.

"Not really," one of the team said. "I bumped into a school friend I hadn't seen in fifteen years in Prague last year."

"Know what hurts the most?" Pilot said. "Mace led me up the garden path, and I was thick enough to let her."

Black clicked his fingers. Back at the riverbank that morning, Chloe had said something that had stuck in his mind as relevant to the case, but until this moment he hadn't been sure of its significance. It wasn't only Pilot who'd been led down the garden path. He grasped Pilot by the shoulders. "Know what mends a broken heart best, son?" he said. "Hours of CCTV."

49

"To go from denying responsibility for either attack to claiming both, is quite a leap, Mme Laurent," Black said. "Let's wind back. Following a chance meeting, Stafford Mills invited you to lunch to discuss your son, an invitation you kept. Stafford greeted you warmly and acted as though the argument, the tail end of which you'd witnessed, hadn't happened. You hadn't been long in his company when he took exception to something you said and flew into a rage. When you tried to reason with him, he physically ejected you from the room. Shaken, you started for home. Does this part of your version of events remain unchanged?"

"It does," Sylvie Laurent said. She was accompanied by her lawyer.

"However, as you waited at the garage for your tank to fill you grew so angry over his behaviour that you decided to return and confront him?"

"Yes."

"And therefore you returned by an entirely different route to the farmhouse than the one you had just used."

"Yes."

"Most people, and without wishing to sound sexist Mme Laurent, certainly most women, would have gone back the way they came. Not you. You headed back cross-country without the help of satnav, to somewhere you'd been only the once, without getting lost."

"I've always enjoyed a good sense of direction."

"A statement which flatly contradicts your earlier one when you put getting lost in Trowchester down to a poor sense of direction," Black reminded her. She didn't reply and he continued. "You parked outside Osborne Tye, changed into an outfit you conveniently had in the car, and walked to the farmhouse, where you climbed through a conveniently open window without leaving a trace of mud, and waited for Stafford. The argument which followed his reappearance was so heated it ended with you hitting him across the skull with a candlestick, yet it was heard by no one. Despite his being more than able to defend himself, he made no attempt to do so, and the blow proved fatal."

"I've told you what happened," she replied tersely.

"I'm trying to get my head around what you say happened, Mme Laurent," Black said. "Have I got my facts right thus far?" She nodded. "Deed done, you left through the open window, leaving no trace of the blood that was on the candlestick you carried, or of any blood that would undoubtedly have spattered on to you when you hit Stafford with it, and made your way across the back garden to the bridlepath at its rear, without being seen by any of the people we know were around. Halfway down the garden you came face-to-face with poor Martin Mills. He took one look at you and the bloodied candlestick in your hand, and fled. You chased him for some distance, and he dropped down dead. You throttled him for good measure, locked his body in a shed, and scarpered. All in broad daylight, and without being seen. You disposed of the murder clothes, which remain missing despite our retracing every conceivable route you could've taken, and calmly arrived at your neighbour's house an hour later than either she or her home help say you did."

"That I believe I can explain. They were trying to help me."

"By providing a false alibi? A serious allegation to make, Mme Laurent."

"I'm not suggesting they lied. Only that they made a genuine mistake, not believing me capable of such an act. I believe they were confused."

"They're not the only ones," Black said. "Our forensics indicate Stafford Mills was sitting down when attacked but you say he was on his feet."

Her lawyer shot her sideways look.

"Your forensics are wrong," Sylvie said.

"Martin Mills wasn't prone on the ground when attacked, as your version has it, but either sitting or leaning against something."

She did no more than shrug.

"Martin Mills wasn't dragged over grass to the shed, he was carried," Black said.

"I carried him. I," she hesitated, "misspoke."

Her lawyer intervened. "Sylvie has admitted manslaughter, Detective Inspector," she said. "We concede there are inconsistencies, but this is very difficult for her. She's doing her best."

"When people act on impulse, they leave traces behind. The lack of any evidence linking your client to the attacks, suggests forward planning. People don't plan manslaughter."

"I didn't plan anything," Sylvie said.

"You've struggled for a long time, haven't you, Sylvie?" Black said. "A single mother on state benefits, without a penny of support from your son's wealthy father. The agony of other people's kids getting all the stuff you wanted for Pierre but couldn't afford. Do the other boys tease him about being poor?"

"Don't you dare use Sylvie's love of her son to trip her up," the lawyer said. "She's told you what happened."

"Your love for your son shines through Sylvie," Black said. "Your willingness to go to jail for a long time for something which couldn't have happened the way you suggest, proves that."

"It isn't a bit of wonder your legs buckled underneath you, Pierre, when you were with your headmaster," Eden said to the boy facing her across the interview room desk, flanked by his solicitor, Kevin Calderstone, and a court-appointed social worker. "Your headmaster gently sat you down and explained your dad had been found with head injuries from which he'd died. How had he ended up with head injuries? You were the last one out the door, and there wasn't a mark on him when you left. In fact, such a clean job had been made of things, there was always the chance it might pass as natural. Not a bit of wonder you dropped your phone."

"My client was at school all morning, gaming, and was in the canteen when his father was brutally murdered," Kevin Calderstone said.

"That was a bit of luck, wasn't it, Pierre?" Eden said. "No wonder you burst into tears. Dad was dead, and you and mum weren't in the frame. Now that's what I call a result."

Pierre cupped his hands under his chin, resting it on them. "Mum killed Dad," he said.

"No she didn't, Pierre," Eden said.

"She did so, and Uncle Martin was alive when she did it. Everything she did, she did for me."

"That I don't doubt for an instant."

"You didn't chance upon Stafford Mills during a visit to Trowchester, Mme Laurent," Black said. "You hunted him down as though a dog. You'd searched his name on-line. Came across his company and the property renovation. The day you and Stafford Mills met in Trowchester was no coincidence."

"Detective Inspector, I've seen your ANPR records for Sylvie's car, and her search history. You've nothing to support this," Sylvie's solicitor said.

"It's difficult to be a brilliant murderer in the modern age. CCTV, Automatic Number Plate Recognition, facial recognition, digital fingerprints, phone masks, on top of everything else. I couldn't figure it out at first, until I heard about an old lady who keeps an unused iPad in a drawer – and the penny dropped. We'd been looking for Sylvie's car, and at Sylvie's Internet history," Black said, "when we should have been looking for Sylvie's neighbour's car, and Sylvie's neighbour's Internet history. The virtually house-bound old lady you visit daily, Sylvie, and whose car I now learn you regularly take out for a spin to keep the battery charged."

"I'm not the only one to take the car out. She gives the keys to anyone."

"You're the only one with a reason to keep returning to Trowchester," he said. Sylvie's lawyer shot another sideways glance at her client. "You stalked Stafford Mills. Hanging around in the waste ground next to the development. Watching him, snapping him through the long telephoto lenses – the kind the Paparazzi use to snap unsuspecting celebrities – we know you bought in your neighbour's name. You saw him come and go. You saw him parked in the drive. You saw him on his phone, on his laptop. You got his access code. Eventually you were ready, and off you went to the show house disguised as a potential buyer. He, oblivious to your identity, not having set eyes on you for years, and your appearance altered for the day, cheerily invited you inside. He showed you around, chatting away, until you asked him if it wasn't about time he did more for his son. He, little realising the request was made on a do-or-die basis, flew into a rage, threatened you with lawyers and threw you out. All recorded by you."

Sylvie clapped. "And why did I want so much to kill my son's father?" she said dryly. "How did I know his younger brother was a secret millionaire without a will or a family and without long to live? Please do explain."

"Good question, Mme Laurent," Black said. "You're training as a textile designer, yes?"

"What of it?"

"Where's the one place textile designers swarm to? The V&A. We know you've been there, more than once. And we know the route you took."

"I'm afraid you're losing me, Detective Inspector," Sylvie said. Beside her, her lawyer looked more and more intrigued.

"It wasn't Stafford Mills you chanced upon in the street, Sylvie. It was Martin Mills. And it wasn't a street, it was the London Underground. South Kensington is the nearest tube line for both the V&A and the Royal Marsden Hospital, where Martin Mills was being treated for cancer."

Black picked up the remote and pointed it towards the screen on the wall where an image appeared of adjacent stairs in an underground station, divided by a railing, with crammed commuters streaming up and down either side. "The suspect is being shown CCTV image marked SM:1659 taken at South Kensington tube station on the date shown," he said. "The man circled in blue ascending the stairs towards the exit of South Kensington High Street has been positively identified as Martin Mills. The lady below the red arrow, descending the same stairs, is you, I believe, Mme Laurent."

In the interview room two sets of eyes watched Sylvie Laurent on the screen suddenly catch sight of someone across the stair rails climbing the station stairs, stop abruptly, stare, take in something, and slowly turn around to push her way back upstairs, against the crowd, her eyes on her target. A different camera catches her hurrying along South Kensington High Street after Martin Mills and Jean Janes. Black stopped the film. "You trailed Martin Mills along Kensington High Street and followed him into the Royal Marsden."

"Even if I did, it proves nothing," Sylvie said. "I didn't speak to him. I wasn't sure it was him. I'd only seen photographs. Just because he was being treated at the Royal Marsden, didn't mean he was dying. Or that Pierre was his heir. For all I knew he had a family."

"Detective Sergeant Hudson showed Martin Mills' landlady your photograph and asked if you'd called at the house. She said you hadn't; nobody had." He called up a recording taken of a waiting area in the Royal Marsden Hospital. In it, Jean Janes could clearly be seen chatting to another woman.

"The suspect is now being shown CCTV image marked SM:1660 recorded by the Royal Marsden Hospital," Black said. "You've changed your appearance a lot since then, Sylvie. The photograph we have of you, the way you look now, quite confused her. Mrs Janes has now identified you as the lady who sat next to her in the hospital waiting room, after Martin had gone in for his appointment, and asked her if she was there with her husband. She told you everything you needed to know, Mme Laurent. She told you her life story, and his. He'd never married. His only hope was a miracle cure. The previous evening's chat about wills. Everything. When you left the hospital it was with one thought on your mind – did Martin still have his mother's Picasso?"

"You're putting thoughts into my client's head, Detective Inspector," Sylvie's solicitor said.

"I knew nothing of this Picasso," Sylvie said.

"Stafford Mills couldn't forgive his mother's favouritism and hated his brother because of it. Your relationship with him was shortly after his mother's death. I don't believe he kept his feelings on the subject to himself. I'm told he didn't stop shouting for a week."

"You can't prove any of this," Sylvie's solicitor said.

"I can prove your client researched Picasso sales on her neighbour's iPad after returning home from London that very day," he replied. He turned to Sylvie Laurent. "Also the rules of intestacy, which you pretended never to have heard of. You knew Martin didn't have a will and that meant Stafford would get the Picasso, unless he died first."

In another interview room, on the other side of the building, Eden said, "Your mum dropped you off at school early, Pierre. You left her chatting to the head, marched upstairs, ran along the corridor, and noisily threw your holdall inside your dormitory and roared off again, ostensibly to meet your mates. In the chaos of cars, taxis, suppliers, buses coming and going on the first day back, no one noticed you slip outside into the extensive wooded grounds. And even if they had, so what? In the woods you retrieved your disguise from its hiding place, and left in its place your PlayStation, carefully setting the timer to run a game you'd played earlier. Disguise on, you slipped out through a gap in the back fence. We found the loosened planks, Pierre, cleverly put back in place. Nobody'd think twice of a schoolboy taking advantage of a gap in a fence – a schoolboy taller than you Pierre, and with longer, darker hair. You met up with your mum, waiting out of sight. On the back seat, you donned protective clothing and hid yourself. At Fenn Farmhouse your mum parked round the corner, changed her shoes and went to the front door, after giving the boot a rap to announce the coast was clear. You jumped out and climbed through the window into your father's room."

"Pierre was at school when his father was attacked," Kevin said.

"Eating lunch," Pierre sneered, leaning back in his seat, legs outstretched, arms folded. "Cottage pie. My fav."

"It's hard enough to get away with murder, Mme Laurent," Black said. "Let alone when there's a connection to the victim and a benefit to the murderer. If Stafford's death didn't bring the police to your door asking all sorts of awkward questions, your son inheriting his wealthy uncle's estate shortly afterwards, was bound to. There was nothing for it, you'd have to hide out in full view. There couldn't be any forensic evidence linking the crime to you, but that was just the start of it. You came up with an idea, and developed it from there. There wasn't much time yet every detail was planned meticulously. A quick search of the local authority revealed plans submitted when the extension was built, giving you a lay of the land. Your plan wasn't perfect, no plan is, but the payout was worth the risk. If enough things fell into place, building a case against you would be difficult, given the imprecise science of the time of death and the lack of forensics."

"You are correct in some of what you say, Detective Inspector," she said. "I saw Martin Mills on the escalator. He looked so ill. I followed him to the hospital. I did speak to that lady. I planned everything. I was at Fenn Farmhouse that day asking Stafford to change his will in Pierre's favour, but he refused. I pretended to leave, doubled back on myself and killed him. That was always my plan. Coming face-to-face with Martin wasn't."

He ignored her. "Having determined to kill Stafford Mills, you had to decide how. Poison? Slipping someone a Mickey Finn isn't as easy as it sounds, and it's detectable. Guns, knives, blunt objects? A forensic dead-end. Stage a car crash? Always opened as a suspected murder. Push the victim from a tall building? Fraught with complications. How to get him or her onto the roof, being just one. Arrange a nasty accident? Might not work. Drug overdose? Highly suspicious in a man who doesn't even smoke. Strangulation? Ah – now we might be getting somewhere. It may leave less evidence than many other methods, particularly at first sight, and leave less forensics on the killer. But strangulation takes strength. Stafford Mills was a big man and you Mme Laurent are a weak and feeble woman. And he was quite a bit taller than you. He'd have fought you off in no time, even taken by surprise."

"I didn't strangle him. I hit him with a heavy object."

"It wasn't only the difference in strength against you, for your alibi to work there had to be witnesses. A voting census search revealed Stafford shared his home with three others, but for that to work, someone other than Stafford had to come to the door to let you in. Stafford had to be engaged elsewhere. You needed someone else on board. You'd never forgotten the publicity following Sarah Smith's tragic death. Tracking down her dad, a clinical research auditor, wasn't too hard. Him going to the police was your biggest risk. The first meeting must've been face-to-face. If he reported you – your word against his. But in the end, he didn't run away in horror."

Tim Smith's voice filled the third interview room: 'You can't imagine what this has been like for me all these years.

Nobody can. I didn't remarry because I don't want to be happy without Sarah and Jayne. I want to stay unhappy. That way I'll never forget them.'

"Sylvie Laurent took full advantage of the empty festering hole inside you, didn't she, Tim?" Judy McDermott said. "She dangled the prospect of revenge under your nose." Judy swung an invisible pendulum in the air. "And it was irresistible."

"No comment."

"What suppressed emotions did she set free in you, Tim?"

"Sylvie Laurent visits Stafford Mills," Black said. "They have a fight. He physically assaults her, she leaves. The body's found, the post-mortem indicates strangulation, the spotlight turns to Sylvie Laurent. But she can't have done it. She's not strong enough, nothing like. Besides, what could she have strangled him with? She came dressed in jeggings, a long-sleeved tight fitting top, finished off with kitten heels. She didn't even have a bag with her. She didn't have anywhere to conceal a ligature, and nothing was found at the scene. Not to mention those witnesses who swore he was alive when she left. The spotlight turns from Sylvie Laurent…" Black waited. She looked him straight in the eye, but said nothing. "You told us you came dressed to impress when we first interviewed you, Sylvie. Dressed to mislead, more like. But wait, I'm getting ahead of myself."

"Little wonder Jenna Nesbitt screaming about Stafford Mills having been found in a pool of blood with his head caved in, rocked you, Mr Smith," Judy McDermott said. "Pool of blood? Head caved in? You left him looking to all the world as though he'd died in his sleep. What the hell had Pierre and his mother got up to after you left? In communication lockdown, there wasn't any way of asking them. You'd just have to bluff it out."

"No comment."

Black continued his questioning of Mme Laurent. "At your neighbour's house you spent hours searching Stafford Mills, but none of those searches would've brought up his Craigslist candlestick advert."

"I knew nothing about those candlesticks until I used one to kill my son's father."

"Oh come on now, Sylvie. Whilst stalking him with those long telephoto lenses we talked about you saw him log into the Craigslist app. He can't have been on his phone. You wouldn't have been able to glean enough detail from that distance, but if he was on his laptop? Ordinarily that wouldn't have told you much more than he used Craigslist, but Stafford Mills was a bit of a security freak. He didn't back anything up, or store passwords on his devices. He logged in from fresh each and every time. It's something we advise. I found a list of passwords jotted down in the back of his notebook. One day, when you were watching, he logged in to Craigslist, and put the candlesticks up for sale. That was a stroke of luck. Gave your accomplice an entirely innocent reason for arriving at the property just before you, that being your biggest hurdle. What brilliant story would you have conjured up otherwise, I wonder?"

"Detective Inspector, I didn't have an accomplice. I acted alone. Stafford Mills was alive when I left the property and alive when I returned to it. There were witnesses, for God's sake," she said.

"The witnesses saw only you, Mme Laurent, not Stafford Mills," Black said. "They were unsighted. They only heard him call through the door, or rather they didn't. What they heard was your son's editing of the recording made on an iPod purchased with your ninety-two-year-old neighbour's credit card. The one you check for her every month."

"I won't listen to any more of this. I demand to be taken back to my cell."

"Did it freak you out, Pierre – coming face-to-face with a dead man?" Eden asked. "Can't have done. You kept your cool and played your part. Tim Smith left. Your dad swearing after him, even though he wasn't in the room." Pierre frowned at her words, confused. She pretended not to notice. "On cue your mum entered. 'Sylvie?' he'd said to her, all those months earlier at the show house when she identified herself, and 'Sylvie?' he said again that morning, the words replayed by you, who, after waiting a few minutes, pushed your own mother out of the door, and replayed at full volume the furious insults your dad had hurled at her months earlier. You gave the door a kick and locked it to be sure. Stafford had his phone with him but he'd left his tablet, allowing you to email: *Show that woman out.* Nice one. After a quick peek out of the curtains, you got out the same way you got in, and jumped back in the car. You must have had a backup plan in case the coast wasn't clear. I imagine your mum would've tripped over or something. Brought people running. Whatever, you got into the car without being seen and your mum dropped you off a few miles down the road and went home. A taxi,

384

booked under a false name dropped you a short walk from your school. You paid in cash and slipped back in the way you'd left, quickly throwing off your disguise. Pierre Laurent again, you collected your PlayStation and ambled back to your room, your disguise and everything you'd taken from the scene, in a rucksack. As soon as the coast was clear you hid the evidence."

"This is all a bit far-fetched, Detective Sergeant," Kevin Calderstone said.

Eden ignored him. "We found these inside your life-sized robot, Pierre," she said, picking up a photograph of a dark wig and platform boots.

"Showing the witness evidence recovered, reference number SM345, dated…" Black said, before showing Sylvie Laurent a black wig. "This wig was recovered from the robot in your son's school bedroom. Strands of the same were found in the boot of your car, Mme Laurent."

She looked disconcerted and glanced away, focusing on the wall behind Black. Making eye contact again, she said, "It's my son's stuff, why shouldn't it be in my car?"

"I'm still not sure where this line of questioning is going, detective sergeant," Kevin Calderstone said. "Pierre was in the school canteen when his dad was attacked."

"All that planning, Pierre," Eden said. "Clandestine meet ups in remote locations. Call as you go phones thrown away every couple of weeks. Letters written, read and burnt. The only digital footprints left behind, those which supported your story. Every detail thrashed out. Everything went according to plan except for one thing. As you tucked into your cottage pie and Tim Smith drank beer in the pub and your mum sipped tea at her neighbours, someone else entered the murder scene, and smashed your dad's head in with a candlestick. Lady luck really was shining, Pierre," Eden said.

"Don't suppose you care much about going to jail, Tim?" Judy said.

"No comment."

"Helping Sylvie and her son secure their inheritance and deprive Stafford Mills of his, gave your daughter the victory over him in death that she didn't get in life. That's what drove you, isn't it? Executing the man you considered responsible for her death came second, otherwise you'd have done it years ago. If you got away with it, well, so much the better. Another victory over Mills. Your history with the man gave you an excuse for a dramatic exit, just as the candlesticks sale gave you an innocent reason for entry. No doubt you'd have come up with another excuse for being there, but the candlesticks were God-given. Had the publican not needed to change the barrel, your alibi would've been unimpeachable. It was the perfect murder. There was only one tiny flaw, Mr Smith. You had no idea what Stafford Mills looked like."

"You might well have got away with it, Sylvie," Black said, "had Stafford Mills actually been in the room that morning."

"Avoiding tax was a game to Stafford Mills. He regularly declared large losses on items he hadn't really sold to set off against the tax owed on his profit, secretly selling the stuff further down the road," Judy explained. "To make sure he didn't trip himself up, he kept a secret record of his transactions. In case the tax office double-checked, he'd get the odd someone to masquerade as a fake buyer, claiming he had to sell more than one item quickly, adding up to a big loss. They didn't need to turn up, a call made to the house booking an appointment made by a staff member was more than sufficient. He'd fill in the blanks. Stafford Mills was never going to sell those candlesticks that day. He was asking a ridiculous price for them. It was one of his declare-a-crushing-loss sales. Not one of his better ideas, as it turned out. The fake appointment left him with spare time and he took himself off somewhere else for a liaison. A liaison which wasn't kept by the other party. Stafford Mills didn't let you in, Mr Smith. He was somewhere else, waiting. Begging the question – how did you really get inside the room?"

"No comment."

Judy rose to her feet and put her hands on the desk, allowing her to lean towards him. "The plan was for you to arrive at the property pretending to be a buyer, wasn't it? It didn't matter whether Stafford let you in himself or one of the live-in staff. Just so long as you got in to see Stafford Mills."

"No comment."

"In the end, no one let you in. No one was about when you turned up. A look in the front window was enough to tell you the hall was empty. You put your head round the corner. No one was there either. You sneaked around the side, and peeped through the first window you came to. And what did you see? Only your nemesis, Stafford Mills, the man you'd come to kill, sound asleep in a chair. This was too good an opportunity to miss. At the window you had a quick look around." Judy looked to one side and then another. "Coast clear, gloves on, you tried the window. It was unlocked. After another shufty," she pretended to look around again, "coast still clear, on went the shoe covers, and in went you, drawing the curtains behind you," This too, she mimicked. "Did tiptoeing across the decking while he slept innocently, feel good? Did it feel even better when you took that tie from your pocket, moved to stand behind him, put it around his neck and tugged?"

"No comment."

"We asked ourselves how could Sylvie ensure she had a witness to her departure from the room?" Black said. "Such an essential part of the plan. I don't doubt there was a backup plan. Pierre ringing the bell and running away, drawing a witness to the front door springs to mind as a possibility. Stafford couldn't very well answer, being dead. As it turned out, Hector came to the door just as the postman arrived. So much fell into your lap. Stafford Mills' offbeat lifestyle gave you a way in, witnesses, alibis."

"The job done, you held your nerve," Judy told Tim Smith. "You heard a car. Two cars! One was Sylvie's, but whose was the other? Never mind whose car it was. You wanted as many witnesses as possible for what was to happen next. You held your nerve. Pierre appeared at the window and climbed in. I imagine you tried to keep him as far away as possible from the body, being at heart a kindly soul. Not that it mattered. Pierre had never met his dad. Just seen a few photos taken way back when," Judy said. "Pierre moved to the door, and as you stormed out yelling, he pressed play,

388

and Stafford Mills' expletives filled the air. Etcetera etcetera etcetera."

Tim Smith smiled ruefully and brushed his hair from his eyes. Judy thought him quite handsome. At this point suspects tended to divide into two camps: the Woebegones, who, realising the game was up, confessed; and the arrogant, who continued lying. Tim Smith fell into neither group. He remained surreally unemotional.

"You're a decent man, Tim," she said. "A million miles from the usual types we have in here. If only life hadn't played such a cruel trick on you. We have a confession. Will you help us?"

"No comment."

"Know your big mistake, Sylvie?" Black said. "There were three people in that murder. It was a bit crowded."

50

"Bridget found Martin on the front doorstep that morning and let him in," Black said. "It's the only thing which makes sense. It wasn't Stafford who told her he had to go in, he'd tell all later, it was Martin. I don't believe she deliberately lied. I think she was genuinely confused. After all, what would Martin be doing on the doorstep? Martin's body turning up like that, just made matters worse. Had she seen him or was her memory playing tricks again? Not trusting your own memory must be a terrible thing."

"If only she'd told me," Brenda Munro said.

"When she and I went for our walk Brenda, she nearly let slip that you and he had been an item. She was about to tell me Martin hadn't let anybody help, even you, but she stopped herself in time, pretending she'd meant his mother. I'm still not sure whether she was protecting you or Martin, but I'm quite sure when she told me Martin didn't do it, she wasn't talking about the car accident, she was talking about Stafford's murder. She was becoming surer of her memory. Him in the house on the morning of the murder, only to then turn up dead nearby, put the two people she loved most in the frame – Martin and you, Brenda."

Eden had provided the final piece in the puzzle. "I just woke up with it in my head," she said. In her hands were two photographs. She held them up, putting one over the other. "This is what they were like in the frame. It looks like one photo. The second one's larger than the front so it's not obvious, even opening the back of the frame." She held the photographs apart for Black to look at. One he recognised as the picture of the woman in fancy dress from Martin Mills' mantelpiece. The one until this moment he'd thought Martin's mother, Cybil. "Martin told Melinka the photograph was of his mother to close down painful questions. Maybe that's why he kept them in one frame?" she said. "Or maybe he just broke a frame and hadn't got around to replacing it. Who knows?" Black looked at the photographs. "Brenda said Cybil Mills was one of the most beautiful women she'd ever seen. But the woman in this photograph," she pointed to the fancy dress photograph, "is attractive rather than beautiful. I don't know why I didn't see it sooner, sir. I've seen Cybil's photo – it was with the plate. That's Brenda," she touched the fancy dress photograph, then the one she'd found below it. "That's Cybil."

Black slid the photograph of Brenda in her younger days dressed up in fancy dress, across the desk. "Martin never stopped loving you," he said. She didn't pick the photograph up, but cupped its edges with her hands and stared fondly at it. "Turn it over," Black said. She did and read Martin's inscription:

Me and Betty Boop in happier days.

"It was his nickname for me. In those days, most people called me Betty, you see. Betty Besthorpe became Betty Boop." She smiled sadly. "We were all set to marry. We had a date, then everything exploded. I never believed it. I told him so. Said I'd stick by him, but he wouldn't see me ruining my life. Said he'd never get a decent job, our children would be shamed. He told me I was still young enough to move on. I didn't let up but my letters all came back." Black's heart went out to this woman. "If only it was me who'd found him at the door? Why couldn't it have been me?"

"What happened, Brenda? When you're ready."

"Dandelion had gone walkabouts and I went outside looking for her, just as he was getting out of his car."

"Are we talking about Captain Jeremy Havelock, Brenda?" Black said.

"Yes, him. I'd recognise that face anywhere, even after all these years. I saw him every day in court. He's got rather fat. I always had him down as the driver. It couldn't have been Stafford – he was somewhere else, that's what everybody said. Couldn't think what he was doing there, but I knew it wouldn't be anything good. The only thing for it was to listen at the window. I decided to give that thing people do in films a go – you know, listening through a glass. I went to the garage for an old paint jar. It was only when I got back that I realised they'd be able to see me. I was going to try it at the other window or the door, when I realised Stafford had drawn the curtains. I heard Aidan and Jen at the front door. I let them go in then snuck up to the window and put the jar to the pane. I was amazed how much I could hear. Not every word by any means, but enough.

"Havelock was saying he had put his neck on the line. Stafford told him to keep his voice down. Heard the words: 'your arse... perjury... Martin...' It was enough. I didn't know what to do. I couldn't face Aidan and Jen so I ran to the outhouse. But I couldn't stay there. That was Bridget's bolt-hole, and she was the last person I wanted to see. It would've taken so long to explain. I ended up in our cottage. I took myself to the bedroom and lay down with a towel over my face. I heard Bridget pottering around. She called out, asking if I was all right, but I ignored her. I heard her leave. It was her who did all the housework. She knew how down I get from time to time, and when I got like that, she always tried to do as much as she could to help out. It was her way of saying thanks. Don't know how long I was there for. I heard Hector shouting across the garden for me. I didn't move. Just lay there, thinking. Stafford had destroyed his brother, and lied for all those years. He swore to me he wasn't in the car when it crashed and I'd believed him."

"When you spoke of the accident to me, I remember you saying: 'You think you know someone.' Was it Stafford Mills you were really speaking of?" Black said.

She nodded sadly. "I decided to confront him. I went round the side of the house so Hector and Bridget wouldn't see me. The hall was empty. I tried the library door, but it was locked. That meant he was inside. Who locks their own internal doors? He did. He didn't trust anyone, that one. I looked through the keyhole, and saw the key. I called out – 'Stafford I know you're in there. I want to speak to you. Now, Stafford.' He'd have known from my tone, I was angry. I thought that's why he didn't come to the door. I wasn't having it. That stuff Hector said about him putting some paper under the door and pushing the key out, was actually me." She touched her chest with her fingers a couple of times. "The wood's so warped it slid out easy. I expected Stafford to jump up asking me what the hell I thought I was doing, but when I went in I saw he was asleep in a chair. I went over to him, to shake him awake, but it wasn't Stafford, it was Martin. I was so surprised to see him. He looked so peaceful. I never dreamed for a minute he was dead. I was trying to wake him up..." she looked away tearfully, "...when Stafford walked in.

He was wittering on. He'd found some email from Hector saying Sylvie Laurent was here. What the hell did she want now? Did my gender ever listen? He stopped in his tracks when he saw Martin. 'Lord in heaven!' he said. 'What the hell's he doing here? First Havelock, then him.' I said we had to call an ambulance, Martin was ill. He checked Martin's pulse and said, 'Too late for that, love.' I told him I knew everything. I'd overheard his conversation with Havelock. Do you know what he said? 'Hardly matters now, does it?' 'Doesn't matter?' I said. 'You betrayed him, and so did I by believing your lies, and now he's dead and I can't make it up to him.'

"He told me to calm down." Typical arrogant rich man, Black thought. "I said I was going to the police and he knew I meant it. He went over to the door and closed it. When he came back, he put his hands on my arms. 'I'm sure we can come to an understanding, Brenda dear,' he said. Come to an understanding," she mocked. "Money. That was his answer for everything. I pushed him away. He didn't push his luck. 'I'll transfer six months' salary, tax-free, to your account straight away, Brenda, and that's just for starters,' he said. I love Hector, Detective Inspector, he's a dear man. He took me and my sister on and never once complained, but Martin and I had our whole lives ahead of us and Stafford stole that from us and his answer was money. People like him don't understand – some things can't be bought. The candlesticks were right there. The sun was beaming right on them. God was telling me what I had to do. He'd just sat down and got his phone out – to make the bank transfer, he said – when I hit him." She smiled to herself. It was a smile of self-satisfaction. "He never saw it coming."

"Yes, Brenda loved Martin, but she loved me too," Hector Munro said. "The way I saw it, she was with me, not him. What was I meant to do? See her jailed or sent to a mental hospital?"

"Could we go back a bit, sir?" Pilot said. "You were on the drive outside, about to take the car to the garage to fill it up."

"Yes. I'd just got to the car when I noticed the curtains were drawn, but the window half open. The curtains were fluttering in the breeze and I saw Brenda standing there, not moving. Thought it a bit odd. I went over to the window to find out what was going on. I saw the candlestick before I saw Stafford. He was on the floor, bleeding. It was like something you'd see on the stage. Took me a while to take it all in. Thank God Bridget was up the lane picking crab apples. I said: 'What the hell have you done?' She didn't move. Didn't take her eyes off him. I knew he must have done something terrible for her to have done that.

"By now I'd seen Martin. Brenda said he was dead too. There wasn't time to ask questions. I swung into action. Told her not to move herself, or the candlestick, an inch –

we had to minimise blood splatter. I've always enjoyed crime. Like the modern stuff best. I knew what to do. I grabbed a plastic bag from the car and held it open through the window. She dropped the candlestick into it. I told her: you came for his lunch, got worried when you couldn't raise him and called me. We got in and found him. I called an ambulance and you stayed with him – that'll explain any blood on you. You thought he'd had a fall, and comforted him. I told her to kneel in his blood, hug him, stroke his hair, like she was comforting him in his final minutes. I told her to get as much of his blood on her as she could. 'We'll say it was burglars,' I said. She wanted to know how we'd explain Martin. 'Burglars wouldn't've have come in with Martin there, would they?' I told her I'd deal with Martin.

"I pulled the curtains, then closed the window. I didn't like to leave her, but there wasn't a choice. In the garage, I threw on the nice new decorator's overall Brenda got me for my birthday and a pair of gardening gloves. I went inside and put Martin inside the bag I use for garden waste and covered him up with some bin bags. She hated that." He lowered his head. "Getting rid of a candlestick is one thing, but a body is another. Couldn't think where I could put it. The park shed came to mind, but it was the middle of the day. Then I remembered the dung heap. It was far enough away not to be searched straight away, and close enough to let me move the body later, after you'd searched my car. I relied on the pong putting the dogs off the scent, which it did. I'd just put Martin's body in the boot when Dandelion appeared from nowhere. Looked over and there was Bridget. Didn't know how much she'd seen. Told her I was just off to get some manure. The dog wouldn't stop yapping, and I chucked her in the back seat. That was

Bridget's dream – I was her 'burglars'. Soon as she told you, I knew. Had a mind to send her on another crab apple trip, but she'd already wandered off. I'd locked the living room door and drawn the curtains, and I left her to it. Her fall was nothing to do with me or my wife, I tell you. She must've tripped over the washing basket and hit her head, poor soul."

Pilot said nothing.

"At the gate I saw the charity bag," Hector continued. "I'd been worrying you'd find evidence of Martin being in the house. I took the bag with me, drove to the dung heap and climbed down. Not exactly where I showed you, along a bit. I put Martin in Stafford's coat and shoes then in three thick bin bags. I left him in some undergrowth. He was as light as a feather. I left the candlestick there as well. Got back wondering what I'd find, but everything was the same. Bridget was nowhere to be seen, having drank herself senseless, I later discovered. I opened the window from the outside. Brenda was kneeling by the body. I told her to stay put and went to the garage for Stafford's telescope. On the way back from the heap, I'd had a brainwave: to use the telescope to scrutinise her for invisible blood drops. I poked the telescope through the window and every time I saw a drop or a splatter, I got Brenda to smudge it, like she'd tried to get his blood off her." He mimicked Brenda wiping her hands across her upper torso, her face, her hair. "All the time we were getting our story straight. 'You came in with his lunch and found him,' I said. 'You called for me. I went for an ambulance and you stayed with him.' She told me how she'd listened at the window and I gave it a wipe. First inside, then out. That's where the paint remover came from. The rim of the jar she used to listen. I had to do one more thing before calling an ambulance. I'd seen his phone on the floor near Martin. The screen had shattered, but it still worked. I've seen Stafford log in often enough. I used his code at exactly 12.57. We gave it another ten minutes, then I called the ambulance. Used the time to make a cheese sarnie and put it on a tray by the door. Before you ask, the delay didn't make any difference, Detective. He was already dead."

"Hector took over," Brenda said. "He thought of everything. All I had to do was stick to my story: we'd had our lunch, I'd gone for his lunch tray, it was still outside untouched, the door was locked, I didn't get any response. Worried, we broke in. He was on the floor, blood everywhere. Hector even dealt with Martin. I didn't like that bit, but what could we do?"

"I was terrified Martin would be discovered before I'd a chance to move him," Hector said, "but he was still there when I went back under cover of darkness. I couldn't move him to the shed straight away – not before you'd search it. You'd already searched the car, so I put him in the boot. He was there for a couple of nights. Lucky we had that cold snap. I moved him in the early hours. I'd earlier slipped Bridget one of Brenda's sleeping tablets and she was sound asleep. I didn't want the dog waking up either and I gave her a quarter of a pill. Knowing you'd find pressure marks – or lividity marks, I think they're called – I made as sure as I could to lay him on the same side and in the same position each time I moved him. To make it look like he died in the shed, I used a knife to draw the bolt across from the outside. That took the longest. I got rid of the candlestick at the same time. Please try to remember, at that stage, we believed he'd died of a heart attack. Neither my wife nor I could believe it when the Detective Inspector told us Martin had been strangled."

"The man Tim Smith believed he'd successfully strangled was Martin Mills not Stafford Mills," Black told Sylvie Laurent. "None of you were there when Stafford was attacked. That happened later and those responsible have confessed."

"I was in the room," Sylvie said. "I'd've known if it wasn't Stafford Mills."

"You didn't go anywhere near the body, Mme Laurent. The body was slumped in a chair, at an angle, head lowered, up on the decking. You could only see it in profile. You didn't get further than the door. You couldn't risk taking a closer look. There couldn't be any forensic evidence linking you to the place he'd been strangled. Not a strand of hair, not a piece of cotton, not a bit of dirt on your shoe. Nothing. The legs and head you saw in profile, from a distance, was Martin Mills, not Stafford. Tim Smith strangled the wrong man. He strangled a man who was already dead. Martin died first. Your meticulous planning was in vain. The Picasso isn't going to Pierre."

"Tell me Detective Inspector," Brenda said, at the end of her confession. "My sister's, death? It was an accident, wasn't it?"

"Mr Munro, what really happened to your sister-in-law, Bridget?" Pilot asked.

"She fell, didn't she?"

Pilot studied Hector. Once confronted with his wife's confession he'd sung like a canary on the subject of the death of Stafford Mills, but on the topic of his sister-in-law's demise, he was closed down and taciturn. Was he protecting himself or his wife? "When she was drunk she could barely remember her name," Pilot said. "She was safe then. But she'd sobered up. Had she started remembering stuff? Was she starting to ask awkward questions? Starting to challenge that dream of hers? Was she getting a bit too close to figuring it out?"

"I wouldn't know anything about that, son," Hector said.

"She'd shown Martin Mills in, to wait for Stafford. She'd seen you put something in the car. The more she dried out, the better her mind worked. Slowly, bit by bit, she was piecing it all together, wasn't she? She couldn't be trusted to stay schtum, and now she was sober people might start taking her seriously. You lured her to the outhouse to talk, didn't you, Hector? You pushed her to her death and planted the money on her, didn't you?" Hector folded his arms and said nothing. "You were only trying to protect your wife, Hector. We know that. What happened to Bridget, Hector?"

"My guess?" he said. "She fell off the wagon, and with everywhere closed went to the outhouse looking for booze, only there wasn't any. Whether she jumped or fell, I can't say. Only, and God forgive me for saying so, she hadn't much reason to go on in this life. She never got over her Ronnie being taken so soon. All she ever talked about was being with him again. Think in the end, everything just got too much for her, poor thing, and she jumped."

51

There were only three people present at the meeting held a week later: Detective Superintendent Judith McDermid, Detective Inspector Guido Black and Mr Dale Seeger – the head of the local Crown Prosecution Service.

On the table by Dale's elbow, lay a pile of buff-coloured files. He moved the top one without opening it. "Jenna Nesbitt has pleaded guilty to causing the wasteful employment of the police by knowingly making a false report, and perverting the course of justice. She's up before the Crown Court next week for sentencing. One-year suspended I reckon." He put the file down and opened the next one. "Presented with the Munro's confession, Tim Smith's brief has offered a plea on his client's behalf. As Martin Mills was already dead when Tim Smith tried to strangle him, he can't be done for murder, only the specific intention to cause the death of a human being under the Queen's Peace. Attempted murder to you and me. He'll plead to that in exchange for a maximum term of five years, and us not proceeding with conspiracy to commit murder. Given the extenuating circumstances, and the out pouring of public support towards him, it's not in the public interest to refuse."

"He's no threat to the community," Judy said. "Can't see him committing another crime as long as he lives."

"He'll get five and serve about two and a half, most of it in an open, I reckon," Dale said.

"Did he implicate Sylvie Laurent and Pierre?" Black said.

"He's steadfastly refusing to confirm details, just that he attempted to murder Martin Mills mistaking him for Stafford Mills, no more. Nonetheless, we can't risk a compassionate acquittal."

"CPS are accepting the plea?" Judy asked.

"We are." Dale removed Tim Smith's file from the top of the pile and placed it face down on the desk, beside his other elbow, and opened the next file. "Hector Munro will only admit to obstructing the police in the course of their enquiries, and preventing a lawful burial," he said, peering across the reading glasses he'd pushed down his nose.

"Nothing about pushing his sister-in-law to her death?" Black said.

"He's continuing to deny involvement," Dale said. "It's the strange case of the dog who didn't bark in the night time, Guido."

"It's the not at all strange case of the dog who was drugged alongside his mistress with her sleeping tablets, so his master could keep a rendezvous and come back again unnoticed," Black said. "That's why it was so dopey when I called round the next day."

Dale removed his reading glasses and placed them on the papers in front of him. This meant he was talking off record. "If Hector lured his trusting sister-in-law to that outhouse and pushed her to her death, you've nothing proving it. CPS are accepting the plea."

Neither Judy nor Black said anything. Dale put Hector Munro's file on top of the file of Tim Smith and turned to the next one.

"Sylvie Laurent," he said, adding, with a tone of admiration, "our mastermind. She's mellowed slightly since you last spoke to her, Guido. Since presented with the evidence. Her solicitor's indicated that she might be prepared to plead guilty to conspiracy to commit murder, and obstructing the police in the course of their enquiries, but only if her son isn't charged."

"With anything?" Black said.

"What've we got on him?" Dale said. "A fancy dress outfit and a recording of his father's voice which she's saying he hid for her in all innocence. The taxi driver who most likely dropped him back at school didn't identify him at the ID parade and we haven't found the ligature used. Unless Smith implicates him, which thus far he ain't…"

"How is Mme Laurent explaining her ejection from the room?" Black said.

"Hurled herself out, with the iPod concealed somewhere unmentionable."

Black gave a wry grin.

"She won't plead if he's charged. We haven't anything on Pierre. Putting any kid on trial risks splitting the jury, but particularly him, given the circumstances," Dale said.

"Have to agree with Dale on this one, Guido," Judy said. "They conspired to commit murder without a doubt, but between the three of them, none of them managed to murder anyone in the end. The crime wasn't seen through. If she goes before a jury, she'll deny everything. Tim Smith isn't going to implicate Pierre. Pierre getting away with it, is all part of Tim's revenge on Stafford. Besides, what's the point? They won't get much longer if convicted than if they plead, with the risk Pierre at least will get off."

"Wouldn't mind reading Pierre's: What I Did In The School Hols, essay," Dale chortled.

"LOL," Black said.

"Which just leaves poor Brenda Munro," Judy said.

"Manslaughter on the grounds of diminished responsibility," Dale said. "Without a shadow of doubt. She's been suffering from depression for years, and on the day was severely provoked."

Black couldn't disagree. The woman had acted entirely out of character. No jury in the land would convict her of murder. He picked Dale's files up from the table and almost immediately let them fall again with a thud. "All those bodies, all those killers," he said, "and not a murderer amongst them."

He was en route to brief the team on the outcome of the meeting with the Crown Prosecution Service, when Janice Burnett called. He assumed she wanted an update, but she didn't.

"I've just been tying up Stafford's estate when I found something which might interest you," she explained. "In the months before his death, Stafford purchased a buy-to-let, which he put in Bridget White's name, presumably to avoid tax further down the line. However, no one can be certain of his intention and therefore the house belongs to Bridget. I'm guessing she didn't leave a will."

"She told me she hadn't two beans to rub together, so I'd guess not. We certainly haven't found one."

"Then the house is Brenda's. May not be the result Stafford expected, but it's what he got."

The revelation that after Brenda got the help she needed, she and Hector would have some security, lifted Black's mood quite a bit. His mind turned to Chloe. Why didn't he whisk her away somewhere for the weekend? Pick her up from the school gates and take her somewhere romantic? Paris or Rome? His good mood lasted until he reached the incident room where, for some reason, his team were gathered in a circle in the middle of the room with looks of astonishment and shock on their faces. Silence descended at his appearance, alarming and deflating him simultaneously.

Eden approached him grimly, clutching a long brown envelope. "A lady from Oxfam rang just as you went into your meeting, sir," she said. "She was going through some clothes left in a recycling bin when she found this envelope in the pocket of a coat." She held the envelope out to him. He took it, but didn't open it, or look at it closely, although aware of handwriting on the envelope. Pilot joined them. "She took a look inside, in case it was something important…" he explained.

"…and realised it was a handwritten will. What's more, she recognised the testator's name," Eden said.

"It's only Martin Mills' last will and testament, Boss," Pilot said. "In the coat Hector dumped."

"You're kidding?" Black said, genuinely astounded at what he was hearing.

Eden removed the will from its envelope. The will was a shop purchased, do-it-yourself one, not dissimilar to the one his landlady, Jean Janes had bought him, but which he hadn't used. Eden turned to the execution page for Black. The will was signed by Martin Mills and dated the day before he died. The names and addresses of the two witnesses were printed below their signatures. Both gave their addresses care of Victoria Coach Station, 164 Buckingham Palace Road, London SW1W 9TP. "He wrote it when they were stranded for hours," she said. She and Pilot did nothing to contain their excitement.

"Good Lord!" Black said, swaying slightly on his heels. "Who's he left what to?" Black half-hoped it was nice Mrs Janes or even the Cats' Home.

Eden and Pilot looked at each other. Eden said: "£15,000 to his neighbour who looked after his cat in Brighton, and £15,000 to Jean Janes, both for their kindness to him. Everything else," she hesitated, "goes to any and all children of his brother, Stafford Mills, in equal shares."

"Pierre gets the Picasso after all," Pilot said. "Don't know whether to laugh or cry."

Black took the will from Eden and quietly read it through. He couldn't see anything which invalidated it. Pilot was right – Pierre got the Picasso. He rocked back on his heels, and started to laugh out loud. "Which just leaves one unanswered question," he said eventually.

Eden and Pilot looked at each other blankly. Neither could think what.

"Will Eden ever call Matt Prichard?" he said.

Printed in Poland
by Amazon Fulfillment
Poland Sp. z o.o., Wrocław

60945018R10247